Praise for *The Bride Insists*

"Perfectly delightful Regency romance… Remarkably executed."

—*Publishers Weekly* Starred Review

"Ashford captures the reader's interest with her keen knowledge of the era and her deft writing. An engaging cast of characters…a charming plot, and just the right amount of sensuality will keep Ashford fans satisfied."

—*RT Book Reviews*, 4 Stars

"A marvelously engaging marriage of convenience tale, and Ashford's richly nuanced, realistically complex characters and impeccably crafted historical setting are bound to resonate with fans of Mary Balogh."

—*Booklist*

"Ashford establishes a
reasons until trust and
For all historical roman

"A solid historical…the heat is palpable."

—*Long and Short Reviews*

"A sweet historical romance that one can enjoy over a hot cup of happy and a warm blanket! Most assuredly a warm and fuzzy read!"

—*The Reading Café*

Praise for *Once Again a Bride*

"A near-perfect example of everything that makes this genre an escapist joy to read: unsought love triumphs despite difficult circumstances, unpleasantness is resolved and mysteries cleared, and good people get the happy lives they deserve."

—*Publishers Weekly*

"A bit of gothic suspense, a double love story, and the right touches of humor and sensuality add up to this delightfully fast-paced read."

—*RT Book Reviews*, 4 Stars

"Ms. Ashford has written a superbly crafted story with elements of political unrest, some gothic suspense, and an interesting romance."

—*Fresh Fiction*

"Well-rendered, relatable characters, superb writing, an excellent sense of time and place, and gentle wit make this a romance that shouldn't be missed... Ashford returns with a Regency winner that will please her longtime fans and garner new ones."

—*Library Journal*

"Mystery entwines with the romance, as Ms. Ashford leads us astray... *Once Again a Bride* is great fun."

—*Historical Hilarity*

Praise for *The Marriage Wager*

"Exceptional characters and beautifully crafted historical details ensure a delightful read for Judith McNaught and Mary Balogh fans."
—Publishers Weekly

"Lively, well-written Regency romance sparkles with wonderful dialogue, witty scenes, and just the right touch of humor, adventure, and repartee."
—RT Book Reviews, Nominated for Best Regency Historical Romance

"A riveting, emotional romance that will garner a place of prominence on anyone's keeper shelf."
—Rendezvous

"You're really going to enjoy *The Marriage Wager*. It is one of the finest marriage of convenience stories I've read."
—All About Romance

"Entertaining, colorful characters, romantic... An engaging and entertaining read."
—Caffeinated Book Reviewer

"An enjoyable Regency romance with complex characters."
—Book Lover and Procrastinator

Also by Jane Ashford

MARRIED
TO A PERFECT
STRANGER

JANE ASHFORD

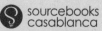

Published by Sourcebooks Casablanca, an imprint of Sourcebooks,
Inc.
P.O. Box 4410, Naperville, Illinois 60567-4410
(630) 961-3900
Fax: (630) 961-2168
www.sourcebooks.com

Printed and bound in Canada.
MBP 10 9 8 7 6 5 4 3 2 1

One

JOHN BEXLEY STOOD AT THE RAIL OF THE HMS *ALCESTE* and watched the gray water race by. Foam streaked the waves under an overcast sky. The sails belled out in a fresh wind, and the current in these narrowing straits, halfway across the world from England and home, pushed them even faster. It wasn't a full-fledged storm, but the weather was certainly what the navy men called "lively." And the roll and heeling of the ship made the small cabin he shared below feel like a cage being shaken by gigantic hands. Far better to brace yourself on deck, endure the salt spray and the roar, feel the full thrill of their swift progress. It was like flying.

He tightened his grip on the rigging as a gust tilted the ship farther toward the sea. Rushing water gurgled and hissed along the timbers. The exultation of this run before the wind was a scrap of compensation for the failure of their mission. They were heading home with nothing accomplished, due to the intransigence of the Chinese emperor. As a junior clerk on the diplomatic mission, he'd had no great role to play in their thwarted attempt to sway the monarch. Still, he'd seen and experienced things he would never have been able to imagine. His mind teemed with new ideas. John grinned in the teeth of the wind. The huge expanse and buffeting energy of sea and sky matched his mood. He had the oddest sense that something had come to life inside him on this long voyage.

There was a crack like a cannon shot. The ship shuddered all along its length and stopped dead in the water, throwing John to his knees. Then the vessel slewed around until it wallowed broadside in the waves, sails snapping like pistol fire. John sprang up and looked wildly around for the source of the attack. The masts shook. There was a grating splintering sound, as of tortured wood. They'd hit something in the sea.

Clinging to rail and ropes, John peered over the side. Foam sucked and surged over a rock just below the surface. The wind pushed at the sails and shoved them harder against it. He could see that the hull was breached, water pouring in. They must have veered out of the channel through the straits. He straightened. Sailors swarmed the deck, some getting in each other's way. Where was the captain? The first mate? Someone should do something, give orders.

He remembered that the senior officers were dining with Lord Amherst and the top members of the diplomatic group. But why hadn't they come up on deck? John looked to the helmsman. He was leaning against the big ship's wheel. The impact had apparently stunned him.

The prow of the ship sagged and dipped. They

were sinking. He was going to die thousands of miles from home, his fate unknown to his family and friends for weeks. And Mary. He and his newlywed wife were just beginning to get acquainted when they'd been separated by this voyage. Now, pulled down into these cold foreign seas, he would leave her a widow. John clutched the rigging so tight his nails dug into his palms.

By God, he was not! Denial rose in John, fierce and fiery, along with a surge of confidence stronger than any he'd ever felt before. He knew what to do. The *Lyra* was following not far behind them. It could pick them up. "Ready the dinghies," he shouted to the nearest sailors. "Everyone must get off the ship. We're going down."

Some of the crew had already gone to the pulleys. At his command, others joined them. John ran for the hatch to see what was keeping Lord Amherst and the others.

The moment he entered the narrow gangway, his fellow clerk Edmund Fordyce careened into him. "Where is Lord Amherst?" John asked.

"How the devil would I know?" replied Fordyce. He pushed John against the wall, trying to get by him. "Get out of my way, you idiot. There's water pouring into my cabin."

"We've struck a rock. We have to find the…"

"All I'm finding is a way off this crate." Fordyce shoved harder, squeezing past John and heading for the hatch.

"Fordyce! We need to…"

"*I* need to not risk my neck. *You* can do as you

like." His tone suggested that he thought John was a fool. Fordyce staggered as the ship leaned, and then he lunged out onto the deck. The hatch slammed shut behind him.

John pushed off the wall and moved farther into the ship. Timbers groaned, and the floor heaved under his feet. Water sloshed out of a cabin on the left. At the end of the corridor, the door to the captain's cabin was shut. A long sliver of wood had somehow become jammed under it, John saw, preventing it from opening. Fists pounded on the inside. A chorus of voices shouted for aid. A knife jabbed through the boards at shoulder height, once, and again.

"Wait a moment," he called. He bent and yanked at the piece of wood. At first, it wouldn't shift, but when he kicked it, it moved and finally came loose. John jerked it free and pushed at the door.

The panels burst open. The captain surged out first, cursing. His first mate and other crewmen were right behind him. Then came Lord Amherst and the senior diplomatic staff. En masse, they jostled toward the hatch. "We hit a rock," John said. He wasn't sure whether anyone heard.

When the knot of men had rushed past, John followed. Water coursed over the toes of his boots. As he went, he checked quickly inside the cabins that lined the corridor. All were empty except the last. Reynolds, one of the troopers accompanying their group, was there, dazed and bleeding from a knock on the head. John put an arm around him and helped him up to the deck.

The scene there had become a more organized

chaos. The captain was shouting orders. The helmsman had recovered. The ship's dinghies were being
lowered into the thrashing sea. John saw Lord Amherst
climbing down into one. The deck was listing badly
now, the stern rising as water filled the front holds.
John helped Reynolds across the shuddering planks.
The grating of timber on rock was even louder now,
audible even over the confused shouting.

A crewman gave him a hand with Reynolds. And
then John was sliding down a rope into a heaving
longboat. He could see their sister ship, the *Lyra*,
standing off not far away, waiting to take them aboard.
Dinghies dotted the waves, rowing toward her. He
grabbed an oar himself as the last men dropped into the
boat, and they pulled hard toward rescue. Curiously,
along with relief, John felt a rising excitement. He was
intensely aware of the pull of his muscles as he rowed,
the lash of spray, salty on his lips, the whistle of the
wind. Had he ever felt this alive, this clear and certain?
All his senses united to tell him there would be no
turning back from this profound moment. From now
on, everything was different.

Minutes later, they made it to the *Lyra*. Crewmen
reached down to help them climb to safety. John
vaulted over the rail and turned to look back at the
Alceste. The ship that had carried them from England
to the ports of China, and partway back again, was
going down. Most of his possessions, including gifts
he'd purchased for people back home, were going
with it. Waves washed over the foredeck. Spars and
coils of rope floated free. The prow went under. The
hull tipped and seemed to hesitate and then slipped

beneath the surging sea. It seemed fitting to bow his head briefly, as if saying farewell to a friend.

"Well, I had to see to it that we got everyone off, sir," said a voice behind him. "Couldn't leave anyone behind."

John turned and discovered Fordyce, speaking to Lord Amherst.

"One has to do one's duty, whatever the risk," added his fellow clerk.

Lord Amherst nodded, eyes on the spot where the *Alceste* had disappeared. John stared at Fordyce, amazed at the man's effrontery. Surely someone had seen him, rushing to the dinghies ahead of everyone else?

As if sensing his gaze, Fordyce's pale blue eyes flicked at John and then away. "I suppose it's just bred in the bone, sir," he said to Lord Amherst. "Family tradition and all that."

John didn't hear what Amherst murmured in response. He was distracted by the captain of the *Lyra*, ordering his helmsman to steer well away from the hidden shoals.

❦

The small Somerset manor house lazed under the June sun, its red brick mellow with age, its bow windows and ruddy chimney pots aglow. Bees hummed in the garden, where summer blooms perfumed the air. Foliage hung heavy in the small park; lawns glowed green.

But in a pleasant parlor at the back of the house, Mary Fleming Bexley felt far from peaceful. Though she had asked her mother to come, indeed insisted that she must, the visit was not going well. "I've been living with Aunt Lavinia for eighteen months, Mama," she said. "I know what she…"

"Well, we had to put you somewhere," said her mother indulgently. "Married a month, and then your husband goes haring off to China." She said it as if the mission that had taken John away was Mary's fault somehow.

What would she have answered, Mary wondered, if John had said, "Will you marry me and then go live with your great-aunt for months and months while I sail off on an important diplomatic journey to China?" Her reply might have been a bit more complicated than "yes." She'd had less than a month as a wife, actually, and then he was gone to the other side of the world and she was packed off to Somerset.

Packed off; there was the crux of it. It seemed she was always being packed off in one way or another. As if she was a misaddressed parcel or a stray shawl left behind at the end of a house party. "I'm twenty-four years old," she began. "A married woman…"

"At last," interrupted her mother. "Thanks to me. Well, and Mrs. Bexley, of course."

Of course, thought Mary. Their families had come up with the match and pushed for it in a united front. Mary understood now, as she hadn't then, that the Flemings and the Bexleys saw their offspring as two of a kind. She, the least promising of five sisters, short on common sense. John, overshadowed by his three brothers' loud accomplishments, stuck in a junior position at the Foreign Office. Mary had actually overheard her mother and John's discussing their similar shortcomings, not long after he'd departed on his voyage. That had been when they were deciding what to "do" with her. She and John had been hustled into marriage like backward children being sent off to school. Why had she let that happen? "Aunt Lavinia is not herself," she tried.

"Really? Who is she then?" Her mother laughed. "Do you remember how your father used to compare her to a frigate under full sail—'prow jutting well out, a nose fit for cleaving waves.' I had to scold him so. I was afraid one of you children would repeat it."

Mary did remember. Her four sisters had feared Lavinia when she visited, sweeping in like a scudding ship, shedding pronouncements and odd gifts and errant barks of laughter. Mary alone had been fascinated, trailing in the older woman's wake like an inquisitive seabird. But sadly, this was not the Great-Aunt Lavinia she'd found when she arrived to stay here. "She's older," Mary said. "And...confused." Worse than confused—uncharacteristically anxious, a shell of her former, formidable self.

Her mother frowned. "Confused about what? She seemed fine to me. A bit tired, perhaps, but as you say, she's nearly eighty. I'm sure her nap will restore her."

Aunt Lavinia had been having a good day. Mary could not regret this, though it did make it harder to convince her mother.

"Really, Mary, don't you think you're the one who's confused? You call me here at a moment's notice, saying I must come, and I still have no idea why. I'm quite busy at home, you know."

Her mother was always busy. She descended like a

striking hawk whenever the least disorder threatened. Mary searched for the right words. But in the face of Mama's all-too-familiar impatience, she couldn't find them. "Let me show you something." Her hand trembled slightly as she reached for her sketch pad.

"Oh, Mary." Her mother sighed and shook her head. "I don't have the time to look at drawings. Please tell me you did not drag me thirty miles over bumpy roads to show me a book of sketches. It's all very well for a *child* to be slow and dreamy and lose herself in fancies, but…" She rubbed her forehead.

Mary felt an old despair. She couldn't stop drawing, any more than she could stop eating. Her mother would never understand this; Mary had given up arguing with her about it years ago. She started to put the sketchbook away. But no. Then her mother would leave without agreeing to her plan. And what would become of Great-Aunt Lavinia when Mary left this house? John had to come home *sometime*. "Please, Mama, if you would just look."

Her mother's tone grew sharper. "Mary, as you have pointed out, you are grown up. You must stop wasting time on such stuff and settle down to more useful pursuits."

Part of her wanted to wilt and slink away, hide the drawings, hide herself, as she had so often done back home. Then, from somewhere, rose a determination that would not be denied. Mary had learned something important in these last chaotic months. In fact, her enforced sojourn in Somerset had brought her a revelation. She'd finally understood that in order to truly understand a situation, she had to draw the people involved. Drawing was her key to understanding the world. Only then did she see the truth of things. Only then could she figure out what to do and find the proper words to communicate it.

She'd known that her drawings captured emotion as well as appearances, through contrast perhaps, or juxtaposition. She couldn't explain how it happened. Sometimes, she had a hint about the feelings already. Other times, she had no idea until the drawing was done. For some reason, she learned subtle things with her hands, as they moved. Not through books, or lectures. No matter how hard she tried, words slipped out of her mind, while shapes and shadows illuminated it. Her mother, her sisters, could look and grasp and comprehend words all in a moment. They could remember all they read with ease. Her sisters found her inability to do so hilarious. Her mother just found it irritating. She looked vastly irritated now. But though Mary trembled under that well-known glare, she had to take the leap. "No, you must look."

Before her mother could object again, Mary flipped open the sketchbook and put two drawings side by side before her.

The first was a watercolor portrait of a middle-aged woman. The face gazed out at the viewer with calm authority. Determination edging toward stubbornness showed in the lines bracketing her lips; pride and imagination in the fashionable cut of her gray curls. Mary had caught a subtle twinkle in the blue eyes, a persistent curiosity in the tilt of the head. More than the sum of its parts, the painting conveyed the essence of a strong personality.

The second portrait showed the same woman, and yet not the same. In this one, the sharp eyes had blurred; though painted, they seemed to shift with uncertainty under the viewer's gaze. This woman's mouth looked ready to quiver with doubt. The skin sagged not just with greater age, but with an uncomprehending anxiety as well. Around this face, the well-kept gray hair and modish lace cap seemed incongruous.

Mary looked from one image to the other, her heart aching for her great-aunt.

"Yes, very well," said her mother. "You've drawn Aunt Lavinia. What do you wish me to say? That it is a good likeness?"

"Can you *really* look, Mama? Please? Try?"

The pleading in her voice seemed to reach her mother at last. She considered the pages again. Her stare went from one portrait to the other. Back again. Gradually, she began to frown.

And Mary felt freed to speak. "She's very forgetful, even of familiar people's names or her own history. The servants were at their wits' end when I arrived." It had been daunting, to be tossed into a floundering household, suddenly surrounded by people looking to her for leadership. She'd had to fumble her way to the idea that she could take charge, if she did it in her own way. "I believe we must find her a companion. Someone who is more than a housekeeper, though she will have to manage the household, too. Someone... patient and kind. We should pay quite well, I think, well enough to attract just the right sort of person." She would fight for this plan, Mary thought. Great-Aunt Lavinia deserved the best.

"We?" said her mother.

"Well, it would come out of Aunt's income, naturally. But as she is not really capable of approving the expenditure, I thought I should speak to you. As her only close relation."

Her mother was looking at her oddly. "You have considered this."

Now that Mary had begun, the words poured out. "I drafted an advertisement that sets forth just what we need." She took the folded paper from the pocket of her gown. "The butler says there is an agency in London that provides ladies' companions. We must be very clear that we require someone…special." Mary unfolded the page and extended it. She was pleased to see that it did not shake in her hand.

Her mother took it and read. "Well expressed," she commented, sounding surprised.

"I thought, if you agreed, we could send it right off."

"Perhaps I should talk to Aunt Lavinia before…" Her mother paused, looked down at the portraits again. "No. That is, I *shall* talk to her. But I daresay you are right. You may put it in the mail." She looked up. "Or…what do you intend to do with the replies?"

"I…I thought I would invite the best candidates here for a visit." Mary faltered a bit under her parent's close examination. "Unless you would prefer to interview…?"

Her mother cocked her head. "You would have to pay their coach fares."

Mary nodded.

"They must be asked about their previous positions and show a complete set of references."

"Yes, Mama."

"Do you really think *you* can find the proper person?" Years of doubt tinged her tone.

Mary sat straighter and met her skeptical gaze. "I do."

The pause that followed went on longer than Mary would have liked, but at last her mother said, "Very well. I shall let you try."

"Th-thank you, Mama," Mary replied, her spirit swelling with triumph.

"I'll give you a list of important questions," her mother added sharply. "And I shall expect a full report on each possibility before the final decision is made."

Mary nodded, her elation a little dimmed. How odd that this success made her feel more lonely, rather than less so.

⁂

John Bexley strode down the gangplank onto the Southampton dock and paused to look over the busy port town. For the first time since he'd left English shores in February 1816, everything felt familiar— the shape of the buildings, the faces and dress of the people, the sounds and scents and voices. And yet, they also felt strangely changed. His twenty-month journey to the other side of the world had reduced England to just one corner of a vast globe. A noble corner, without doubt, a corner with a proud history and admirable ideals, but still just a smallish island among continents. And so his home looked not only natural and welcoming but also a bit…constricted.

Speaking of constricted, John wiggled his shoulders, trying to get more comfortable in a coat that no longer fit. He'd gained more muscle than his clothes could accommodate. The binding cloth contributed to the mixed emotions of this moment. He'd outgrown his raiment. What about his old routines, or the wife he'd left behind?

John looked at the English faces on the docks around him, pale even under the August sun. For almost two years, he and Mary had led separate lives—his active and public, hers domestic and small. So many things had happened to him that she would never comprehend. And a thousand domestic details that newly married persons usually shared had gone by on opposite sides of the world.

Worse, John wondered now whether he'd done the right thing, giving in to his family's plan for him. The young man he'd been before this voyage had let his family urge him into a lifetime bond without really thinking. If the foreign secretary's letter about the China mission had come a few weeks sooner, would he have offered for Mary? The answer was too uncomfortable to contemplate.

John looked out over the town. His world of two years ago seemed like a dream to him now, pale and insubstantial, the people distant shadows. Swept away on a grand journey, he'd found inner continents as surprising as the discoveries of ancient explorers. The impulses that had risen in him and answered the challenge of storm-wracked seas still burned—more vibrant perceptions, fiercer ambition, a determination to make his mark.

But a suitable wife—one with important connections and social skills—was practically required for advancing through the ranks of the Foreign Office.

A bale of silks rose from the ship's hold, pulley creaking as the navvies hauled on the rope. The heavy cargo swung out over the dock and plunged down just as a street urchin emerged from between two stacks of crates. John took three steps, snatched the boy from its path, and pulled him well out of the way. "Careful there," he said.

Pale and wide-eyed, the grimy child nodded his thanks and scampered away.

The planks of the dock vibrated as the bale thumped to the boards. A brawny dockworker rounded the corner of a warehouse and hefted it—no easy task, John knew. He should head into town, find transport, and begin the last sixty miles of his journey. To Mary. But his tumbled thoughts kept him standing near the ship.

He remembered his first sight of her at the Bath assembly. Neither of them came from the sort of grand families who went to London for the Season; Bath was the center of their social world. She'd stood with her mother by the wall—a small, delicate girl with chestnut brown hair and huge dark eyes; a full lower lip that seemed made for kissing; pretty little hands. She'd looked as sweet and timid as a sparrow. In that moment—which now seemed long ages ago—his family's mandate that she was the wife for him had seemed no burden at all. He'd walked over, been presented. Mary had smiled at him…

After that, events were a bit of a blur. They'd danced, walked the streets of Bath together, taken teas and dinners at their families' tables. He had offered for her; that moment had been between the two of them.

At the time, it hadn't seemed as if he had a choice. But once the words were spoken and she had accepted, their mothers had swooped in and taken over. He didn't remember being consulted about a single item after that. He was simply told things. Mary's father had lectured him about how the combination of their two inherited incomes would allow them to live very comfortably, as if John couldn't work that out for himself. His brothers had teased him relentlessly, as usual. He'd overheard his parents agreeing that this was a good enough match—for him, for Mary—and for some reason, incomprehensible to him now, he'd made no remark.

There'd been a whirl of a wedding and a seaside week in Weston-super-Mare, with dolorous rain and intimacies that had been clumsier than he'd have liked. Then the Foreign Office summons had arrived to take over his thoughts and change his life.

John sighed. His life, not Mary's. What would a little sparrow like Mary think of the intricacies of Foreign Office etiquette? What would she think of him, now that he'd…come alive? He took a deep breath of the seaside air. That's how it felt—as if he'd been half-asleep for years and finally woken. Now, he intended to plunge into the drive for advantage and jostling rivalries he'd generally ignored in his three years on the job. Work was going to occupy much of his time. Where did Mary fit in all this?

John loosened his shoulders, chafing at the tightness of his coat once again. Done was done. Mary was his wife. She would have to fit. She was young, unformed, eager to please. Though she didn't have the family connections that were so useful in government work, she was a taking little thing. She'd welcome his guidance. Indeed, she would probably be awed by his new sophistication. There was a curiously attractive notion.

John fell into a pleasant reverie. In the long months at sea, men had talked, and inevitably one of their topics had been women. John had heard a lot of nonsense and endured a load of empty boasting. But some of it had been eye-opening and, when one winnowed through the sources and considered the characters of the speakers, quite intriguing. He looked forward to trying out some of the...

"Ah, here he is!"

John stiffened at the sound of that affected voice. He'd thought he was the last passenger off the ship.

"Bexley can deal with the trunks," the voice drawled on. "It's just the sort of thing he's good at."

John turned to face the two men stepping off the *Lyra*'s gangplank. Beside Lord Amherst's admirable, capable private secretary sauntered the recent bane of John's existence, the Honorable Edmund Fordyce.

Since the shipwreck, Fordyce had made it his mission to harass John. Before that, they'd had little to do with each other, despite the smallness of their party. Fordyce, equally junior in the diplomatic group, had pursued more exalted company. A foppish, supercilious son of an earl—as John had learned in recent weeks—Fordyce had constantly dropped names and attempted to reminisce with Lord Amherst about lavish country house parties and fashionable town balls.

But following their encounter in that narrow

gangway of a sinking ship, the man had focused almost obsessively on John. He'd created opportunities to highlight the difference in their backgrounds or cast doubt on John's abilities. It was wildly irritating. And ridiculous. What did he think John was going to do—run and tattle about his cowardice like a sniveling schoolboy? Try to tell their superiors that he, John, had made sure the *Alceste* was clear? That Fordyce had misrepresented his own behavior? There was no way to initiate such a conversation, even if he wished to.

John had even tried to say something like this to Fordyce, with no effect. It was as if the fellow didn't even hear him. By this time, the mere sound of his voice affected John like the screech of tortured metal.

"If you wouldn't mind, Bexley," said the secretary. His expression showed a certain amount of sympathy. "I must follow Amherst to London immediately, and there are a number of confidential items still in the hold."

"John will be happy to play footman," said Fordyce. "Won't you, John? Oh, I didn't think. Are you familiar with footmen? They stand about front halls in *important* houses, waiting to run errands and carry packages, that sort of thing." He smiled, the picture of toothy falsity.

Fordyce laced his arm with the secretary's as if they were bosom friends. The secretary didn't quite shake him off. But John read distaste in his face, which took some of the sting out of Fordyce's words. Confidential items required careful handling, by someone who could be trusted. The task was significant, whatever Fordyce's silly prejudices. "Certainly, sir," John said.

The secretary nodded his thanks as the two men moved off down the dock. "See you in London, Bexley," he added.

John's spirits rose at this acknowledgment. More than his own inner landscape had changed with this voyage. He was known now; from among the vast army of junior functionaries in the Foreign Office, he'd been noticed. His future prospects were immeasurably brighter than they had been before this journey. That, and Fordyce's sour expression, considerably lightened the job of seeing that each trunk was properly labeled and sent off with a reliable carrier to its correct destination.

❧

Sitting at her easel in the back parlor of her great-aunt's house, Mary was swept by a wave of loneliness so strong it made the brush tremble in her hand. How long was this "visit" to go on? she wondered. It already felt eternal. In this household, she had no one to talk to or laugh with. No one within a decade of her age. Instead of a house of her own with a husband and perhaps by now a tiny addition to their family, she had a group of elderly...charges. There was no other way to look at it.

A shriek rent the air. Mary's brush twitched. A streak of yellow flicked across the painted face, muddling one eye, slashing across a cheek like war paint.

Mary lowered her brush, sat back, and sighed. Apparently, she would never become inured to these disturbances. Who could? Yes, she no longer leaped to her feet and ran, heart pounding, to discover the emergency. But she couldn't help reacting when Alice the housemaid screamed. It could only be Alice; past forty, and she still delighted in shrieking at the least excuse. Setting her brush in a glass of water, Mary rose and went to see what it was this time.

She found her Great-Aunt Lavinia, Alice the housemaid, and Voss the aged butler in the morning room, looking down at a shattered vase, a scatter of pink roses, and a puddle of water. The once formidable Lavinia Fleming was wringing her hands and trembling. Humid August air wafted through the open French doors.

"Drat that boy!" said Voss.

Mary didn't question his attribution because…well, there simply was no question about the origin of the disturbance.

"Something must be done," Voss added, clearly addressing Mary.

Mary looked back at him with wry resignation. When she'd first arrived, into this household that had lost its rudder and fallen into chaos, she'd hung back, of course. She was a guest, and anyway she hadn't known what to do. But then it had risen in her, like a great wave looming from the sea, an irresistible need to set things right. Perhaps it was an inheritance from her mother—not an entirely comfortable thought. But she found she could no more resist than she could alter the deep brown color of her eyes. The household had been like a workbasket jammed with snarled thread. She'd been forced, really, to discover her own way of untangling it. She'd been surprised at her daring and then amazed at how eagerly her intervention was welcomed.

"Ma'am?" said Voss, waiting for her to solve the household's most recent problem.

"I'll go and speak to him," Mary said, and she walked into the hall toward the front door of the manor.

Outside, she scanned the parkland for her quarry. There was no sign of him on the lawn or in the front garden. Mary turned toward the stables, rounded a corner, and there he was.

Ten-year-old Arthur Windly squatted at the edge of the stable yard, searching for more round pebbles. Here was the one remaining source of mayhem in her great-aunt's household.

She walked over to Arthur, who pretended to ignore her. The son of Great-Aunt Lavinia's supremely competent estate manager, Arthur was a constant conundrum. Mr. Windly was vital to the workings of the manor and must not be offended. He was also a prickly, distant man, especially, Mary had been told, since his wife's death three years ago. Her attempts to speak with him about Arthur had confirmed this characterization. He'd treated her like a nuisance and a busybody, and she was certain he hadn't listened to a word she said. Using her own newly discovered skills, Mary came to understand that Arthur was desperate for his father's attention and that the boy would take a whipping if that was all the notice he could contrive.

Trailing from Arthur's pocket was a length of brown cord with a woven pouch in the center, the source of many recent disasters. The local vicar had taken it into his head to show his young parishioners the instrument that had vanquished Goliath. The man had a passion for practical demonstrations of biblical subjects and seemingly no notion of the havoc a sling-shot could wreak in the hands of a mischievous little boy. Mary sometimes thought her great-aunt's entire neighborhood was barmy. She held out her hand. "You'll have to give me the sling, Arthur."

The boy sprang to his feet and glared at her. "No, I don't."

"That was our agreement—the last time."

"I never agreed!" Arthur's lower lip jutted out; his hazel eyes narrowed. Rebellion showed in every line of his skinny little body.

Suppressing a sigh, Mary stood and thought. She could threaten to go to his father, and Arthur would dare her to do it, and they would repeat a cycle of punishment that accomplished nothing. Arthur wasn't a bad child. Still, he couldn't be allowed to break vases, or knock ripening apples from the trees, or crack glass windows on the upper stories. Providentially, a scrap of overheard conversation came back to her. "I understand the hayricks in the north field are infested with rats."

"What?" Arthur frowned at the non sequitur.

"Still, I don't suppose you could kill a rat with that sling."

Arthur stiffened in outrage. "'Course I could."

"Really?" Mary strove to look merely interested. "Your father is desperate to be rid of them. Indeed, the idea of a whole colony of rats…" Her shudder did not require much acting. "But it must be much more difficult to hit a moving target than, oh, a vase or a window."

"I could, though." Speculation and hope passed visibly over the boy's triangular face. "I could do it!"

"I'm sure *everyone* would be very grateful," Mary replied.

Without another word, Arthur rushed from the stable yard. Mary walked back to the house with some bounce in her step and cautious optimism in her heart.

Inside, all was quiet once more. Great-Aunt Lavinia dozed on a sofa, the strings of her lace cap fluttering with her breath. Mary returned to her painting to see what could be salvaged but found herself picking up her sketchbook instead. She wanted to capture the image of Arthur sifting through stones in the stable yard, with his intent expression and irrepressible cowlick.

She opened the drawing pad and came upon a portrait of John, done during their brief honeymoon journey to the shore. For a disorienting moment, memory wavered in Mary's mind. But that was ridiculous. Of course she remembered her own husband. Here he was. Medium height, wiry, with reddish brown hair, a broad brow, straight nose, and crystalline blue eyes. The direct gaze of those eyes had been one of the first things she noticed about him.

She stared at his image. He'd been away longer than all the time she'd known him. And with the great distances involved, they'd had only occasional dispatches to let them know he was alive and well. What would it be like when she saw him again? Mary's heart beat faster at the question. With anticipation, or worry? She felt nothing like the heedless girl who had married him. She didn't know what she felt like as she gazed at the man she was expected to live with for the rest of her life. The rest…that might be forty years, fifty, all resting on one unconsidered choice.

Pushing such unsettling thoughts aside, she turned to a blank page. At once, her fingers itched to draw. Under the golden afternoon light slanting through the open casement, her soft pencil moved over the paper as it so often did, as if it had a mind of its own.

She didn't know why she'd loved to draw since a teacher first put a pencil in her hand and explained some of the principles of art. She didn't know why she had a talent for capturing human figures, particularly faces. Her landscapes were wooden and characterless, her still lifes stiff and uninteresting, while people sprang to life on her pages. The process held a kind of magic that she was reluctant to probe.

Using her pencil and the tip of one finger, Mary shaded and sharpened, added detail, and clarified line. A sharp, foxy little boy emerged on the page, scrabbling for stones to fill his pouch, ready for any sort of mayhem. He looked as if he would leap up in the next moment and set off on yet another escapade.

When she felt finished, she surveyed the result. Arthur's likeness was accurate, the expression true to life. It was good.

Sadness jumped from the page. Although she'd been thinking of the Arthur who continually disrupted the smooth workings of the household, her pencil had found more in the angles and lines of him. The poignancy of the boy's life tightened her throat and stung her eyes. A kindred loneliness plucked at her. It was time—past time—for her real life to begin. But had she chosen the right life? Looking back at the… girl she'd been, she didn't feel as if she'd chosen at all.

Mary set the drawing of Arthur aside, along with

the self-pity. Done was done. She'd made her vows. And right now there was plenty of work awaiting her, chiefly readying quarters for the housekeeper/companion she'd hired for her great-aunt. The woman was due to move in next week, and Mary wanted everything perfect for her arrival. Mrs. Finch had seemed the perfect solution to the problem of Great-Aunt Lavinia and all her household. She wanted her to feel warmly welcomed and pleased with her situation.

Alice came in with a letter, brought by courier, she said. Mary opened it quickly, fearing bad news, then caught her breath. "John's ship has landed at Spithead. He's home."

Two

JOHN BEXLEY REINED IN HIS HIRED HORSE ON A SLIGHT
rise and gazed down at the redbrick manor, somno-
lent under the August sun. Eager as he was to get to
London, he'd felt he must detour west into Somerset
to fetch Mary. Her family's decision to put her under
the care of a great-aunt while he was away just showed
he was right to fear that such a shy, quiet girl couldn't
arrange a journey on her own. And now that he was
here, the sight of this place soothed him; it looked the
very essence of English country comfort and peace.

John clapped his heels and rode down the hill.
Dismounting, he tied his horse to a shrub near the
front door of the house. He'd get someone to take
the nag to the stables, and he had no significant luggage. Most of his belongings rested at the bottom of
a foreign sea.

John's knock was answered by an aged butler. He
gave his name, stepped in, and inhaled the familiar
scents of beeswax polish and potpourri. The place
reminded him of his own home farther north. Golden
light pooled on the wooden floor and gleamed on the

stair rail. In the rooms on either side of the entry, the furnishings were classic and inviting. Mary had certainly had a beautiful and serene spot in which to wait for him. "Mary's husband," he added when it seemed as if the old man didn't know what to do with him. "I believe I am expected."

"Yes, si—"

A filthy, hysterical chicken shot through the rear door of the dining parlor on his left, skidded in a turn around the table, and raced past him, neck extended, screeching, flapping its mottled wings. A little boy slathered with mud came racing after it, careened off the doorjamb, and staggered across the entryway, leaving streaks and globs of dirt in his wake. The old butler stiffened in horror.

The bird hopped across a flowered sofa in the front parlor, stitching it with muddy tracks, circled the delicate carpet, and looped back toward John. The boy in pursuit slipped, fell, jumped up, and turned to follow. He flapped muddy hands at the fowl in an inept attempt to trap it.

What seemed like a herd of adults jostled into the dining parlor, then surged forward. "Arthur!" snapped a young woman, her voice crackling with authority.

"It isn't my fault," the boy shouted over the wild squawking. "I pulled her from the mire. Fox was after her. I never shot her or nothing."

The chicken swerved away from his snatching fingers, bug-eyed and still screeching. The boy lunged, missed, and fell flat. "I was taking her back to the pen," he said as he scrambled up and continued the chase. "She savaged me right by them 'French' doors, the devil." He exhibited a bleeding cheek. "Which shouldn't ought to be left open," he finished, aggrieved.

As the crazed chicken surged past him, John bent, reached, and snatched hold of its legs. When he straightened, he held the muddy bird upside down, at arm's length, well away from his clothing. It flapped and protested; flakes of dirt dropped to the floor.

"Good!" said the managing female, striding from the dining room into the hall. "Take it from him, Alice, and put it outside at once."

The middle-aged maid jumped to obey like a subaltern responding to a commanding general. The butler relaxed. The boy stood to attention. "It wasn't me, I swear," he repeated. "I rescued 'er. I killed three rats as well. Would have been four, but I…"

"Very well, Arthur," the woman replied. "Go now and get cleaned up."

The boy finally noticed the mud sliding from his clothes to the polished floor. His face shifted from defensive to horrified, and he slunk out. In the same moment, John realized that the woman with a voice like a sergeant major was his meek little sparrow of a wife. Which could not be. This woman was older than Mary; she must be older. She was definitely taller. Wasn't she? Her face was set in stern lines rather like those he'd seen on…Mary's redoubtable mother. John blinked.

The maid tugged at John's hand. He relinquished the chicken.

"Outside," commanded Mary.

The chicken lunged, its tiny yellow eyes crazed. John backed up a step as the servant bustled out the front door with the bird. John's unrecognizable wife turned with a wry smile and held out her hands. "Oh, John, what a poor welcome for you."

Confused, John took her hands. He didn't know what to say. His gaze settled on Mary's mouth. It was still a lovely little mouth, shaped for kisses, not commands. Indeed, this new Mary had a compelling quality, a bewildering allure. But he had no memory of that militant glint in her deep brown eyes or that decisive set of her pert chin.

An old woman entered the parlor. Though beautifully dressed and coiffed, she looked lost, anxious, and vague around the eyes. Seeing John, she stopped short. "Oh…hello," she said.

"Aunt Lavinia," said Mary. "Here is John, my husband. I told you he was arriving today."

"John." She obviously did not remember. Then her blue eyes brightened. "Have you returned from India so soon?"

"China," said Mary, as if correcting her elders was an established custom. "John, this is my great-aunt Lavinia Fleming."

John dropped his wife's small hands. This was the wise elder guardian who had had charge of his wife all these months? He bowed. "Pleased to meet you, ma'am."

"Has no one offered you any refreshment?" The old woman looked around as if food and drink might materialize out of the air.

"Only an outraged chicken," said Mary, a laugh in her voice.

The old woman smiled as if she was quite accustomed to hearing incomprehensible phrases. John stared down at the girl he'd married, who'd shown no previous signs of a warped sense of humor.

"Come and sit down," Mary added. She moved toward the sofa, noticed the line of muddy chicken tracks, and turned. "In the morning room, I think. Voss, have someone see to John's things."

The old butler snapped to attention.

Half an hour later, John had a glass of Madeira, a plate of sandwiches, and the persistent feeling that he was conversing with a stranger. He hadn't felt this stiff and artless with his wife when they first met, let alone after their wedding vows. To make matters worse, they were interrupted every few minutes by servants with problems or questions about the household. They seemed to feel unable to make a move without consulting Mary. For her part, she rattled off instructions without hesitation, with no reference to her great-aunt, who had lost herself in a plate of cakes.

John's mind reeled. The Mary Fleming he remembered had deferred, quite prettily, to all his opinions and requests on their honeymoon trip. And during his preparations for the China mission, she'd bustled about helping him, doing whatever he asked. As far as he could recall, she hadn't offered a single suggestion. This woman—dominating the household, hostess, and staff—was not that girl. Not by any measure. She sat and spoke and reacted quite differently. The disorientation built in him until words had to escape. "What has happened to you?"

Mary pulled back in her chair. The husband she remembered did not bark at her like an enraged parent. He was polite, quiet, gentlemanly. This John's mouth was hard with authority; his blue eyes bored into her. The planes of his face were harsher. He seemed larger, stronger, taller, though it was hardly likely he'd grown several inches at the age of twenty-six. He was…disturbingly riveting. As far as she could remember, her newlywed husband had never compelled her attention so completely. It was hard to look away from him. What had his travels done to the John Bexley she'd married? "Happened to *me*?" she replied.

"You act as if this were *your* house," he said. "Giving orders without any reference to…others' opinions."

With a sidelong glance at Lavinia, Mary said, "My great-aunt is…afflicted…"

John's mind was teeming with recollections of being chivied through his courtship and marriage ceremony by two relentless mothers. He'd let it happen then, but never again! Not in his worst nightmares had he expected to be living with a woman like that. "Nobody likes an encroaching, managing female," he said.

"Actually, quite a few people seem to."

John was startled by her wrongheaded notion but even more at Mary's dry tone. She sounded…acerbic, argumentative, and as if she might be laughing at him underneath those alien attitudes. Her pretty chin had come up, and she was looking down her straight little nose with something very like disapproval.

"In fact, they seem only too happy to push their problems off onto someone else," she added.

More than acerbic, she sounded quite critical. John couldn't believe it. "That's ridiculous. I can't conceive where you got such an idea."

"From living in a household plagued with upsets like the one you just witnessed," came the prompt reply.

She met his eyes squarely, no hint of apology in their depths. She seemed to have a comeback for anything he said. Where had she gotten this caustic tone of voice? From nowhere rose the sneering image of Fordyce, on the hunt for ways to discredit him. People said a tactless spouse was death to a diplomatic career. He had to get the old Mary back, at once. "Perhaps we might speak privately," he said, standing.

"Indeed." Mary rose as well. She had no wish to talk in front of Aunt Lavinia. Setting aside the rudeness of it, her aged relative had flashes of lucidity, when she suddenly understood far more than Mary realized.

John followed his wife upstairs to an untidy bedchamber. Accustomed to the enforced neatness of shipboard life, particularly once they were all crowded onto the *Lyra*, he found the disarray galling. The silk stocking flung over a chair back and the straw hat in the window seat might have been suggestive under other circumstances. Now they seemed of a piece with the general disruption of his universe. His sweet young wife had kept their quarters in good order. Hadn't she? He couldn't quite recall. He flicked a monitory finger at the litter of papers on the table near the window.

Mary stiffened, then relaxed when he didn't look into the pile of sketchbooks. She started to tell him that she'd been jerked from sleep by one of Alice's ear-piercing shrieks and that everyone had been too occupied since then to straighten the room.

"I hope it is understood that our home must be kept tidy." He shouldn't have to say it. She should have the habit of neatness; indeed, the wife he'd left behind *had* had it. He was almost certain she had.

Mary didn't respond at once because she was struggling with a surge of anger. She didn't remember being this angry ever before in her life. She felt as if words might erupt from her, like lava spewing from a volcano. It was daunting. She didn't throw tantrums. She never had, not even as a small child. Now, it felt as if her eyes were shooting lances of flame.

John missed them. His attention had been snared by the bed in the corner. Its covers were just slightly rumpled; he could almost smell the lavender scenting the linen. With extraordinary vividness, he saw himself sweeping Mary up in his arms and thrusting her into those fragrant sheets, drowning her unacceptable pertness in kisses, watching the unsettling spark in her dark eyes melt in the throes of passion.

John was so startled by the power of this vision, and by how much it aroused him, that he took a step backward. But the move had no effect on his imagination or on the way his body was responding to the images it conjured. Bits of talk he'd heard on shipboard, in those long, long months at sea, urged him on. He would slip his hand beneath the hem of that pale muslin gown, let it slide up the silk of her leg, finding its way to what one shipmate had called "the key to the kingdom." John's heart pounded with the thought; other bits of him throbbed in rhythm.

"Ma'am?" called someone from the hallway outside. "Mrs. Bexley, ma'am?"

Mary growled.

No. She couldn't have, John thought. His pretty

little wife did not growl like a caged tiger. He would never have married a woman who made a sound like that, no matter how goaded by his family. His mind was playing tricks on him. He was losing his mind. "I'll see to my horse," he muttered and turned away.

Mary nearly grabbed his sleeve and spun him around to stop him, set him straight. But before she could move, he was gone. She heard Alice give a startled yelp as he pounded down the stairs.

Mary started to follow, paused, and then paced the bounds of the room, her skirts swirling around her ankles, hands clenched at her sides. This was how her husband greeted her after all these months? This was the way he spoke to her? When she'd imagined their reunion, it had included a kiss, an embrace, some sign of affection at least, mention of missing her, an expression of gladness at being reunited. And what had she gotten? Nothing like that! Carping and insults from a man who knew nothing about the situation in this house. Mary pressed her hands to her cheeks. She'd worked so hard to be helpful here; she felt ready to burst at the injustice of John's criticisms.

She looked at the stocking draped over the chair back. She *would* have put it away if she'd had a single free moment today. Alice would have straightened the room if *she* hadn't had one of her fits of the vapors. Aunt Lavinia had been deeply distressed by Alice's weeping. And then came Arthur and the chicken. John simply had no idea.

Mary reached for the stocking…and somehow

found herself sitting, sketchbook in hand, the pencil nearly poking through the paper with the vehemence of her strokes.

Quickly, a face emerged under her hand, the one that had gazed at her so steamily a few minutes ago. Mary drew like one possessed. In slashing lines, she shaped and shaded, added detail. The pencil lead broke. She had to scrabble through the pile on the table for another. When at last she felt finished, she threw down the sketchbook and stared at it. Heat flooded her cheeks, washed over her neck and chest, and pooled further down. Her body came to attention like a whole troop of grenadiers. She put a hand to her throat and felt her pulse beat there.

Hands trembling, she rifled through the pile and pulled out another sketch pad. She flipped to the portrait of John on their honeymoon and set the two images side by side.

They looked like different men. Of course the outlines were the same—the cheekbones, the jaw. But the older sketch showed an amiable fellow indulging the whim of the artist who wished to capture him. His eyes held mild benevolence and…distance. Mary somehow hadn't noticed before, but her honeymooning husband appeared…detached, as if his thoughts were elsewhere and wouldn't be returning anytime soon, as if the deepest part of him would always be… veiled. Why hadn't she seen this when she first drew him? she wondered uneasily.

She turned to the new sketch, and her pulse jumped. This man sprang from the page. There was nothing mild about him, yet also nothing withheld.

He…wanted things. And he would take them. He knew just how to take them. Mary swallowed.

Her gaze went back and forth between the two portraits. The same face, hairline, nose, and eyebrow arch. But it was as if…a new person inhabited the old outlines. She was married to a stranger. A most compelling and vibrant stranger, yes. A man who demanded attention…and much more. Did he deserve it?

Mary crossed her arms on her chest. The reflection of her movement in the vanity mirror caught her attention, and she met her own wide eyes there. She looked shaken and…uncertain. The man in her second sketch roused far more tumultuous, and complicated, feelings than the respect and mild regard she felt—had felt?—for the first. She wanted to set him straight, to make him apologize, to throw her arms around his neck and pull those authoritative lips down to her own. Mary shivered again at the bolt of sensation that raced through her with that thought. It threatened to sweep all else before it.

She raised her chin and let her arms drop. No. She wouldn't let it. John had to see that he couldn't speak to her as he had earlier. Going away and changing didn't mean he got to ride roughshod over her or spout his mistaken opinions as if they were gospel. She would tell…

The door opened, and John strode back in. His eyes scanned the untouched stocking and hat, skipped over the two portraits, and settled on the bed. Quickly, he turned and faced her. His blue eyes burned into hers.

Mary's rational arguments went up in smoke. She

struggled to regain her train of thought. "It was… wrong, the way you spoke to me earlier," she said.

A low noise emerged from John.

"Did you hear me?" Mary's voice shook a little.

Catching the tremor, John wondered if she was afraid of him. John was a bit afraid of himself in his current state. The life he'd plotted out during the last days on the ship seemed to teeter in the balance. Reason battled for supremacy—and lost. He moved toward his wife, and the bed, and everything his imagination had promised.

"Are you refusing to talk to me?" Mary's dark eyes glittered; her cheeks burned a tantalizing rose red.

He reached for her.

Knuckles rapped on the bedroom door. Unlatched, it moved a few inches. "Excuse me, ma'am?" came the voice of the housemaid. Why hadn't he locked the cursed thing? John thought.

"Not now, Alice," said Mary breathlessly.

"But that delivery's here, the one you particularly wanted to check. For Mrs. Finch's room?"

"Voss can do it," said Mary, her eyes fixed on John.

"But, ma'am, you said you had to make sure it's right before we let…"

"Later!"

Even he would have retreated at the snap in her voice, John thought. But the door edged a little farther open. The housemaid was either foolhardy or utterly deaf to nuance. "The man said as how he had to be on his way to the next…"

"All right!"

She was giving in, walking away from him. John's

hands curled closed, then open. This place was bedlam. He had to get away, get Mary away, before he did something irrevocable. "We're leaving for London as soon as you can get packed," he commanded. He thrust aside the annoying inner voice that pointed out he had no carriage to transport her.

Mary paused on her way out. "What? I can't go now. The new housekeeper doesn't arrive until next week. I can't abandon Aunt Lavinia."

Raw with emotion and desire, John snapped. "You haven't managed to install a housekeeper in twenty months?"

His tone was like a lash. Mary's anger blazed up again. "Like a 'managing female,' you mean?"

"You might have gotten help for this one simple task."

"One…simple…?" The myriad upheavals she'd dealt with while he was away crowded Mary's mind. Not to mention the fact that finding just the right person had been far from simple. He had no idea what she'd faced or what she'd accomplished. "That's not fair."

"Must you argue with everything I say?"

"When you're mistaken, yes!"

"Ma'am?" came a plaintive voice from beyond the door.

Goaded beyond endurance, John turned and flung it open, making Alice jump and shriek. Did the silly woman do nothing but jump and shriek? He pushed past the aging maid, speaking to Mary over his shoulder. "I must be back in the office by Monday." This wasn't precisely true, but he didn't care. "If your aunt's housekeeper is more important to you than

I am, I'll go alone." With some slight satisfaction at venting his frustration, he strode from the room.

Mary ran after him. She might have caught him at the front door, but it had been left open. Voss stood on the step berating a large mustached man leaning against a furniture delivery wagon. The old butler turned when Mary appeared, like a child welcoming the arrival of a parent. Mary lost precious minutes fending off his complaints.

In the stables, John spotted his saddle and threw it over the back of his hired horse even as a startled stableboy ran to help. The long summer daylight would last for hours, and the nag had had a bit of rest.

Mary hurried in as he fitted the bridle. How had things gotten so completely out of hand? she wondered. "John, you mustn't go like this."

"Don't tell me what to do!"

He sounded rather like Arthur in a sulk. "But it's ridiculous. We should talk…"

"Ridiculous!" John felt as if his head might explode. "You're the one who's formed ridiculous notions while I was away making a *real* contribution to the world."

"A real…?" Mary couldn't find the words to respond.

At last, the horse was ready. John mounted and looked down at his errant wife. "The next time we meet, I expect you to have mended your ways."

"Mended…?" In her glare, John caught another glimpse of the cadre of mothers who had pitched him into his present predicament. He kicked his heels and urged the horse out of the stable yard. He was conscious of Mary's eyes on him all the way down the lane and of a sinking sense of disaster. What sort of devilish marriage had he gotten himself into? Was it going to drive him quite distracted?

He'll turn back, Mary kept thinking. He'll realize how pigheaded he's being and change his mind. But he didn't. His mounted figure receded farther and farther into the distance until he disappeared over the crest of the hill above the house.

Three

THREE WEEKS LATER, MARY FLEMING BEXLEY TRAV-
eled east to London. Though she rode in a comfortable post chaise and the early September days were
warm and golden, she was almost too preoccupied to
notice. All through welcoming her great-aunt's new
companion, getting her established in the household,
more turmoil over Arthur Windly, and packing her
own things, Mary had thought of John's brief visit.
How had it gone so wrong?

The two letters she'd received from John during
this period were short and informational, as cordial as
if their quarrel had never happened. And since he told
her about their new home without asking for opinions
or answering questions she sent about staff and furnishings, Mary wasn't moved to send an apology. He
seemed to think she was incapable of deciding details
about her own household. Indeed, it had all felt a good
bit like being bundled off to Aunt Lavinia's months
ago. She tried not to be angry, because John also said
how very busy he was in the aftermath of the China
mission. But it was difficult. Mary had to believe

that things could be smoothed over once she was in London, because to think otherwise was to despair.

She arrived in the afternoon, when John was at his office. As the carriage pulled up at the correct address, and she examined the house that he'd leased, Mary realized that part of her wanted to find fault, to discover that John's choice was quite unsuitable. That would prove him arrogant and incapable and *wrong*. It was not an impulse she liked in herself.

In fact, the tall, narrow, gray-brick edifice looked comfortable, the sort of place she might have chosen, given the opportunity to do so. It sat on the south side of a leafy square. Dwellings to either side had beds of fall flowers in their small front gardens. She knew the place was close enough to the Foreign Office that John could easily ride there on the horse he kept at a nearby livery stable. She knew that the lease terms he had arranged were reasonable. She knew she was looking at her home, that perhaps she would be living here for many years. Someday, she might recall this first sight of it and think…what would she think?

One of the postboys opened the carriage door, and Mary stepped out onto the cobbles. A small, skinny figure, bouncing with energy despite the long journey, had already jumped down from the box. Arthur Windly circled the chaise, gazing around the square with bright curiosity. Mary sighed. The boy's presence was another complication, when she didn't need the ones she already had.

"This one?" Arthur asked, pointing at the house. When Mary nodded, he skipped up the two stone steps and knocked on the front door. Mary mounted them behind him. After a rather lengthy delay, the door was opened by a housemaid. "No one home," declared the young woman, and she shut the door in their faces.

Astonished, Mary blinked at the wooden panels.

"What the…?" Arthur pounded on the door.

It opened more quickly this time. "I told you…"

"This is Mrs. Bexley," said Arthur. "It's *her* house, ya daft creature." He pushed at the door.

Mary put a hand on his shoulder to restrain him. "I wrote that I would arrive today," she said.

"Oh." The maid stood back, opening the door. Arthur darted inside.

Mary waited for embarrassment, an apology. None came. "And what is your name?" she asked in her best Great-Aunt-Lavinia-in-her-prime manner.

"Kate…ma'am." Belatedly, the maid dropped a curtsy.

"Kate." Mary looked her over. The young woman had blond hair and blue eyes that were a bit small for her round face. She was several inches taller than Mary, probably a bit older, with square shoulders and a stubborn-looking jaw; her print dress and apron were superior examples of a housemaid's garb. She might have been attractive if not for the sullen set of her mouth and general dissatisfied air. "Well, Kate, that is not the way callers are to be greeted at *my* house."

The maid leaned a little toward her, as if to emphasize her greater heft. Perhaps she expected her new mistress to be cowed. Two years ago, she might have been, Mary thought. But much had happened since then. She took the time to find the right words. "I require that everyone who knocks be treated with courtesy. And spoken to with respect, whoever they may be. You are not to shut the door in people's faces. Ever."

Kate's eyes fell. She muttered something about not being used to answering doors and turned her attention to the postboys and driver as they carried Mary's trunks inside. The maid followed along to show them the way upstairs and to exchange flirtatious remarks with the youngest. Once Mary had paid the boys off, Kate seemed prepared to trail her about the house as well and to make slighting remarks about the size and decoration of the place. Mary had to dismiss her quite firmly before she was left on her own.

At last, Mary stood alone in the small entry, able to really look around. To the right was a reception room with an attractive tiled fireplace. She recognized the sofa and two armchairs as castoffs from her parents' house. The Flemings and the Bexleys had taken it upon themselves to send furnishings, and she knew John had not discouraged them from doing so. The faded rose pattern on the chintz was familiar and fit well enough in the paneled space, however.

Mary looked left. The dining room was smaller, as the house's front door was offset from center. A dining table and six chairs filled it to overflowing. They, and the red Turkish carpet, must have come from John's family. She didn't remember them.

This was *her* house, Mary told herself as she started up the stairs at the back of the entryway. Not her mother's undisputed domain or her great-aunt's abdicated kingdom. No authority would be looking over her shoulder, reminding her how things *should* be.

Though she hadn't gotten to choose the place—or the furnishings, for that matter—she could order life as she imagined it here, set routines that suited her and John, of course—the changed John who had come back from the other side of the world, who might not be the sort of man Mary would have chosen to marry at all.

Mary shoved aside this thought and moved on. The second floor offered three rooms. One was already set up as a study/library and showed signs of John's occupation. Another, also overlooking the square, would make a cozy parlor for her use. The last, just now empty, was quite small. Here she found Arthur Windly peering out the window over the sea of rooftops receding into the distance.

"So many houses," he marveled. "I never thought there'd be so many."

"London is very large," Mary said.

"Where am I to stay…ma'am?"

She sighed. She had made a deal, and she must stick to it. "Upstairs."

Arthur trailed her to the third floor, where she and John had connecting bedchambers. Her trunks sat ready for unpacking in hers. A smaller room was empty. He followed her again up to the top level of the house, which contained servants' rooms. Two of the small bedchambers showed signs of use. Mary gave Arthur his choice of the other two. He opted for the one at the front, and ran off in search of his bag.

Mary walked slowly back down the stairs. The place was a bit stark and drab, in need of draperies and other touches of warmth, but she didn't mind the lack.

She wanted to choose those things herself. Her luggage included lengths of cloth from both her parents' and aunt's houses, handed along for her use.

Descending to the basement kitchen, she found Kate huddled with a thin, pinch-faced woman of perhaps fifty. The older woman wore a cook's apron and a sour expression. "This place isn't what I'm used to," she said as soon as Mary appeared. "Everything's old-fashioned and near worn-out. The kitchen stairs are so narrow, it's a penance to carry a tray up 'em. There's no proper pans or knives…"

Mary interrupted the flood of complaint with, "How do you do? I am Mrs. Bexley."

"Catherine Tanner," the woman supplied, scarcely missing a beat. "*Mrs*. Tanner. And I don't know how I'm to cook under these conditions."

Mary, whose mother had given her a solid grounding in household economy, took stock. The brick-floored kitchen had space for cooking and preparation and a large table off to the side where servants could dine and sit in their off hours. There was a scullery and pantry behind, and Mary just glimpsed an outdoor stair up to the back of the house. The woodstove set into the huge old fireplace seemed to be working well. There was a hot water reservoir and a grill. The walls had been recently whitewashed, and she was happy to see that everything looked clean. It was true that pans and utensils were few. She would have to remedy that. But as far as she knew, the woman had been cooking here successfully for two weeks. She remembered her mother's list of questions for new staff. "Where did you work before this?"

Mrs. Tanner drew herself up and crossed her arms on her meager chest. "We came direct from the Duchess of Carwell's household. And let me tell you, I didn't have to scrub roasting pans or peel potatoes *there*. Two scullery maids and a potboy, we had. Not to speak of kitchen maids and one cook just to do the bread and pastry."

"You were head cook for a duchess?" Mary marveled. Why in the world was she here, in that case?

"Second undercook to 'Monsewer Danyell,'" said Kate, earning a glare from Mrs. Tanner. "He's landed on his feet, he has. Working for an earl, is what I heard."

"Why did you leave your positions?" Mary's mother had emphasized that this was a question one always asked, perhaps the most important question.

"Her Grace's precious son gambled their fortune clean away, didn't he?" replied Kate, with obvious relish. "They had to sell the town house and let all the servants go. All his fancy racehorses as well. Family's run off to hide in the country. I wouldn't wonder if them down there was to lose their places, too."

"Kate!" snapped Mrs. Tanner. She pulled a folded packet of paper from one of her apron pockets. "I have a very good reference from Her Grace's housekeeper," she said. "Worked in the household all my life, I have…did."

She didn't mention references for Kate. Mary took the pages and read the references under two pairs of resentful blue eyes, two similar sullen expressions. When she'd finished, satisfied that Mrs. Tanner had been honest about the recommendations, she suppressed a sigh. This was not the sort of staff she'd imagined in her new home.

The packet went back in Mrs. Tanner's pocket, and she resumed her litany of complaint as if it had never been interrupted. "I'll be needing more help as soon as may be. And what's to be done about the bread, I do not know. I only have two hands. As for that butcher down the street…" She sniffed. "Not a partridge to be had, he tells me. It's all chickens with him. Scrawny ones, too. And mingy bits of beef you wouldn't feed a spaniel."

Did she even know how to cook for a small household? Mary wondered. It was quite a different job from feeding a peer's huge retinue. Or her spaniel. Something would have to be done about this.

"Who's that boy?" Kate asked, with no sign of deference. "Is he staying?"

"That is Arthur," Mary replied. "He will help out." Or else, she thought.

"He can do the scullery work," replied the cook. The spark in her eye did not bode well for a peaceful future.

ॐ

John arrived home after six to find his wife established in the parlor with some sewing. There was a small fire burning in the grate, candles throwing a warm light over the walls, and a cozier feel to the room somehow. More color, John thought; she'd thrown a shawl over the back of the sofa, draped some cloth at the windows. Relief washed over him. This domestic picture seemed to herald the old Mary, the sweet compliant

Mary, rather than the militant creature he'd encountered in Somerset. Perhaps, in his disorientation at being back in England, he'd imagined the latter?

Dropping into an armchair, responding to her quiet greeting, he profoundly hoped so. Because right now, he could not stomach any more aggravation. After two hours, he was still seething, and longing to kick something. That idiot Fordyce had tipped a bottle of ink over John's carefully composed twenty-page report, wrecking two full days of effort. And when John had protested, the overbred twit swore it was an accident, even though John had seen him pause beside the desk, check to see no one else was watching, and flip a finger at the bottle. When he'd sworn at him, Fordyce claimed his coattail must have brushed it. Pure chance, due to John's carelessness, really, to be leaving ink bottles about uncorked. John found that he was clenching his teeth.

He'd thought that once they were back in London, taking their former places among the army of clerks at the Foreign Office, Fordyce would disappear from his life. He hadn't been aware of the man before the China mission. He didn't expect to see him after. But Fordyce had other ideas and a positive genius for malicious little incidents like today's, where a protest was impossible. Insisting that Fordyce had done it on purpose would only make John sound like a bleating schoolboy whose homework had been spoiled. Or a tiresome grind. Fordyce was a master of the raised eyebrow, the mocking gesture, the pitying smile that said caring too deeply was just so tiresomely middle class. John would have dismissed his antics as ridiculous, except that this was the pervasive culture of the Foreign Office—the glorification of the aristocratic amateur.

He was going to have do something about Fordyce, make him stop these infuriating games. John had big plans and no time for his nonsense.

The hiss and crackle of a log falling in two in the fire called John back to the parlor. Mary's needle had gone still. She looked wary and as if she might have said something that he didn't hear. The disaster of their last encounter came flooding back to him. Another tangle he had to unravel. "How was your journey? Not too tiring, I hope?"

"No, the weather was fine and the coach quite comfortable."

They might have been distant acquaintances meeting in the street, John thought.

"The plantings in the square are quite lovely," she added. "I walked all around it earlier. There was no one else about."

His wife was looking quite lovely herself, John realized. Her rose-pink gown emphasized the warm color in her cheeks and lips. Her dark hair shone in the firelight. She'd been hemming a handkerchief, he saw—a picture of domestic tranquillity, of the gentle Mary he remembered from their wedding journey. Had that scene in Somerset really happened?

She raised those huge brown eyes and met his gaze. The color in her cheeks deepened a bit. "Are you hungry?" she asked. "I ordered dinner for seven, but we could move it up a little. Or perhaps you'd like a glass of wine?"

He was ravenous, John realized. He hadn't had time for a bite since breakfast. "Starved," he said. He rose and held out a hand. Mary took it. She set her sewing aside and stood to face him. Her fingers were small and warm in his. A hint of her scent reached him, subtle and flowery. Was it violets? He breathed it in. He thought it was violets—the shy, secret blooms hidden under fallen leaves and bracken deep in the forest. Her cheeks looked soft as violet petals, softer even than the hand he held. The pink cloth of her gown moved with her breath, the modest swoop of its neckline making him think of what was underneath. If he bent forward only slightly, he could place his lips at that edge.

Down in the kitchen, something fell with a resounding clang. A spate of unintelligible words followed the sound. Mary turned her head, frowning. "Oh, what can it be now?"

It was the voice she'd used in Somerset, the sergeant major chivying the troops.

"I'd better go and see. I'll tell Mrs. Tanner we're ready to eat."

John let go of her hand. And with a last breath of violets, she was gone.

They sat down to dinner a short time later. It was roast chicken again, but John didn't complain. Mary had no way of knowing that he'd had chicken three nights out of five since the servants arrived. The maid reached past him with a serving platter. A carving knife slid along the edge and dropped off, spearing directly toward his lap. John barely caught the handle as she set the platter down with an audible thunk.

"Kate!" said Mary. "Take some care."

A dish of potatoes from the maid's other hand hit the tabletop even harder. One bounced out; she snatched it up and replaced it.

She was a ham-handed servitor. John had noticed it before, but now that Mary was here, the maid's clumsiness seemed somehow his fault. He started to carve the chicken. "I trust your great-aunt is well settled?" he asked.

"Yes, I was quite right about Mrs. Finch. She is perfect for the position. Both kind and efficient. And the staff all likes her."

"That's good."

The maid's footsteps coming up the kitchen stair and back into the dining room sounded like the tromp of a whole platoon. Something soft and creamy plopped to the floor behind John, followed by a muttered imprecation and scrabbling sounds. There seemed to be far more noise from below than he was accustomed to as well. Had the cook begun talking to herself?

"Leave it till later, Kate," said Mary, who was in a position to see what was going on.

"I can get it back in the dish," replied the maid pertly.

"We won't have it now."

"But it's hardly dirt—"

"Just bring up the tarts I made," Mary commanded. With a muttered, "Yes'm," the girl departed.

"You made?" John said.

"Yes, I quite enjoy baking. I often…"

"You shouldn't be cooking."

"Why not?"

"You have servants for that."

A crash from the stairs was followed by an audible curse. "Should I not pick up the tarts either?" shouted Kate from the nether regions. Shattered crockery stirred. "They're mostly broke," she allowed.

"Never mind," called Mary, her teeth clenched around the words. "We don't need anything more right now."

John recognized the annoyed glitter in her eyes from Somerset. "The registry said these people had worked in the household of a duchess," he said. "I assumed they would know their business, add a touch of elegance to the place. Apparently, I was deceived." This was just a cap to his truly wretched day.

"I'll take care of it."

"The maid is hopeless. I see that." The words came out sharp and impatient, driven by his pent-up anger.

Mary didn't want to talk about dismissing the servants within their hearing. Indeed, she wasn't eager to begin any significant discussion. John had come home so grim and fierce, so utterly unlike—again—the man she'd thought she married that she hardly knew what to say to him. And then he'd stood in the parlor gripping her hand and staring at her as if he'd never seen her before. It was very unsettling.

"Do you wish me to admit I made a mistake in hiring them?" John snapped. "Very well, I admit it. Satisfied? Now you have an opportunity to show that you can *manage* much better than I can."

"I was not thinking any such thing!" Though she certainly *could*, Mary thought. She reined in her temper. "I will talk to Kate about her serving…"

"Our house is not a training ground for incompetent

servants!" He was spoiling for a fight, John realized. Though he knew it was Fordyce he wanted to throttle, and not his unsuspecting wife, he couldn't seem to stop himself. "You will dismiss them at once."

"I am in charge of the house. I will decide what to do."

"Do you take pleasure in contradicting me?"

The sarcasm in his voice eroded Mary's resolve to be amiable. She would not be treated like a lackwit in her own home. "You are being unreasonable."

"*You* are being infuriatingly stubborn! Why will you not simply do as I ask?" It was a question for John's whole world at this moment. It seemed that every element of his life strove against him.

"The servants are *my* responsibility," Mary countered. She knew that the women below stairs would be straining to hear every word they said. "I'm quite good at running a household."

"Indeed? And that is why there is…" John turned to look behind him. "…something green and slimy seeping into the carpet."

Mary lost her battle with annoyance. He was really being quite unfair. "*You* hired them!"

"And now *you* refuse to be rid of them! Why? I suppose you will enjoy shoving my mistake in my face each and every day?" Just as Fordyce created opportunities to make him appear incompetent.

Mary was shocked by the idea. "I would never do anything like that." How could he think such a thing?

They stared at each other across the table. The tension in the atmosphere stretched and tightened until Mary thought she would scream. Then it seemed to slowly drain away. John's gaze shifted to his half-eaten dinner. "I can't stand constant brangling," he said. "I have more than enough of that at the office."

"I hate it," said Mary, wondering what in the world his office could be like.

They contemplated one another through a further silence.

"We were married off by our families," said John finally. It was a stark statement; all the emotion had disappeared from his voice. The flat tone so depressed Mary's spirits that she could only nod. It felt as if the fragile fabric of her marriage might be coming apart at the seams.

"We'd just begun to get acquainted, and then we were apart for a long time, leading quite different lives."

"Yes."

"We don't know each other very well."

It was true that the man who'd returned from his long journey seemed like a stranger. And sometimes, lately, Mary felt she scarcely knew herself. Yet the way he said it was so dispiriting. "I suppose not."

"But we're married," he said.

She didn't like the "but." Not at all. It sounded resigned, and not particularly hopeful.

"So…I think we need to…make allowances."

"That's a horrid word." It came out of her mouth without premeditation. She didn't blame him for looking startled. Mary licked her lips and searched for clarity in the jumble of her thoughts. "Making allowances" was for inescapable predicaments or disagreeable relatives. "More like…starting fresh?"

John cocked his head, raised an inquiring brow.

An errant impulse brought Mary to her feet. She came around the table, stood before him, and dropped a small curtsy. "Pleased to meet you, Mr. Bexley."

After a moment, a smile tugged at his mouth. He rose and bowed politely. "Mrs. Bexley."

Mary offered her hand. He took it and, as in the parlor earlier, heat seemed to suffuse the air. She felt his gaze on her. His eyes looked bluer, somehow. She was newly aware of his height, the breadth of his shoulders, the strength in the fingers around hers. He raised her hand toward his lips.

Audible grumbling and loud footsteps heralded the appearance of Mrs. Tanner, still in her soiled cook's apron. She looked startled to find them standing together, then defiant. "We've run out of kindling," she declared, "and the coal bin's near empty as well."

John dropped Mary's hand and stepped back. How had he endured these servants for two weeks? They were insupportable.

Mary frowned at her. "I'll see about ordering new supplies first thing tomorrow," she answered. "You might have waited until then to tell me…"

The cook just stood there with crossed arms. "Mr. Bexley said he'd do it today."

John cursed silently. He'd said he would try to see about this, but with all that had gone on at the office, he'd forgotten. He opened his mouth to defend himself.

"Mr. Bexley is far too busy to deal with household orders," Mary replied crisply before he could speak. "I said I would take care of it."

"I suppose there's money for coals and all?" was

the incredible response. John gaped at the woman's impertinence.

"Yes, Mrs. Tanner, there is. And for whatever else I decide that we require."

Mary spoke like a duchess herself, John thought. And the obstreperous cook responded at once to her tone. She took a step back, dropped a curtsy, and said, "Yes, ma'am." She left the room much more rapidly than she'd come in.

Relieved, and impressed, he turned to gaze at his wife. There she stood, looking just like the pretty little thing he'd taken to the altar two years ago, the sweet girl he'd imagined molding to his revised requirements. Only she wasn't. She was somebody else entirely, currently watching him with uncomfortably sharp brown eyes. It was a fine idea, starting fresh. He liked it; he approved. But just now it felt like another task in a long list on his plate.

"I have a good deal of work to do." He had to recopy his report, deciphering and reconstituting the ink-spoilt pages. It would take hours, but he couldn't let Fordyce's stupid trick make the document late.

"Oh." Mary felt dismissed, as if she no longer had any place in his thoughts. "Shall I bring you a cup of tea?"

"Yes, thank you." John smiled. "And perhaps some of those broken tarts?"

For a disorienting moment, Mary thought he'd said "broken hearts."

"If you can pick out the bits of china," he added.

He was joking, Mary told herself. He was trying to be pleasant. She nodded and smiled back. Amity trembled into existence between them once again.

What if she simply embraced him? Mary wondered. If they could cut through the thicket of words that seemed to entangle them every time they spoke...

And just at the moment she would *not* have chosen, Arthur Windly erupted into the room from the kitchen stairs. "That Kate is a regular caution," he said. When the Bexleys turned to look at him, he added, "She said to come and ask you. Cook wants me to scrub all the pots. There's a great mound of 'em. Must I really? Ma'am?" The boy wilted a little under their combined gaze. "Sir?"

"Who are you?" John asked.

"This is Arthur," Mary supplied. She turned back to the boy. "You know the agreement, Arthur."

"But they're all crusted over. And Kate burnt a whole pan of..."

"Nevertheless. You must do as you're told." Mary's sergeant major voice was back.

John got it finally. "Aren't you the boy who was chasing the chicken in Somerset?"

Arthur's skinny shoulders drew together. "That devil! I never meant to go in the house. If those dratted doors hadn't been left open..."

"Go on to your work," Mary told him. "You promised." With a scowl, he turned and walked—very slowly—out of the room.

"Who exactly is he?" John asked again. "And what is he doing here?"

Wishing she could have chosen a better moment for explanations, Mary plunged in. "Arthur is the son of Great-Aunt Lavinia's steward. He and his father are having...a difficult time of it. They cannot seem to get along. The chicken, uh, incident was the last straw for Mr. Windly, after a number of other…mishaps. He insisted that Arthur must be truly punished, so as to learn his lesson once and for all." Mary tried to read John's face, to see if he understood. "Arthur cannot seem to do anything right in his father's eyes. I was worried that his measures would be…too severe. But when I tried to speak to him about it he…didn't wish to listen. So I thought…"

"That you would bring him here," John said in an odd voice.

Mary nodded. "Arthur is set to go off to school next year. I think he will do quite well once he is away…" She left that thought unspoken. "His father decreed that he spend the time until then as a lower servant, in order to understand what he might come to if he didn't, uh, straighten up. He thinks that blacking boots and scrubbing pots and…oh, obeying orders will…"

"Turn Arthur into a paragon of virtue," said John.

Mary couldn't fathom his dry tone. He didn't seem angry, as she had feared he would be. "More or less." She shrugged. "I promised him that Arthur would be put to work. But I thought it would go better here than directly under Mr. Windly's eye…" She'd also thought, in the end, that Mr. Windly had suspected as much, even known that she would treat Arthur with more sympathy than he could muster himself.

"There can be no doubt of it," John declared. "You did quite right."

Mary had expected annoyance at the least, a battle at worst. This response confused her. "So, you don't mind if he is with us for a few months?"

"On the contrary. He's quite welcome." The smile he gave her was one of the most open and sincere she'd seen since his return.

Mary watched her husband head for the stairs, surprised and grateful. He'd been so irritated about the servants. Why was he suddenly amenable? Truly, she didn't understand him. And now that the hurdle of Arthur was successfully passed, she felt a tinge of guilt. She was sure the boy had his slingshot packed away in his bag.

When she took up the tea and broken tarts a bit later, she found John settled at his desk, deeply engrossed with pen and ink. Oddly, a bulky document covered with ink was spread before him. He barely acknowledged her arrival, though she could see it was from distraction.

Later still, Mary climbed into her unfamiliar bed alone. Though she was worn by days of travel and her rocky arrival, she didn't fall asleep right away. She was acutely conscious of John on the floor beneath, directly below her pillow—almost as if she could hear the scratch of his quill across the page, see the look of concentration on his handsome face. She remembered the way his strong, shapely hand had gripped hers earlier, how he'd looked at her with such unsettling intensity. That look had been…thrilling. And fleeting. And confusing. John had never looked at her that way before he went away. The girl she was then wouldn't have wanted him to, really. Now, she hoped he would do it again, soon.

Indeed, what if she went downstairs this minute, as she was, in only her thin nightdress, and stood before his desk…? A flush began in Mary's cheeks and burned all the way to her toes. Where had that idea come from? A host of others, equally new and enthralling, bubbled up as she imagined what might follow.

But, no, he'd been so completely taken up by his document. If he turned her away… She punched her pillows and turned over.

This stranger husband roused such a welter of emotions in her—anger and fascination and frustration and spikes of desire. Had she known what any of those words meant before? She'd felt more, it seemed, in the past few weeks than in her whole previous life. Which was…disconcerting. To say the least.

Mary turned over again. Starting fresh; they were starting fresh.

The sheets and coverlet felt heavy, stifling. What should she do? What did she want? Everything, declared a new inner voice, one that she scarcely recognized. She was no longer the docile creature who went along with what others decreed—the follower of stronger-willed sisters, the obedient, if disappointing, daughter. Mary's hands curled as if to grab and hold. She'd discovered a self absolutely brimming with wants. The only question was how to satisfy them.

Four

MARY DIDN'T HEAR HER HUSBAND LEAVE THE following morning; he was up and out so early. This was his invariable habit, Kate told her, setting down a plate of toast at breakfast. "Up with the birds," she said, in a tone that suggested a proper master would loll away the morning in his bed.

Mary ignored her. She took her last cup of tea upstairs to the room she'd chosen as her own retreat and set about putting down roots in her new home. There was work to be done, tasks she understood and was good at; there was a certain thrill in beginning them.

And so she started her first full day in London making lists—things needed and where to get them. In many cases, she had no idea where to purchase the items she wanted, but she was confident she could find out. For the draperies and other furnishings, she would consult friends of her family or John's who lived in London. Her mother had given her some names and also written to her particular friends. The most pressing needs she dealt with by the simple expedient of knocking on the doors of three of her neighbors and asking the servants who answered where these households purchased their wood and coal and staple groceries. Since she got the same answers at all three, she sent Arthur off to the designated vendors with written orders for immediate delivery. If the skip in his step was any measure, the boy was delighted to be given this outdoor mission. Mary wondered how long it would be before she saw him again.

In the afternoon, having ticked off a satisfying number of lines on her list, Mary went out to walk in the central garden of the square. This was a surprisingly spacious stretch of vegetation, beautifully landscaped. Local residents had keys to the gate in the tall wrought iron fence that surrounded it, so casual walkers couldn't enter. The rectangle of trees and late summer flowers and gravel walkways felt quite private and exclusive for a patch of city.

After she'd taken a bit of exercise, Mary sat on a bench and opened the sketchbook she'd brought along. She had no plan other than to let her subject come to her. Fancy and intuition would lead her down their own pathways, directing her to anything she needed to discover. She took out her pencil and waited for her hand to move.

It soon did. A head and shoulders began to form on her page, and then another. The features of Mrs. Tanner and Kate the maid gradually emerged as Mary lost herself in the process. She used her hands, her heart, the techniques her mind had learned, the impulses of her spirit.

Fifteen minutes later, Mary gazed down at a dual portrait. Her cook and maid stared out at her, wearing their customary sullen expressions, pure embodiments of disgruntlement. Mary sat still and let the images sink into her consciousness. Though she hadn't noticed it before, the two faces revealed similar lines. And that called up memories of certain ways they spoke to each other, small gestures that she'd noticed without noticing. Mrs. Tanner and Kate were related, she concluded. Mother and daughter, most likely.

With that insight came a cascade of others. Mary realized that these two women were humiliated and afraid. They'd lost their familiar place in the world, tumbled down many ranks in their social scheme. They were terrified of falling further, furious at the workings of fate, and fighting their fears with belligerence. Her idea of dismissing them in the next few days and hiring more amenable servants withered and died. Seeing them exposed in her drawing, she couldn't think of turning them out. She also couldn't suppress a sigh at the thought of the complicated negotiations that lay ahead.

"That's very good," said a voice above her head.

Mary jumped. Her hand moved instinctively to hide the drawing as she turned.

A woman stood behind the bench—old, small, a little bent. A fine lace cap covered her snow-white hair, and her pelisse was beautifully tailored. Pale blue eyes gazed from a wrinkled face, backed by the fine bones of persistent beauty. "And you don't even have a model," she added. Her expression was all bright interest and admiration.

Mary made herself straighten out of her defensive hunch and remove her hand from Mrs. Tanner's face.

"I…can draw pretty well from memory," she said. She smiled. "Although, you don't really know whether it's a good likeness."

"The feel of it tells me it is," the old woman replied, smiling back at her. "It has great vitality." She took a step closer to get a better view. "Two women outraged by life, wishing they could make someone pay for whatever's happened to them. Yet fearful, because they can't."

Mary blinked, surprised to hear her thoughts so clearly echoed.

"It's really remarkably lifelike." The woman walked around the bench to sit beside her, taking a small sketch pad from under her arm. "I draw a bit, too." She opened her tablet on a charming scene, a view of the circular flower bed in the center of the square, the greens and purples picked out in watercolors. "Landscapes only, I'm afraid. Something about faces makes my pencil go off. Perhaps it's a sense of being overlooked. I dislike being watched while I draw."

Mary certainly understood that. "I think of it as watching *them*," she offered.

The old woman shrugged. "Perhaps I've just been too…encumbered by people in my life." She glanced at a house on the other side of the square from Mary's. Her smile returned, impish and youthful despite her wrinkles. "These days it's my servants. They will hover. It's all I can do to escape to this bit of garden. I promise you that two or three of them are peering out the windows right now, wondering who you are and what in the world I think I'm doing. Outdoors without a bonnet! Or my gloves. Scandalous!"

Her lighthearted tone made Mary dare, "What *are* you doing?"

The old woman laughed. "Teasing them a little, perhaps. But chiefly making the acquaintance of a new neighbor. I haven't seen you here before. And I'm quite brazen, you see. No waiting for a 'proper' introduction."

Her roguish look made Mary laugh as well. "I'm Mary Bexley. We just moved into number thirty-six. My husband John and I."

"Eleanor Lanford. I've lived in this square for six years."

"I'm so glad to meet you…Mrs. Lanford. You are my very first acquaintance in London. Indeed, this is my first day in town."

"Is it? Ever, you mean?"

Mary nodded, wondering if she had sounded countrified.

But her companion was examining her with every appearance of cordiality. "You rather remind me of one of my great-nieces. You must call me Eleanor. Mrs. Lanford…" She waved the label aside.

"That's odd. I was just thinking you were rather like my Great-Aunt Lavinia." As soon as the words popped out of her mouth, Mary wondered what she meant by them. There was no resemblance. Except… perhaps in the feel of her new neighbor. She had the sort of self-assurance and marked presence that Aunt Lavinia used to have. "Are you acquainted with everyone who lives in the square?" Mary said, to change the subject.

Eleanor Lanford looked at the row houses surrounding them. "Not really acquainted. I know most of the names and some of the professions. There are several senior barristers and a banker or two. They are all closer to my age than yours. And rather... punctilious. You are quite a breath of fresh air for the neighborhood."

This was flattering, but disappointing. Mary couldn't imagine making friends among people like that.

"This garden could use some children playing," her companion added wistfully.

A woman came out of the house Eleanor had pointed out as her own. She looked like a superior lady's maid. She started toward the garden gate.

Eleanor rose. "I must go. You are very talented, my dear. I hope to see you again soon."

The servant marched over to the wrought iron fence and stood waiting. She looked militant.

"I hope so, too," said Mary. The servant's frown made her add, "I hope I haven't caused you any trouble."

"Not at all, my dear. I am quite able to control my household." Eleanor's straight back and raised chin were suddenly the picture of aristocratic hauteur, dissipated a moment later by a twinkle in her pale blue eyes. "I keep all the keys to that gate, and my staff are reduced to peering through the fence and beckoning." She gave Mary something very like a wink before slowly, with great dignity, walking away.

Mary watched her meet the maid at the garden gate and saw that Eleanor was treated with marked deference. Even at a distance, Mary thought she could see affection as well as concern in the fussing. The servant took Eleanor's sketchbook, offered an arm, and shook her head good-naturedly when it was refused. They walked together into Eleanor's house. Mary sat back with a smile. She had made her first friend in this new place, and that made a great difference.

She sat for a while longer, enjoying the autumn sun. She was just about to go in when her idyll was interrupted by a spate of furious barking. This was soon joined by the sound of racing footsteps and an inarticulate shout. Curious, Mary rose and went to look through the fence in the direction of the noise.

Arthur emerged from one of the streets that gave onto the square. He was running as hard as he could, his skinny arms pumping, eyes wide and wild. The barking grew louder as a huge yellow dog appeared behind him, getting closer with each lunging stride. It was about to catch him.

"Arthur!" Mary ran over to the gate as the boy's head swiveled toward her. She waved. He spotted her and veered in her direction. Mary pulled the gate open. Arthur hurtled through, and she shut it right on his heels, only just in time. The gigantic dog slammed sideways into the wrought iron pickets, bounced off, and stood slavering and barking, inches away. Its teeth were daunting, long and sharp.

Mary backed up several steps, even though the animal couldn't reach them through the fence. "What have you done?"

"I never meant to hit him," Arthur cried. "There was a ruddy great rat right outside the market stalls. Biggest rat I've ever seen. You think the London rats are some kind of special…?"

"Arthur!"

He danced in place. "So I was going to kill the rat,

see, as a favor to the hawkers." His air of put-upon virtue was laughable. "And I'd've done it, too, but *this* great brute walked in front of me just as I let fly."

Now Mary saw the strings of the slingshot sticking out of his pocket. "You shot this dog?" She looked at the huge creature. It had settled into pacing and growling just outside the fence.

"By mistake," Arthur insisted. "An accident, like."

"Who does it belong to?" Mary couldn't decide if the appearance of an irate owner would be good news or bad news. He could call off the dog, but he might want to drag Arthur to a magistrate.

"Don't know," Arthur replied. "Didn't see anybody with him."

Mary examined the dog. He had no collar. His yellow coat was rough, but he didn't appear underfed. She gazed up the street. No sign of anyone looking for him. Nor was there any reaction from the nearby houses, despite the earlier barking. She moved closer to the fence and slowly held out a hand. The dog rushed up and stuck his muzzle between two of the bars. He snapped and growled. Mary jumped back.

"Have a care!" said Arthur. "He ain't what you'd call friendly."

"I see that." Mary scanned the streets again. They were empty; still no signs of life from any of the houses. It was certainly a quiet neighborhood. Or perhaps just a cautious one. From this angle, Eleanor's house was blocked by a bushy evergreen. "Kate will see us eventually and come out."

"Her?" Arthur jeered. "She wouldn't lift a finger against a dog like that."

Mary was afraid he was right. And what would she have done if she'd looked out her window and seen such an animal? Rushed out to confront it?

"Reckon I could scare him away," Arthur said. He took out his sling. The dog erupted in a frenzy of barking.

"Arthur! Put that away."

He shoved it back in his pocket, and their jailer quieted. "What are we going to do?" For once Arthur sounded like a small boy rather than an apprentice wreaker of havoc.

"We'll wait. The dog will get bored and wander off." Or so Mary hoped.

"But I'm hungry!" Arthur was always hungry. In Somerset, the cook had made it her mission to fill him up, but she never managed it. Huge quantities of sustenance disappeared into his rail-thin little body without perceptible effect. "I gotta eat."

"Shh. You're upsetting it."

Arthur subsided with a mumble that sounded very much like, "It's upsetting *me*."

They sat down on a bench. Arthur fidgeted. After a while, the dog lay down on the cobbles and rested his formidable jaw on his forepaws. Thinking he might have calmed, Mary rose and slowly approached the gate. The dog jumped up, growling, and started to bark. "Stupid mongrel," muttered Arthur as she retreated again.

The sun inched down behind the western roofs. A breeze rustled the autumn leaves. A passerby indignantly declined to become involved in their dilemma, moving off at a blistering pace when he spied the dog.

This was ridiculous, Mary thought. She would

simply walk through the gate and across the square to her front door. It was well-known that dogs responded to an air of command. Her father's dogs always did so. But when she put her hand on the latch, this animal lunged at her with a growl and snap so threatening that she pulled away again.

&

John's mood was far lighter than yesterday's as he headed for home. His report had been handed in on time and welcomed with a mention of his good work on the China voyage. He hadn't encountered Fordyce. He left his office with a solid sense of accomplishment and a mind full of the plan he intended to put in motion in the next few days. He was even able to get away a bit early.

Passing a flower vendor outside the Foreign Office building, he paused and looked over her small selection of late blooms. When he told her he wanted something for his wife, the woman helped him put together a charming little bouquet. It seemed a good idea to arrive home with a...not a peace offering. It wasn't that. It occurred to John that one often sent flowers after being presented to a young lady. He'd sent something—roses?—the day after he and Mary first danced together at a Bath assembly. Remembering her curtsy and introduction last night after dinner, he smiled. Recalling the feel of her hand in his, the visions it conjured, he let out a breath. The bouquet could be a tangible sign of their fresh start.

Their lives had shifted like one of those newfangled kaleidoscopes that Scottish fellow had invented, John mused as he walked to the livery stable. One of his colleagues had showed him how the bright pieces turned and slid into a new configuration. The change was disorienting, uncomfortable but also rather...intriguing.

Every time he saw Mary his mind slipped that way. She looked very much as she had before he left; that was one view. Then she felt so different; that was the turn of the cylinder, the pieces falling into a startling new order. He was tricked by old assumptions to act as he had before, and then he got a prickly, unsettling response. Like reaching down to pet your cat and touching a...a hedgehog...or a...dragon. It was... sometimes...quite exciting.

As he retrieved his horse and rode homeward, his thoughts were full of Mary. She contradicted him and confused him. But it was all of a piece, he realized suddenly, with the alterations his long voyage had stirred up. His interior life now seemed to be a matter of surges and sparks, waves of intensity, rather than a placid stream he scarcely noticed. He'd become something of a stranger to himself.

John left his horse at the livery near home and strolled off, indulging in a pleasant reverie about the moment when he had thought to drop a kiss just at the edge of Mary's pink bodice. He'd touched that silken skin on their honeymoon, but not, he knew now, with the care and attention it deserved. He had a host of ideas about how to remedy that lapse, if only they could...renew their acquaintance. The idea made him smile. He walked faster, eager to be home. It was almost as if he could hear Mary calling to him.

John stopped and listened. She actually was calling

his name. Shouting it, really. Here, outdoors. What the deuce?

Searching for the source of the sound, he discovered his wife and the boy she'd brought from Somerset waving to him from the garden in the center of their home square. He waved back. Rather than heading for the gate to join him, they embarked on a series of frantic motions, pointing and beckoning mysteriously. They looked quite agitated. John walked toward the fence.

"Look out!" shouted the boy, gesturing frantically at the cobblestones. What was his name? Arthur, that was it. Chaser of filthy chickens, at odds with his father. "He's vicious," the lad yelled. For a disorienting instant, John wondered if he referred to his parent.

"Be careful," Mary called.

A few steps nearer, John was able to see past a bush and spot a large yellow dog near the garden gate. The animal rose to its feet and bared its teeth.

"Watch it, sir. He's savage," Arthur said.

"This beast has kept us pent up here for hours," Mary added.

The two of them peered through the iron bars like little lost waifs. The dog eyed them with what looked to John like malicious satisfaction. He had to laugh.

"This is not funny!" cried Mary.

"You've been in there for hours? Really?" The dog glanced at John, then it turned back to its captives. John would have sworn that he was enjoying himself. Laughter overcame him again.

"Please get us out!"

She sounded genuinely distressed. Suppressing his

smile, John moved slowly closer, examining the dog. It was acting threatening but showed no signs of derangement. Its eyes were vigilant, but clear. Since he went back and forth to the livery stable alone every day, sometimes well after dark, John carried a cane. He did not raise it, however. He kept it at his side, in reserve, as he took a few slow steps closer to the dog. A growl rumbled in its chest.

John squatted. With a firm grip on the cane, he extended his other hand and only then recalled that it held a bunch of flowers. This actually proved fortunate, for the colorful petals seemed to rouse the dog's curiosity. Sniffing, it came closer. "You like flowers?" John said. "Be good, and you may have them." The animal crept nearer. "Down," John commanded.

The dog sank onto its belly. John extended his arm and set the flowers before its nose. At once, the beast began to paw and mouth them.

Moving swiftly but smoothly, with no sudden gestures, John rose and went to the gate. The dog gnawed on the blossoms. Mary was already opening the bars. "We will walk quickly but steadily to the house," he said. Seeing Arthur poised to spring, he added, "Do not run!"

Mary grasped Arthur's arm and guided him. John took rear guard, his cane ready. But it wasn't necessary. For some reason, the dog remained transfixed by the flowers and paid them no heed. In another moment, they were through the front door and inside the house.

"That was champion!" said Arthur.

John set his cane in the stand and looked at the

freed prisoners. He had to smile again. "Where did that animal come from? I've never seen it around here."

Arthur's demeanor shifted from open admiration to guilt. His mouth turned down, and his thin shoulders slumped.

"Arthur shot him," Mary said with some asperity.

"Shot…?"

"It was an accident!" The story spilled out of the boy, with running commentary from Mary. Aware of her annoyance, John pressed his lips together to restrain his laughter. When the tale was finally told, however, and Arthur dismissed to the kitchen, a burst of mirth escaped him.

"I'm *so* glad we could provide you with such a cause for amusement," said Mary.

Her sarcasm had no effect on his laughter. "I fear your jailor ate the bouquet I brought you."

"May he choke on it!"

John's snort earned him another searing look.

"I've been trapped out there for ages. I must go…" With a gesture toward the back premises, Mary rushed off.

Half an hour later, as they sat at the dinner table, John was still subject to random grins. "Didn't you see that your mistress was…having difficulties this afternoon?" he asked the maid. She'd been managing to set dishes before them without a single thump or spill, but now the buttered parsnips threatened to tumble onto the tablecloth.

"Difficulties, sir?"

"With a dog." Mary made a sound, a kind of *hmph*, and he felt his smile broaden.

"I didn't notice any dog," Kate said, evading his gaze. With a sketch of a curtsy, she hurried out.

"I don't believe that for a moment," declared Mary. "And I don't care who hears me say so."

"I suppose she might have been afraid. Of the dog." He did not add the words "You were." He was not so foolhardy as that.

From her flashing look, Mary heard them anyway. "The wretched animal was tired of the game by the time you got home."

"You are probably right." John sampled the roast beef. He was hungry, and whatever the faults of the maid, Mrs. Tanner was a fine cook.

"I am certainly right!" When he didn't venture to dispute this, Mary sighed. She rubbed a hand over her forehead. "I must get Arthur under control," she said. She spoke as if she expected him to blame her for the boy's escapade. "He seems to have a genius for doing precisely the wrong thing."

Without warning, a memory sprang into John's consciousness—vivid, full-blown—four boys lazing on the moss under a trailing willow, the chatter of a shallow brook. He and his brothers in one of their favorite summer haunts. He saw himself at, what, five? And there was his oldest brother Frederick, looking as he had just before he went off to school. George would be eight then. Roger, a toddler, was tied to the willow with a long cord so he couldn't get near the water.

It was the day that Frederick had been reading to them from a life of Sir Francis Drake. And John had muddled up this ancient history with a British ship that attacked Spanish Puerto Rico. He saw himself launching a twig and leaf vessel into a tiny rapid, slashing the air with an imaginary sword, and declaring his plan to be a noble privateer and capture Spanish gold in the Indies.

Frederick and George had laughed so spontaneously, so heartily, over these words. Even little Roger had laughed, though he couldn't have understood why.

They'd found the idea simply ludicrous, that their hapless brother John would embark on a marvelous adventure. It had been somehow established in the family, even that early, that John was a limited and bumbling creature. Their parents had said so; his brothers knew it to be true. He didn't have a shred of greatness in him—not like Frederick with his intellectual skills or George with his stubborn courage. Even Roger, later, had been granted talents to be admired, while John remained the goat.

The affectionate gibes of twenty more years piled onto the memory. How had it become a family joke—poor old John, who always does the wrong thing?

"John?"

From the way she was gazing at him, it was clear that Mary had asked him a question. "What?"

"Do you think it best to send Arthur back to the country? Perhaps my idea was just not…?"

"No! Let him be." It came out more strongly than he intended.

Mary blinked and sat back a little.

"He didn't do any real harm. And he apologized."

"If you're sure?"

"Positive."

Mary looked both relieved and puzzled. She turned

her attention to her dinner, and silence fell as they both ate. It was several minutes before she broke it, saying, "I wondered...I'd like to know more about what you do all day."

The question pulled John's thoughts out of the past like the hands of the *Lyra* crewmen yanking him to safety after the shipwreck. He'd sailed, on a real vessel, to the other side of the globe. He'd seen exotic places, spoken to men so different they almost seemed another species. His analyses were valued throughout his department. "Various kinds of reports, from around the world, come into the Foreign Office. I—among others—read them and, ah, boil them down for the foreign secretary's personal staff."

"Picking out what's important and what isn't?" Mary replied.

John nodded. She'd gotten to the crux of it right away. "In order to make decisions about the country's policy, and actions, Lord Castlereagh must have the best possible information. It's one way England can uphold standards of justice and fairness."

Mary looked admiring. "Isn't it difficult to decide which bits to include?"

John leaned forward a little, the remains of his dinner forgotten. "You get to know the style of the writers, you see, so that you can...feel really when they're onto something important. We have to keep up on developments in our areas, too, of course. The sensitive spots and potential threats."

"Areas?"

"There's so much information coming in, we

have to specialize. Conolly and I are East Asia. And Fordyce." The latter name was sour on his tongue.

"That's why you went to China," Mary concluded.

John nodded. He still marveled a bit at the luck of being chosen, with no influential backers to push his candidacy. It had nearly killed Conolly to remain behind, and he would have been twice as useful as that damned Fordyce.

Mary's gaze was openly admiring. "It sounds like vital work."

John couldn't help preening a little. "I like to think I make a contribution to the process of good government." That sounded pompous. If his brothers heard him talk like that...

"Tell me something you saw on your journey," Mary added. "It must have been such an amazing adventure."

Struck by her choice of words, John stared at her. Mary was leaning forward. They inclined toward each other across the dining table. Her dark eyes glowed. Those kissable lips were curved with anticipation. He wanted to make her marvel. He wanted to boast and amaze. "On the voyage out, we stopped at the southern tip of Africa," he began. "It was autumn there in March, because the seasons are opposite to ours, you know. There were birds that looked like patchwork quilts, all different colors." Urged on by her obvious interest, he talked, his anecdotes punctuated by appreciative exclamations from his wife. She seemed to take every tale he told as true and wise and enthralling, which was rather a new experience for John Bexley.

"You learned so much on the trip," Mary commented after a while.

He nodded, caught up in memories. "More than I ever expected. About the job as well as the world."

"The job?"

"Hard work isn't enough." He shook his head, recalling a host of observations during the journey. "Though if you work harder than anyone else, it is noticed. And personal initiative—of the right sort. But success at the Foreign Office often depends on social position, or personal connections."

"Connections outside the office, you mean?"

John met her dark eyes and came back to the present. He nodded.

"So, why don't we invite Conolly to dinner?" she added.

"How do you know of Conolly?"

"You mentioned him several times as you were explaining, as if he was a friend."

"We get along well. We work closely together." Conolly was the opposite of Fordyce in every way.

"I'd like our house to be a place where your friends feel welcome. And perhaps it would be helpful, too."

It wasn't a bad idea. He and Conolly had never seen each other outside the office. Of course, John had never had a home to invite him to before. "I'll see if he'd care to come."

"Next Wednesday, perhaps? We'll have done the baking. Or Thursday would do as well. Is he married?"

"No." John realized that he had no idea how Conolly spent his time away from work. He'd never asked. Their conversations were always absorbed by the details of their analyses. Yet Fordyce's ludicrous antics, along with things he'd learned on the voyage, had made him see that people who rose higher in the

Foreign Office had a whole network of social ties, some reaching back into childhood. Perhaps they could be built as well as…inherited. Perhaps the plans he'd been hatching weren't the only resources he had for success. "I'll ask tomorrow," he vowed.

Mary smiled at him. It was such a beautiful smile that John couldn't look away. He lost himself in its present loveliness, its promise for the future.

"Would there be anything else, ma'am?" asked a pointed voice behind him.

Mary realized that the remains of their dinner were congealing on their plates. They'd been talking for almost two hours, and without a single dispute! She'd been fascinated, and impressed, by her husband's exploits—the stories he told and the bravery and ingenuity so clearly implied in what he did not say. "No, Kate, you can clear up." She turned back to John. "Shall we sit in the parlor?"

They moved across the entryway into the sitting room. Candles Mary lit from the ones burning on the mantelpiece shed a golden glow over the comfortable furniture. The day had been warm, so they had no fire. But when they'd settled on the sofa, half-turned toward one another, the easy rhythm of conversation had dissipated. The silence felt awkward, and their long separation yawned between them once again. Mary thought of asking more about his journey, but that seemed contrived. Did they have nothing else to talk about? "I met one of our neighbors in the square today," she said finally.

"Before the dog?" John smiled slightly.

Mary wrinkled her nose at him. "Before, yes. An

older woman, perhaps sixty. Have you seen her walking in the garden?"

"I don't know. Many of our neighbors seem to be elderly."

"Her name is Eleanor Lanford." John was looking at her so fixedly. She spoke more quickly. "Her house is on the other side of the square."

John shook his head without shifting his gaze.

It was as if his eyes were lit from within. Like a gas fire Mary had once seen, they seemed preternaturally blue. She had to look down, but then her attention was caught by his hands. They were very attractive hands, strongly made, so much larger than hers. They looked...terribly skillful. "It's good to know somebody nearby," she said inanely. It was silly to be nervous, alone with this man. They'd shared a bed on their honeymoon, lived together for weeks. But that was two years ago, and he was so changed. It occurred to her that a honeymoon now might be quite different from the awkward groping at their seaside lodgings.

Mary blushed. John shifted a bit on the sofa cushion. His shoulders were straining the seams of his coat, Mary noticed. And very fine shoulders they were. He needed a new coat to set them off properly.

He reached out and touched her hand, then he ran his fingertips lightly up her arm and down again. Sensation shivered through her, like a hot breeze. He turned her hand over and caressed the inner side of her wrist. Mary's breath caught as he raised it toward his lips.

The thunder of footsteps in the entryway could not have been more unwelcome if they heralded news of disaster. Perhaps they did. It was Arthur. He stood in the open doorway and said, "That dog is still out there." He danced from one foot to the other, brimming with energy, as always.

Much as she liked the boy, at that moment Mary wished him a thousand miles away.

"He's walking round and round the garden fence. You think maybe he's lost?"

"I'm sure he can find his way back where he came from," Mary replied. Her voice sounded sharp in her own ears.

"Why don't he go then?" Arthur wondered.

"I'm sure he will…"

"I feel like it's my fault he's out there, see. I shoulda been more careful where I was shooting. I do try to watch out. But it seems like things just go…" He flapped his hands to show he deplored the random eruptions of mayhem in his life. "Anyway, I think I oughta make amends."

"Amends?"

"Help him get back home," Arthur elucidated. "Or back where I saw him first, anyway."

John stood up. Mary blinked at him, startled. "Let's find a piece of rope," he said. "We'll tie him up behind the house for the night. And then in the morning, you can return him to where you first encountered him."

"By myself, sir?" replied Arthur in a small voice. He looked at the floor and shuffled a foot. "It's only…he was that angry at me. For hitting him with the stone. Accidental."

John looked down at him. Though Mary couldn't see her husband's face, she had the sudden sense that it was full of compassion. She heard it in his voice when he said, "I will go with you. It has to be quite early, mind."

"Yes, sir! Early as you like. I'll be ready."

They left the room together before Mary could speak. She didn't know what she would have said in any case, only that her heart felt full.

The capture of the dog developed into an epic chase around the square. Mary was amazed that no one came out of the neighboring houses to inquire about the racing footsteps and the barking and the coordinating shouts. The hour grew late, and what with one thing and another, the delicious moment that had been trembling between her and her husband was gone.

As the night ticked over into morning, John Bexley undressed in his bedchamber. He was tired yet keyed up by the chase around the square and by all that had passed between him and Mary. His senses remained full of her, and he wanted far more than sleep.

Shirtless, he went to the door of her bedroom and opened it. Mary was asleep. She always slept deeply; he remembered that. Breathing softly and evenly, she looked younger, with no sign of the "managing female" in her lovely face.

He could go over and wake her and assuage this ache. He was a married man. It was his right. He'd done it before.

John flushed a little, remembering those nights after their wedding. There had been a bit of fumbling, but mostly he'd simply taken what he wanted. If he'd thought about it then, which he had not, he would have said that Mary preferred it that way. His upbringing had given him the idea that women were not much interested in the physical side of marriage.

Talk among the men on shipboard had shown him his mistake. And now, gazing down at Mary's sleeping form, he was even more enflamed by the idea that she could want him as much as he did her. He'd glimpsed signs of desire in her eyes. Hadn't he? He craved more of that—to watch them blur and drown in the throes of passion.

John's hand went out of its own accord. His fingertips had nearly brushed her cheek, when he caught a whiff of sweat from his run after the dog. He didn't want to drag her from sleep and demand his rights. He wanted much, much more. Pulling back, he decided he would take the time, and the care, to get it. Jaw tight with control, he turned away and left her.

Five

In the office they shared, William Conolly watched his colleague Bexley take off his coat and fold it carefully. He traded it for quite a different sort of garment from a portmanteau beside his desk. Though this new garment was still a coat, Conolly supposed, it was a shabby, threadbare example of the species, long and bulky and the color of mud. John buttoned it up so that it hid his good shirt. The cloth cap he pulled out next was equally disreputable. He'd already pulled off his top boots and donned ancient buckskin breeches instead of pantaloons; now he slid his feet into a pair of scuffed clogs. "Is it really necessary to dress like a beggar?" Conolly wondered.

"I'd make nothing as a beggar in a coat as fine as this," John replied.

"You call that fine!"

"It isn't hanging in strips from my shoulders," said John. "I have shoes. And no deformities or scars. Far too 'prosperous' for a beggar. On the other hand, I don't appear worth the effort of robbing. That's the point. That, and the people I want to speak to can't be seen with a 'toff.'"

"Are you sure this is a good idea?" Conolly asked.

"We need better information about the countries in the East."

"We do." Conolly watched, fascinated, as Bexley took a jar out of the portmanteau and unscrewed the lid. It appeared to contain dust. His enterprising colleague used a bit of it to smudge his face. He had clearly thought this through down to the last detail. "You really think you can find out anything useful?" he asked.

"Only one way to find out."

"I'm not sure." Conolly eyed the disreputable figure that had recently been his neatly dressed office-mate. "Can you really trust this interpreter fellow?"

"*Bù hǎo.*"

"What?"

"That means 'no good,'" John informed him. "I can't trust him completely. But I've given him the impression that I know more Chinese than I actually do, which should keep him at least a bit honest. Along with the payments I make to him, of course."

"Say something else," said Conolly.

"*Nǐ hǎo,*" said John.

"What's that?"

"How are you?"

"It sounds…do you sort of…sing it?"

John nodded. "The tones are as important as the words. Get the intonation wrong, and you'll be saying something completely different, as I learned to my cost a time or two in China."

"Where you took the time to learn some of the language. Unlike any of the others."

John shrugged. He wasn't ready to tell Conolly all his reasons for tonight's foray. The government did need a better information network, and he did believe this was a way to improve it. But he had other motives as well. He intended to show his superiors that he possessed the intelligence, the initiative, and above all, the ability to get results that could take the place of aristocratic connections in the hierarchy of the Foreign Office.

"Did you find this interpreter through Rolfe?"

"*Hěn hǎo.*" At Conolly's raised eyebrows, he translated. "Very good." The captain of the *Lyra* knew all manner of seafarers and had given him some contacts to pursue. John made a quick bobbing bow.

"You're a marvel, Bexley."

"What do you mean?"

"Look at you. When you put on that gear, you stand differently, your face is…you look like another person entirely."

"That's the idea."

"Still, venturing into the slums… I suppose I'm to rally the troops if you don't show up tomorrow."

"I'll be here," John replied. But the truth was, he'd confided in Conolly for this reason exactly. Someone had to know where he'd gone.

John slipped out of the mostly empty Foreign Office building. He paused to make certain his coin was well secured and that the pistol in the deep pocket of his coat was easily accessible. Then he made his way carefully through dark streets.

London's Limehouse slums were full of sailors from across the world. Hired in their native waters for their knowledge of local currents and hazards in port, they were set down in London when the voyage ended, abandoned until they could sign on with another ship. They needed money, and many of them were willing to tell whatever they knew in exchange for small sums.

Over the years, some of these sailors had settled and opened grogshops or doss houses or brothels to cater to this continually shifting population. They gathered news from the tide of men who washed through their establishments, and they might be persuaded to pass it along to John for a price. Only once they met and trusted him, however. Such men had an aversion to writing things down—those who could write. Notes could go astray. Throats were slit for less.

As arranged, John met his translator at a tavern called the Red Dragon at the edge of the district. He had discovered Henry Tsing, son of a Chinese sailor and a Limehouse whore, through an acquaintance of an acquaintance of Rolfe's. Henry had learned Chinese dialects as a potboy in a grogshop, and John judged him suitable as a general ear to the ground around Limehouse. "Shen may have something," he said when John appeared.

John nodded. "*Hěn hǎo.*" And they set off.

Midway through the evening, it began to rain, turning the filth and litter in the narrow streets to a disgusting mush. John turned up his collar further and kept going. The hope for useful information just barely kept his spirits from sinking in the endless succession of dark, dirty holes, where men clutched their rotgut liquor or opium pipes in a desperate quest for solace.

The circuit Henry led him through took longer than John had expected. They couldn't hurry from place to place without drawing unwanted attention. Their progress had to appear dawdling and random. He'd planned to return to the office and change his clothing before going home, but by the end of the night, he was worn out. As he left Henry at the edge of a less disreputable district, John told himself that everyone would be asleep and he trudged homeward.

Well after midnight, he crept through the alley behind the house and let himself in the back entrance. Shedding the filthy clogs and shapeless hat, he was filled with gratitude for this warm and peaceful refuge. How many men had he seen tonight who would never know such a haven? He dropped the ancient coat and stripped off mud-spattered stockings. He'd come down very early tomorrow and gather them up before they were noticed.

Barefoot, he crept through the house and up the stairs. At the door of his bedchamber, he nearly jumped out of his skin when candlelight fell over him as Mary opened her door. "John?" she said.

She stood in the opening, the small flame throwing golden light over her thin nightdress, her dark hair tumbled about her shoulders. Even bone-tired and dispirited and cold, he was stirred to his depths by the sight.

"I was worried."

"I told you I'd be out late tonight," he said.

"Yes, but…where are your clothes? Why are you wearing…?"

"I…was caught in the rain. I left my wet things downstairs." He would have to go back down as soon as he placated her, John thought, and hide his disguise. The scent of violets drifted around him. There could be no greater contrast with the places he'd passed through tonight. He ached to touch her, to feel her softness and warmth, but the sights he'd seen tonight had left him feeling soiled within and without.

"You went to a reception?" Mary said.

She was looking at his mud-spattered buckskins, obviously inappropriate for a Foreign Office gathering. He'd implied, without actually saying, that such was his destination. Her face showed bewilderment and hurt. John shook his head. "It was something else."

"What?"

"It's confidential. I can't talk about it." This wasn't absolutely true, but he didn't want to talk to her about the dark things that went on in other parts of their city. To link Mary, even in thought, to that bleak world of men bereft of home and family, of no women except whores… He shook his head.

"You don't trust me?" Mary said. The candle wavered in her hand.

"I do. But much of my work simply can't be discussed. That is its nature."

"Work…in the middle of the night. Half-naked."

That final word seemed to echo on the narrow landing. John became acutely aware of his bare feet and legs, his shirt hanging open. It would take less than a moment to shed the rest. The bone-deep chill of his long trek evaporated in a surge of heat, a wave of arousal. He had to have her. He couldn't wait an instant longer.

"You have dust on your face," Mary said. She touched his cheek, her fingertips light as a butterfly on his skin, then she looked at the smudge left on her fingers.

Though that gentle touch enflamed him almost beyond bearing, John's hands fell to his sides and curled into fists. He'd been splashed with all manner of filth tonight. He'd held dirty glasses of rotgut that he had to pretend to drink. He'd been pawed by a drunken lightskirt and forced to endure one mucky kiss before he could be rid of her. A gin-crazed lascar had spit on his sleeve. He wasn't fit for his marriage bed, no matter how he ached for it. "I'm exhausted, Mary," he said. "I must get some sleep."

Mary's face fell. She turned away. John's hand came up of its own accord and reached for her. He forced it down, remorseful yet resolute. Mary's realm was this gracious house, this serene square, in the safe, respectable district he'd chosen for her. Mary was clean crisp linens, the scent of violets and baking bread, warmth and laughter. She must never be touched by London's black underside, the remnants of which spattered him now. He waited for her to close her bedroom door, then he waited another few minutes before retrieving the sodden clothes from the scullery.

❧

Mary didn't see John the following morning. He was up and out earlier than ever, before even Mrs. Tanner could glimpse him. And oddly, when she inquired about his wet clothing to send to the laundress, none could be found. Whatever he'd been doing—certainly not a Foreign Office reception—he'd removed all signs of it. Just as he'd refused to tell her anything.

Sitting at the breakfast table, she broke a piece of toast into smaller and smaller pieces as she went over last night's encounter in her mind. She couldn't see how the work he'd described to her over dinner could ever require creeping around barely dressed in the night. But where had he been then? What were the secrets she couldn't be allowed to know?

She crushed the last bit of toast to crumbs. He'd been here for weeks on his own, after they'd parted in anger in Somerset. Had he found someone…? The thought made her feel sick. But she couldn't believe he'd be so clumsy and…blatant about it. And… Mary frowned. His look and manner had pointed to something more mysterious, and more sinister, than an affair.

Mary's cheeks burned with humiliation. She'd stood before him in nothing but her nightdress, offering… everything. He must have seen that in her face. How could he not? She'd longed to throw her arms around him, lose herself in the kind of kiss that had begun to tantalize her imagination in the dark hours. He'd been so alluring, half-dressed in the candlelight, his bare throat rising from the open shirt. When she closed her eyes—and even when she didn't—she could see him there, barelegged, primal. But he'd turned away.

Mary left her uneaten breakfast and went to sit in the front parlor. A bit of sewing unheeded in her lap, she watched rain run down the windows. The season was turning. Leaves had fallen in the square, and the garden looked much less enticing with bare branches tossing in the autumn wind. The flowers had withered; puddles dotted the gravel paths. It seemed a mirror of her marriage—waning. At one moment they had seemed about to come together, and the next they swung far apart. What should she do? Would she ever truly come to know this stranger who was also her husband of almost three years? What if she didn't?

When she'd agreed to marry, she saw now, she hadn't expected a great deal. An amiable companion, a settled home, her parents' approval for her obedience. She could hardly comprehend that Mary now. Why had she asked so little of life? Why hadn't she known, felt, that there could be so much more? The Mary she'd become since then yearned for…things she could scarcely define. A fervent, vibrant, passionate existence. If she couldn't have that, her heart would break. All would be empty and bleak and…

"Stop this at once," Mary said aloud. She swallowed the threat of tears. John was her husband. He would be here every day for…forever. She would figure something out. Even the old Mary hadn't been a moper. She would not sit here feeling sorry for herself. There were plenty of tasks waiting to be done. She put aside the sewing, stood, and shook out her skirts.

In the kitchen, she found Kate and Mrs. Tanner sitting at the large wooden table near the warmth of the stove. The cook was peeling apples from a bowl. Arthur was set up in the corner blacking a pair of John's shoes. None of them rose when Mary appeared. The women's expressions, each line of their bodies, declared that she was no duchess. Well, she wasn't. But she was the mistress of this house and not the least bit intimidated. It was time to have a frank talk with her staff.

"You said you wanted a pie," Mrs. Tanner remarked, making a small gesture with her paring knife. "But I told you I bain't much of a hand with pastry."

"I am," Mary responded. "I'll make it." She enjoyed baking. Beyond the tactile pleasure of it and the delectable results, it had been one skill her mother praised in her.

"I'm mortal fond of pie," put in Arthur, licking his lips.

"You're mortal fond of *food*," replied Kate. "It's a wonder you're not fat as a flawn."

"He needs feeding up," said Mrs. Tanner. "I swear they must have starved the lad in Somerset."

Mary sat at the table, ignoring the women's surprised looks as well as Arthur's soulful acceptance of the cook's sympathy. "You and Kate are related," she said to her.

"She's my mam," said Kate.

"For my sins," murmured Mrs. Tanner.

Mary nodded. Since drawing the two women, she'd found the words for this necessary conversation. "This is a small household and will remain so. No peers of the realm, no large staff with specializations. I don't plan to hire anyone else for now. If you wish to remain here, you'll have to turn your hands to many different tasks."

Mrs. Tanner stiffened with apprehension. Kate merely sulked.

"If you find that prospect too unpleasant…"

"No, ma'am," the cook interrupted.

Mary looked at Kate. "You will have to take more care serving dinner."

Arthur hooted, and Kate shot him a glare.

"Particularly because we are planning to have a guest," Mary continued. John's colleague couldn't be subjected to thumping crockery and falling knives.

"She will," said Mrs. Tanner. "I'll see to it."

The maid tossed her head. "I'm no footman to be hauling trays. As soon as may be, I'm going to marry a man who'll keep me. Owner of an inn maybe."

"Who'd marry you?" Arthur wondered. "Anyhow, you'd be serving at all kinds of tables at an inn."

"He'd hire people to do that," Kate replied.

"The wife of an innkeeper either cooks in the kitchen or serves at the bar," her mother declared. "Haven't you seen as much yourself?"

"A shop then," Kate said.

"What, a grocer or a notions store?" Mrs. Tanner wrinkled her nose. "You'd be serving at a counter there. You have to work, my girl. You may as well accept it."

"Too lazy," said Arthur, who had abandoned the shoes in his interest in the conversation.

Kate turned on him. "Be quiet, you wretched boy! I don't mind working. Nobody understands that. It's the kind of work."

"What sort do you like?" Mary asked, genuinely interested.

"The stillroom," was the prompt reply. "I like concocting things. Her Grace showed me how to make a lovely hand lotion and an herbal mixture to clear out phlegm."

MARRIED TO A PERFECT STRANGER

"There's no place for a stillroom in a small house like this," said Mrs. Tanner.

"Don't I know it." At her mother's glare, Kate subsided. "I'll do better with the serving," she muttered.

Satisfied for now, Mary let it drop and went to the pantry to get the ingredients for a piecrust. "What happened to the dog?" she asked Arthur as she cut in shortening and mixed.

Arthur's rag stopped moving again. "We took him back to the market square. There weren't many people about, so Mr. Bexley said I was to wait a while so's I could ask about an owner."

"Talking of lazy," Kate accused, pointing at the shoes.

Arthur went back to rubbing at the leather. "I didn't want to be left alone with that great brute. But Mr. Bexley gave him his orders and he lay down like a lamb." The boy's tone was admiring. "Finally a feller came along and said it was his dog and what was I doing with him."

Mary sent up a small prayer of thanks. She'd dreaded hearing that the animal was in need of a home. "And what did you say?" she wondered, rolling out her dough on a slab of marble she had purchased for the purpose.

Arthur assumed a look of pious virtue. "Said I'd found him wandering and was afeered he was lost."

Kate snorted.

"So you returned him?" Mary said.

Arthur nodded. "The fella was that glad. He gave me a sixpence."

When Mary looked at him, he grinned. There was

no need to point out the irony of being rewarded for shooting a dog. Obviously, he was well aware.

෩

The lingering awkwardness between the Bexleys had somewhat dissipated that evening when Mary learned that William Conolly had accepted their dinner invitation. "Shall we invite your brother George as well?" she asked her husband. "I've only just remembered that he's stationed in London."

"No."

Mary blinked. "He isn't station—?"

"He's very busy with his own friends."

"Surely you count yourself among…"

"We can ask him when we're completely settled," John interrupted.

"But we are…"

"He and William Conolly wouldn't get on."

At his curt tone, and third objection, Mary fell silent. It seemed that John did not intend to confide in her about his family either. She felt her temper rising. Did he imagine that they would confine their exchanges to practicalities and commonplaces? That he could continue to push her away? Was this his conception of a marriage?

She'd met the Bexley brothers at her wedding and retained only a general impression of three young men who resembled her husband. She knew that Frederick, the oldest, managed the family property in Somerset. George was in the military, and Roger, the youngest, had gone off to India to make his fortune. The brothers had seemed cordial after the ceremony. Mary got no sense of friction among them. Yet John had not even mentioned George since she arrived, she realized. If one of her sisters lived in London, Mary would have haunted her household.

She examined John's set expression. "How can you be so sure that they won't?" she pressed.

"Because I know them both. As you do not," he snapped.

Mary put every bit of the irritation she felt in a look. As far as she could see, it had no effect. That evening it was she who retreated—to her parlor studio and sketchbooks—leaving her husband to go to his study without protest.

❦

William Conolly came home with John on the appointed day, and Mary was introduced to a slender man of medium height with black hair, hazel eyes, and an engaging, mobile face. Though his clothes seemed designed not to call attention, he had a definite presence. There was a French phrase Mary had once heard—je ne sais quoi: an indefinable quality of... assurance. John's friend possessed this. Perhaps it was his easy smile as he bowed over her hand or the slight lilt in his voice, just an echo of—Irish, or Welsh? Most importantly, it was clear that he liked and respected John, and Mary would have welcomed him for this if he'd been half as pleasant.

He admired the neatness and comfort of their house as he drank a glass of the sherry John had bought specially. Mary was glad she'd hung new draperies in the front parlor. Kate appeared in the doorway right on time, curtsied correctly, and signaled that dinner was served. "Shall we go in?" said Mary. She savored the role of hostess in her own home.

She was also proud of the meal she put before them. There was salmon in a pastry crust, roast beef and potatoes, and just the right array of side dishes—plentiful but not ostentatious. Kate actually was taking particular care with her serving. And Mary was secure in the knowledge that there was a Chantilly cream to finish. She'd managed it out of a cookery book. It looked and tasted lovely. Her eyes met John's, and he smiled. Mary felt an odd little flutter in her chest as she smiled back.

John held Mary's gaze and felt a moment of perfect amity with her. It had been a bit strange to leave the office with Conolly and traverse the familiar streets in his company. Now, here he sat at the head of a laden board, his beautiful wife at the other end. She created a gracious setting, a fine meal. He'd never been the householder, the host. He rather liked it.

"Do you enjoy living in London?" Conolly asked Mary. "You've been here only a short time, I believe?"

She nodded. "I'm still getting accustomed to town life. There's so much to see. This square is a very pleasant place to live, a little patch of country, with the trees and the garden to walk in. And I've met one kind neighbor, Eleanor Lanford."

"The Dowager Countess St. Clair? Someone said she'd moved out this way."

"Countess?"

"They claim she's become a hermit." Conolly smiled as if to show he knew the label was ridiculousness.

"She was the toast of society years ago, you know, during the American war."

"They?" said Mary, then she flushed as she realized she'd spoken aloud, repeating words like a parrot.

"Well, her old friends. They like to pretend there's no existence outside Mayfair. Lady Cast…" Conolly appeared to notice that he'd astonished his hosts.

"Lady…?" Mary prompted.

"Castlereagh." For the first time all evening, Conolly looked self-conscious.

John took a sip of wine to mask his surprise. He'd heard that Conolly had some family connections, though he hadn't paid much attention at the time. He had *not* known that his colleague was acquainted with one of the chief arbiters of London society and the wife of the foreign secretary himself. "You know Lady Castlereagh?" he couldn't help asking.

Their guest seemed embarrassed. "I'm not a friend, or anything of that nature. Just a distant connection of her mother's. Very distant—fifth cousin, eight times removed, or some such thing." He made a deprecating gesture. "On the Irish side, to boot. I get the odd invitation, pick up this and that bit of gossip. I'm the sort of sad creature who enjoys hearing it."

Obviously he'd thought John was aware of this relationship already. Abruptly, John felt as if he was back at his job, navigating the shoals of the Foreign Office's internal politics, rather than monarch of his own small homely kingdom. It seemed he'd made quite a clever move, inviting Conolly. He simply hadn't done it on purpose.

Conolly singled out the Chantilly cream for special

compliments. He praised the wine John had chosen, working hard to restore their earlier ease. When they'd finished eating and Mary rose to leave the men to their port, he suggested they all retire to the front parlor. "It's not as if we want to drink ourselves insensible," he said with a laugh. "And why should you go and sit all alone?" He made it seem a jolly scheme rather than a deviation from etiquette or an acknowledgment that their house was so small, Mary would hear everything they said unless she retreated upstairs. But nothing put the evening back on a relaxed footing until he shifted the conversation to China. "I don't see how we can ever establish proper diplomatic relations with a ruler who insists on the *kǒutóu*," he said. Noticing Mary's blank look, he added, "Anyone granted an audience with the Chinese emperor has to kneel before him and bang his forehead on the floor."

"Even foreign ambassadors?" Mary wondered.

John nodded. "Lord Amherst couldn't agree to it, of course."

"I should think not." She tried to imagine an English nobleman in such a humiliating position before a foreign ruler, and could not.

"You can't even present credentials in a situation like that," John added. "So how we'll redress complex commercial grievances, I don't know." He spoke with calm authority. This was a side of him that Mary hadn't seen.

"We could give up tea," Conolly suggested humorously.

"Perhaps Englishmen should stop drinking it," replied John, smiling to show he knew it had been meant as a joke. "A boycott would erase the trade imbalance in a matter of months."

Their guest shook his head. "We'll never let go of our tea at this point. And it's too late anyhow. The opium trade is established, and so profitable it will go on whatever the diplomats do."

John made a sour face, but nodded.

Mary was fascinated by the way her husband came to life talking to a knowledgeable colleague. He sat straighter; his eyes glowed with a relish for debate. He looked absolutely confident of his ability to contribute She wanted to see more of this man. "What does tea have to do with opium?" she asked.

Conolly smiled at her and sat back to allow John to answer.

"Just this," her husband replied, ticking off points on his fingers. "Tea from China is the largest single item in Britain's trading accounts. Every Englishman wants his tea. Of course we sell goods to the Chinese as well, but not nearly enough to offset the amount we purchase. Some years ago, tea imports finally became so expensive that there wasn't enough silver to pay for them. So traders looked for a profitable product to compensate for the loss."

"And discovered that many Chinese like opium," said Conolly.

"Which is illegal in China by imperial edict," added John.

He and his coworker were like a practiced chorus, Mary thought. Obviously this was much discussed at the Foreign Office.

"However, opium is produced in India and sold there anyway."

"By private agencies, not the British government,"

her husband assured her. "But the trade is silently condoned by the East India Company."

"Because it brings in piles of money," Conolly supplied, "with which to buy tea."

Mary nodded. "I see."

"We're rapidly reaching an impasse," John concluded. "And it will end in war."

"Do you think so?" If he had begun the conversation out of politeness, Conolly was wholly engrossed now. Mary could see how much he valued John's opinion.

Her husband nodded. "All sides are obdurate. Communication is slow and uncertain and often contentious. Somebody will call out the troops in the next few years."

Mary understood better now why John cared so much about his work and devoted so much time to it.

William Conolly looked glum, but he didn't argue. "There must be some way we can stave it off."

"By doing our jobs," replied John. "Get the most accurate information to the right people. Lay out the implications as best we can. I haven't much hope, though."

"Do you think that your new explorations will…?"

John made a quick gesture. Conolly bit off the end of his sentence. The two men had been leaning forward, gripped by the intensity of their discussion. Now they sat back, the rhythm of the exchange broken.

Conolly glanced at the mantel clock. "Is that the time?" he exclaimed. "Lord, I've overstayed my welcome abominably." He turned to Mary. "I can only plead the excellence of your hospitality."

"Don't be silly. It's not that late." She looked from one man to the other, trying to figure out what had just happened. What had Conolly meant by "explorations"? Why had John cut him off?

Conolly rose to go. The Bexleys stood to walk with him to the door. Mary rang for Kate as she passed the bellpull. When Kate brought their guest's coat and hat, Conolly turned to Mary, smiled, and bowed. "Thank you very much for your kind hospitality, Mrs. Bexley. It's been a most enjoyable evening."

"Good," said Mary with a smile. "I hope we will see you again soon." When the door was shut behind him, she added, "I like him. I'm so glad we invited him."

John nodded and turned back to the parlor.

"What did he mean by 'explorations'?" Mary asked as they sat down again.

"Nothing." John had retreated behind a barrier of hooded eyes.

She felt a spark of irritation. "It didn't seem like nothing. It seemed as if you didn't wish to have it mentioned."

"Nonsense."

Mary's irritation increased. It was as if John wasn't really paying attention, now that their guest was gone. "Wasn't it surprising to find that Conolly is related to Lady Castlereagh?" From his reaction, she was sure John hadn't known.

His laugh was curt. "That's one word for it."

"What's another?" Mary wanted the John of an hour ago back again. How could he be so clever and confident about his work and so dense about everything else?

He paused and then said, "Complicated," in a dismissive tone.

But Mary didn't wish to be dismissed. "In what way?"

John's gesture seemed to say that she couldn't possibly understand. And that he had no intention of trying to explain it to her. "The dinner was very good."

"Well *managed*?" snapped the part of Mary who wasn't going to be labeled negligible ever again.

John stiffened, but he really looked at her, rather than at some indefinable object beyond Mary's grasp. "You aren't going to begin some sort of brangle, are you? Because I'm really not in the mood."

"And have far more important things on your mind?" said Mary, responding to his tone.

"Yes, Mary, in fact, I do. As I think a wife might have the sense to know."

Afraid of what she might say if she stayed, Mary turned on her heel and walked up the stairs to her bedchamber. Her solitary bedchamber. Where she vented her temper by pounding an innocently ruffled pillow into complete submission.

Six

MARY TOSSED AND TURNED ALL NIGHT AND WOKE FULL of confusion. The new Bexley household had received formal calls from several sets of family friends. All of them belonged to their parents' generation, however, and Mary had struggled to find common ground for conversation, beyond news of home. Though the exchanges were cordial, it was quickly clear that these visitors would be acquaintances, sources of practical information perhaps, but not friends. Their visits made Mary feel her distance from her family more acutely. She had no one to look to for advice.

As a solace, she took her watercolors to the garden. She had a lidded jar for water and a neat little case for the paints. She wanted to be outdoors, even though the day was cool and overcast.

The space was empty when she unlocked the gate and went in. She sat in a secluded corner and opened a small folding easel her father had given her years ago. Uncapping the jar, she wet her brush and swept it lightly over a sheet of paper. Then she held it poised over the row of colors and waited. Soon her hand began to move. Color and shape flowed over the page. A face began to form. Gradually, it revealed itself as her youngest sister, Petra.

Mary smiled as she added detail. Petra always joked that their father, Peter Fleming, had finally given up on having a son when he named her. Petra hadn't turned out boyish, but she was certainly the liveliest of the five Fleming sisters. Mary added a highlight to capture the twinkle that animated Petra's hazel eyes. The portrait showed the characteristic tilt of her head, the mischievous quirk of her mouth.

Mary's hand slowed as she acknowledged how much she missed her. They'd been able to exchange occasional visits while she lived at Great-Aunt Lavinia's, but that wouldn't be possible now. London was too far. Her older sisters Eliza, Lucy, and Sophia, all married, the first two with small children, were too busy to make such a journey. And Petra was being presented to Bath society when the season began there next month; she'd be fully occupied. Mary wouldn't see any of her family any time soon.

And with that thought Mary acknowledged that she was terribly lonely. She'd been shoving aside the emptiness that had been building in her since she arrived in town, refusing to examine it. She was married; she was settled; this was her life. But she still felt so cut off from her husband. When they'd first married—it seemed so long ago now—they had talked more. Hadn't they? She was sure they'd talked more. About…she didn't remember specifically. Indeed, the memories of those first weeks of married life felt dim and pallid.

Much of their talk had involved preparations for

his long voyage, she realized. There had been so many details to settle and items to procure. They had worked together to gather them all in the short time he'd been given. Then he'd gone away for months and months, and he'd come home a different man.

But still absorbed by his work, she thought. Or... even more absorbed.

When his orders for the China mission first came, he'd been amazed. She was sure she remembered that properly. He'd marveled about the significance of the opportunity and his great good luck in being named to the group. Hurrying to prepare, he'd included her in the decisions about what to pack. He'd asked for her opinions; she was certain that he had. She'd struggled to come up with some; she remembered that, too.

Now, he seemed more deeply involved than ever in his job. He'd come to life last night, talking to William Conolly. But, beyond mere anecdotes of his travels, he didn't want to talk to her about it. He'd pointedly excluded her.

She remembered the two drawings of John she'd compared in Somerset, and she wished she had them with her to study again. The John who had come home in August was so much more compelling than the one she'd married. And what would portraits of her own face from two years ago and now show? Just as much change perhaps. No, certainly. Because she wanted so much more than she'd dreamed of then. She wanted John—all of him.

It was all such a muddle. What was she going to do?

Stop feeling sorry for yourself, replied a stern inner voice, so strong she could almost hear it in the still autumn air. It sounded rather like her mother. Mary sat back and took a breath. She wasn't the meek girl who waited for orders and did what she was told. What was she going to do? She was going to decide precisely what she wanted and find a way to get it.

Sitting straighter on the bench, Mary noticed that Eleanor Lanford—or rather, the Dowager Countess St. Clair—was walking slowly along one of the garden paths toward her. Here was another person in her life who had turned out to be someone else. When she caught Mary's eye, the old woman raised a hand in greeting. Mary composed herself and went to meet her. "Hello, uh, my lady."

The old woman's smile shifted. "Ah, someone told you."

"Yes, my…"

"Please. I thought you were going to call me Eleanor."

"That was before…"

"My dear, if I cared about such things, I would have announced the title myself. If I'd even bothered to speak to you." Her smile grew larger. "Or come to live here, for that matter, which I would not have."

Mary had to laugh. Still, it was different knowing her neighbor's rank. She wouldn't have felt so comfortable when they first met if she'd been conscious of talking to a countess.

"What have you been painting today?" Mary shrugged, not certain she wanted to show her sister's portrait. The glance she got in return was uncomfortably keen. "Walk with me a little," said Eleanor, and she took Mary's arm.

They strolled a path that curved around the far end

of the garden. The wind had been freshening, and now a gust shook the branches above them. Yellow leaves swirled through the garden. "There will be rain soon," Eleanor said. "I must go in. You should, too."

Watching the scudding clouds, Mary had to agree. Would she see her new acquaintance at all once winter descended? She'd barely begun to know her.

"My granddaughter Caroline is coming tomorrow to stay with me for a while," the old woman said.

"Have you many grandchildren?" Mary replied politely.

"Six. Caroline is the oldest girl. Nineteen."

She spoke the final number as if it was ominous. Her tone, and wry expression, roused Mary's curiosity. "You'll be happy to see her."

"Very," was the firm reply, as if the remark had been a challenge. "Come to tea tomorrow and meet her. I think you'll like her."

"I…thank you. I'm sure I shall."

With a smile and a nod, Eleanor turned toward the gate. Mary went to collect her painting gear, her mood buoyed by the invitation.

Back home, she returned her paints to the parlor across from John's study. She'd set up this chamber as her retreat, studio, and sitting room, and now she traded her brushes for a pencil and sketchbook. Eleanor's face emerged on the page, Mary's hands confidently filling in a portrait that spoke more than she could ever have put into words. She was unaware of all else until the impulse to draw had spent itself. Then she stood back and looked at what she'd created.

Here was her new friend—gracefully aged, elegant,

and…sad? No, that wasn't the right word. Weary… pensive…distressed? No…troubled. That was it. That fit what she saw in the face on her page. Troubled about what? Slowly, Mary tidied her materials away. Probably she couldn't help. Eleanor seemed far wiser than she. But she would keep an eye out for any opportunity.

❧

"You know, I don't see why I was chosen over you to go to China," John said to Conolly as they left the office to find sustenance at midday. He'd been chewing over this puzzle in the back of his mind since Conolly revealed his ancestry.

"I expect they wanted the best man for each place," Conolly replied, with no sign of discomfort at the frankness of the question. "They knew you'd do well on the voyage, and they knew I could manage all the information flooding into our offices alone. Because I am a 'blinkin' marvel' at the job."

John smiled at his friend's cocky grin. "You are that. But that's not how it's done, Conolly. Men get preferment based on who they know."

"Less now than in the past. British interests are more far-flung and complicated every day. You can't run that kind of enterprise strictly on patronage."

John hoped this was true. Indeed, he was counting on it. But just this morning he'd heard of a senior appointment that was clearly based on lineage rather than ability. He named the man now, "LaRoche."

Conolly shrugged. "There is the way things were done, and there is the future. We are betwixt and between. Family connections matter. I'm sure they always will. But they aren't everything." If he realized why this topic might be of particular interest to John he didn't show it, for which John was grateful. With a nod, he let it drop.

Near the end of the working day, he went to hand in an important report. "What's the gist of it, Bexley?" asked his superior Harkness as he took the pile of pages.

"We need more information sources inside China," John said. "Someone with access to the emperor's court, preferably. Perhaps one of the mandarins who disagrees…"

"No nobleman would betray his sovereign for pay," said a drawling voice from the outer office. John hadn't seen Fordyce come in. "It's called honor, Bexley. Noblesse oblige. Not something you'd know anything about, I suppose."

"A mandarin isn't a noble," John replied. Fordyce's ignorance was almost as galling as his insults. Almost. "He's a bureaucrat. And often quite susceptible to bribery."

"Very true," said Harkness. "I must read this." He waved them both away.

John walked out. Unfortunately, Fordyce followed. "I suppose you have to memorize facts when you don't know any important people," he said.

"Memorize?" The word so misconstrued and belittled the nature of his work—their work, actually, if Fordyce ever did any. It was what they did with the flood of facts that inundated the Foreign Office that mattered. "Can you really not bother to use whatever brainpower you have?" he said.

"I beg your pardon?"

"If I thought so, I might grant it."

"What?"

"What indeed? I haven't time for this."

Back in the room he shared with Conolly, empty just now, John couldn't quite settle into the pleasure he usually found diving into waiting stacks of intelligence. Fordyce might be a snob and an ass, Conolly might be reassuring, but it was still true that a powerful family made a vast difference to a man's prospects. Hearing news like LaRoche's appointment could be discouraging.

John sat back in his chair. He didn't have aristocratic parents, but he had ideas. He'd discovered that he had more energy and determination than Fordyce could imagine.

He shook his head. Before his trip to China, he'd pottered his way through his workdays, the Foreign Office merely his lot in life. He'd ambled through life without significant highs or lows, not giving anything much thought. How had he stood it? Would he really have gone on like that for…decades? John's mind crackled with denial. The point was moot. He'd… woken up, and nothing was going to stop him now.

❧

After they finished dinner that evening John headed for his study, leaving Mary alone in the parlor. When he went up to his desk, he always said it would take him only half an hour or so. Perhaps he even believed it. But once he started working, he hardly ever emerged before she went up to bed. She pointed that out. He denied it.

Restless, annoyed, Mary couldn't settle to a book or sewing. On impulse, she fetched a warm shawl and her bunch of keys and let herself quietly out the front door.

Their neighborhood was deserted at this time of night. Still, she wouldn't have considered lingering outdoors if she hadn't had a key to the private garden. No random passerby could get in there, and none of the neighbors were likely to be out.

She walked quickly across, unlocked the gate, and slipped inside, closing it securely behind her. As she moved along the gravel path to the center of the space, a late September moon lit her way. Puffs of wind set the tree branches rustling. It was a world of black and silver, secret and separate from the everyday. A thrill went through Mary; she'd so seldom been outside alone in the night. It felt daring and yet safe in this secluded enclosure. She pulled her shawl close around her and sat down on one of her favorite benches.

Shadows dipped and shifted. The lighted windows around the square seemed to recede. Mary began to feel unmoored, like a boat adrift on a powerful current.

A strong gust of wind lifted a branch higher, and Mary realized that she could see into the study on the second floor of her house. She stood and moved around the tree. There was John, outlined by golden candlelight, bent over his papers. She couldn't make out his expression from this distance, but she imagined he was intensely focused, his thoughts a thousand miles away from her. Her connection to her husband felt like these windblown branches. They swayed a little closer to each other and then away, pushed by forces beyond her control.

Above, in the window, John rested his forehead in his hand, a tired gesture. Of course his work was important. She would never argue that it was not. She only wished to be included, to enter more fully into this pivotal part of his world. He had to understand this.

Mary walked back to the gate, unlatched it, and stepped through. As she did, she thought she saw someone crouched near their front parlor window. She stopped, staring, trying to separate a human figure from the general darkness. No one should be about at this hour. She stared at the house. Nothing. It must have been a bit of shadow shifting with the wind.

She gazed up at John one last time. He straightened as if he could feel her gaze and looked around. Though she knew she couldn't be seen, Mary looked back at him, willing him to recognize her presence. Of course, he didn't. She walked swiftly across the pavement and back inside.

Upstairs, John gazed at his reflection in the black glass of the window. But the feeling of being watched had gone. And it was high time he dispensed with the illusion that someone was looking over his shoulder and criticizing his work, a lingering relic of his school days. It was ridiculous. There was never anyone there. He turned back to his report, trying to concentrate through his fatigue.

Footsteps on the stair signaled that Mary was going up to her room, although it was rather early. It was a melancholy sound, John thought, and then he was surprised at himself. Perhaps he ought to get up and…

The footsteps stopped outside the study door, followed by a knock. "Yes?"

Mary came in and stood before his desk, hands clasped before her. "This is unacceptable."

"What?"

"You up here so many evenings, leaving me alone downstairs during the only time we have together."

"I've explained to you that I have work…"

"And I know your work is important, but I don't see that it needs to separate us so."

There was a slight tremor in her voice. Moved by her wistful expression, John rose and walked around the desk to take his wife's hand. "I know it's been difficult, moving far from your family. Once you have some friends of your own…"

"Is that what you wish?" Mary interrupted. "That I find my own friends apart from you? Perhaps you would like me to go out with others in the evenings and let you be?"

Sharp denial spiked in John's chest at this picture and called up a quick shake of his head.

"What then? I won't be pushed aside as if I were stupid or…simply negligible. I'm not going to sit back and let that happen again."

"Again?"

Mary pulled her hand free and paced the room— once, twice. The folds of her skirt rustled with the sharp movement. Her hands moved as if to grasp something floating just out of reach. Then she stopped and faced him, her expression now fiercely resolute. "It is just that I do things in my own way. I'm perfectly capable of helping you."

"Helping? With what?"

"Wasn't our dinner for William Conolly a success?" She waited for his nod. "You're trying to make our country just and fair as well as great. I want to…"

"You give me too much credit," John had to say, though he hardly minded the admiration in her dark eyes, in the lines of that eminently kissable mouth.

Mary shook her head. "I saw how Conolly respected your opinions. There must be more I can do."

The resolute set of her chin was charming. Her resolute gestures, all of her was so distracting, so… arousing. He took a step closer. In this mood, she was really irresistible.

"I want to be part of it all," Mary said, spreading her hands.

John took another step and yielded to the overwhelming impulse to pull her into his arms. She looked up at him with wide startled eyes. She felt slight and soft and thrillingly pliable under his hands. He bent and took those enchanting lips for his own.

There was a haunting familiarity in the taste of her. But the memories of their brief month together were rapidly submerged in new sensations. He was a different man, kissing a different wife, in an altered world. His heart raced as she melted into him.

Mary had never been kissed like this in her life. It surpassed any fantasies she'd indulged in. John held her with an authority and demand that took her breath away. She'd felt his body along the length of her own before; she'd kissed these lips. But not like this. Her knees went weak. Her hands closed on his shoulders and clung. She nearly whimpered when he drew back. But then he pulled her closer and kissed her even more thoroughly. The second time he raised his head, they were both breathing hard.

John found that he'd pushed his wife right up against the desk. She was bent a little backward above it, and one of his knees had slid between hers. His pulse thundered in his ears. An errant thought made him picture the papers shoved to the floor, Mary on the desktop unclothed. She gazed up at him, her eyes huge and nearly black, her lips slightly parted. One shoulder of her gown had slipped, and he was ready to tear the rest away.

"Oh my," she breathed. "That was so much... better than before."

"Before?"

"At the seaside, when we first... I wasn't sure I would ever like it then. I didn't realize it could be like this."

John felt as if she had thrown some of that cold seaside water in his face. "I didn't realize it had been so bad," he said.

"Not bad. I didn't mean... Just...awkward. You know. And a bit, um, uncomfortable."

John moved a little away from her. Of all things, he did not want to think about this now.

"It was just...we seemed to be always bumping elbows and..."

She trailed off, looking worried. John remembered one of the fellows on the China ship saying that there was nothing worse than a woman who chattered during intimacies. He hadn't much cared for that man.

He'd found his conversation coarse and disrespectful. But right now he felt a certain sympathy with this remark. Had Mary really needed to point out his previous inadequacies? Right at this moment? John stepped back. That awkwardness of two years ago almost seemed to enter the room.

"John, I didn't mean... I *said* it was better. Much, much better. Wonderful!"

She reached out to him. But the instinctive certainty of moments ago had evaporated. He didn't want to do anything that would evoke past clumsiness. His gaze brushed the pages on the desk. Firmly, familiarly, anchored on the desk. "I must get back to work."

"Now?"

The incredulous reproach in her tone stung. *He* hadn't been the one who brought up old grievances. "Yes." He returned to his chair, picked up a page, and pretended to be able to read it.

The door to the study opened and closed with an angry snap. John put down the report and bent his head. His breath came out in a long sigh. He felt as if he'd been thrown from a cantering horse—from headlong to a slamming stop all in an instant. Knowing it was irrational and unwarranted, he wanted to hit something.

Alone on the stairway, Mary put her hands to her forehead. Why must he be so difficult? All right, she'd said the wrong thing. Yet again, unconsidered words had gotten her into trouble. But hadn't she *told* him how much better those kisses had been than the half-forgotten ones from the past? All she'd wanted was another, and more, far more than that.

She would go back in right now and tell him. Or shake him until he admitted he was being an ass.

Mary reached for the doorknob, started to turn it, and balked. It had felt so dreadful to be pushed away— like a blow to the heart. She saw her hand tremble and drew it back. She listened for some sound from within. All was quiet. Had John actually gone back to work, as if the kisses had never happened? As if she didn't matter?

She stood on the landing for long minutes, her stomach churning. She couldn't make herself go in. She couldn't bear another rejection just now. Blinking back tears, she crept silently up the stairs to her room.

Seven

WHEN MARY CAME DOWNSTAIRS THE NEXT MORNING, John had already left the house. No one remarked on this, since it was his established habit. Mary ate her breakfast, conferred with her staff about the day's tasks, and went about her own—all as usual. But through the routine her mind seethed with determination to make a change.

At eleven, she walked into her parlor studio and set up her watercolors. She would rely on her own unique abilities to find her way through the thicket of emotion where she floundered. She sat before her small easel, cleared her mind, and, instead of waiting for a subject to arise on its own, called up a memory of William Conolly's face. This was a new thing for her, and she worried a little that insisting on a particular image might not work. But Conolly was the only person she knew from John's work life, her only avenue into this crucial part of his world. She didn't know how else to enter it.

Her fears proved groundless. Her pencil began to move over the paper in response to the visualized image. Conolly's face started to form, and Mary was soon lost in the process of creation. After a while, she abandoned the pencil for a watercolor brush and began adding color and highlights. The man's crisp black hair, bright hazel eyes, narrow face, and mobile features emerged. She worked quickly, surely, happily, immersed in her natural element. Time became irrelevant. Detail accumulated, bit by bit forming a greater whole. Mary reveled in the sense of rightness and harmony that came when she drew.

Finally, with a long breath, she sat back and considered the portrait she'd produced. She'd clearly captured Conolly's jaunty presence. The man looked out at her much as he had over their dinner table. She could almost hear a quip drop from those smiling lips. But what else was there to see, if she looked deeper?

Trustworthy—that word came to her. She was already aware of his intelligence. And he had demonstrated ample good humor during their evening together. Under all that, though—a spark of rebellion and…anxiety? Tension? Resentment? It seemed like a mixture of all three of those. Like every person Mary had ever drawn, he wasn't one simple thing.

So did this portrait help her? Mary stared at it and willed it to tell her what steps to take about John. This was his friend. They had formed a connection working together. Out of all those employed in the Foreign Office, John had singled out this one man. What did that say about him? She stared and pondered and racked her brain. But she hadn't found an answer to these questions when the time came around to walk across the square to Eleanor Lanford's for tea.

The inside of her neighbor's house matched Mary's expectations. Like its owner, it was quietly elegant and rich without undue opulence. The old woman awaited her in a chintz-hung parlor at the front overlooking the sodden garden. Roses in the wallpaper countered the dismal weather. A lovely young woman with golden hair and bright green eyes stood beside her. "Mary Bexley, this is my granddaughter Caroline."

The young woman looked surprised.

Eleanor cocked an eyebrow at her. "Did you wish me to say Lady Caroline Lanford, eldest daughter of the Earl of St. Clair?" she inquired.

"People usually do," the other remarked.

"I am not 'usually.'"

"I know, Grandmamma. That is why I'm so delighted to be here." Caroline dropped a tiny curtsy. "Pleased to meet you, Mary Bexley. And since I am introduced as Caroline I hope you will use my name." She opened her arms in an expansive gesture. "Let us throw formality to the four winds."

Mary returned the curtsy. She could trace some resemblance to Eleanor in Caroline's oval face and sublimely regular features. The twinkle in the old woman's eyes escalated into mischief in her young relative's gaze, however. They sat down, and Eleanor poured tea and offered tidbits.

"I suppose Grandmamma has told you that I am in disgrace," Caroline continued blithely.

"Disgrace?"

"You didn't tell?" Caroline gave her grandmother a roguish look.

"My dear, I am not a gossip."

"Or perhaps you wished to keep my transgressions a secret from your friends?" Caroline's eyes sparkled, and Mary wondered what sort of disgrace could make her so lively.

Eleanor did not rise to her bait. She merely waved a hand as if to say, do as you like.

"My family thinks I am being subjected to quite a dire punishment," Caroline went on, "to be sent here so 'out of the world' for the whole hunting season. If I'd known that was the penalty, I'd have misbehaved far sooner."

"You did," commented Eleanor dryly. "Just not quite so outrageously."

Caroline grinned. She had dimples. "I must tell her. It was such a coup."

Despite her confident manner, Caroline clearly waited for her grandmother's permission to speak, which came in a nod.

The younger woman turned to Mary again. "I trained one of the ratter's ferrets to drop acorns on Papa's stuffy guests at the dinner table." Smiling, she waited for a reaction.

Mary tried to picture it. "Acorns? Ferrets?"

Caroline leaned a little forward. "Ferrets are quite clever, you know. They love games. Some of them, anyway. So I taught the smartest one to bring acorns from the big oak outside the dining room window along the picture rail near the ceiling and toss them onto the table." She paused as if waiting for applause. "One landed in the Duke of Portland's soup with such a splash that his shirtfront was soaked. He was livid."

"He has a limited sense of humor, as I recall," put in Eleanor.

Caroline giggled. "Another one dropped down the front of Lady Serence's gown. She has quite the embonpoint, as you know, Grandmamma. I thought Lord Ferring was going to dive in after it, but he stopped himself just in time. Felix laughed so hard he snorted soup out his nose." She glanced at Mary. "My brother," she explained.

"Your father didn't find it so amusing," said Eleanor.

"Well, he couldn't admit it, nor could Mama."

Mary was picturing the scene. A grand dinner party with flowers and silver and a fleet of servants; a small animal running along the picture rail tossing acorns. The resulting mayhem. How had she ever thought up such a scheme?

"It is astonishing how hard you will work to set up a prank and how little effort you expend on anything else," Eleanor told her granddaughter.

Caroline showed her dimples again. "Now everyone's terrified I'll kick up some sort of scandal in my second season," she said to Mary. "So they've sent me here to contemplate my sins and repent. And for Grandmamma to talk some sense into me, of course. As if she would."

"Oh, I shall," responded Eleanor.

Caroline looked briefly dismayed.

"My kind of sense."

Mary realized that she would very much like to hear this. She said so.

"That I should do as I please," suggested Caroline. "Isn't that what you've done, coming to live 'way out' here?"

"After a lifetime of doing my duty, I came here, yes," said Eleanor.

Caroline's face fell. "You aren't really going to tell me to get hold of myself and do my duty to the family, are you?"

Eleanor looked out the window, her face remote. "I'm going to tell you something much more difficult. Discover your passion and embrace it, Caroline."

"But I have…"

"Pranks are not a passion. They are a diversion." Her tone was so definitive that her granddaughter was silenced. "If you allow yourself to be diverted—by what others see as your duty or anything else—you will end up filled with regret."

"As you are?" Caroline wondered.

"By no means!" The snap in Eleanor's voice set both young women back. "Children were my passion. I longed to be a mother from my earliest years. An admirable mother, who gave her offspring what they needed in all ways. The choices I made were guided by that desire."

"And you had Papa and my uncle and aunts," said Caroline.

The old woman nodded. "Fine people whom I love dearly."

Mary noticed that she didn't mention her husband. Had she loved him dearly, too?

"I have regrets, of course. No one goes through life without some regrets. But I am *not* filled with them." Eleanor's expression softened. "And once I'd launched my children successfully—happily—into the world, I did as I pleased." She gestured around the cozy room in this "remote" neighborhood. "Who stops me?"

"Nobody," acknowledged her granddaughter with feeling.

Eleanor nodded. "Look at Mary," she continued. "She has great artistic talent, and she has cultivated it."

Mary wasn't entirely comfortable being held up as an example. "I draw a bit…"

"We both know it is far more than that," said Eleanor.

Mary met her penetrating gaze and bowed her head in acknowledgment. She was surprised by the flood of gratitude that followed. Drawing was her passion, she acknowledged. But what exactly did it mean—to embrace it?

Caroline was too involved in her own thoughts to notice this silent exchange. "That's all very well if you have a talent," she said. "I haven't. Or…my talent is for pranks. For shaking people up." She brightened. "Isn't that a good thing? Society is so staid and dull."

Eleanor raised skeptical eyebrows.

"Well, parts of it," amended her granddaughter defensively.

Caroline could see high society that way because she'd been born into the midst of it, Mary thought. Perhaps you had to be a secure part of something in order to mock it.

"What shall my passion be?" Caroline mused, her attention firmly on herself.

"You don't choose it like a new bonnet," replied her grandmother. "It finds you."

The girl bit her lower lip, frowning. "That's all very well to say, Grandmamma. But I know scores of people who clearly have none. You may have always known what you wanted, but you are quite…special. Perhaps I'm not."

"You are my granddaughter," declared Eleanor imperiously.

Caroline laughed. "And thus obliged to be special?"

"You are intelligent, courageous. You have enough spirit for three girls. You will find your way, my dear."

Her granddaughter jumped up and kissed her cheek. "How I love you, Grandmamma!"

Mary observed the obvious bond between the two women with a pang of envy.

❧

When John arrived home that evening, the parlor off the entryway was empty. A small fire burned in the grate, but there was no Mary sitting before it, her hands busy with some sewing project. He was startled at how much he missed that sight; he'd become accustomed to her greeting as he came in, to the air of tranquil domesticity she created, antidote to any upheavals he'd endured at his work. Searching, he went upstairs and found her in the room she'd chosen for her own use. She stood before a table scattered with painting materials, lost in thought. "There you are."

"Oh, John. I lost track of the time." She turned as he stepped farther into the room. He hadn't really been in here since she'd arrived in London, and he saw now that she'd made the space truly her own. There were colorful hangings, a comfortable armchair by the fireplace, and interesting little objects scattered from mantelpiece to windowsill. The long table under the front window was crowded with sketchbooks, watercolor paints, one jar of brushes and another of pencils, a pretty pottery bowl for water, and a small wooden case for transporting these items. Though the surface was crammed full, it seemed quite an organized clutter. The room felt at once cozy and sharply individual. It seemed to John like a glimpse inside his wife's personality.

He took another step and saw around Mary to a portrait resting on a tabletop easel—William Conolly to the life. The face was so familiar and so well done that it pulled him closer. "That's very good, Mary." The painting caught his colleague's quirk of a smile and alert intelligence. "I'd forgotten that you like to draw. You did me on our wedding trip, I remember."

Mary blinked and looked self-conscious. Recalling the last time their honeymoon had been mentioned, John half-turned away. Wanting some occupation for his hands, he picked up a sketchbook from the table. Mary's hand twitched, then fell back to her side. Opening it at random, John came upon a drawing of an older woman, a stranger.

"That's our neighbor," Mary said. "The one Mr. Conolly knew, the dowager countess. She's very kind. She invited me to tea today. I met her granddaughter. Caroline. Lady Caroline Lanford, I should say. She's quite a lively person. Caroline. Not Eleanor. She insists I call her Eleanor, although I know it is not…"

She was babbling. "Is something wrong?" John asked. Belatedly he wondered if he was intruding in her private sanctuary. Did she expect he would ask permission to enter a room in his own house?

Mary took a breath. "I…I'm not accustomed to showing my drawings."

John gazed at the image of Conolly. "But they're quite lifelike." He tried to be encouraging. "No need to be shy."

"My mother always thought I wasted far too much time with my paints."

Her voice was hurried, breathless. John didn't understand it. "Well, but young ladies are meant to have accomplishments, are they not?" he said heartily.

"Accomplishments."

She said the word as if it was some sort of insult, which made no sense; he'd praised her blasted painting.

"Like playing the pianoforte or the harp," Mary added. "But not seriously, of course."

He had no idea what she was getting at. The decorative pursuits of young ladies weren't serious. Wasn't that the whole point? They were designed to make life more gracious and...pretty. His wife moved a step closer, and he caught a hint of the sweet scent she always wore—violets. Thoughts of art and accomplishments fizzled and scattered and disappeared from his brain.

"My drawings...I see things in them sometimes. Insights? I was thinking it could be helpful..."

John was transfixed by the way her cheeks had reddened, like living roses. He scarcely heard the words or noticed her tentative tone and diffident gesture. A glossy brown curl had fallen across her forehead as she gazed at him so earnestly. His hand came up of its own accord and pushed the curl back. It lingered. His fingertips brushed her cheek.

Mary stopped talking, lips tantalizingly parted. She met his eyes and held them for what seemed like forever. "What I said yesterday, when we..."

John's hand dropped. "There is no need to discuss…"

"But I didn't mean… I said the wrong thing. I was just so surprised."

"Surprised?"

"At how amazing, how splendid it was." She moved, and John found he had a fragrant armful of wife.

Her arms came up and around his neck and tightened. Without a thought he pulled her closer. This kiss was as intoxicating as the last, as different, indeed, as it was possible to be from the tentative clumsiness of their honeymoon. She'd been right about that.

John pushed this thought aside as Mary's lips parted under his. Blood began to pound in his veins. He let his hands roam over her and brought his fingers up to cup a curve of breast. Her small moan as he teased it thrilled him. There were ways, he'd learned on his travels, to drive a woman distracted. He was newly inspired to try them all.

"Mr. Bexley! Sir!" John raised his head and discovered Arthur Windly standing in the half-open doorway.

Drat the boy, couldn't he see that he was emphatically not wanted in this moment? "Go away…"

Arthur hopped from foot to foot as if the floor were covered with hot coals. "The kitchen's on fire!" he cried.

"What?" said Mary and John simultaneously.

They ran, John with an eye out for whatever might be useful against a fire. He snagged his greatcoat from a chair in the entryway and raced on. Arthur was right behind him, babbling, "It weren't me. I didn't touch that chimney or the stove or nothing. I was scrubbing a great dirty pot in the scullery. I didn't even see how it…"

Mary was directly behind Arthur as they hurtled down the last stair. She stopped so suddenly that she almost toppled over, as the scene in the basement kitchen was terrifying. Mrs. Tanner stood well back from the big old fireplace, wringing her hands and watching flames run along the soot on the inside of the chimney and dart out into the room. Her screech when she saw them arrive was earsplitting. Kate had a broom and was beating at the tongues of flame on the hearth, without much effect. The acrid smell of burning filled the room, along with puffs of black smoke. A lick of flame burst out and threatened the walls, and Mary nearly shrieked herself.

Before she could move John had snatched up a large pot from the woodstove. He lunged right inside the fireplace and heaved its contents upward in a wide spray. Soup—was it soup?—splashed over the bricks, dousing some of the fire. The pipe running up the chimney from the stove hissed and steamed.

Arthur grabbed a second pot and thrust it toward John. Mary thought this one contained mashed potatoes. John waved it away and began beating at the remaining flames with a cloth he'd found somewhere. He leaned further into the chimney and reached up, thumping at the accumulated soot, bringing down a shower of black fragments and more smoke. "Watch out!" Mary cried, terrified he'd be burned.

He showed no sign of hearing. He kept on long after Mary could see any sign of flames, reaching higher, ducking when he loosened more flakes of soot, blinking it out of his eyes and leaning in again. Finally, he stood back, breathing hard, and let the scorched and blackened cloth drop to the brick floor.

Mary hurried over to him, but he held up both hands to forestall her. John's face, hands, and shirtfront were coated with soot. His hair was black now rather than brown. His greatcoat—the cloth he had been using, as she saw now—was ruined. "Is it out?" Mary said.

He nodded, then bent, putting his hands on his knees.

"I couldn't even think, and you just…you leapt in and saved the house."

"There was no time to summon help," he said.

Chimney fires could easily destroy a dwelling. Indeed, they often did in London. Mary started to shake. "You could have been badly burned!"

John straightened and, amazingly, grinned at her, his teeth a startling white against his sooty features. "I wasn't. Only a trifle scorched." He looked positively energized by the emergency.

"What are you doing, you wretched boy?" exclaimed Mrs. Tanner.

Balancing the pot he still held in one hand, Arthur had jerked open the oven door and tossed the mashed potatoes inside. When he turned to find everyone staring at him, he said, "I saw smoke coming out."

"My roast was burning," wailed the cook. "And now you've covered it with the potatoes. A proper mess you've made, which you will be cleaning up, you young devil. And the dinner all spoiled."

Arthur ignored her. "That was beyond anything great!" He gazed at John with hero worship shining in his eyes.

Mary surveyed the streaks of soot twisting up the whitewashed walls, the soup pooled in the hearth, and the hissing, dripping stove. The place smelled dreadful.

She took deep breaths to still her trembling. "The chimneys should have been swept before this place was leased," she said.

"Be sure I'll be speaking to them about that," said John. "I was told the house had been completely refurbished after the last tenant." After a final look up the chimney, he strode into the scullery and put his head under the pump.

"My kitchen!" Mrs. Tanner threw up her hands and gave way to hysterics.

Kate moved to put an arm around her mother. Her rare show of sympathy seemed to encourage rather than assuage the wailing, however. John finished scrubbing at his face and hands and hair and edged toward the stairs. "I must change out of this shirt," he said. The cook's noisy weeping seemed to affect him far more than a potentially lethal fire.

Mary nodded amid the wreckage. "Arthur can fetch some food from an alehouse."

The boy accepted his mission with alacrity. Turning to deal with the cook's vapors, Mary rather wished she could go with him.

Eight

THE NEXT FEW DAYS WERE CHAOS IN THE BEXLEY household, wholly taken up with repairs to the kitchen. A chimney sweep was summoned first thing, but the pipe from the stove had to be removed before he could do a proper job of cleaning. Which meant no cooking could be done—not even a cup of tea or a boiled egg. The household subsisted on bread and cheese and roast fowl and ale from a nearby public house. Mrs. Tanner used the opportunity to take to her bed on the top floor, "prostrate" with nerves.

To Mary's surprise Kate seemed merely amused by the disruptions, and she rallied round to help. She and Mary worked side by side with Arthur and some hired cleaners to scrub the soot off every surface and utensil in the kitchen and put a new coat of whitewash on the walls. After this long and exhausting chore was at last complete, the maid even coaxed her mother downstairs to see the new closed stove Mary had purchased. Kate made the first pot of tea in the refurbished kitchen, and Mary felt more in charity with her than she ever had before, when the harrowing episode finally came to a close.

The disruptions meant that she fell into bed exhausted each night, however. There seemed no moment in those hectic days to revisit the thrilling scene the fire had interrupted. They didn't sit down to dinner together, as there was no proper dinner. They didn't sit cozily in the front parlor of an evening, because there was always another task calling out to be done. Add to that the fact that Arthur had taken to dogging John's footsteps, his skinny frame practically vibrating with admiration. As often as John kindly sent him away, he was soon creeping back, wide-eyed, reverent, and…intrusive. And so they had scarcely an instant alone. Mary might dream of her heroic husband's hands on her every night as she slept, but the reality remained otherwise.

Thus, Mary was more than delighted to leave the house for an evening out. William Conolly had invited the Bexleys on an expedition to Vauxhall Gardens as a return of their hospitality. "I thought you would enjoy the illuminations," he told Mary as he helped her into a hired carriage to begin the journey to the south side of the river. "And Vauxhall closes at the end of September. So you must see it now or wait until spring."

"I've heard a great deal about the place," said John. He looked very handsome in a new evening coat and snowy shirt.

"What are they like?" Mary wondered.

Conolly would only smile. "Wait and see."

When they walked under the great paneled archway

into the pleasure gardens, the first thing Mary noticed was the crowd. Despite the coolness of the evening, throngs of well-dressed strollers peopled a tree-lined walk stretching into the distance. She could see them perfectly by the light of thousands of glass lamps hung among the branches. The effect was dazzling; the sound of a thousand conversations was a surprising roar in the outdoor setting.

They joined the revelers. With Conolly as guide they walked past fiddlers in cocked hats playing under the gilded cockleshell in the midst of the gardens. They paused to hear singers of comic and sentimental ballads. They watched a group of country dancers, earning applause with much jumping, thumping, and laughter. They marveled over a lady in a spangled costume walking a tightrope and solemnly observed the hermit sitting in his illuminated hermitage. John remarked on the unlighted walks off to the sides, and Conolly told him they were known as places for amorous adventures.

Their host had hired a box for supper, and when they'd tired of walking, they retired there, admiring the mural at the back. Servitors brought the thinly sliced ham for which the place was famous. "They say that a Vauxhall carver slices so thin he could cover the whole garden from a single ham," Conolly said.

"Making it hardly worth eating," John replied, prodding the near transparent serving on his plate.

"Still, you must have it," replied his friend. "You can't come to Vauxhall and not have the ham."

"If I must, I must." John smiled, wrapped the tissue-thin meat around his fork, and ate the whole slice in one bite. "It tastes"—he paused, letting the others wait—"like ham."

Their mingled laughter buoyed Mary's heart.

Conolly had also ordered assorted biscuits and cheesecakes and a bowl of the notorious arrack punch. "Take care," he teased Mary when he dipped her out a cup. "This will go straight to your head."

Gingerly she tasted the mixture. "What's in it?"

"I have it on the best authority that it's made by mixing grains of the benjamin flower with rum."

"What is benjamin flower?"

"I have no idea."

"There was some journalist fellow called Benjamin Flower," John put in. "Ranted against the French war at the beginning. I think they put him in Newgate for sedition or libel or some such thing." He tried the punch and raised his eyebrows. "Not likely he had anything to do with this mixture."

"Your husband is a veritable encyclopedia of political knowledge," Conolly said to Mary. "We are in awe of him at the office."

This made John laugh. He had the most wonderful laugh, Mary thought. She didn't hear it nearly enough. She raised her glass to him. "As you should be," she replied. "He saved our house quite heroically, you know." She met her husband's eyes and found she really couldn't look away.

Smiling, Conolly drank from his own cup. The story of the fire had been fully explored on their way over. "Ah, there's the Duke of Wellington in that box directly across."

Mary tore her gaze away from John's sparkling

blue eyes and observed an upright man with a jutting profile. He looked every inch the soldier.

"And that is Wrotherton, one of our leading dandies, four boxes to the left."

"What happened to his neck?" John wondered.

"A fashion faux pas of a neckcloth," was the reply.

"It looks like a bandage."

"Very like," Conolly agreed. "It's probably sturdy enough to support a broken neck."

John laughed again. He was far handsomer than the famous dandy, Mary thought.

Their host pointed out other notables. He seemed to know everyone. Mary began to wonder about his particular friends and habits. "You seem so familiar with the place. Have you been here often?" she asked.

He shrugged. "Fairly."

"Was there no one else you wished to invite along this evening?" she asked.

He wiggled his eyebrows at her. "A lady, perhaps? Why are married people always so eager to promote matches? Enough that you are happily settled." It was said with a smile to remove any suggestion of real complaint.

"You don't wish to marry?"

"My wishes don't really come into it," Conolly replied.

"What do you mean?"

"That's his own affair, Mary," put in John.

"No, no." Conolly gestured expansively. He'd had three full cups of the punch. "It's my family's position, you see. Creates rather a conundrum for me. The young ladies I meet are looking for a far bigger fortune than I have to offer. They expect to live in the sorts of houses they grew up in and have the same sorts of…comforts. And why shouldn't they, eh? No doubt they deserve it. But I can't provide 'em. This or that one may like me but not well enough to give up their luxuries. Yet I'm expected, nay commanded, to get leg-shackled to a girl of my own rank."

She and John were lucky, Mary thought. Though they didn't come from excessively wealthy families, they'd each inherited a competence. Put together, the amount was ample for a comfortable life. How would it be if they lived in a set of rooms—as she'd been told Conolly did—with no servants except a landlady. Cramped and…insupportable, she thought. She would hate it. "Perhaps an heiress will fall in love with you," she joked a bit uneasily.

Conolly's wry shrug made her feel gauche. "Their mothers see that they don't get the chance. And there's also the little problem of my reputation."

"Your…?" Was this what she'd sensed in the portrait? Mary wondered. She saw that John was frowning at his friend.

Conolly's expression shifted. He looked impish. "I played the odd prank at school. My mind just runs that way. The Irish in me, perhaps."

"Ah, I'd nearly forgotten." John turned to Mary with another heart-melting smile. "Not only at school," he said. "I must tell you that Conolly sometimes informs new employees in our office that they are required to provide their own chairs, as the government budget doesn't cover such expenditures. I actually bought one and was hauling it up the stairs when he took pity on me and told me the truth."

"And a fine chair it was," declared Conolly,

laughing. "Much better than the poor things they give us to sit on."

"At least no one else saw me," said John.

"Didn't I make sure of that?" protested his friend.

"You did," John agreed. "And got the porter to let me leave it with him until the end of the day."

"Is it the chair at your desk in the study?" Mary wondered.

"The very one," John confirmed.

She laughed. "It's odd; I recently met someone else who loves playing pranks."

"Who's that?" Conolly wanted to know.

Now that she'd said it, she wondered if she shouldn't have shared this information. But she didn't see what harm it could do. Caroline hadn't seemed at all shy about her antics. "Lady Caroline Lanford." Both men looked surprised. "Our neighbor's grand-daughter," she reminded John.

"The Golden Minx?" Conolly said. "That's what society calls her," he added in response to their puzzled expressions. "Nickname."

"Do you know her?" Mary asked.

"Oh, quite above my touch," their host replied.

Something in his tone made Mary glad that the conversation was interrupted just then by the begin-ning of the fireworks. They got up and went to watch the display from a better vantage point.

John relished the play of colored light over Mary's face as the rockets burst above them. She looked lovely tonight in a pale yellow gown and dark blue cloak. After the drudgery of putting the house to rights, she deserved a good time, and she looked like she was having fun. So was he, he realized. He must see that it happened far more often.

Immediately, his thoughts filled with other ways that they might enjoy each other's company—if only their life wasn't so crammed full of people. He let his gaze rove along the beguiling line of her neck. He watched her chest rise as she oohed over a burst of color above and could almost feel the soft curves beneath the cloth. Tonight, he vowed, when he got her home he would sweep her upstairs before anyone even knew they were there. His body reacted to the thought and the pictures it roused of what would follow. It was time—far past time—to make his marriage whole.

At last, the fireworks ended. They turned away and headed for Vauxhall's gate. They had nearly reached it when John spotted Fordyce, strolling languidly toward them. His mellow mood evaporated. He took Mary's arm to steer her away, but the blasted man had seen them.

"Bexley, Conolly," came the irritating drawl. "How odd. And a…lady."

He made it sound as if there was something disreputable about Mary's presence. John felt as if his head was filling with hot coals.

"Mrs. Bexley," provided Conolly smoothly. "This is Edmund Fordyce. He works with us at the Foreign Office."

"You're *married*?" Fordyce said to John, scarcely acknowledging Mary. "How very…daring of you."

Mary was examining the newcomer with interest. Fordyce turned and surveyed her, looking insultingly unimpressed. "I don't suppose I know your people?"

"I don't suppose you do," she replied.

Fordyce's pale eyebrows went up. "Oh my, do you fancy yourself a wit?"

John just barely stopped himself from going for his throat. Slights to himself were one thing; it was quite another to see this damned coxcomb talking to his wife as if she were a presumptuous nobody. Conolly's tug on his arm did little to divert the fury pumping in his veins.

"We were just going," Conolly said. "Good night, Fordyce."

The fellow twiddled his fingers in an insulting farewell. He didn't say it had been a pleasure to meet Mary or make the least effort at politeness. Something like a growl vibrated in John's throat. Conolly tugged at his sleeve again. Perhaps he had heard it. "Come along," he said.

Fordyce turned and walked away from them. John started to let Conolly steer him away. "You know he is *trying* to vex you," Conolly murmured, too low for Mary to hear. "Ignore him."

It was fine to say so. And it was what John habitually did. But with Mary involved…rage burned through him again. That Fordyce would dare treat her so slightingly. The man should be horsewhipped! John pulled his arm from Conolly's grasp. "You go ahead. I'll be along in a moment."

"Bexley. Don't do anything…"

John ignored his wife's curious glances from him to Conolly and back again. He turned and strode along the path to catch up with Fordyce. Fortunately, the man was still alone. "You are never to speak to my wife in that way again," he said to him.

Fordyce raised his thin pale brows. "I beg your pardon?"

"You don't and never will. Just hear this, should you ever encounter my wife in future…"

"I can't imagine why I would."

John just barely resisted grasping the man's neckcloth and choking him. "…you will treat her with respect."

"Such heat." Fordyce made a flicking gesture, as if brushing a speck of dust from his coat. "You may call me out if you think I've insulted your little wife." He put a sardonic twist on the last two words, clearly designed to enrage.

John caught a hint of eagerness in his eyes. Fordyce was just the sort of fellow who would study fencing and keep a pair of dueling pistols. "I'm not going to call you out," he said contemptuously. "I'm not some creaking antique. Even if dueling weren't illegal, it's idiotic. I'm simply telling you that you've gone too far. You will stop all your stupid tricks and stay away from me."

Under John's glare, Fordyce backed up a step, but he still sneered. "And if I decline to do so?"

John's rage was like a fine brandy, distilled down to a biting intensity. "I will write a full account of your behavior when the *Alceste* went down, every cowardly bit of it."

"No one would believe you…"

"I will produce numerous copies and circulate them around the office, like a broadsheet sold in the streets." John didn't particularly like making this threat, but he was mortally tired of Fordyce and his juvenile attitude. "It will create quite the sensation, I imagine. Our colleagues do love to gossip."

Fordyce stared at him, hatred in his light blue eyes. "You're a nobody. You wouldn't dare carry through on that…"

"Oh, I think you'll find that I will." John put all his resolve in his voice and expression and watched Fordyce quail. "If you had left me alone, I would have done the same for you," he added. "I have no interest in telling tales. But you would keep on. Believe me, I will do this unless you disappear from my life."

Fordyce's hands closed into fists and opened again. "I can't help seeing you at the office," he said, a hint of fear in his tone.

"You know what I mean," replied John. Satisfied that he was understood, John turned to catch up with his party.

"Not a very pleasant man," Mary tried when John found them again outside the gates. The tension between John and Fordyce had been palpable.

"He won't trouble you again," said John.

"I wasn't troubled, particularly." What was the glitter in John's eyes? "He was just rude."

"Rude! He spoke to you as if…"

He broke off, and as Conolly asked a Vauxhall footman to summon their hired carriage, Mary realized that her husband wanted to protect her from this Fordyce person. Though she hadn't felt much affected by the snub of a complete stranger, John's response touched her deeply. It made her long to throw herself into his arms and show him how much she admired and appreciated him. She would do exactly that, she vowed, the moment they reached home.

Unfortunately this was not soon. There was an

interminable wait for their carriage. Everyone seemed to be leaving Vauxhall at the same time, and the servitors gave precedence to the carriages of the noble guests. Vehicles jostled and blocked each other until none of them could move. Coachmen shouted and cursed; horses shied and snapped. Impatient revelers added to the chaos by wading in and pulling at bridles and reins, making things worse as far as Mary could see.

The hour grew later. Their carriage was nowhere to be seen. After her intense exertions of the last few days, Mary grew tired. She tried not to be impatient. Conolly was doing his best to hurry matters, but there wasn't much he could do. It was more than an hour before they found their vehicle, and then they were forced to weave slowly through the press of carriages, all trying to be first away.

And when at last they were free of the mass, even stops and starts and cobblestones couldn't keep Mary from falling asleep on the long ride across London. She fought the fatigue and the effects of the Vauxhall punch, but sleep dragged at her with a power like the sea. She couldn't help but succumb.

John carried his sleeping wife through their front door and up the stairs to her bedchamber. At the feel of her body in his arms desire dizzied him. He could not wait any longer. Undoing the clasp of her cloak and letting it fall, he laid her on her bed. "Mary?" He untied the strings of her bonnet and eased it off.

She stirred and muttered but didn't wake.

"Mary?" He slipped off her shoes.

She let out a long languorous sigh that roused him further.

"Mary," he said more loudly. He shook her shoulder gently.

She murmured again, threw out an arm, and turned away from him, curling into her pillows. He shook her softly once more, but she wouldn't wake.

The Vauxhall punch had done for her, John thought. She wasn't used to drinking more than a glass of wine. She was dead to the world for tonight.

His hands hovered over her. He could have her. He was her husband. No one would blame him. Mary might not even know. And that was the trouble. It didn't feel right. And it wasn't the way he wanted it to be. Damn it all!

Carefully, he undid the buttons at the back of her gown. Each time his fingertips brushed her soft skin, they shook with the effort of restraint. Easing the garment off her almost broke him. This had to end. He was desperate. Quickly pulling the coverlet over her tantalizing form, he fled the room.

Mary woke in her bed, in her underclothes, shoeless. She stretched, sat up, and noticed her cloak and evening dress lying on the floor. Heat suffused her face as she realized that John must have carried her upstairs and removed her gown. The picture this evoked was so vivid that her breath caught. Her mind conjured up the image of John undoing buttons, sliding the cloth gently off her shoulders, down along her body. Mary cursed the Vauxhall punch; it had added the final straw to her tendency to sleep like one drugged. Her sisters used to marvel that she could slumber on through thunderclaps and barking dogs and late night upsets. And now it had caused her to miss what could have been a…truly delicious process. Why had John not shaken her awake?

Because he was thoughtful, perhaps a bit too scrupulous. Or still smarting over her stupid remark about their honeymoon? Why had she blurted that out? Why must unconsidered words be her nemesis? Mary dressed quickly and hurried downstairs, but as usual John had already gone. She couldn't suppress a curse, which led Arthur Windly to gape at her openmouthed and then grin.

❧

At his desk in the Foreign Office, John Bexley was equally frustrated and finding it damnably difficult to concentrate on reports from intelligence agents. His mind was full of Mary—her small frame in his arms as he carried her up the stairs, setting her on the coverlet, and loosening her clothes. He remembered how he'd envied her ability to sleep so deeply on their honeymoon. No lumpy bed or chorus of roosters had disturbed her then, and with the addition of the punch… If only those dark eyes had opened, and discovered him, and…

"Bexley?"

John looked up to find Harkness in the doorway. His superior was looking at him rather oddly. It seemed likely that he'd spoken more than once. "Deep into it, eh?" the man added.

"Sorry, sir." John straightened and half rose. He hadn't slept well.

Harkness waved him back to his chair. "Your focus and dedication is appreciated. Would you please write

up a précis of your last report? I want to pass it along."
He put the report on John's desk as he spoke.

"Of course. Right away." With a nod, Harkness
departed. John folded away the document he'd been
reading and pulled the report closer, elated that his
analysis had impressed Harkness. "Passing it along"
meant that Harkness thought his work important
enough to be reviewed at the highest levels. He
needed to clear his mind and do his job, John thought.
And his marriage needed to be a support, not a distraction. No matter what, tonight he would have to make
a move to see that it was.

⁓

Mary was more and more restless as the day wound on.
And as so often when she felt that way, she soon found
herself with a sketchbook. Of course. She must draw
Fordyce; she must find out all she could about the man.
Was he merely John's rival? His enemy? Excited by the
thought of discovery, she went to work. Her pencil
moved quickly, outlining Fordyce's remembered features
and filling in detail. Then, in a corner of the page, she
sketched a full-length study of the figure they'd encountered last night. An hour passed unheeded as she drew,
softened stark lines with her finger, and added highlights.

When at last Mary sat back, there was Fordyce
gazing at her—his long face and hooded eyes, his pale
blond hair and light blue eyes, and his wide mouth
seemingly made for sneering. He was just above
medium height, Mary remembered, and…sinuous was
the word that floated up. His shoulders weren't much
wider than his hips. Like an eel…or a snake.

She contemplated her work. She knew from Conolly that Fordyce was the third son of an earl. She'd asked him as they waited for John. He'd also told her that he and John had traveled together to China. She knew from her own observation that John didn't like him. She suspected William Conolly didn't either. And having met the man she could see why. His manner had been taunting, sarcastic.

Mary set herself to look deeper. Whereas Conolly's portrait had appeared trustworthy, the man in this drawing seemed the opposite. You would never want to confide in him. He would find a way to use it against you, she was somehow sure. His eyes, half-hidden as she'd recalled them, held an empty glint. Which was an odd combination of words, Mary thought. Yet it seemed right. The shimmer in his eyes didn't feel like vivacity or humor—definitely not sympathy. It signaled a kind of...intelligence, perhaps? Curiosity? No, here was a man keenly interested in others, but only so that he could root out what they didn't want revealed. He wanted secrets, desired them as a drunkard longed for drink. He wanted them to use, to betray, to advance himself at others' expense.

Mary stepped back from this latest product of her art, and she felt a strong desire to escape its intrusive stare. She closed the sketchbook and left the room.

Wanting the company of more amiable people, Mary headed for the kitchen. There she found Kate sitting at the big wooden table leafing through what looked like a sheaf of recipes. Mrs. Tanner was bent over a pot on the stove. "There you are," the cook said before Mary's foot left the final stair. "That dratted boy's gone missing."

"Arthur? He's missing?"

"He's just out having a bit of a lark," said Kate, as if she wished she was doing the same.

"I sent him up to the greengrocer for carrots, which I needed twenty minutes ago." Mrs. Tanner stirred glumly. "And now he's been gone a good two hours." She made a sour face. "And, no, Kate can't go looking for the little devil. She needs to do a bit of work for a change."

Kate grimaced at her mother's back. Not for the first time, Mary thought that these two should have taken positions in different households when they left the duchess's employ. In a peeress's large group of servants they had evidently gotten on well enough. Here, they rubbed together every moment, and the older woman was often irascible.

In many ways, Mrs. Tanner seemed to have adjusted to her changed situation. She'd delved into the cookery books Mary had purchased and appeared to enjoy being queen of a smaller kitchen, now that she was accustomed to its ways. Their baking days had become a pleasant cooperation. All would have been well, Mary thought, if her maid weren't Mrs. Tanner's daughter. Mrs. Tanner was more critical of Kate than she would have been of a stranger, and Kate was more rebellious. The maid showed no signs of becoming reconciled to her position, yet she couldn't be dismissed without offending her mother. Mary was sympathetic to their situation, up to a point. But she wouldn't be spoken to in this way in her own kitchen.

She held Mrs. Tanner's gaze until the cook dropped her eyes and murmured, "Sorry, ma'am."

Mary nodded. "I'll go out and look for Arthur," she said. "I'd like a walk, and I have some errands." Ignoring the cook's renewed muttering, Mary fetched her cloak and a basket and went out into the brisk September afternoon.

Nine

MARY WENT FIRST TO THE GREENGROCER THEY patronized to inquire about Arthur. He had been there and bought the carrots, but that had been more than an hour ago, she was told. She went on to a spice merchant in a nearby street. Once she'd made her planned purchases, she walked to the market square where Arthur had encountered the dog, but she found no sign of him there. Thwarted, she wondered where else to search. She wasn't terribly worried about the boy. Their neighborhood was quite safe. Arthur was fascinated by London and had stretched out the time of his assigned errands before, though not for as long as two hours. She was more concerned about what he might have shot with his sling or other mischief he might have gotten into. He could be lost, she supposed, though for a country boy he'd demonstrated a keen sense of direction in town.

Mary made some looping circuits of their neighborhood. People bustled in and out of local businesses, carried parcels wrapped in brown paper under their arms, and chatted in front of the butcher's and the tea shop. But none of them was Arthur. She ranged a bit farther. Turning down an unfamiliar street, she came upon a crooked lane of small shops. She knew she wasn't far from home, but she'd never seen this rather charming thoroughfare before. Walking along, noting the businesses and their various wares, she came upon an intriguing display in a bow window.

She stepped closer. Small colored bottles held labels that described tinctures and medicinal concoctions. There were packets of dried herbs as well and flower-based lotions. The sign above the door read, "Jeremiah Jenkins, Apothecary." Intrigued, she opened the door and went in. A bell on a spring heralded her entrance.

Inside, there was far more than the rows of patent medicines and tank of leeches one found in a commonplace apothecary shop. The place smelled lovely—like all the flowers Mary could imagine in one bouquet.

A young man came through the arch at the back and gave her a polite smile. "Yes, ma'am, how may I serve you?"

"Are you Jeremiah Jenkins?" asked Mary.

"I am."

He was young to be the proprietor of his own shop, perhaps twenty-five, and very handsome indeed, Mary thought. His black curly hair grew in a dramatic peak above dark eyes; his square chin promised determination, his wide forehead intellect. "The display in your window interested me," she said. "Do you make your own tinctures?"

"Mostly I procure them from country people with

generations of experience in finding and combining the proper ingredients."

She smiled at his prompt promotion of his products. "I'm sure I could supply any compound you might require."

Mary forgave the touch of pomposity in his voice. She was pretty certain he used it to counteract his youth. "Do you have a family?" she asked

"I beg your pardon?"

"I…ah…I prefer to deal with family men. You have a wife? Children?"

"I am unmarried," he replied stiffly. "But I do not see… I assure you this has no effect on my ability to provide satisfactory service."

"Indeed. Still, you are rather young…"

He grew even stiffer. "My father owned this establishment before me, and he thoroughly educated me in every aspect of the apothecary's trade. He was a master of his craft."

Mary liked the emotion in his voice when he spoke of his father and his apparent devotion to his profession. This unexpected encounter had given her some intriguing ideas. "Well, your shop is very interesting."

Still prickly and now disappointed at her failure to purchase anything, he sketched a bow as she turned toward the door.

Basket on her arm, Mary walked to the end of the lane and around another corner, finding herself back in familiar territory. She was a little distance from home and out of ideas for finding Arthur. The afternoon was waning. She could only hope he'd returned in her absence. If he hadn't, they would institute a more serious search.

It was nearly dusk when she came into the square and saw the candlelit windows of her house ahead. She was hurrying toward home when she heard her name called and turned to find John striding toward her. "What are you doing out alone at this time of day?" he said.

"I was looking for…"

"You must take Kate or Arthur with you when you go out." He took her arm and pulled her along toward home.

Mary thought for an instant that she saw someone at the entrance of the square behind him, but then it seemed it was just a moving shadow. "I often do. The trouble today was that Arthur…"

"I won't have you out alone in the dark!"

While she appreciated his concern, Mary also felt it a bit unreasonable. "I don't go out alone in the dark. I…"

"What do you call this?" John gestured at the growing gloom.

"Our neighborhood is quite safe. I was trying to find…"

"Until that single time when it isn't!" He hustled her toward the front door. Mary already had her key out to open it, and in a moment they were inside. John faced her with an intense look. "I can't worry about you while I'm out. I have to keep my mind on my work."

"There's no need for you to worry."

"You have no idea what London is really like. I've seen things…" He broke off with a haunted expression.

"What things?"

"Never mind, Mary. I want your word that you won't go wandering the streets alone."

She started to say that she hadn't been "wandering the streets" and that he was making a great case out of nothing. But something in his face made her bite back the words. "I won't."

John wanted a more specific promise. He wanted a guarantee that he would never arrive home to find her missing, hurt, or dead in an alley somewhere, dragged off by villains… Something twisted in his chest at the idea; for an instant he felt he couldn't breathe. Then he forced these unlikely scenarios out of his mind. They didn't live in Limehouse. Their neighborhood was, in fact, quite safe. Why else had he chosen it? She'd said she would do as he asked. She hadn't argued. He had to accept her word. He nodded, managing a smile.

Only then did he notice Kate at the back of the entryway, standing ready to take his coat and watching their exchange with bright interest. He took off the coat and gave it to her.

"Has Arthur returned?" Mary said.

"Yes, ma'am," said the maid. "A good hour past."

Mary sighed and nodded. "I'll speak to him later."

Something in the exchange caught John's attention. "Returned from where?"

Mary looked at Kate. "Did he say?" When Kate shook her head, she added, "He was out for hours on a simple errand. I must tell him that he is not free to pursue 'adventures' all over town."

Mary spoke lightly, as if to assure him this was a trivial matter. But the word "adventures" struck like a gong in John's head. "I'll talk to him," he said.

"You?"

Nettled by Mary's surprised look, he said, "I was a lad myself. I understand the breed."

"I know, but…"

"You have some objection?" He was angry, and he had no idea why.

"No, of course not. I simply didn't want you bothered with domestic problems."

"Perhaps this is neither a problem nor domestic!"

"What?"

Confused by his own reactions, John turned toward the parlor. Irritatingly, Mary followed him in. She put a hand on his sleeve. "It's very kind of you to think of speaking to Arthur," she said. "I know he admires you very much." She smiled, her dark eyes warm.

John's vexation evaporated in a breathless rush. In its place came memories of all the times he'd touched her—the feel of her lips, her pliant body responding to his hands, the gasp of startled pleasure he'd once roused. Desire flooded every inch of him, as if he'd been plunged into scalding water. Unthinking, he reached for her.

In the parlor doorway, Kate cleared her throat. "Dinner is served…ma'am."

❧

Their meal that evening was weighted with nuance. They talked of commonplace things, but John's mind was still full of the times he'd held his wife in his arms. Their process of getting "reacquainted," adjusting to their new situation, fresh start—whatever you wished to call it—had gone on far too long. Tension had begun to burden the very air. Why should it seem such a great step from this pleasant table to the bedchamber? But Kate was serving parsnips, and Mary was talking of some spice merchant, and there was a whole routine to be gone through before they were alone. It seemed like hours before the meal ended and they retired to the parlor.

John settled beside his wife before the fire. He told himself not to be impatient or clumsy, but desire pulsed in at him. He could wait no longer. "Mary?"

Something in his tone seemed to arrest her attention. She gazed up at him.

"I know we said we would keep a certain distance until we were better acquainted…"

"I didn't." Mary bit her lip.

"What?"

"I didn't say it."

Heat ran through John, as if he'd stepped into flames.

"We're…we're married," Mary added. "We've been married for two years. It's not as if…I mean…"

In one swooping move John pulled her into his arms. Her eyes burned into his for one thrilling moment, and then he kissed her.

Her eager response added to the fire coursing through him. He coaxed and caressed, his hands moving across her back, drifting up to brush her breast and rouse the breathy sigh that so delighted him. Their time apart had altered them both. They'd found their way to inner fires as life challenged them, and now the two together promised conflagration.

Mary couldn't have said how long the kiss went on; she only knew that she felt bereft when it was interrupted by yet another cough from the parlor doorway. "Was you wanting tea or…anything else?" Kate asked. She didn't even try to hide a grin.

Mary jerked back, but John kept his arm firmly around her. "Nothing," he said to the maid. "Go… wherever you like. Away."

Kate giggled, dropped a saucy curtsy, and went.

Mary put a hand to her reddened cheek. "What she will tell her mother…"

"That I was kissing my wife? And she was kissing me?"

"In the parlor, right in front of the window where anyone…"

"I don't actually care." He smiled and let go of her long enough to rise and hold out a hand. "I do think we should move upstairs, however."

His fingers closed over hers like a pledge. His arm slid around her once more as they walked up the stairs side by side.

John closed the door of Mary's bedchamber firmly behind them and locked it. He pulled her back into his arms with all the fervor that had been building in him for weeks. Yet he told himself not to rush. Here was the moment to practice the intimate lore he had gathered on his long voyage. Here was the chance to redeem the awkwardness of their honeymoon for all time.

He dropped kisses along her cheekbone and then captured her lips again. Slowly, he insisted, though his body vibrated with the urge to tear at clothing and fall into bed.

Mary gave herself up to the kiss. Her body felt like a cascade of gateways opening, one and another, sensations and demands coming alive. His lips drifted down her neck; he pushed the sleeve of her gown off her shoulder and followed the retreating cloth with his mouth. Even as her senses swam, Mary remembered hurrying into her nightdress on their first night together, so worried about being caught in the midst of disrobing. Why had she cared? Tonight, she tangled her fingers in John's hair and urged him onward.

Their clothes came off in fits and starts—unlacing and unbuttoning for themselves and each other, hands brushing, lips trailing along newly bared skin, more and more urgent. She could touch him, too, Mary thought. How had she not thought of that before? Somehow, in their months apart, she'd come to understand the authority of desire, the beauty of acquiescence. She could ask and offer even as John did the same.

They fell together onto Mary's bed, fingertips tantalizing heated skin, exchanging a flurry of kisses. Mary slid her leg over his. John gathered the remnants of his wits and recalled that shipboard assurance—there was a sure way to drive women wild. Shoving aside the memory of avid lantern-lit faces and lubricious laughs, John let himself experiment. He slid his hand along Mary's inner thigh. And up, up to a hot liquid center. His fingertips glided over it, teasingly drew back. Mary moaned and arched toward his touch. Exulting at his success, aching with desire, he kept on until she tensed beneath him and cried out in release.

John had one long glimpse of his wife's dark eyes drowned in desire, just as he had wished, and then she was pulling him closer. Her hands were urgent, insistently enflaming. And then he was with her as never before—moving in harmony, breath and pulse quickening as one. Together, they rode a wave of pleasure right to the glorious crest. And it broke and engulfed him, and rational thought dissolved in a burst of glory.

Afterward, they lay entwined, panting. Mary's senses swam back to something like rationality, and she started to say how very glorious that had been. Then she pressed her lips tight and kept quiet. That hadn't gone well the last time. And she certainly meant no comparison to their awkward honeymoon intimacies. There *was* no comparison! So she simply nestled against John's shoulder as they made themselves comfortable in the bed. When his eyes closed some time later and his breath deepened into sleep, she felt as if her heart would burst with happiness.

Ten

THE NEXT MORNING, MARY WENT DOWNSTAIRS SING-ing. Even though John was gone from the house, from her bed, her mood was ebullient. Today, she wanted everyone on Earth to be happy. Thus, at midmorning, she summoned Kate to accompany her on a round of errands. The discontented housemaid looked surprised to be asked, since Mary most often sent her on her own or employed Arthur. But she fetched her cloak and a basket without demur, and they set off together in the crisp autumn air.

Mary chose a new spool of thread at one shop and a pound of tea at another, following a route she had plotted out in her mind. Kate walked beside her, look-ing increasingly puzzled by the nearly empty basket she carried. As they turned the final corner, Mary hung back a little to watch the maid's expression when they came upon the apothecary's establishment.

Kate was eyeing the narrow street with her cus-tomary dissatisfied expression. Her mouth was turned down, her blue eyes restless in her round face. Then she glimpsed the jars and bottles in the display window. She moved toward the place as if drawn by an invisible string. Mary watched her examine the labels on the tinctures, the packets of herbs, and the bottles of lotion. Her gaze rose to the sign above the door, then moved back to the array of products.

"I was thinking of purchasing some rose-scented lotion I noticed here," Mary told her. "I thought you could advise me."

Kate looked down from her superior height. For the first time Mary could recall, she seemed confused, or uncertain, and it softened that stubborn-looking jaw. "Advise you."

It wasn't a question. Or, at least, it wasn't a simple question. Mary moved forward and entered the apothecary shop, the bell above the door jingling. The mingled scents of many flowers rose around her again.

Kate was right behind her, scanning the shelves and displays with an eagerness Mary also had never seen in her before. When the proprietor came out from the back, Kate turned, blinked, and went still.

Mary gave her a moment to absorb the man's handsome face and figure before she said, "Mr. Jenkins, I have returned, you see, to inquire about the rose lotion."

With a small bow, he went to the display and picked up a bottle. "A fine choice, ma'am. Many of my customers swear by its soothing qualities. And of course the scent is most pleasing."

"When I was here before, Mr. Jenkins told me that he gets his tinctures from country people with a great deal of experience in concocting," Mary said to Kate. She turned back to the apothecary. "Kate has worked in the stillroom of the Duchess of Carwell." Mary told herself that this was quite true. If it implied that the stillroom had been Kate's main job, well, that was not what she meant.

"Indeed," replied the apothecary.

The two faced each other. Though Kate was tall, Jeremiah Jenkins was taller. Though her shoulders were rather square, his were broader.

Kate stepped closer, picked up another bottle of the rose lotion from the display, opened it, and sniffed. "Do you use almond oil?" she asked.

She sounded curt, almost suspicious.

"This particular lotion is made for me by a respected herbalist in Essex," he responded. "She is pledged to use only the finest ingredients."

"So you don't even know what they are?"

What was Kate doing? Mary wondered. She'd been sure the maid would admire Jeremiah Jenkins. He was so appealing. And unmarried—she should have mentioned that before they came in. Couldn't Kate see the possibilities for her future?

"All my sources are highly skilled and completely trustworthy," replied the man sternly and rather like an advertisement.

"How can you be sure of that if you can't make up the preparations yourself?"

She was being positively annoying, Mary thought. "The lotion seems very nice to me," she put in. Neither of them paid the least attention.

Kate put down the bottle, without replacing the top, and moved along the counter to a display of small dark vials. She opened one, again without asking, and sniffed. "Tincture of lavender. Brandy based. Vinegar is better. Good for the skin."

She really was knowledgeable, Mary thought. But she was so arrogant about it. Was she *trying* to antagonize the apothecary? To what imaginable end?

Kate went through the same process with several other concoctions. Jeremiah Jenkins trailed along after her, replacing lids and tidying displays. Finally, Kate returned to the open bottle of rose lotion. "This seems well enough made," she said to Mary, with a careless flick of her hand.

Not knowing what else to do, Mary purchased the lotion. Mr. Jenkins took her coins with a small bow. His thanks sounded slightly strained. And then they were out the door and on their way home. "I thought you would be interested in that shop," Mary said to her maid.

"It was very interesting…ma'am."

"Weren't you…rather critical, though?"

"I have to say what I think," was Kate's firm reply.

There was no trace of doubt in her tone. Mary had known that her reluctant maid had little subtlety or tact. But she'd thought the various attractions of Jeremiah Jenkins—personal and practical—would work on her. It had seemed a perfect fit, a place for Kate to find contentment, even happiness. Apparently, she was off the mark.

❧

At his office John found himself prey to random smiles. He forced himself to concentrate, but images from the previous night would drift back and tantalize him. Thoughts of Mary floated up between him and reports from Shanghai and Kowloon. Informants' notes were superseded by memories of her silken skin and ardent responses. When Conolly commented on his buoyant manner, John tried harder to hide his smugness. He finished his reports from the previous day and turned to the stack of mail awaiting their attention.

Right on top he discovered two heavy envelopes, one with his name written on the outside, the other with Conolly's. This was unusual. Information did not come in directly to them. Indeed, their names were not known to the far-flung sources of the Foreign Office. Quite the opposite.

Opening his envelope, he found a formal invitation for him and his wife from Lord and Lady Castlereagh to a Foreign Office reception in honor of the ambassador from the United States of America. Astonished, John checked the envelope again. It was indeed his name inscribed there.

Conolly had opened his as well. "Got the official summons, I see," he said.

Dazed, John nodded.

"It'll be one of their crushing squeezes," Conolly went on.

"I've never been invited before." The words escaped John before he could censor them. Fortunately, only Conolly was there to hear.

Triumph swelled in John's chest. This stiff square of paper was an unmistakable sign that he'd been noticed and marked for advancement. He looked at the curlicues of text again. The date was two weeks away. He had time to procure a new coat. "Regular evening dress, I suppose," he said, trying to sound casual.

Conolly nodded.

John attacked his work with renewed enthusiasm for the rest of the day, then he hurried home to tell Mary the news. Her reaction was all he could have wished. Her face lit, and she threw her arms around him. "It's a sign that they see how wonderful you are."

"It's a step…"

"The foreign secretary himself has noticed you. That's far more than a step."

He lifted her off the floor and spun her around, both of them laughing. "Buy a new evening dress," he urged her. "Spare no expense."

"I'll do my best to be a credit to you."

John set her down and looked into her dancing dark eyes. "You'll be the loveliest woman there."

Their lips met as naturally and joyously as if wild kisses had always been their gift. John pulled Mary tight against him. The feel of her body eagerly molded to his was dizzying. In that moment, he felt he had everything to celebrate and nothing to regret.

He dropped kisses down her neck. Impatiently undoing a row of tiny buttons, he pressed his lips into the hollow of her throat, let them wander over the swell of her breasts. He reveled in the way he could make her breath catch.

"Oh." It came out on a gasp. "John." A sigh. "Kate…will be…announcing dinner…"

"Deuce take dinner. Let's go upstairs."

"Now?" Mary drew back a little, gazing at him

through eyes blurred with desire. "That is a positively scandalous suggestion, sir."

He cupped her lovely bottom and pressed her closer still. "Would you refuse me?" he whispered.

"Nothing," she breathed, rousing him to an almost intolerable pitch.

Holding her close, he swept her up the steps and into her bedchamber. Turning the key in the lock, he faced her, absorbing the lovely, utterly enticing picture she made.

Mary felt as if his blue eyes were burning into her, heating her skin, igniting sparks of desire all through her. It made her want to throw off every stitch of clothing. For a moment she was shocked at herself, then she tossed her scruples to the four winds.

Holding his hot gaze, she finished the task he'd started with her buttons. Her gown fell open and slid to the floor. She sent her petticoat after it and stepped out of her shoes. Unfastening her chemise, she cast that aside, as well, and stood before him in only her silk stockings.

"Mary," he groaned.

She found that some part of her delighted in his arousal. "I won't do all your work for you," she murmured.

In two steps, John was before her. He knelt and untied one garter and then the other. Slowly, he slid her stockings down her legs and off one foot, the other. He looked up and caught her eyes again as his hands rose, caressing her calves, moving featherlight over her knees, and slipping along the sensitive skin of her inner thighs. Mary's legs turned to jelly. She swayed.

John stood and lifted her onto the bed. Then he

resumed his previous occupation, his clever fingertips moving higher still, until they made Mary cry out at the incredible pleasure of his touch. She wanted more, and more. But she forced herself to pull back and sit up. "You too," she panted, pushing his coat off his shoulders, down his arms. With a breathless laugh, he discarded it. Her fingers clumsy with longing, Mary unbuttoned his shirt, shoved it after the discarded coat, and turned her attention to the fastening of his pantaloons. She delighted in her husband's moan as she tugged them down.

John stepped back long enough to pull off his boots, and then he was with her, bared to her on the bed. He touched her again, and she went up in flames. Mary tried to reciprocate, but desire was overwhelming her now. She could only give in to the wave of sensation that rose and crested in a cascade of glorious release. She clutched John, urging him on; she wanted everything.

John's every faculty was saturated with passion. He fell into warmth, his wife's eager hands pulling him closer. She moved with him as he found his way toward an unbearable peak, and cried out with him as he lost himself in a torrent of bliss. He never wanted to let her go, he thought as it reverberated through him. He wanted this moment to last forever.

Afterward, they lay together, enlaced, as their pulses slowed and their breath lengthened. Mary's brain slowly regained rationality. "What will the servants think?" she murmured.

"It isn't their business to think," said John. His stomach growled. "I'm starved," he added.

Mary laughed. They untangled themselves and retrieved their scattered clothes. Downstairs, some minutes later, Kate smirked as she served them a somewhat dried-out dinner. Mary couldn't help but blush under her knowing gaze. In the kitchen below, pans rattled and banged, indicating Mrs. Tanner's displeasure at having her cooking spoiled. Mary felt self-conscious until she caught John's teasing look. Her cheeks reddened further then, but not with embarrassment. If the cook objected to her making love to her husband whenever she liked, the woman could find another position, Mary decided.

After eating, they settled on the sofa before the parlor fire, Mary's head on John's shoulder. She felt thoroughly sated and content. There seemed little need for conversation. They had said so much without words an hour earlier. She could stay right here, just like this, forever, Mary thought.

And so, of course, one of her household chose that moment to knock at the closed door. A rather tentative knock, to be sure, but perfectly audible.

"Yes?" said John.

The door opened and Arthur Windly appeared, skinny and subdued. "Kate said as how Mr. Bexley wished to speak to me," he muttered.

Mary sat up straight. Kate had a malicious sense of humor, she thought. She had mentioned John's offer in the kitchen earlier today, when the cook was complaining again about Arthur's waywardness. But that did not give Kate the authority to send him up. "This isn't a good time…" she began.

"No, it's all right," said John. "Come in, Arthur."

"I never meant to eat the carrots," he blurted out. "It was just that I got so hungry."

John looked at Mary with raised brows.

"Arthur was sent out to purchase carrots on the day he stayed away so long," she explained.

"There was a man in the Parish Hall talking about steam engines. He had pictures and all."

"You were in the Parish Hall?" Mary hadn't dreamed of looking there.

"Perhaps we will make this man to man," John said. He looked at Mary.

It took her a moment to realize what he meant. "Oh." She rose. "Very well." She walked to the door and pulled it almost closed behind her. Then, a bit guiltily, she lingered. She didn't think John would be too hard on Arthur, but she couldn't help but make sure. "I suppose everyone has told you that you did wrong," she heard John say.

"Yessir." Arthur's voice was barely audible.

"The household will always worry if you are out for such a long time and they don't know where you've gone. There are dangers in the streets, even though this neighborhood has few of them."

"Yessir."

"But it is *not* wrong to long for adventures."

"Sir?"

"Let no one tell you it is or discourage you from dreaming of great things." Mary was touched by the sympathy in her husband's tone.

"Like when you put out the fire in the chimney?" Admiration filled the boy's voice.

Satisfied that they were getting on well and a bit ashamed of her eavesdropping, Mary slipped away.

In the parlor, John saw the adulation in Arthur's eyes. It was a new experience, to be held up as a hero by a child. "Not exactly like that."

"The way you jumped in and beat out the flames, that was a wonder."

"Sometimes you have to act quickly." They were getting off the point John had set out to make. "You understand what I said? You can pursue what you imagine…"

"Well, I don't reckon there'll be another fire," Arthur replied with a tinge of regret. "Not that I'd wish for one," he added hurriedly.

"What interests you?" John asked, trying to get him off this subject. "Do you imagine traveling the world or…"

"This fella at the Parish Hall said they were putting a steam engine on steel rails to move right over the ground," Arthur answered.

John almost sighed. It was difficult to keep the lad focused on their conversation. "When people try to tell you that you aren't capable of getting what you want…"

"I'd like to see one of them steam engines up close," Arthur answered.

John felt as if he was offering a bit of treasure from his own experience, and it was being wholly disregarded.

"Have you ever seen one working, sir? There's a great noise, I hear, and…"

"I have not."

"You'd like to, though, I reckon." Arthur's eyes gleamed. "And they'd be glad to let us…you see, if you asked. There's to be a demonstration next month in…"

John gave up. "You understand that you are not to wander off for hours and worry everyone."

Arthur's face fell. "Yessir. I'll pay more attention, like."

"Good."

"I never meant… I hope you're not angry with me any longer, sir."

Why did the boy imagine he was angry? John wondered. He'd never been angry at him. "Not at all."

Arthur slumped with relief. Only then did John understand the tension that had been animating his skinny frame. The reason for it remained a mystery. "You should get to bed," was all he could find to say.

The boy nodded. "Thank you, sir." With a small bow, he went out.

John sat before the fire, ruminating, for some time. But review it as he would, he could not comprehend why their exchange had been so fruitless.

Eleven

THE FOLLOWING AFTERNOON MARY WAS GLAD TO glimpse her neighbor Eleanor and her granddaughter walking in the garden in the center of the square. Mary got her cloak and hurried down the stairs to catch them.

She nearly ran into Kate, who was climbing the steps, and they tottered for a moment on the landing to regain their footing. "I wanted to speak to you... ma'am," said the maid then.

"I was just going out." Mary didn't want to miss the opportunity to talk to Eleanor.

Kate stood straighter. Her expression was stern, and she spoke in a rush. "I only wanted to ask if I might order a...a few ingredients to make up some creams and tinctures. A matter of a few pounds. I'll sell them and pay you back. That is...I'm sure I can."

She hated asking, Mary realized—hated being obliged to ask. "To Mr. Jenkins?"

Kate nodded.

So the maid had been more interested in the apothecary shop than she chose to appear. Mary still found her attitude incomprehensible, but it had been her idea for something like this to happen, after all. "Very well," she replied, aware that it was best to make no fuss over the request. "Order what you like. Just keep a tally."

Kate didn't smile. She gave a brisk nod and turned to descend the stairs. Mary was right behind her, heading for the front door.

September had passed into October, but the air was mild enough today, smelling of dry leaves and coal smoke. Caroline waved when Mary came through the wrought iron gate, and Eleanor looked pleased to see her as well. It turned out to be easy to ask them for advice. "I want a gown that is…splendid," she said when she'd told them about the invitation. "But… perfectly suited to the occasion, you know."

Caroline clapped her hands. "Oh, you must let me dress you. Say you will. I know exactly the sort of thing you want."

Mary had a moment's doubt. "I don't wish to… attract undue attention," she said. Caroline seemed to enjoy having all eyes upon her. Mary merely hoped to fit in and make John proud.

"Gauze the color of a ripe peach," Caroline replied, as if she hadn't heard. "Or perhaps dusty rose. Either of those will look wonderful on you. With the tiniest sleeves and a cascade of ribbons. Cut a bit low." Caroline swept a hand across her bosom. "I will take you to my modiste at once."

Mary felt as if she'd unleashed a monster. "Not low," she objected. "Regular sleeves. A…a proper evening dress."

"You have a lovely figure," Caroline said. "You should make the most…"

"Perhaps I should come along on this expedition," put in Eleanor. She looked amused.

"Oh yes, please." Mary couldn't hide her relief.

Caroline pouted. "Don't you trust my good taste?"

"She doubts your restraint," answered her grandmother.

"Restraint!" Caroline fluttered her fingers in disdain at the word. Then her face lit. "I'm going to wangle an invitation to this party. I have to be there—to watch your great success."

At first uncertain, Mary realized how comforting it would be to know someone in the sea of people at a large reception—someone who was familiar with society and very comfortable there. She smiled and accepted as they settled the details of their shopping expedition.

❧

Mary returned at five, her mind awhirl with satins and gauzes, tucks and ruffles, and a vast variety of trimmings. The exclusive dressmaker in Milsom Street had received her with enthusiasm because of her companions, and she'd been brimming with ideas for a ravishing toilette. Once Mary had secured Eleanor's approval of her choice, she'd ordered a gorgeous, expensive design. Indeed, the cost seemed a bit worrisome. But when she told John about it at dinner, he waved her concerns aside. "You deserve to be wearing the most beautiful gown in the room," he said.

They retired to the parlor after the meal and had just begun a fascinating game, a tantalizing toying with button and laces, when there was a staccato knock on the front door. In the quiet, cozy house, it was startlingly loud. "Who could be calling at this hour?" John wondered. He rose, frowning. "Can it be someone from the office?"

The parlor door opened. Before Kate could speak, two young men came in right on her heels, as if there could be no question of denying them. "Mr. Frederick Bexley and Mr. George Bexley," said Kate. Realizing with chagrin that the top button of her gown was still undone, Mary turned quickly away to fasten it before greeting them.

Would she have recognized these two as John's brothers in another context? she wondered. She'd seen them only once before, at her wedding. Both did have John's striking blue eyes and brown hair. On George, the military man, the hue was darker. His face was rounder, too, to match a frame with a good deal of muscle. Something about his expression and the way he held himself reminded Mary of a bulldog. Frederick, the eldest Bexley brother, was taller and slenderer, with sun-touched hair and craggier features. He looked as if he had a healthy sense of his own consequence. Mary supposed being the oldest of four brothers would foster such an attitude. She stepped forward, happy to have an opportunity to get to know John's family better. "Bring some wine," she told Kate quietly.

"Well, John," cried George. "It seemed you were never going to invite me, so I decided to come along and beard you in your den."

"I was shocked, shocked, to learn that you hadn't entertained your brother even once," put in Frederick.

"So, as I was in town on a bit of business, I decided to call and set you straight."

A bit surprised at the way they spoke to John, Mary made a welcoming gesture. "Please sit down," she said, doing so herself.

George appropriated the other end of the sofa. His stocky frame seemed to require a wide expanse of cushions. Frederick sat in one of the armchairs as John took the other. "Not a bad little house," said Frederick, looking around. "A bit cramped for my taste."

"Rather out of the way," said George. "The cab had a deuce of a time finding it."

"It's convenient for my…" John began.

"Not too dear, I suppose," Frederick interrupted.

Did he expect John to make an accounting of their lease expense? Mary wondered. It almost seemed so.

"It suits us," John said.

"Oh, well…" Frederick's wave was oddly dismissive.

"The garden in the square is very pleasant," Mary added.

Kate came in with a tray, and the brothers accepted glasses of wine. Frederick raised his in a mock toast. George stood and examined the ornaments on the mantle, looking unimpressed. He drained his glass and helped himself to another from the bottle Kate had left.

"So why have you been avoiding your family?" Frederick said then. "Mama says you've scarcely written since you first returned."

"Nor has she written me," John replied. He shifted in his chair. "I've been quite busy with the aftermath of the China mission."

"Oh, your 'job,'" said George.

Mary couldn't keep silent in the face of his dismissive tone. "John's work is extremely important."

John made an abrupt gesture. Mary didn't understand the look he gave her.

George and Frederick exchanged a smile. "You don't want to be taken in by John's wild notions and fancies," said the elder.

"Indeed, we can give you the real picture." George laughed. "Reveal all his youthful peccadilloes. Give you the ammunition you need to keep the upper hand, eh?"

Mary blinked in surprise at this very odd idea of her.

"Remember the time he got stuck up the stable yard oak?" said George. He grinned.

"He does tend to get stuck in things," Frederick told Mary.

"He went up after the cat," George continued. "Thought *she* was stuck, you see."

"She was," protested John. He sounded younger than usual.

"Well, the cat jumped down and left him bobbing at the end of a branch." Frederick laughed. "And then he couldn't get himself turned around to climb down."

"Sheba ran along my arm and shoulder when I reached for her," said John, as if he'd said these words many times before. "That's how she made it down. She wouldn't have been able…"

"I had to get a ladder to fetch him, he was so far up," interrupted Frederick. "Swaying there like an overripe fruit, yelling for help."

"Did…not…yell," said John, playing his part in the recitation. It was a practiced story, Mary thought.

"Cat sat at the bottom of the tree, cleaning her fur, watching," said George. "If a cat could laugh, she would have been. Roger nearly wet himself."

Frederick nodded, laughing himself.

"And what about that time in Brighton?" added George. "When John set off on his 'adventure'?"

It wasn't so much the things they said, Mary thought. Brothers did tease each other; she knew that. It was their tone. They spoke of John as if he was… always faintly ridiculous.

Frederick took his cue with a nod and a grin. "We'd been reading *Robinson Crusoe* in the school holidays," he told Mary. "And John decided to go off and find his own deserted island."

Mary thought he might have had reason to want one.

"He went trudging off with a knapsack of warm clothes and a packet of bread and cheese," said George.

"There was no knapsack," put in John. "You know you've embroidered this tale out of all recognition. I was merely interested in discovering…"

"He tried to get a place on a fishing boat," interrupted Frederick. "The owner made a great joke of it when he'd dragged John home to Father." The eldest Bexley brother altered his voice to a higher pitch. "'If you please, would you take me to a desert island.'"

"He said nothing of the kind. You were standing right there, Frederick."

John's brothers didn't seem to really hear him when he spoke, Mary thought. Or…they heard, but the words had no effect on long-established anecdotes.

George slapped his knee and guffawed. "When that failed, our John decided to make a raft out of some bits of driftwood and rubbish on the beach."

"It was an experiment…" John began.

"He got right out into the sea," Frederick told Mary. "The thing was sinking under him when a sailboat spotted him and brought him back."

"That sounds dangerous," said Mary. George and Frederick showed no sign of hearing her either.

"He was positively woebegone when they brought him home that time. We called him Friday-Face for a bit after that."

"For four or five years," said John. He was smiling, which Mary thought odd.

"Friday, you see." Frederick didn't seem satisfied with her reaction. "That was the name of the savage in *Crusoe*."

"Your mother must have been so worried," replied Mary, ignoring his invitation to laugh. "He might have been swept away."

"Oh, she was accustomed to John's misadventures by that time," said George carelessly. "Quite resigned to it. You'll see for yourself soon enough. He's continually hatching some harebrained scheme or other. And then we have to rally round to the rescue. Brothers, you know."

The look he gave John was fond, yet Mary still found it annoying. "I don't think so," she replied, unable to keep the coolness from her tone.

"No, no, you'll see. Everyone does," Frederick assured her. He and George laughed again.

From their smiles, they truly believed that this

chafing was all in good fun. And they didn't appear to notice that she wasn't amused.

"That girl from the hotel next door thought you were romantic as anything after that," George continued. "A regular heartbreaker."

John looked surprised, then he laughed. "She did, didn't she? I'd forgotten about her."

"What was her name?" wondered Fredrick.

John thought about it. "Sarah? No, Susan. Susan Fielding."

"That was it. Trailed after you like a mooncalf for the rest of the holiday."

George nodded. "Kept telling people you were just like the chap in that Byron poem. What was he called? Childe Harold." He frowned in concentration, then added, "'Sore given to revel and ungodly glee.'"

"I can't believe you remembered that," Frederick exclaimed.

"Well, she was always spouting random bits of it," said George.

"Which you appear to have listened to," John said. "I *thought* you were rather taken with…"

"What a peagoose that girl was!" George interrupted.

Again, it was as if John hadn't spoken, Mary thought. His contributions were not part of the rhythm of the story.

"The first bit of that poem had just come out," Frederick mused. "Everyone was talking about it."

"She thought you quite the brooding hero," added George, as if it was a ludicrous notion.

"Too bad I was only eleven and not really prepared to appreciate it."

"Susan was about fifteen and had a very…" George realized he'd brought his hands up to his chest, and quickly dropped them. "…was quite pretty."

"You seem to remember her far better than I do," said John. He raised his eyebrows at George, who waved this comment aside.

"I can't think how she was allowed to read that drivel at her age," put in Frederick.

"She stole the book from her aunt's boudoir," John answered. "They blamed it on a houseguest. She kept it hidden with some of her schoolbooks."

"Told you all that, did she?" marveled George. "And what else did you get up to when we weren't around? Or don't you want to mention it in front of your wife?"

"Wouldn't you like to know," John said.

They all three laughed. But it didn't seem to Mary as if they were laughing together. John's brothers seemed to have an ingrained habit of…disrespect. Why didn't he set them straight? "John has quite an important job, you know," she blurted out.

They looked surprised at this sudden change of subject.

"They…they rely on him at the Foreign Office. And he was singled out to go on the China mission."

"Spare my blushes, Mary," said John. He shook his head.

"Singled out for a shipwreck," said George. "If Amherst had known about the raft, he'd never have taken John to sea."

Frederick found this hilarious.

"His opinions are highly valued. His friend Conolly told me that he…"

"By Jove, you've found yourself another Susan," George interrupted. He grinned at Mary. "Fond of Byron, are you?"

"No, I am not." Mary had to turn away and pretend to fuss over the refreshment tray lest she say something cutting.

"How are things at home?" John asked his eldest brother. "Did you manage to buy that lower field from Jasper?"

This set Frederick off on a long oration about the family estate, including every tiny detail that had arisen in the last six months, it seemed.

"What news from Roger?" John said when he had at last run down.

George and Frederick alternated reports of their youngest brother's successes in India.

"Mama is well?" John said as soon as this topic was exhausted.

Frederick allowed that this was so. "She expects you at Christmas," he warned.

"My family has invited us for the holidays," said Mary, even though it was rather rude. She'd had as much as she could take of this conversation.

"Yours." The visitors looked at each other as if they'd forgotten she had a family.

"Well, but…" George frowned. "The Bexleys always celebrate Christmas together."

"Indeed? Will Roger be there?" Mary asked.

"He's in India," Frederick replied. His tone suggested that anyone halfway intelligent should be aware of that.

"And we will be in Somerset," snapped Mary.

George and Frederick looked at each other. Their bewildered expressions were so similar that it was almost funny.

"We haven't made a final plan," John said.

She couldn't believe he was being conciliating and contradicting her in front of these two.

"Ah, well then…" His brothers nodded.

Mary could see them thinking that John would bring his unruly wife into line. She felt like shaking them—all three of them. "I didn't realize it was so late," she said in her Great-Aunt Lavinia manner.

John gave her a look. But George and Frederick took the hint. After some backslapping and a flurry of coats and directions to a cab stand not too far off, they departed on a last gust of boisterous laughter. In their wake, the parlor felt unnaturally silent.

"How can you let them speak to you that way?" Mary had to say.

"What way? And did you need to hustle them out…"

"So…dismissively."

"They were just joking." John frowned at her. "Retelling old stories, as families do."

Mary suddenly thought of her sisters. Yes, they told stories, too—much softer, more…caressing—of her dreamy inattention and social blunders. The details were different and yet akin. She too had been subjected to years of good-natured laughter. "You should tell them it's not funny."

John gazed at her, uncomprehending. "Why would I do that? Everyone enjoys hearing family tales."

"About Frederick? And George?"

"Of course."

"Tell me one." Mary felt positively militant.

"What is the matter with…?"

"I want to hear a 'funny' story about Frederick."

John let out an exasperated breath, then he shrugged. "Oh, very well. Ah…" He considered. "At school, Frederick was first stroke on the rowing team. During one race, one of the other boats floundered, and he was struck on the arm by an oar. It hurt like the devil, but he managed to keep rowing, and they won the match. Later, the doctor discovered that a bone in his forearm was cracked." He looked at her as if to say, "There you are."

"That's not the same."

"What do you mean? You wanted a story…"

"That's just praise." How could he not hear the difference? "Frederick wasn't the butt of a joke. That's just…history."

"Well, it's all history. Family history."

"John, it's not the same."

He came over and put an arm around her. "I think you're tired." He drew her close. "They should have sent word before stopping by."

"It isn't that."

"Come to bed," he murmured.

Mary wanted to tell him how she'd made her mother truly see her drawings of Aunt Lavinia and prove to him that old stories could be changed. But he didn't understand what she meant. And he wasn't listening.

He bent and kissed her. It was so hard to keep up a train of thought when she was drowning in the taste and feel of him. Mary's breath came out in a long, languorous sigh. His hands moved, and it felt so very good. She would tell him later, some other time, when her senses weren't swimming. "Oh, John."

Twelve

SEATED AT HIS DESK THE NEXT DAY, JOHN TOOK A report from the stack of papers awaiting him. There was always so much to absorb, such an unruly mass of information to boil down into a concise report. Could he even manage it? Had he been overambitious when he'd promised the summary in two days' time? Would Conolly have finished by now?

John glanced at his colleague, who was bent over another document on the other side of the room. That was silly. Conolly worked no faster than he did. What was wrong with him this morning? John read on, underlined a significant passage, and made a note. He was well on the way to making his mark, demonstrating his skill to...everyone.

It was time to visit Limehouse again and dig for information that others hadn't found. Why had he heard nothing from Henry Tsing? Why hadn't he contacted the man himself? He'd allowed domestic concerns to distract him, but that couldn't be. There was no room for slacking and no margin for error. He would get in touch with Tsing today and schedule further expeditions. And right now, he *would* absorb the pertinent facts in this stack of paper and produce the perfect report. He bent his head and kept working.

❧

This would be one of the last days to sit outside this year, Mary thought as she set up her small easel in the garden at the center of the square. The air was chill, with a premonition of rain, and the leaves were almost all gone. There was no wind, however, and the autumn sun shone with enough warmth to let her take advantage of the outdoor space.

She was uneasy and restless after yesterday. And her house felt overfull, even when she was shut away in her private parlor. Pungent odors rose up the steps from the kitchen, where Kate was concocting lotions and tinctures. Mrs. Tanner had followed the vapors upstairs to complain that her daughter's work made a great mess and hindered her cooking. Mary imagined that this was partly true and partly just resentment at being superseded in her own domain.

Meanwhile, Arthur bounced between the bickering in the kitchen and his room on the top floor. He had no qualms about knocking at her studio door as he passed to see if she had some errand or task for him. He didn't have enough to do to absorb his boundless energy. Finally, she'd sent him out for a packet of straight pins she didn't really need.

So this chance to escape to the garden and her paints was more than welcome. She set out her colors and opened the jar of water, prepared the paper, then sat back and waited. Very soon, her brush began to move. Quick strokes over the damp page outlined a head with short hair. She blended brown with white and a dash of red to color a face. Blotting her brush on a cloth, she added the eyes, mouth, nose. Alternating clean lines and the subtle washes that watercolors offered, Mary elaborated the portrait. It was the eldest Bexley brother as he'd appeared on his visit yesterday. She wasn't surprised. Thoughts of him, and George, had been running in the back of her mind, or seething might be a better description.

An unknown while later, Mary lowered her brush, finished, and contemplated what she'd done. The features were accurate. The blue eyes gazed out directly, smugly. The jawline jutted with complacent belligerence. Here was a man who was perfectly content with his own opinions, she decided, looking deeper into what her talents had produced. He would laugh at attempts to challenge or change them, secure in the knowledge that he knew better. If you needed him to think differently, well, you might have taken on an impossible task; if you wanted him to actually listen to John, for example, or recognize his brother's many talents. Mary was afraid that the eldest Bexley brother had acquired all the ideas he wanted at an early age. He was certainly unlikely to accept any from her.

She gazed at the face she'd drawn, searching for more amiable traits. She saw no touch of malice or deceit. Frederick would not comprehend grudges, she thought, because he never held one himself. He had no need to, because he was always right.

"Ah," commented a familiar voice from over her shoulder. "You've done it again—captured a character. A most self-satisfied young man, I'd say. You simply itch to smack some sense into him."

Mary turned to find Eleanor, warmly bundled against the chill, standing behind her bench.

"A friend of yours? Oh dear, not your husband, I hope?"

"No." Mary hesitated. But Eleanor was unlikely ever to encounter Frederick. "His brother."

"Well, that's a relief for the sake of my manners. But not such good news for family harmony, I expect."

Mary shook her head. Her mind was full of the Bexleys and the way they'd acted with one another yesterday.

"Older brother," said Eleanor. It wasn't a question. "Eldest, I imagine. It's the usual look."

"Usual?"

"I was here first. I learned everything before you. You can tell me nothing."

Mary had to laugh a little. Eleanor had described Frederick's attitude so perfectly.

"At least he's not a duke," the old woman added. At Mary's surprised look, she explained, "It's far, far worse when all the world is toadying to them."

It must be, she supposed. Mary had never encountered a duke—unless you counted seeing Wellington at Vauxhall, which she didn't.

"Does he live in London?"

"No."

"Fortunate." Eleanor smiled at her. "Well, you are being discreet, which is admirable. And you haven't asked for my advice. However, I shall exercise the prerogative of the old and give it to you anyway. Keep this young man…" She raised an eyebrow.

"Frederick," Mary supplied.

"Frederick. Keep Frederick at arm's length in the nicest possible way. Don't tell him what you're up to or what you think about any great matters. Don't ask him what you ought to do, unless you are fully prepared to comply with his orders. Follow these precepts and peace will reign."

"You seem very certain." The rapid spate of advice was startling.

Eleanor's expression grew impish. "Oh yes. I am an eldest child myself, you see. I kept my brother quite under my thumb until he cheated and ran off to Eton. They convinced him of his own importance there, and he no longer listened to a mere girl."

Mary laughed, even as she thought that Eleanor was very likely right about Frederick. "You are alone today?"

Eleanor nodded. "Caroline has gone off to call on a friend. I believe she is wangling that invitation we spoke of. I hope so, actually. Otherwise, she is up to some mischief."

"Oh."

Her neighbor's smile said that she heard Mary's misgivings in that one word. "Caroline has a good heart, you know. She just needs a bit of reining in."

That was all well and good for her grandmother. But if Caroline required reining in at the Castlereaghs' reception, what was Mary supposed to do? How did one subdue an earl's daughter? Then she realized that her new acquaintance's antics were unlikely to involve her. Caroline would more than likely disappear into a circle of her society friends.

"My lady?"

Eleanor's maid came up to the gate in the wrought iron fence. She didn't rattle the bars, but she looked as if she'd like to. "It's cold, my lady," she called. "You're going to take a chill."

Eleanor smiled and raised a gloved hand to show she'd heard. "I must go."

Mary's fingers were icy by this time. She started tidying her paints. "I shall miss sitting in the garden."

"As I do, every winter." Eleanor cocked her head as if she'd had a thought. "Perhaps you would come over, now and then, and paint with me? Not as good as being outdoors, but still pleasant perhaps."

"I'd like that very much," Mary replied.

"Good." With a smile and a nod, her neighbor departed.

⁓

In his empty office, John once again prepared to venture out into the slums, trading his neat coat and pantaloons for shabby, threadbare garments and emptying his purse of all but the coin necessary to pay for information. This time, he'd made sure that everyone had gone before starting his transformation. He didn't want Conolly's commentary or another colleague's questions. Indeed, the thought of *any* cautions or objections chafed unbearably. He knew what he was doing. He did not require oversight or interference from those less familiar with the situation.

He set off on foot. A fellow such as he was pretending to be would not arrive in a hackney even at the far edge of the slums. He walked with shoulders slumped, a man with nothing to steal, while carefully scanning the streets around him. He would not be taken by surprise by lurkers waiting for easy pickings.

His ancient stuff coat, buttoned up to the neck to hide his good shirt, was surprisingly warm. And the wind had died down, so the air was less chilly. In half an hour, John reached the Red Dragon tavern, sidled inside, and spotted Henry Tsing at a battered table in the corner. He walked over—not too fast, not too slow—and joined him, settling in the most shadowed chair, and pulling his cloth cap well down on his forehead.

"New ship in from Shanghai," Henry muttered, his words covered by the babble of drinkers around them. "Dumped four Chinese sailors with no work."

"They are here?"

The other man shook his head. "Two over at Shen's. The others at Dora's—till their pay runs out."

John nodded. It was no use trying to interview foreign sailors at Dora's bawdy house. Their attention was all on her girls. And in any case, the men were not usually interested in his offers until they'd used up all their wages from a voyage.

They stayed at the Red Dragon long enough to nurse one drink at a believable pace. John sloshed some of the rotgut out onto the table and tipped more into the corner behind him when no one was looking. He did his best not to swallow any of the harsh liquor.

Henry Tsing spoke to this man and that as they passed the table. He offered greetings and bits of gossip and asked for news. They uncovered no single significant fact in this manner, but John was convinced that the accumulation of data would prove useful in the end.

Leaving the Red Dragon, they took a circuitous route that led them into several other grogshops, where their routine was the same, before ending at Reginald Shen's impressive establishment. Shen was the most promising contact that Tsing had found for John, and this was the place where he expected, eventually, to turn up something important.

Like Henry, Shen had been born in England to a Limehouse slattern. But unlike John's guide, Shen's Chinese father had taken an interest in his existence. Moreover, the elder Shen had a secure post on an East Indian trader, because of his wide knowledge of currents and shipping lanes across the eastern routes. His vessel docked in London every year or so, and he visited his son and checked on his welfare when in port. Before the voyage from which he didn't return—for unknown reasons—he provided funds for Reginald to open a business in these dark streets. Perhaps he also bequeathed a measure of cleverness, because the young man made a success of the venture.

Shen's became known as a haven for Asian sailors. It offered cheap lodgings, a taproom with food prepared by a Chinaman, and a place where a variety of transactions could be safely completed. It was not a shop or a market; it was a space where men could sell or trade trinkets and possessions to raise the funds to live while they searched for a berth on an outgoing ship. Shen took a percentage of every deal, of course. He'd also told John that he maintained the service because it allowed him to acquire interesting objects, while drawing customers for his other services.

The surprising thing, to John, was Shen was a

patriot. He revered England as his home, as the land that had given him opportunities, and he was happy to provide information to England's government. He did require payment, but as he explained it to John, this was entirely reasonable. Did he not have to pay the servers who manned his enterprise and the cadre of toughs who protected it? And without them, there would be no flow of sailors and no information.

Shen's help had other conditions. Secrecy, of course. To be known as a conduit would not be good for business. But he also insisted on meeting John in person. Sending spoken messages back and forth with Tsing or another was too risky, in Shen's opinion. And he certainly didn't care to leave written evidence.

And so John had begun a series of clandestine visits, late at night, when Shen's patrons were deep in their cups and more alert neighbors sound asleep. He and Tsing wandered the district, as they had tonight, and came to Shen's only when Limehouse's lack of interest in them had been thoroughly demonstrated.

As before, Tsing was left behind in the taproom. John was spirited up an unfamiliar set of stairs and around several corners before being led into the room where he'd visited Shen before. The man's headquarters was hidden within a maze of corridors with more ways in and out than John had been able to count.

The office itself was like a comfortable parlor, with little sign of business about it. Shen sat in an armchair before a crackling hearth, thin hands held out to the flames. He wore the dress of a prosperous English merchant. They exchanged greetings, and John sat in a chair on the other side of the fireplace. "What news?" he asked.

Shen smiled, as he always did, at his visitor's bluntness. "Limehouse is still enjoying the tale of how the emperor tricked the English over the *kŏutóu*."

John tried to curb his impatience. The proprietor of this place was a handsome man, neat and spare with dark hair and eyes slightly tilted from his heritage. He was intelligent and quick to see irony. Some part of John always expected a foreign accent, but Shen spoke like a London native. "It's surprising how widely that story spread among common sailors."

Shen shrugged. "Servants, courtiers, spiteful mandarins—someone is always jabbering. Is this not how you hope to discover important information?"

John nodded. "I wish the emperor had received Lord Amherst. If they could have talked…"

"The dragon throne is angry about all the opium traders are bringing into his country and the arrogance of foreigners."

John leaned forward. "I want to find out if China will go to war."

Shen shrugged again. "A sailor may be on a ship where high officials travel and hear things, but it would be a very lucky coincidence for that sailor to turn up here."

"I know." John sat back.

"War might be less likely if Westerners showed more respect for the emperor."

"The Chinese court doesn't respect us," John pointed out.

"I believe they feel they have an ancient culture, more refined than those of outsiders." He made a graceful gesture. "This is what I hear, at least."

"Pottery and philosophy won't matter in the face of gunboats."

Shen looked grave. "That is quite true, Mr. Bexley, and another reason I try to help you." He put the tips of his fingers together. "There is word of some new... presence lurking in our streets."

"Presence?" It was an odd way to put it.

"Someone who appears and disappears like smoke, who hides so skillfully no one can find him. Even I do not know where he stays. But the rumor is, he also will pay for information."

"Also?" Had Shen revealed his visits to others?

"I say this only to you," the other man assured him.

"Tell me all you have heard," replied John, preparing to concentrate. Shen did not allow him to make notes as they talked.

❧

John left Tsing with his payment at the edge of Limehouse and headed back toward the office. The farther he got from the slums, and from suspicious eyes, the more briskly he moved. At one point he heard footsteps and the clatter of something falling behind him, but when he looked there was no one there. He was tired out and more than eager to finish this task and go home.

A retired sergeant major manned an unobtrusive side door to the Foreign Office building, an entry for staffers when a crisis loomed at night. Recognizing John, he admitted him with raised eyebrows at his shabby dress. John took a candle from a store kept there, lit it at the sergeant major's lamp, and hurried through empty corridors to his office. He would have liked a thorough wash, but there was no way to have that here. He was not going home in these clothes, however, no matter how tired he felt.

John changed and bundled away his slum disguise. He sat to pull on his boots, then he took up a pen to make notes about what Shen had told him. He rested his cheek on one hand as he wrote. His eyelids drooped. He pushed himself to keep going.

Fatigue, and the bit of alcohol he hadn't been able to avoid drinking, dragged at him, urging him to rest his head on the desk. His head drooped. He jerked upright, fought the impulse to sleep, and kept writing. The words swam under his exhausted gaze. He had to rest his eyes, just for a moment. Only a moment…

❧

John woke to an exclamation from a servant who had come to sweep out the office hearth and light the day's fire. "Sorry, sir. You startled me," the man said. "I didn't expect to see anyone here so early."

John straightened in his chair, stifled a groan at the complaints of his stiff muscles, and gestured for the man to go on with his task. The room was cold; dawn light shone through the windows, exposing his scribbled notes. The candle had long since burned out. His shirt was creased, his neckcloth crushed. He ran a hand over his jaw and felt the rasp of stubble. Conolly would exclaim at finding him in this state.

John formulated excuses as he rose to go in search of cold water to splash over his face and tea. He very much wanted tea. Then he stopped, grimaced, and

sank back to write a note to Mary. He'd send it with
one of the office messengers as soon as they arrived.

∽

An hour later, Mary held this missive in her hand and
tried to contain her anger. When John had sent word
yesterday afternoon that he wouldn't be home until
late, she'd been irritated but resigned. He was kept
at the office now and then, with work he couldn't
discuss. It had happened several times since she'd
come to London. Lately, she'd started waiting up for
him on those nights. She enjoyed greeting him with
a hot drink and a smile of welcome. She was certain
he liked it, too.

But last night, she'd waited to no avail. John
never returned. She'd passed a sleepless, increasingly
frantic night, wondering where her husband could
be, imagining an attack in the streets, a fatal accident.
She'd been half-mad with worry and ready to visit
a magistrate this morning. And now came this note,
with barely an apology. John was sorry that he'd fallen
asleep at his desk. Why should he do so? Why had he
not sent her further word if he was being kept so late?
Should she even believe this story?

Mary crushed the page in a shaking hand. She didn't
think John would lie to her. But what was the difference between an outright lie and a partial truth? What
was he hiding from her? She was going to find out.

Thus, as the afternoon waned, Mary lay in wait for
her husband, watching at the front window for him
to appear in the square. As soon as he did, she threw
on her cloak and hurried out the front door. "Mary.

Where are you going?" he said when she accosted him. She grasped his arm and pulled him over to the garden, key ready to unlock the gate. "What are you doing?" John said.

Urging him through the bars, Mary rushed onward until they stood in the center of the space, well out of earshot of any passersby, far from the interested audience of their household. Then she turned to face him. There was just enough light left in the sky for her to see his face. "Why did you not come home last night?"

"Mary, I'm very tired. I didn't…"

"I waited and watched for you all night. I was afraid you were dead…"

"Why should you imagine anything so silly?"

"Haven't you told me about the dangers of the London streets?" Mary demanded. "How I wasn't to walk alone…"

"You. I am perfectly capable…"

"Why should you sleep at your office?" Mary asked.

"I was out later than I meant to be."

"Where? Doing what?"

"It doesn't matter…"

"Who did you go out with?" Mary asked. Her voice shook.

John stared at her. "No one. Or not… It wasn't that sort of 'out,' Mary. You can't think that I would…"

"What am I supposed to think?"

"That I am your husband and would not lie to you or betray you."

Mary looked deep into his blue eyes. "All right. But you do hide things from me."

"You know I cannot tell you everything about my work."

"So, if you told me where you were last night, it would endanger the…country, the government?" John shifted from foot to foot and looked away. Mary waited for an answer. He said nothing. "Or it would *not* endanger England," she prodded. "It must be one or the other." She struggled between anger and sadness.

John ran his hands over his face and up through his hair. He was so very tired. "Can't we go inside? It's cold."

"Do you want the servants to overhear this conversation? You won't even tell me where you were."

John sighed. He looked around, spotted a bench, and went to sit on it. He pulled his scarf tighter around his neck against the evening chill. When Mary joined him, he weighed his words. If he meant to continue his information-gathering trips into Limehouse—and he did—Mary would have to be told something. She clearly wouldn't be satisfied with secrecy, and she should not be made to worry. John looked at his wife in the dimness. She was leaning forward, hands folded tight in her lap, frowning. Her eyes were pools of darkness. He realized that he didn't want to fob her off with evasions and half-truths, even if he could think of plausible ones. He let out a breath and said, "I was out in the city, looking for information." And he explained his expeditions with Henry Tsing and the reason for them.

Mary was silent for a moment when he finished. "Isn't it dangerous, going into the slums?"

"There is some risk, but I take great care," he assured her.

She didn't look convinced. "You didn't want me walking alone even in this neighborhood…"

"The cases are entirely different," John said again. "And I am not alone."

"I don't see how it's that different. A gentleman moving among the poorest classes is surely a target for robbery, if not worse."

"I don't go as myself."

"Not…?" Mary looked startled. "Oh. You wear a disguise?"

He nodded. "You'd laugh to see my worn coat and ancient clogs."

"How clever you are!"

Though night was coming on, John could still see the glow of admiration on her face. It warmed him.

"And you think you will get important information from these foreign sailors?"

He leaned toward her and spoke quietly. "I don't know. But I feel I must try every way I can to fill in the outlines of the situation in China. If there is any way to prevent England from being plunged into a far-off war over the opium trade, I have to find it."

Mary reached for his hand. "Yes, I see! You must let me help you."

John sat back. He was relieved to have the confession over with, but this was unexpected. "There is nothing you can do to help."

"I could! I could…take care of the clothes you use as a disguise. Conceal them from Kate and Mrs. Tanner when you come home afterward. You must come home, John, or I shall worry myself sick."

"It would be easier to leave and return from

here," he admitted. And there would be no chance of encountering any colleague who might hamper his efforts.

"You must! And then I will know where you've gone. Someone should know, in case of…trouble." Mary frowned. "Are you sure there won't be trouble?"

"It is necessary." He believed it was. Some sense of the flow of events, a current in the tides of information that washed through his office, urged him on. But it was a good idea to have someone trustworthy who knew where he'd gone. He could give her Conolly's address and tell her about the sergeant major who manned the door of the Foreign Office at night.

"It is so brave of you. So brilliant."

Her hand was warm in his. Her face was a pale oval in the dusk. Then the moon rose over the buildings across the square, and he could see her more clearly.

"And so resourceful. No one else thought of it, or learned the language, or was willing to risk himself."

"It isn't that…" But John's impulse to play down his achievements was cut off by the admiration in her eyes. Had anyone ever gazed at him with such respect and appreciation? Not that he could recall. It was heady stuff. All he could do was lean forward and kiss her.

The touch of her lips—so soft, so yielding—sent a thrill through his body. He slid his arms around her and pulled her tight against him. This was outrageous; they were outdoors, in public, an inner voice objected. But another declared that no one would see them in this dark garden and to hell with the proprieties. As he slipped a hand under Mary's cloak and found the intoxicating curve of her breast, John marveled at how his life had changed since his long voyage. These inner fires that burned so hot were a gift and a delight. And then all thought dissolved as Mary's hand crept beneath his greatcoat and moved in a way that was profoundly arousing.

Some indeterminate time later, the click of footsteps sounded on the cobbles outside the garden. Both of them went still. Mary stifled a giggle. They sat there—buttons undone, laces hanging loose—until the sound faded on the opposite side of the square. Then Mary giggled in earnest. Laughter rose in John's chest as well. "I'm shocked, shocked, Mrs. Bexley, at your levity in these scandalous circumstances."

"It's my husband," Mary murmured in his ear. "He is so…masterful. I can deny him nothing."

Though the words were like gunpowder to the flames of his arousal, John had to say, "We must go in."

Mary nestled against him in a way calculated to drive him to distraction. "Must we?"

"We have a warm fire and a bed ten yards from here."

"Well, of course we will use that later. Too."

"Mary…"

With stifled laughter, she pulled at cloth barriers, shoved aside folds of her gown and his coat, and shifted until she sat astride his lap.

"Mary!"

She tented her cloak around them, kissed him, and wriggled.

John's objections evaporated on a gasp. His wife rose a little onto her knees. He guided her back down, and they came together in a white heat of daring and desire.

She buried her face in his shoulder to silence her gasps of pleasure. He clenched his jaw to keep in his own. They danced together up to a peak of ecstasy and plummeted together into glorious release. In its aftermath, they held each other as if they would never let go.

It was some time before they raised their heads, laughed again, and stood to adjust tousled clothing and run across the dark lawn hand in hand.

Thirteen

JOHN MADE SEVERAL MORE FORAYS INTO LIMEHOUSE over the next two weeks. He was slowly amassing a thick file of facts and suspicions. Though they didn't add up to anything definitive as yet, he had hopes that they would in time. He made particular, discreet, inquiries into Shen's story of a mysterious newcomer in the slums. Rumors of such a person persisted, even grew, but it was impossible to pin down details. The whispered tales dissolved in his hands like the shreds of mist that drifted in from the river to blur the outlines of buildings in the twisting lanes and hide the hunched figures who scurried past. It was frustrating to feel a possibility so close yet out of reach.

He did now have the pleasure of being greeted by Mary when he came home tired and cold. It really did help to know that she watched for him from the dark house. When he had changed out of his shabby disguise, she brought hot drinks and listened admiringly to the stories of his searches. During these quiet talks late at night, it was as if they were the only two people in the world. John had never felt closer to anyone.

And he had never felt prouder than on the evening of the Castlereaghs' party.

He had ordered full evening dress from his tailor, and as he walked down the stairs in his black coat and snowy linen, he heard female voices from Mary's room. Lady Caroline Lanford was in there, helping Mary put the finishing touches on her ensemble. The earl's daughter had taken to visiting his wife. They seemed to have become real friends, and she was going with them tonight. John was glad that Mary would have her company. No doubt it would ease her entry into this new rank of society.

When the ladies came down, however, he saw only Mary. She wore a gown of peach gauze over satin of the same shade trimmed with ribbons in a darker hue. Her cheeks glowed; her dark eyes sparkled. She seemed to him the most beautiful creature he had ever seen.

"Is she not gorgeous?" asked Lady Caroline. "I'm taking full credit for Mary's appearance. I told her that color was perfect."

John looked at their guest—a pretty blond girl in a green gown. But his eyes went immediately back to his wife. He felt ready to burst with pride and affection. "You are exquisite," he said, and she flushed under his gaze.

John had hired a carriage for the night, and it took them from their out-of-the-way address to St. James Square, in the heart of fashionable London. The Castlereaghs' town house blazed with light, with ranks of candles in every window of the lower floors and torches burning beside the wide front door.

Vehicles streamed in from both directions, disgorging richly dressed people to mount the steps and enter. Where would all these equipages go while their owners reveled? John wondered. Should he have some instructions for his driver? Then he noticed a pair of stableboys directing the coaches as they emptied. There must be some place set aside for them to wait.

At last their carriage made it to the entry. John helped the ladies down and followed them inside. Footmen waited to take their wraps and pass them into a set of large reception rooms already crowded with people. The glitter of jewels and roar of conversation was a bit intimidating. Bath assemblies were nothing to this.

"Come over here," said Lady Caroline. Fully at ease, she led them away from the archway where they'd entered to a less populated spot near the wall. "This is a good vantage point. We can look around and plot our route," she added.

"Route to where?" Mary asked.

"The people we wish to speak to, those we don't, the food," the girl replied. She surveyed the chattering crowd with an eagle eye.

"I don't know anyone to speak to," Mary said. "Oh, yes I do. There is Mr. Conolly."

John's colleague was approaching and soon greeted them with a bow. "Mrs. Bexley. John."

"How nice to see a familiar face," said Mary. "This is Lady Caroline…"

"We've met," said Conolly with another small bow.

"We…?" Lady Caroline looked blank, then quickly hid her reaction. "Of course. Good evening."

"At the Massingtons' fete last season," said Conolly, clearly not fooled.

Caroline cocked her head, considering, and then her green eyes lit and her lips curved upward. "Conolly. You're the one who put the goats in the garden."

"I?" His face was carefully neutral, but a spark danced in his hazel eyes. "I can't imagine why you say so. I don't believe the…er, perpetrator was ever established."

Seeing that sparkling gaze, John had no doubt that Conolly had been involved in whatever had happened with the goats.

"Never established, but certainly suspected. *Strongly* suspected." Caroline examined Conolly for an interested moment before turning to the Bexleys. "Gerda Massington is a frightful pill," she continued in a low voice, expertly pitched to reach no further than their small circle. "She's famous for making girls cry at their debut balls and then spreading dreadful stories to explain the tears. Every year, she has a garden party to show off her roses, though everyone knows they're all due to her gardener. But last year, when they threw the doors open to reveal her triumph, they found a herd of goats eating them."

John pictured the scene—a carefully manicured London garden ravaged by yellow-eyed invaders. He had to smile.

"It's surprising how odd goats look with their mouths full of pink petals," said Conolly, his tone cordially commonplace.

"She shrieked like a yowling cat," said Lady Caroline. Her accompanying smile was rather feline.

"So it was rather like the ferrets at dinner?" said Mary.

John turned to look at her. What ferrets? At what dinner?

"Oh, better than that," Lady Caroline replied.

John watched Conolly and Lady Caroline exchange a long appraising look. It went on until Conolly blinked and turned back to face the crowd. "Ah, hmm," he said. "Well. The diplomatic corps has turned out in force tonight. There is the Prussian ambassador, Wilhelm von Humboldt." He discreetly indicated a burly man with a chest full of honors.

John looked him over. The people in these rooms represented the highest echelons of the profession he'd chosen. It was fascinating to see them all gathered and to know that weighty matters could be settled here in a few sentences, rather than dragging on for months at a conference table. The place buzzed with possibilities as well as conversation.

"And over in the corner there are the Count and Countess Lieven," Conolly continued. "He represents Russia."

"Or they both do," murmured Caroline. "They say the countess is a far better ambassador than her husband."

"'They' are great gossips," replied Conolly with a smile.

"Dorothea von Lieven is a patroness of Almack's," Caroline continued. "Along with Lady Castlereagh, of course."

Mary tried not to be overwhelmed by the volume of chatter surrounding them. There were dozens of people in these rooms, perhaps hundreds, all talking while casting critical glances about as if searching for someone more important to engage. She sorted the possibly important information Conolly had shared from the irrelevant. She would never be going to Almack's.

"The Esterházys are here somewhere," Conolly said. "Austrian ambassador. And a Swede or Dane or two. Those are the main ones."

"No one from China?" Mary asked.

Conolly and John shook their heads.

"There's Lady Castlereagh." Caroline tugged at John and Mary. "Come. I'll introduce you."

Mary hung back. "She seems quite occupied."

"Nonsense. Don't you want to thank your hostess? And isn't the point to get noticed?"

John stood straighter. Mary thought of his career and allowed herself to be led. "But she's talking…"

"To the American ambassador, Richard Rush," Conolly supplied.

"Everybody says he quite gentlemanly," Caroline murmured. "It's much appreciated after the last one, that dreadful little man. What was his name? John Quincy Adams." She wrinkled her nose. "Why should an American insist on three names?"

"Mr. Rush's father was one of the signers of the former colonies' Declaration of Independence," John murmured.

"Trust you to know the odd fact," said Conolly.

"Well, he has the good sense not to mention it," Caroline commented.

They approached their hostess and lingered nearby, waiting for a break in her conversation.

"Yes," Lady Castlereagh was telling the American ambassador, "we have several North American animals in our menagerie. Down in the country, you know. A mockingbird and a flying squirrel."

Richard Rush nodded politely.

"The mockingbird does not sing, however. Would you know how to make it do so?" She cocked her head, rather like a bird herself, Mary thought. A hungry hawk, perhaps.

"I fear not, your ladyship," replied the ambassador.

"Ah, too bad. I should like to discover the problem. For, you know, I have been wanting to procure a hummingbird from the United States, but I'm worried that, once on English soil, it will not hum."

Mr. Rush choked and cleared his throat. "Um, I've heard you have a tiger in your collection, ma'am."

"Yes, he's quite vicious, always growling at us." Lady Castlereagh seemed to relish that fact. "We have kangaroos as well, all the way from Australia, you know, and some ostriches."

An aide approached the ambassador. "Here we go," said Caroline as the man excused himself and moved away. She practically pushed the Bexleys up to their hostess, then dropped a small curtsy. "Good evening, Lady Castlereagh."

"Evening." Her tone was cool.

"I'm Caroline Lanford," she added with a bright smile.

"Ah, St. Clair's girl, isn't it? And William." Lady Castlereagh nodded at Conolly.

"Yes, ma'am," said Caroline. "May I introduce Mr. John Bexley and his wife Mary?"

"Ah?"

John bowed. Mary curtsied. Should she say anything? she wondered. Or was it like being presented to the queen?

"Friend of mine from the Foreign Office," Conolly added.

"Oh? So, you work for my husband, Mr. Bexley?"

"Yes, my lady."

"In what capacity?"

"Analysis, ma'am, the same as Conolly."

"He was with Amherst in China," Conolly prompted.

"Indeed. Robert hoped for so much more from that effort."

Her disapproving look put a brief damper on the conversation.

"Mrs. Bexley is a talented artist," Caroline said then. "She draws the most wonderful portraits. In just a few strokes. So very lifelike."

"Really?"

As Lady Castlereagh turned to examine her, Mary felt her cheeks blaze. What in the world was Caroline up to? She felt horribly exposed. John looked startled, too, and not pleased. She felt ready to sink under Lady Castlereagh's hawkish eye.

"You don't say so?" drawled another voice. "How very interesting."

Mary's heart quailed further as she saw Edmund Fordyce lurking behind Conolly. She watched her husband stiffen and scowl, then quickly hide his reaction.

"I have the greatest *respect* for such gifts," Fordyce added. He slid closer to Lady Castlereagh. "Almost a…reverence, you might say. We should have a demonstration. I'm sure your guests would find it most entertaining, my lady."

He spoke as if she weren't standing right here, Mary thought. And he looked her up and down as if she were a juggler or conjuror hired for the night. Mary saw John's fists clench. "I wouldn't presume…" Mary struggled to find the right words to pass this off lightly. She glanced at Caroline for help.

"She is not here for your entertainment," Caroline began.

"Of course we would not ask…" Conolly said at the same moment. Their words overlapped and were lost in the general din.

"Something a bit out of the common way," Fordyce inserted smoothly. "I've not seen anything like it at an evening party."

When a flicker of interest passed across Lady Castlereagh's face, Fordyce flagged down a passing footman and demanded paper and pencil. The servant looked to his mistress. Lady Castlereagh cocked her head as if curious and gave a shrug and a nod.

Praying that no drawing materials would be found, Mary tried again. "I really cannot…I mustn't take up your time, when you have so many guests."

"Indeed," John added. "If your ladyship would excuse us. It was a great pleasure to meet you…"

"Nonsense," interrupted Fordyce. "We must not allow Mrs. Bexley to be so modest. Not when we have such *respect* for her talents. Look, here we are."

The footman was returning. Mary cursed his competence as Fordyce intercepted him, snatched the sketchbook and pencil he carried, and thrust them at her. She had to take them or let them fall to the floor.

"A portrait of our hostess," declared Fordyce, "by an exceedingly gifted young lady." He spoke loudly, attracting the attention of a number of nearby guests.

"Really, Fordyce," said Conolly.

"Edmund," said Caroline at the same time. "You are being quite…"

"Rather like a game," said Fordyce, ignoring them.

Lady Castlereagh looked around, took in the circle of interested guests, and gave another tiny shrug. "Why not?"

She looked at Mary. Everyone looked at Mary. The beady stare of all those eyes made her feel a little sick. There must be some way to escape this trial, even now. Lady Castlereagh made a small gesture, urging her on. It seemed to Mary that she could not refuse without giving offense.

She grasped the pencil and held up the sketch pad. She would be quick. A few minutes, and it would be over. How she longed for her own cozy parlor! She began to draw.

Once she'd laid down the first outlines, Mary's self-consciousness began to recede. She no longer noticed the noise of the crowd. The jostling of people around her faded from her mind, as her focus narrowed to the page. Lady Castlereagh's face took shape—round cheeks, straight nose, lower lip a little thin. As always, Mary lost herself as her hands took over. Ringlets dangling beside the lady's ears, a shadow beneath her eyes. Mary's fingers moved with confidence now, creating highlights and shading. This was her gift. She knew how to do it; she was meant to do it.

And then the image felt finished. Mary's drawing hand went still. She took a deep breath and let it drop. The sense of the room flooded back as people crowded forward to see the result. Abruptly, Mary felt hemmed in hard, stifled. She felt John's hand on her elbow. He was right behind her, looking at the drawing.

Fordyce darted forward and snatched the sketch pad away from her. He held it up for Lady Castlereagh to see, making certain it was visible to a large segment of the surrounding crowd as well. Lady Castlereagh examined the image, and as she did, Mary stared at the picture she'd created. The resemblance was striking. It was their hostess to the life. But the woman gazing back at her from the page wasn't smiling. She wasn't the chattering, assured center of this glittering gathering. Her mouth was tight; her eyes were deep and…haunted. The portrait gave off a sense of terrible sadness and fear.

Mary looked up and found the actual woman's eyes burning into hers. She didn't have to wonder whether Lady Castlereagh had noticed these nuances. The answer was dismayingly plain.

"What's all this?" asked a male voice. The foreign secretary himself wove through the press of people around them. At fifty years of age, Lord Castlereagh was a large handsome man, with pale hair and even features. He stopped beside his wife and looked at her portrait. His eyes flew to her face, back to the image. Then he turned and, without a word, walked away.

Murmurs swept the crowd around them. Many of them saw the mysterious anguish in the portrait, Mary thought. It was all too plain. Others were approaching from the far corners of the reception, asking each other what was happening.

"How dare you?" whispered Lady Castlereagh. She jerked the sketch pad from Fordyce's hands, slapped it closed, and thrust the object at a footman. "Take this away," she ordered. The man fumbled with the tray of glasses he was carrying, got the tablet under an arm, and hurried off. With a final glare at Mary, Lady Castlereagh swept away, parting the gaping crowd like a knife through soft butter.

"Oh dear," said Fordyce, his voice oozing satisfaction.

John stepped toward him. "I warned you," he hissed under the buzz of speculation sweeping the gathering.

"But I spoke of your wife with the utmost *respect*," was the mocking reply. The man's pale eyes glittered. "And she certainly justified my…esteem. I don't think anyone will heed your 'stories of the voyage' after that little performance."

Mary had never fainted in her life, but she felt as if she might right now. Every complaint her mother had ever made about her came back in a dizzying rush. She was heedless, dull-witted, and wholly lacking in common sense. Her dreamy immersion in art would lead to a bad end. And it had. She had offended the Castlereaghs! She had been stupid and careless and… Her knees threatened to give way and leave her in a heap on the polished wooden floor.

"Come."

Caroline's arm laced through hers and supported her. Mary let herself be pulled toward the arched doorway. She saw Conolly pull John away from Fordyce and urge him along behind them. John's jaw looked so tight Mary thought it must hurt. Faces loomed and passed, staring and jabbering, as if they would drink in every particle of her humiliation. It was like a nightmare.

They passed into the entryway. Caroline kept moving. And then they were outside in the chill of late evening. Footmen and linkboys peered at them. After a moment, Conolly came out with their wraps and threw Mary's shawl around her shoulders. Where was John? He hadn't gone back…? No, there he was, coming behind.

"I'm so sorry," Caroline said. "So sorry. I meant to help you by mentioning the…"

"Help?" John's voice was like a lash. "Where do the carriages wait?" he snapped at a servant.

"I can send a message to your…"

"Where?" John interrupted.

"Over yonder," supplied a linkboy. "Down that street on the other side of St. James."

John pulled Mary away from Caroline. When she swayed a little, he put an arm around her to guide her along the pavement. "You shouldn't come with us," he said to Conolly when the other man started to follow. "No need to be linked with me."

"Of *course* we will…" Caroline began.

"We will come," Conolly replied.

The four of them walked in silence across St. James Square. Mary found she was shaking so hard it was difficult to move.

Conolly's voice came out of the darkness. "You know, Bexley, this may not be so very bad…"

John snorted. "It's a disaster!"

Mary stumbled. Only John's arm kept her from falling. Despair engulfed her.

They found the mass of carriages in the designated street, along with a cluster of drivers waiting for their charges. After a brief hunt, they located their own conveyance and got in. Mary huddled in the corner of the seat and tried not to cry.

"I only meant for Lady Castlereagh to hear how talented you are," Caroline said when they had been under way for a while. "What a wonderful artist. So that you—both—would be noticed."

"Noticed!" John's tone was savage.

"I'm sorry," Caroline repeated. She sounded near tears herself.

"It wasn't your fault," said Conolly. "If Fordyce hadn't pushed in…"

"I could kill him," John snarled.

Mary thought of the ruffians John had encountered in the slums and what they might do for pay. Her hands grew icy. "You mustn't…you can't…"

"We all might like to, but of course we cannot," replied Conolly, his tone all calm reason.

"More's the pity," Caroline said.

"This incident will pass off as a mere triviality," Conolly said.

Mary didn't think any of them believed it. At any rate, no one responded. The journey back home was mainly silent.

Fourteen

JOHN SAT IN HIS STUDY IN THE SILENT HOUSE, FORE-head resting in his hand, and wondered about fate. Were his brothers actually right? Had he somehow been born a bungler? Was he cursed? He saw now that he'd been naive to imagine he'd defeated Fordyce. The man would never forgive John for having witnessed his cowardice on the ship. He'd merely grown more subtle, lying in wait for a chance to ruin John's career.

Something like a growl rumbled in John's throat. He sat up straight, his hand moving in an impatient gesture, rejecting exaggeration and self-pity. Let us not overdramatize, he thought. Ruin was not the word. He wouldn't be dismissed. No one would go so far as that. But his dreams of serious advancement...

John nearly laughed. He'd longed to rise from obscurity, to distinguish himself from the rank and file of Foreign Office functionaries. And so he had! He'd become the man whose wife had offended Lady Castlereagh, without even being acquainted with her. If social connections were vital to preferment, social destruction must be the death of such hopes. He could remain in his current junior position for as long as he cared to be employed there. As years passed he would age into one of those wizened clerks he sometimes encountered in the furthest corners of the offices—knowledgeable but negligible in the grand scheme of international affairs. Frederick and George would be round to tell him how right they'd been, to offer their misguided comfort.

And he didn't see, just now, anything he could do to mend matters. Draft an apology? What precisely was he supposed to say? Lady Castlereagh, I'm very sorry that you did not like my wife's portrait of you? She…she what? What had Mary been thinking? And who cared about a drawing anyway? It was infuriating to be thwarted by something so petty and silly… But wars had been started over events that looked quite petty and silly in retrospect.

John sat back and stared at the opposite wall. Fordyce had outdone him at the game of underhanded swipes. If John circulated the story of his cowardice now, the fellow would easily pass it off as a vengeful lie. Perhaps he'd been emboldened by a sense that John had never wanted to do it anyway. He disliked having to be devious. And clearly, he wasn't much good at it.

He could practically hear Fordyce's voice, murmuring down the corridors of the office, insinuating, pretending to be sorry even as he shared every detail of this incident. Or…not every one. Details selected, or made up, by him, designed to put John in the worst possible light. What could John's wife have been up to, he would wonder, all wide-eyed innocence. What had John told her to make her draw such a strange likeness? He would probably plant the idea that John told tales about his work at home. He would hold John up as devious, and spiteful, and...bungling. John closed his eyes briefly.

The door opened halfway, and Mary looked around it. Traces of tears showed on her face. "I'm so sorry, John."

The tragic look in her dark eyes bothered him. And yet the question erupted, "Could you not have found a way to refuse?"

"Everyone was looking at me," she faltered. "It seemed it would be so rude."

"Perhaps. But perhaps that would not have been as bad as what actually happened?" She flinched, and he regretted it. Yet he couldn't refrain from asking, "Why the deuce did you draw her in a way that... annoyed her so?"

"I can't help it," Mary said. Her mouth trembled, and she blinked back further tears.

This made no sense. "What do you mean?"

"When I draw, it just happens."

"What happens? What are you talking about?"

It was always a struggle to explain this. "When I draw, something...occurs," Mary tried. "It lets me see deeper into people, and that becomes part of the portraits I create. It's my...talent." The last word seemed inappropriate in this moment.

John shook his head, bewildered. "All sorts of girls play the pianoforte at parties, or sing. God knows, some chit is always being pushed forward to sing. You could have just drawn a pleasant picture. Why not make her ladyship a bit prettier than life, as portrait painters can do?"

"It's not like that for me."

"Why the devil make her look so...haunted?" Remembering Lady Castlereagh's reaction to the image Mary had produced, John felt rather haunted himself.

"I didn't set out to do it!" Mary cried. "I can't help it if that is how she feels...inside."

"Inside?" John gazed at his wife. He hated to see her so distressed, but he had no idea what she was talking about. He couldn't control the annoyance that rose. "For this, my career is destroyed?"

"You are not destroyed! They can't be so unfair!" Mary sounded frantic. "It was my hand on the pencil. What I did should not hurt you!"

John said nothing. They both knew that a wife's actions always reflected on her husband. And it was even more true in this case. The memory of her face when Fordyce snatched away the sketchbook and Lady Castlereagh stared at her portrait returned to him. She'd looked devastated. She looked devastated now. He fought down his temper and, finally, sighed. "The furor will pass, Mary. Some other cause for gossip will arise, and interest will...lessen." He couldn't suppress a hint of regret. "I'll fall back into the larger mass of Foreign Office staff..."

"You shouldn't! You're so good at what you do! You work harder than anyone else. People know that. They've praised your work..."

"I don't expect Lord Castlereagh will want to hear me praised now."

Mary winced. She came further into the room. "John, we'll find a way to fix this."

Just now, he couldn't see it. But her eyes were pleading. He nodded.

"You're tired," Mary added. "Come to bed."

"Not yet." There was no sleep in him.

"Please." She came over and took his hand.

Gently, he disengaged. "I can't rest just now. Or... anything else. I need to think." Tears pooled in Mary's eyes. John rose and embraced her. "Don't cry. We'll get through this. I'll take care of you."

"You don't have to take... I want to help *you*!"

"I think you've done enough." He regretted the words as soon as they escaped him. Mary winced as if from a blow. "I'm sorry," John added quickly. "Go and sleep."

"Won't you come...?"

He had to refuse. He was full of tension and afraid other harsh words might pop out. He couldn't take this mood to her bedchamber. "Things will look better in the morning," he told her.

❦

The old adage was bunk, Mary thought the next day. Things did not look better, not in the least. She still felt as if something dear to her had died. No, she had killed it. Her insistence on drawing had brought a load of trouble down on her husband.

Mary paced the front parlor, hands clenching and opening in distress. Her mother had been right after all; she should have resisted indulging in her peculiar talent and kept it hidden. Here was what came of revealing yourself. If she hadn't let Eleanor see her drawings, then Caroline couldn't have pushed her forward. And that wretched man Fordyce couldn't have taken advantage of the opportunity to embarrass her. And everything would still be all right.

John had gone off to his office, as usual. She could imagine the unpleasantness he'd face there. How many of his colleagues had been at the party? And how many more would be listening, agog, to the story of what had transpired? Imagining John's exposure made her stomach twist with regret. If only there was something she could *do*.

Unable to be still, Mary went upstairs. But she found no comfort in her studio retreat. She would not be sitting at her easel today. Back out on the landing, she noticed Arthur Windly through the open door of John's study. To her surprise, he was placing a sheet of paper on the desk. "What are you doing?" Moving into the room, she saw that the page held a sketch, some sort of diagram. "What is this?"

"It's a steam engine," the boy replied. "How it works, like."

"How it works?" Mary picked up the page and examined it. "I don't understand."

Arthur pointed at a double square in the top corner. "That's meant to be the boiler, see, with the firebox underneath." His voice gathered enthusiasm as he spoke. "Once the water in the boiler heats enough, the steam goes up this pipe and drives a piston, right there." He pointed to a cylindrical shape. "That turns a shaft. Or runs a belt. You can power just about whatever you like that way."

"I see." And she did. "You explained that very clearly."

Arthur merely nodded. He looked glum.

"How did you learn all this?" Mary wondered.

"I heard a man talk at the Parish Hall. There was a fella visited back home, too. He'd seen the powered looms up north."

This was a whole new side of Arthur. "So you've always been interested in engines?"

Head down, he shrugged. "Dad says they're 'the bane of the working man.' Taking their jobs away, you know."

Must Arthur's father belittle everything about his son? Mary wondered.

"I thought I'd show Mr. Bexley, in case he'd like…" The boy broke off with a sigh. "It's not an adventure. I couldn't think of a good adventure."

"Adventure?"

"He said I should have adventures. But it ain't that easy to come upon a fire to put out or somebody to…rescue, like. I was thinking…inventions could be a kind of adventure. Don't you think? Perhaps? I wanted to ask him."

"I'm sure he'll be very interested." Remembering her husband's glum mood last night, Mary added, "He is rather busy just now."

"He's always busy," said Arthur, as if he was all too familiar with that excuse. "And I'm stuck in the kitchen, with Kate and Mrs. Tanner arguing over the stove. It's gotten to be a proper donnybrook down there."

A spark of real interest penetrated Mary's gloom. "Kate is making concoctions?"

Arthur nodded. "She's got a vast deal of bottles and

such, but she says she needs more. They were all over the table. Mrs. Tanner came near to smashing the lot yesterday, so Kate put some of 'em in her room."

Mary hadn't foreseen such friction when she introduced the maid to Jeremiah Jenkins. Here was something else she'd gotten wrong. She ought to go downstairs and speak to her staff, she supposed. But she didn't want to.

Then she realized that there was one person she might ask for advice. Fetching a cloak, Mary walked across the square to Eleanor's house. She was admitted at once and ushered into her neighbor's private parlor. Eleanor turned from her easel and smiled. "You're out early. How was the reception?"

"You haven't talked to Caroline?"

"She's still in bed. What's wrong?"

Sinking into an armchair, Mary poured out the story. The old woman's face grew more and more concerned as she talked. "Sad and anxious," she murmured when Mary was done. "I wonder what weighs so heavily on Emily?"

Mary was briefly abashed. She hadn't considered Lady Castlereagh's state of mind and what might be troubling her. But after all, how could she be of help? She wasn't really acquainted with her.

"Well, there will clearly be a storm of gossip," Eleanor added.

"I suppose I can be thankful that we won't hear it, since we don't move in those 'exalted' circles." And never would, Mary thought.

"My family will complain about Caroline's part in it."

Another factor Mary hadn't considered. Social calamity apparently made one quite self-centered and sarcastic and just generally despicable. She rose from her chair. "I'm sorry. I mustn't drag you any further into…"

"Nonsense," said Eleanor. "I was just thinking aloud. Sit down."

She did. Eleanor gazed out the window, lost in thought.

Mary stayed quiet as long as she could, then words burst out of her again. "I must find a way to help John."

"It will be very hard for him," her neighbor acknowledged. "Men can be far worse gossips than women, no matter what people say."

"I want to *do* something," Mary exclaimed. "What can I do?"

"You may leave everything to me," declared Caroline from the doorway. She strode into the room like a Valkyrie. Her green eyes sparkled with defiance. "I shall go and see Lady Castlereagh this morning and explain how…"

"No!" said her grandmother and Mary at the same moment.

Caroline put her hands on her hips and glared at them.

"It's just…" Mary didn't want to offend her, but she thought it only too likely that Caroline would make things worse rather than better.

"A young lady with a reputation for playing pranks, who had a clear hand in last night's events, is not the ideal emissary," said Eleanor.

Caroline looked stricken. "No one could think that I meant this to happen."

"People may think whatever they like," responded

her grandmother. "But after the ferret, and the brandy in the schoolroom tea, and the 'ghost' in the spinney…"

Caroline sank onto the sofa next to her and took the old woman's hand. "I would never set out to hurt someone—anyone—with my pranks. Particularly not Mary and her husband. You must believe that, Grandmamma!"

"I do." Eleanor squeezed her hand and let it go. "But then I know you very well and love you very much."

Caroline slumped onto the cushions. "I caused this tangle. I should fix it."

"From what Mary has told me, you were not the sole cause."

"Edmund Fordyce." Caroline wrinkled her nose in disgust. "The toad. And I used to think he was rather witty. But whyever did he…?"

"He and John do not get on," interrupted Mary. It hardly mattered now why. "What can be done?" she asked Eleanor. "I will do anything, grovel and beg if need be."

Eleanor rose. "I shall go and talk to Emily. We are of different generations, but we are friends of a sort."

Mary clasped her hands tight in her lap. "Could you tell her…that I'm sorry…that I never meant to cause her any pain. That I just… Oh, she will never understand what happens when I draw."

"What does happen?" asked Caroline. "I mean, I did wonder why you made her so…"

"Mary learns and, in a way, 'speaks' with her hands," replied Eleanor, reaching for the bellpull.

Mary's mouth fell open in surprise. She stared at her hostess.

"It's simply a different way of dealing with information."

"How did you know…?" Mary couldn't find words to convey her amazement.

Eleanor smiled at her. "It happens to me, just a bit, also. Enough so that I can recognize and admire it."

"Admire!"

"Your hands? How can they?" Caroline looked brightly curious. There was no censure in her gaze.

Mary ventured an explanation. "When I begin to draw…they somehow know what to do without my thinking about it. They draw what…I might not be able to understand…otherwise."

"Really?" Caroline gazed at Mary's hands. "How interesting."

The butler came in answer to Eleanor's ring. "I need the carriage, Jenson," she said.

"It's quite cold and blustery outside, my lady." It wasn't quite an objection, but there was a hint of reproach in his tone.

Eleanor gave him a stern look. "The carriage. Immediately."

He surrendered with a bow. "Yes, my lady."

Caroline begged Mary to stay and await the result with her, and so the two young women tried to occupy themselves for an endless hour. Caroline asked further questions about the drawing process. In the face of her uncritical interest, Mary talked about portraits she'd done and the ways they'd helped her. After a while Mary began to hope that she could explain what had happened at the party to John as well.

When the sound of carriage wheels finally came

outside, they leaped up and met their hostess at the front door.

But Eleanor shook her head as the servants took her hat and gloves and cloak. "Emily has gone down to the country for two weeks," she said.

They walked back into the parlor, closing the door on curious eyes.

"As far as I could discover, her departure had been planned for some time," Eleanor continued. "Hunting season, you know. There will be parties invited to Waletts for sport."

Mary sank into a chair, shaky from the release of tension as much as disappointment.

"I was thinking on the way back that this may be just as well," said Eleanor. "Over that time, the talk will decrease. We can consider what…"

"So we do nothing!" exclaimed Caroline.

"To think and plan is not nothing," was her grandmother's mild reply.

Caroline paced the room, her skirts swirling around her. "It feels like it."

It did, Mary thought. She longed to put everything back the way it had been yesterday, when they'd been anticipating the party with such high hopes.

"Scandal fades away," said Eleanor. "Emotions cool. It will be far better to speak to Emily when she is…"

"Not furious with me," finished Mary.

The silence in the room confirmed her judgment.

Mary rose. "Thank you for trying to help," she said to Eleanor. She nodded to Caroline to show that she included her in this, despite a niggling wish that Caroline had stayed silent at the reception. "I must go home." She moved to the door. Caroline started after her, but Eleanor seemed to sense Mary's need to escape and called her granddaughter back.

Mary found several of the dowager countess's servants in the entry. As she waited for her cloak to be fetched, the lady's maid sidled up to her. "Quite a brisk wind today," the woman said. "There's talk of snow by morning."

Mary nodded.

"If there was anything you could do to discourage her ladyship from going out in the cold…"

Another thing to regret, Mary thought. There was no end to them just now.

"Her family is always urging her to visit in the winter, when town is so grim and empty," the maid confided.

Empty of the *haut ton*, Mary thought. Yet thousands of people remained in London going about their lives as usual.

"Her son the earl would be glad to have her," the maid continued. "Or Lady Frist, her younger daughter, you know. Not Lady Caroline's family perhaps…"

"Her ladyship makes up her own mind, Jenson," was all she could find to say as she gratefully pulled on her gloves and cloak.

❧

All through the afternoon, John felt like a zoo animal. So many of his coworkers made an excuse to pass by their office and peer inside. Conolly kept them out, for the most part, but John could feel the news of last night spreading through the building like an acrid fog. John was more than ever grateful that fate had made William

Conolly the other inhabitant of this small room. The man knew when conversation was unwelcome.

John buried himself in his work. And there he found some salvation. The tasks were familiar, and he knew he did them well. The pile of intelligence reports awaiting his scrutiny both challenged and reassured him. Exercising his faculties in analysis restored his spirits and renewed his determination. He would find a way through this. He would keep his head down, do his job, and endure. Tomorrow would be better, and the day after more so, as the talk subsided.

Still, he was relieved when the day ended and he could head for home. Riding through the darkening streets, he bowed to a raw wind that found all the crevices in his scarf and coat. Small, sharp snowflakes raked his bare face like tiny knives. It was wonderful to reach the house and be welcomed by warmth and golden candlelight. His house felt like a sanctuary, far from Fordyce, rumors of war, and the slums where so many wretches shivered this night.

He gave Kate his things and headed for the fire, holding chilled hands over the flames. Mary came to stand beside him. "John, I would like to explain about the drawing," she said. "How it happened…"

"Please." His hand came up, unthinking. He was sick of the whole subject. "Going over and over the thing will do no good." He smiled at her. "Let us talk of something else tonight."

"But you don't understand!" She reached out a hand, looking agitated.

He took it and squeezed her fingers. "I know very well that you meant no harm."

"Of course I didn't." Her tone had a snap now. "I need you to see…"

Above all, he didn't want to quarrel. "Must we do this now? I had very little sleep and a trying day." He tried another smile. "I'm quite hungry as well, looking forward to one of your excellent dinners."

Mary gazed at him for a long moment. He wished she wouldn't look so sad. "I'll tell them to serve as soon as may be," she said and went out.

Dinner was stilted at first. John searched for a topic that would raise his wife's spirits. "How is your family?" he asked. "Have you had letters from your sisters?"

"I had one from Lucy," Mary replied.

"What news from her?" He was surprised at the depth of his relief when Mary began to smile.

"Her little boy is teething, and he got hold of the dog's bone and began chewing on it before she noticed and took it away from him."

He laughed, partly to encourage her to go on.

"She washed out his mouth with lavender soap. And then he was sick. And she doesn't think that he will ever forgive her."

"More likely he's too young to remember the indignity."

"The dog was quite aggrieved, also, when she threw away the bone."

"What is the name of this ferocious child? I fear I've forgotten."

"Daniel."

"That's right. He sounds rather like Frederick's eldest."

Through the rest of the meal, they diverted themselves with stories of the upcoming generation in their families. Mary had five nephews and nieces, to his two. When they removed to the parlor after dinner, however, conversation tailed off. They sat on the sofa before the fire, its crackling a counterpoint to the scratch of snow at the windows.

The silence had grown long, and awkward, when Mary turned to him and said, "I *will* find a way out of this tangle." Her tone was fierce. Her dark eyes glowed with resolve. Then she laced her arms around his neck and kissed him, holding on as if for dear life.

The intensity in her voice and her touch shook him, fired him like a match set to tinder. He slipped his arms around her and drew her close, murmuring her name against her lips. The world drew in around him, a sheltering cloak, until nothing existed but their embrace.

Some endless time later, John surfaced. Mary's hair was tousled, and her eyes were smudged with desire. Her gown was falling off one white shoulder. He pulled his wife to her feet. "Upstairs."

In the sanctuary of the bedroom, they shed clothes with hurried tugs and low murmurs. Firelight gleamed on glimpses of skin and then on bare bodies yearning for each other.

John let his hands run over the curves that he'd learned to savor and teased out the gasps that had come to thrill him as much as his own surges of desire. His breath caught, too, as Mary's fingers found ways to tantalize him.

Falling into bed, they urged each other on, and on, until desire beat through them like floodwaters at a dam. John hung at a vibrating edge, until he felt Mary shudder and open under his touch, and then he plunged and let the whirling urgency take him away. There was nothing, then, but this, the exquisite joy of shared release. He felt Mary with him as the wave rose to an impossible peak, broke in glory, and slowly, deliciously, ebbed.

Wasn't this enough? John thought, over the gradual slowing of his heart. Still holding Mary, he turned on his side and kept her close. Need a man ask more than to be happy in his home? Wasn't the rest of it just empty posturing? There were other desires, yes—to be useful and admired by one's fellow man. Yet how could they match…? His mind blurred; he tried to think about the question. But last night's sleeplessness caught up with him and pulled him down into oblivion.

Lying beside him, still encircled by his arm, Mary heard her husband's breathing slow into sleep. His body relaxed against the pillows, and his face looked peaceful, younger than when awake. Tears burned in her eyes, and a sharp ache pierced her heart. She'd never regretted anything so much as the trouble her drawing had brought him. It was so unfair that he should suffer, so undeserved! And that she should be the cause…

She desperately needed him to understand how it had happened, to understand *her*. They were no longer the strangers who had reunited after his long absence. But the steps they'd taken toward each other had simply made her want more.

Mary traced her husband's handsome features with her eyes. If they could lie here forever side by side… But that was not the way of the world. Morning would come, and he would go out to contend with the difficulties her drawing had caused. She bared her teeth at the thought. She would do anything, she realized, anything to make this right for the man she…loved.

Mary rose on one elbow and looked down at John. Her heart seemed to expand in her chest. She desperately loved this husband who had returned to her a stranger and gradually become the center of her life. She *would* find a way to help him. She didn't know how just now. But she'd find a way.

Careful not to disturb him, Mary turned to blow out the candle on the small table beside the bed. She lay in the darkness a long while before sleep finally came.

Fifteen

AT BREAKFAST THE NEXT MORNING, KATE WAS unusually attentive, offering to freshen Mary's tea or fetch more toast. Instead of appearing only if called, she positively hovered. Instead of her customary sullen stoicism, her expression seemed full of purpose, her movements crisp. When Mary had finished eating, Kate stood before her like a workman who has completed his assigned task and now expects payment. "Ma'am, would you go with me back to the apothecary shop? I've finished all the samples I wish to show Mr. Jenkins."

"You can have leave to go on your own, Kate."

"I don't want to go alone." The maid's tone was adamant.

What was this? Kate had never been shy of any deliveryman or shopkeeper. Not that Mary had seen. "Why not?"

"This is an...official visit, like."

"Official?"

"And I don't want Mr. Jenkins thinking I'm the sort of girl who goes gadding about the streets on her own, getting up to mischief," Kate added.

Mary was tempted to ask her what sort of mischief she had in mind, but she was too intrigued by this new Kate—focused and intense, clearly determined. The lackadaisical, discontented servant she'd endured for all these weeks had disappeared. The transformation almost made Mary forget her own troubles. "All right, I will go with you," she said.

An hour later they walked out of the square together, warmly dressed against the morning chill. Kate carried a large basket that clinked softly as she moved, though she had swathed many of her samples in cloth.

Eager to promote the success of her own plan, and remembering their last visit to Mr. Jenkins, Mary ventured a hint. "Perhaps you should be a bit more… umm…accommodating when you explain your concoctions today."

Kate's chin came up, and her lips turned down. In an instant, she looked like her old sullen self. "I've no need to be 'accommodating.' His shop'll be better off with my lotions and tinctures. I'm very good at concocting, if I do say so."

"Well, but he doesn't know…"

"He will after today." Kate shook the basket slightly. "And I'm right here in London and can make up special orders in a day. No sending down to the country."

She'd clearly thought this through. Mary was impressed, yet she had envisioned a rather closer relationship for Kate and Mr. Jenkins. "Yes, but if you seem to be puffing yourself off…"

"No one else will if I don't," was Kate's brisk reply. "Old Alice in the stillroom used to say, 'The only way to get respect is to insist on it.' And I reckon she was right."

Insist on it? The words seemed to echo in Mary's ears. Insist on recognition for one's talents? She tried to imagine doing that with her family and saw a row of astonished faces gazing back at her. Yet, she had insisted when it came to Great-Aunt Lavinia. She'd made her case, and her mother had agreed. But the drawing of Lady Castlereagh…that was different. People were angry at her. Even John… That struck to her very heart.

"Here we are," Kate said.

Mary had nearly walked past the apothecary shop. She saw Kate take a deep breath before opening the door and realized that the maid might not be quite as confident as she was trying to seem. They walked in, the bell jingling to herald their entrance, and handsome Jeremiah Jenkins came out from the back.

Kate marched up to the counter and set down her basket. "I've come to show you some things," she declared, pulling back the cloth covering.

For the next half hour, Kate talked with surprising authority. She explained her concoctions in detail, verifying the quality of the ingredients and detailing their uses. She smeared lotion on her wrist and offered it to Mr. Jenkins to sniff. She commandeered Mary's wrist for another, so as not to mingle the aromas. She extolled the efficacy of several herbal tinctures and flower essences. She noted how carefully they'd been made. When a customer entered, Kate paused and stepped back, then picked up right where she'd left off when the customer was served. Mary was amazed by her fluency and assurance. This was a different creature from her dissatisfied, mumbling housemaid.

As she talked, Jenkins's expression slowly shifted from surprise to wariness to enthusiasm. When at last Kate ran down, he said, "These are first-rate." He held a tincture up to the light. "Not a crumb in the suspension. Very well made."

"Didn't I say so?" replied Kate.

Mary winced at her truculent tone, but the apothecary merely nodded. "I assume you mean to offer them to me for sale here?" he said.

"Yes. I could do special orders as well. If a lady wanted a lavender-scented lotion or rose. Whatever her favorite is."

Jenkins nodded again, more thoughtfully.

"You could run advertisements," Mary suggested, "like the ones in the fashion papers for Denmark Lotion and Olympian Dew."

Her companions did not appear to hear her. They were leaning toward each other across the counter. "I suppose you could supply new concoctions fairly quickly?" said Jenkins.

"Not like the days it must take from the country," Kate agreed. In the face of his interest, she smiled, and the smile transformed her somewhat plain face, giving it beauty and life. Mary was startled. Had she ever seen Kate happy in all the weeks she'd known her? Not that she could recall. The change in her expression suggested a far more engaging, attractive creature than the sullen maid she knew. She could see Jeremiah Jenkins noticing it as well.

"I do believe we can work together," he said. He

held out a hand. Kate grasped it. They shook on the bargain and did not immediately let go. From the way Kate's smile broadened, Mary suspected that she wouldn't be asked to accompany her to the apothecary shop again.

❧

At the Foreign Office, another awkward day crawled past. John chafed at his situation and did his best to ignore it. He would go out with Henry Tsing tonight, he decided. That was one initiative he could control, and who knew, a few calculated risks might yield important information and counterbalance his current…not disgrace. That was far too strong—and foolishly self-indulgent—a word. Notoriety?

Whatever you called his plight, it didn't change the fact that he wanted to help England and that he had valuable skills to apply to this goal. He dashed off notes to Tsing and to Mary, letting her know of his plans, then settled to work in somewhat better spirits.

Trudging through the slums that evening was actually a relief. The sailors and ruffians John observed in grog houses and taverns knew nothing of society gossip and wouldn't have cared a fig if they heard it. Whatever shifts they were put to in their struggle to survive, they weren't idle and bored. Their lives had a…gritty reality that altered his perspective on his own problems.

Ending his tour at Shen's establishment, he sat for a while with the man and had a real drink. No need to tip Shen's fine brandy into a dark corner or under the scratched boards of a grog house table. It was finer than what John had at home. They discussed ships newly in from the Orient and the activities of the latest crop of stranded Chinese sailors. "Not much news tonight then," John concluded.

"Ah."

The tone of this one word made John sit straighter despite his fatigue.

"Two of my fellow…proprietors have become quite elusive of late. They haven't dropped in for a chat, as you are kind enough to do." Shen's tone was ironic. "Or responded—except uselessly—to my inquiries."

"Who?" John asked. And when Shen named the owners of a sailors' doss-house and a low inn, he said, "They're in the habit of calling on you?"

"From time to time. It's good for business to be acquainted with your…competitors."

Shen was being charitable. John knew these other two were far less influential. "Perhaps I should call upon them…"

Shen shook his head. "Unwise. A whiff of a stranger, and any odd doings will be swept away. Let me inquire. I shall tell you what I learn."

"You expect it to be significant." John could hear it in his host's voice.

"I do. Though there is nothing I can put my finger on, I have a…feeling that they may have the answer to the elusive 'presence' we have been pursuing."

John had a healthy respect for intuition. Many of the reports he read from far-flung spots spoke of hunches that paid off. Still, who mentioned those that did not? "I shall leave it to you then."

"You may."

John nodded his thanks. This scheme of his would be impossible without this man, he thought. It was a piece of luck that he had found him.

⚉

Mary sat in the front parlor of her home with only the light of the fire to illuminate the room. She was watching for John's return, and it was far easier to see the square outside without a lamp or candles reflecting off the window glass. And though she knew it was much too early to expect him, she found the dimness soothing. It let her feel hidden, secret, safe. In the dark the sense of a battery of accusing eyes upon her lessened.

The clatter of a carriage brought her to her feet. Peering out, Mary watched a hackney draw up in front of Eleanor's place across the way. A man alit and paid the driver. When he turned, the carriage lamps washed his face, and Mary recognized William Conolly.

John's friend knocked and was admitted, though this was hardly a conventional time for calls. He must have an appointment, and Mary doubted he'd come to see Eleanor. Caroline was a much more likely attraction. Mary wished him well if that was where his interests lay.

She returned to her chair and watched the wash of orange firelight on the walls. The evils of her situation cycled round and round in her brain. She'd tried a book, a pile of mending, but nothing diverted her from the desperate desire to help her husband.

Sometime later, Mary heard Kate and Mrs. Tanner

go up to bed. As the hour passed midnight, she moved to a straight chair by the window.

Finally, at what seemed the middle of the night, she heard footsteps in the silence of the square. Peering out, she spotted John. He carried a small lantern to light his way. She now knew that he had a pistol in his pocket, too, which was both a worry and a reassurance.

The light of a half-moon silvered the landscape, and just as Mary was rising to go to the front door she saw another figure, lingering at the corner of the street that led into the square, fifty feet or so behind her husband.

This person carried no lantern, and so was a mere outline. He—she was certain it was a man—edged over to the fence bordering the square's garden. There, he crouched, harder to see against the wrought iron bars and bare branches beyond.

At the sound of John's key in the lock, Mary looked away for a moment. When she turned back, she could no longer see the dark figure, no matter how hard she stared. Cursing that brief inattention, she hurried out to the front door.

John started when she appeared in the entryway. "Were you sitting in the dark?"

"To watch for you." She moved past him and through the still open doorway.

"What are you doing?"

Mary rushed over the cobbles and scanned the line of the fence. John came up behind her, the light of his lantern illuminating an empty scene.

"Mary, what the deuce are you...?"

"There was someone following you. I saw him."

"Following?"

"He came into the square behind you, and then went over to the garden fence."

John looked around and held the lantern higher. "There was no one behind me. I kept a careful eye out."

"There was."

John turned, casting the beam of light over the pavement and running it along the iron fence. "See, no one."

"But I saw someone!"

John walked back into the house. After a moment, Mary followed. He closed the door and extinguished the lantern, setting it down on the floor. "If you saw anyone, it was probably a late reveler or a neighbor who couldn't get to sleep," he said.

Mary let the "if" pass. "Why would anyone like that hide by the fence?"

"A call of nature?"

This use for the fence hadn't occurred to her and was an unappealing piece of knowledge. Mary shook her head, remembering something. "I've seen someone before. Nearer the house. Watching or…"

"The neighborhood is full of people, Mary."

He didn't believe her. Mary wanted to argue, but he looked so tired. She would leave it for now. Though she knew she was right.

❧

The next day was Sunday, and the Bexleys attended the local church, as had become their habit. After Mrs. Tanner's Sunday roast, they'd barely settled in the parlor when there was a sharp knock at the front door. "Are you expecting anyone?" Mary wondered. John shook his head. Since she'd given her small staff leave to go out, she went to answer it herself.

She found John's brother George on the doorstep. He didn't wait for an invitation but walked in as if he owned the place, saying, "Mary," with a curt nod. He was peeling off his coat when John appeared in the parlor doorway. "There you are," said George. He handed his hat and coat to Mary and walked into the parlor.

Mary looked at her husband. His jaw had tightened. As he turned back toward the parlor, she tossed George's things over a chair and hurried after him.

George Bexley stood before the hearth, with his hands out to the warmth of the fire. His ruddy face was creased in a frown. "What the devil have you been up to?" he said to Mary.

"I beg your...?"

"From what I hear, you've managed to insult Lord Castlereagh." He shook his head. "Mama thought that getting John leg-shackled would put an end to his scrapes. Now we find all it's done is double the risk of his falling into them."

"That is absolutely not..." began John.

"So I've come round to pull *both* of your chestnuts out of the fire," George interrupted.

"How do you even know...?" tried Mary.

"Friend of mine was at that party, gawking at some drawing of yours." George let out an aggrieved sigh. "Why in God's name were you drawing before all those people? Idiotic thing to do. Pushing yourself forward."

Mary found that her throat had gone rather dry.

George frowned at her. "And if you had to draw...

which of course you did *not*. What sort of feather-brained chit makes an unflattering picture of…?"

"Enough!" snapped John.

His brother drew back, looking startled.

"You will not speak to Mary in that tone."

George bridled. "Someone needs to. She seems to have made you a laughingstock, if not an absolute pariah. If Mama had realized that she's as hopeless as you—or worse!—when it comes to…"

"She is not!"

Mary's heart swelled at the outrage in John's face. He was defending her even though he had said some of these same things about her drawing.

"What's got into you?" George said.

"A sense of justice?"

"What? Don't begin spouting some sort of non-sense. I've come all the way over here to save you from your own folly."

"And what do you imagine you can do?" said John.

Under his brother's cool inquiry, George sputtered. "Give you a sense of your…tell you what Mama says…talk some sense into your dratted wife."

"Enough!" The command in his voice silenced George. "I will say it again. You will *not* speak of Mary in that way."

Mary blinked back tears. No one had ever defended her so fiercely or so completely.

"Ever," added John. He frowned at his brother. "Moreover, your 'help' is not required. Nor is Frederick's, nor Mama's, nor Roger's from halfway across the world, for that matter. I will take care of this myself."

"Really?" George retrieved his customary condescension. "The way you did when you fell off the barn roof? Or when you…"

"Will you *stop* talking to me of things that happened when I was a child? All of you seem to be…obsessed with the past. Did I need your help at school? Did I need it when I took up my position at the Foreign Office? Did I need it on a voyage halfway around the world? No, I did not!"

Mary was so proud of him that she thought her heart might burst.

"You'll be sorry for flinging my offer back in my face like this," snapped George.

"Indeed? And what is your grand plan to make all right?"

"Well…" George obviously had no idea.

"Are you going to fetch a ladder? Or simply rant at me about my shortcomings? And laugh yourselves sick, of course. That's always a great deal of help."

"John, what the devil is wrong with you? I was only…"

"You—all of you—may leave the ordering of my affairs to me from now on."

"Really? What's *your* plan then? If you have one." George's face had gone crimson with anger by this time.

"There's no need for you to know that," John replied.

"No need or no chance. Because you haven't the least notion what to do. You're hopeless, the pair of you."

"Mary, get George's coat," replied John.

"Are you throwing me out?" His older brother was incredulous.

"This conversation is fruitless."

"You are not the best judge of what is…"

"This is *my* house. I fear it is not a convenient time for a visit."

Mary brought George's things. Practically steaming from the ears, he snatched them and stamped out of the parlor. A moment later, the front door slammed.

John let out a long breath. "I've never spoken to any of my family in that way."

"And it's due to me." Mary felt as if another black mark had been ticked up against her, even though George's attitude was undoubtedly insufferable.

"Yes."

He might have denied it, she thought. Or said more than that one stark word. "I'm sorry."

"When he attacked you, I could see how unreasonable he was being." John shook his head. "I suppose I'm used to being the family goat. But when George turned it on you, it was so clear…" He nodded as if acknowledging some obvious fact. "I should have spoken up long ago. I can't imagine now why I didn't." He moved his shoulders as if easing into a coat that fit him to perfection. "I could have been a bit more temperate…"

"I don't think George would have heard anything quieter," Mary suggested.

"No." John stood even straighter than usual. "I must say it felt rather…good." He met Mary's eyes and grinned. "Quite…extraordinarily good."

She smiled back, delighted.

"I daresay I shall have to apologize…"

"Not until your family admits that you are extremely intelligent and very well able to manage…anything," Mary insisted.

"That could be quite a long time," he said, still smiling.

"Well, they are great fools then."

John put an arm around her and led her back to the sofa. "I shan't be in a hurry to recant," he admitted as they sat down. "Now if only I had the plan I claimed just now."

"We could make one together." Filled with relief at his willingness to talk about it, Mary rushed on. "Eleanor...our neighbor, the dowager countess, is going to speak to Lady Castlereagh as soon as she's back in town. They are friends. She will have some influence."

"That is kind of her," John acknowledged.

Mary gathered her determination and went further. "It's even more than that, because Eleanor understands about my drawing. She said it's because it happens to her also, that drawings reveal things without her... purposefully setting them down."

"Reveal?" said John.

He looked puzzled but not annoyed as he had the last time she'd tried to tell him. Mary strove to call up Eleanor's words. She'd said it so well. "I learn and 'speak' with my hands. It's simply...a different way of dealing with information."

"I don't understand."

Mary groped for the right phrases. She so desperately wanted him to understand. "You get so much from reading," she tried.

"Of course."

"But it is not 'of course' for me," she told him, leaning forward in her urgency. "It is quite difficult. Sometimes...nothing goes into my mind from a printed page."

He frowned as if trying to imagine such a thing.

"But when I begin to draw…my hands know what to do…somehow…without my thinking about it. They express what…I might have noticed or sensed but have not understood."

John was still frowning but not angrily. "Are you talking about a kind of…intuition? Comprehending things without reasoning them through?"

"Yes, only it happens in a drawing."

He gazed at her. "Like an idea that just pops into your head out of nowhere…"

"Or shows in a picture without my planning it."

"It seems rather…odd." But he said the word as if he was trying to take in the thought, not as a criticism.

"So, that is what occurred when I drew Lady Castlereagh," Mary finished, to make certain he saw the whole.

"You can't help it?" he asked.

Mary quailed inside. It seemed she'd been urged to "help it" for most of her life. She shook her head.

John seemed bemused. "Well, perhaps our kind neighbor can explain that to her ladyship." He didn't sound convinced.

Was he skeptical about Eleanor's ability to explain or about what she had told him about herself? Mary wasn't certain. She longed to ask but wasn't sure she wanted to hear the answer.

"Meanwhile, I shall continue to search for information in Limehouse. There are indications that I may be onto something important."

"You'll find it, and the Foreign Office will see what a prize they have in you," Mary said.

"Indeed."

Was he humoring her? "Both our ideas will work," Mary insisted. "And things will go back to the way they were. Or...they will be even better. Your brothers will treat you with respect..."

"Don't ask for the moon." John laughed.

"Why not?" she demanded. She wanted so much, more than she could say just now.

"Never give up?"

"Never!"

Still laughing, he kissed her.

Sixteen

WHEN JOHN ARRIVED AT THE OFFICE THE NEXT MORN-
ing, he was surprised to find William Conolly entertaining a group of colleagues, including Fordyce,
in the corridor outside their room. The gathering
wasn't unprecedented. Foreign Office staff sometimes
lingered in clusters and chatted before settling to work.
It could be an efficient way of connecting important
facts that originated in different departments. But in
his present circumstances, it was a bit uncomfortable,
and he wished Conolly had found a different place to
hold forth. But there his friend leaned, against the wall
near their doorway; as always, he seemed polished and
at ease.

"Indeed," Conolly was saying as John passed, "Lady
Castlereagh is very proud of her menagerie."

John suppressed a wince at the lady's name and
walked through to his desk. As he reached for a report
to begin reading, Conolly's voice floated in.

"FO staff stationed abroad often send animals home
to her," he said. "I heard she was vastly pleased with the
tiger some chaps shipped from India a few years ago."

"That's the one that roars at everybody and tries to bite," said Fordyce. Whatever the topic and however ill-informed he might be, he always tried to sound as if he had special knowledge.

"How else is a tiger supposed to behave?" replied Conolly. "You wouldn't want a tiger that's tame as a pussycat. What's the point? I heard some lads in New Spain sent over an armadillo."

"What the devil is an armadillo?" asked one of his listeners.

"It's Spanish for 'little armored one,'" offered another.

"That fits," Conolly responded. "I think the thing's rather like a badger in chain mail. Ugly. But both the Castlereaghs were pleased with it, I believe. Jeffries insists the gift of an exotic creature is the way to their hearts."

John listened more closely as Conolly laughed to show this was a joke. He knew that laugh, and William's whole tone, come to think of it. His friend was up to something.

"I've heard her ladyship is longing for some special sort of monkey," Conolly added. He appeared in the office doorway, turning away from his audience. "Well, best get to work, hadn't we?" He came into the office and settled at his desk.

"What was that all about?" John asked.

"I'll tell you tonight."

"What's tonight?" John wondered.

"You'll see."

"Are you planning some prank? Involving Lady Castlereagh? This hardly seems a time to stir things up further…"

"Don't worry," interrupted Conolly with an airy gesture. "Would I do anything you didn't like?"

"Yes!"

Conolly put a hand to his chest. "You wound me. When have I ever…?"

"You put that sign on our door…"

"You were supposed to be out that afternoon," his friend protested. "You told me you would be."

"And Weeks came by while *you* were out—to 'Uniform Supply,' as evidenced by your grand sign—and asked me for his Foreign Office dress uniform."

Conolly struggled with a smile. "It was his first day on the job."

"So you simply had to give him a false chit for a powder blue coat and scarlet pantaloons." John felt his own lips turning upward.

"He actually *believed* we would all wear a rig like that on formal occasions." Conolly spread his hands, marveling.

"I can see how that would be irresistible." John had to smile.

"There you are then."

"What are you up to, William? With everything that's happened lately, you must tell me."

But Conolly wouldn't be drawn, no matter how John pressed him. His only response was a mysterious smile. Experience had taught John to view that particular expression with caution.

When the workday ended and John drew on his greatcoat, Conolly was right beside him. He walked with him out of the building and over to the livery where John stabled his horse during the day. "What are you doing?" John asked.

"Coming home with you" was the jaunty reply.

John stopped in the middle of the street. "Why? What's going on?"

Conolly laid a hand on his arm. "As soon as we get there. Trust me, John."

"Do I have an alternative?"

Conolly's laugh was so lighthearted that John had to join in.

At his house, John found Lady Caroline Lanford sitting with Mary in the parlor. One look at Mary's face told him she was as bewildered as he. John sent Kate off with their coats and closed the parlor door. "All right," he said. "Confess. What have you done, Conolly?"

"Is there some bad news?" asked Mary.

"Not at all," Conolly assured her.

"Then why…?"

"We have been discussing a variety of plans," Conolly went on. John frowned at him.

"You and John?" Mary said.

"Lady Caroline and I," was the reply.

"We are going to get revenge on Edmund Fordyce," said Caroline, green eyes sparkling.

"Revenge?" Mary leaned back on the sofa.

"We're not entirely sure how as yet," Conolly admitted. "That's why we have called a council."

"Council?" John looked from his colleague to his guest and back again.

"We've been thinking it should involve animals."

"Because they offer such tempting opportunities," added Caroline with an impish smile.

"Like the ferrets?" Mary said.

"Ferrets?" John wondered if he was going a bit

mad under the strain of the past week. "Why are you always linking Lady Caroline and ferrets?"

"Caroline trained a ferret to drop acorns on stuffy people at the dinner table," said Mary.

"What?" He could not have heard correctly.

"One went down a high-nosed lady's dress," Mary added.

"A ferret?" He struggled to picture it.

"An acorn." Mary laughed.

"Oh! If I had trained him to retrieve them…" began Lady Caroline.

John frowned at them both. "We are not introducing ferrets into…anywhere."

"No, no," replied Caroline. "Although…"

The sly expression on the girl's pretty face seemed ominous.

"…but no," she continued. "Ferrets are too common. Too English. All the animals in the Castlereaghs' menagerie are exotics."

"Menag…oh, she was talking about that at the party." Mary grimaced at the memory of that event. "She spoke about a…mockingbird that wouldn't sing. What is a mockingbird?"

"Any bird that overhears this ridiculous conversation," said John.

Lady Caroline wrinkled her nose at him. "Don't be stuffy. We've been trying to think of the perfect scheme. Fordyce is a toady at heart, so…"

"So we thought we would give him an irresistible opportunity to ingratiate himself with the Castlereaghs and make sure that it goes badly wrong," said Conolly.

"Perhaps with a monkey," Caroline added meditatively.

"A…monkey." John sat back and stared at them. His guests smiled winningly in response. Mary looked uncertain. "What in God's name would you do with a monkey?"

"Well, that is the question," Caroline replied with an encouraging nod. "That's what we've gathered to figure out."

"Don't we have enough trouble already?" John wondered. He'd never become directly involved in one of Conolly's schemes.

"I suppose monkeys can be quite…trainable?" said Mary.

"Did you hear me?"

"Of course," said Caroline to Mary, as if she hadn't. "Haven't you see them in their cunning little hats and jackets collecting coins for their masters?" She nodded reminiscently. "That's why we've nearly settled on a monkey. I was thinking of a crocodile, but it would be harder to procure. And Mr. Conolly said it wouldn't…"

"There will be no monkeys or crocodiles or elephants or creatures of any kind," John declared. His brain reeled with visions of chaos. "Fordyce isn't worth the trouble you might get into."

"No one will know who did it," Caroline said. As if it might be a reassurance, she added, "Mr. Conolly and I are quite good at pranks. Did you know that he once…?"

"Do you want to see me thrown out of the Foreign Office once and for all?" At last the room went quiet. They were all looking at him. John felt his cheeks redden. "We have been the subject of quite enough…

attention," he continued. He saw Mary's wince and regretted it, but he needed them to understand. "We are not going to manufacture another opportunity to be…singled out for criticism. Purposely."

Caroline's chin came up. Suddenly, she looked every inch the aristocrat. "You can't stop us from doing whatever we please."

"Caroline," said Mary. "If John does not wish you to…"

Conolly gazed at John. "Have my pranks ever truly damaged anyone, Bexley?"

John hesitated. The victims he could bring to mind had all seen the jest in the end. Even he, with his superfluous chair, had laughed. "Reynolds," he remembered.

Conolly nodded. "Ah, yes, Reynolds, who meant to…um…take advantage of that émigré girl who'd come for help in finding her parents."

Reynolds was a blackguard, John admitted silently. He'd more than deserved to be…curbed.

"We only mean to give Edmund Fordyce the *opportunity* to behave badly," Caroline wheedled. "He needn't do so. It is his free choice."

John's mind was a muddle. The impulse to risk warred with the fear of failure. A desire for justice clamored against the caution that had been drilled into him in his childhood. And through this churning indecision, he kept seeing the look on Mary's face when Lady Castlereagh snatched her drawing away from Fordyce. If Mary was involved in a scheme of revenge against Fordyce and he found out, he would turn on her like a poisonous snake. "No. I want to make a serious effort to come about from this recent… setback. Not indulge in…high jinks."

"How can you be so tedious…?"

Conolly interrupted Caroline's protest. "I understand." When Caroline started to argue, he held her eyes until she subsided. "I will escort you to your grandmother's house," he added. He took her arm and practically dragged her away.

When they'd gone, John and Mary sat down to a belated dinner. They ate in silence for a while, and then John said, "We have made our own plans. Fordyce is…a creeping nothing. He isn't worth a thought."

Mary nodded. "Although the thought of wiping that smug look off his face is tempting."

"He'll be quite downcast if I succeed."

Mary nodded. She looked wistful, but as John saw it, Conolly—and still worse the unpredictable Lady Caroline—threatened to bring her more pain, not less. It simply wasn't worth the risk.

෴

After dinner, John went up to his study for a while. Mary drifted into the front parlor, but she couldn't sit still. After poking the coals of the fire, straightening perfectly orderly cushions, and staring with loathing at her basket of mending, she gave up and went to her sitting room studio. So often in her life drawing had made her feel better. It had also made her feel many other things, of course. Drawing was her solace and her bane, her gift and her burden. She turned to it now, closing the curtains over dark windows, lighting lamps, sitting at the long table before her easel, holding a pencil, and waiting.

At first it seemed that inspiration had closed up shop for the day. Her hand did not move. To encourage the flow, Mary doodled along the edge of the paper—a flower, a bucket, a series of interlocking triangles. The next image turned into a monkey, creatures she'd seen only in pictures. She remembered the long limbs and tail, though, the projecting jaw and liquid eyes. Her monkey squatted in the corner of the page, hands on its knees.

When finished it was a creditable likeness of the breed, even charming, she thought. However, it had none of the resonance of her human portraits. Mary wasn't certain whether this was because her talent was limited to people or because she had no *particular* monkey in mind. They must have some individual characteristics. And one would never draw a generic "human being." She *had* once produced a portrait of Petra's cat that plumbed the depths of Tomasina's arrogance.

Her pencil moved on, outlining the little monkey in another pose. Then bold strokes swept into the center of the page, heralding a larger image. Wiry frame and furry tail, hands so like a person's—only this monkey's face emerged differently. It came out as a distorted version of Edmund Fordyce's long countenance. Mary's lips curved as her hand moved faster and added details. The man's hooded eyes fit right in; she went ahead and made them blue with a bit of chalk. Fordyce's sneering mouth appeared, lengthened into a simian snout. She gave the figure ears, flattened against the sides of the skull, and some incongruous tufts of yellow hair. With a soft laugh, she added shadows to a squashed nose, a furtive hunch to sinuous shoulders.

When she was done, she had a face and figure that screamed of low cunning and sly malice. She'd never done anything like this before—and it was an insult to the breed of monkeys—but she was thoroughly enjoying herself. She rubbed out some lines with her fingertips and began to sketch in a little costume, like the ones Caroline had mentioned. Soon, this version of Edmund Fordyce wore a frogged jacket and pipe-stem trousers; he held out a little cylindrical hat, begging for pennies.

"Mary?" called John's voice from outside the room. There was a knock at the door, and then he was looking around it. "There you are." He came in, holding a sheet of paper. "I found this…" He spotted the drawing on her small easel, and his eyes widened.

Mary put down her pencil and waited.

John took a step closer. His lips parted in astonishment. Then they curved up at the corners. His penetrating blue eyes started to sparkle. And he laughed.

It was a joyous, wholehearted laugh, the easiest she'd ever heard from her husband. And it went on, and on. Delighted, and a touch relieved, she joined in.

John pointed at the image. "The hair," he gasped and went off again. He laughed so hard that tears came to his eyes.

Mary laughed along with him, delighted by this evidence that her drawings could make him happy as well as cause trouble.

It was quite a while before John's mirth finally ran down, reduced to occasional chuckles. "I didn't know you drew caricatures," he said.

"I don't. I didn't. I suppose it was something about the conversation tonight…"

"The way he holds out the hat..." Laughter overtook John again. "How I wish I could hang that in my office for all to see," he said when he'd recovered again. "Can we even show Conolly, I wonder?" He shook his head. "Far too tempting for him. How he would relish it, though."

"I won't keep it," Mary replied.

"No, you must. We'll take it out when we feel low and laugh again." He grew more serious. "Don't show it to anyone else, though."

Mary nodded. Did he think she would be rushing out to show off her drawings, after the last time? "You said you'd found something?" she asked, pointing at the sheet of paper in his hand.

John looked down and seemed surprised to find it there. "Oh, yes. This...diagram was on my desk. Is it yours?"

Mary took it. "No, Arthur did this. It shows the workings of a steam engine."

"It does?" He gazed at the nest of lines scrawled over the page. "Why was it in my room?"

"He wanted to show it to you. I forgot." She'd been preoccupied with her own problems again, Mary thought. She'd overlooked Arthur's confidences. "He was eager to impress you, I believe," she added.

"With this?" John retrieved the paper and looked at it more closely. He turned it around to get another angle, frowning.

"He's quite knowledgeable about how the engines work."

"Indeed." The word vibrated with John's lack of interest in mechanics.

"He said something about not being able to find a proper adventure."

"Proper…?" This appeared to arrest his attention.

"He seemed rather downhearted," Mary went on. "And I forgot all about it. I've been so selfish, involved in my own concerns."

"Nonsense," John said.

"But I was. Arthur wanted to speak to…"

"He's probably forgotten all about this by now." John put the page on the table.

"I don't think he will have."

"I'll speak to him."

"I know you have a great deal on your mind, but it would be…"

"Don't worry, Mary, I will take care of you," he replied.

The tenderness in his eyes sent a tremor all through her. But she wanted to do her part, not simply be protected. "We'll care for each other," she said.

Then he took her in his arms and kissed her, and her reasoned arguments were lost in a flood of desire.

Seventeen

SEVERAL DAYS PASSED WITH NO MORE TALK OF MONKEYS, or of Edmund Fordyce. Routine took over and, with it, a measure of calm. Yet the shadow of disappointment lurked in the background. As Mary went through her days, a question constantly echoed in the recesses of her mind, "What else can I *do* to make things right for John?"

This preoccupation so distracted her that when she went out on Tuesday morning to replenish her supply of watercolor paints, she forgot her reticule. She had to turn back to fetch it. The artists' supply shop would give her credit, but she had other errands as well and needed her purse.

She let herself in quietly, not wishing to pause for household concerns. She had one foot on the stair to go up to her bedchamber, when she heard Lady Caroline Lanford's voice from the kitchen. Which was odd. Had Caroline come to visit and found her out? But why would she go downstairs?

Mary started for the basement steps.

"Have you mixed it up for me?" she heard Caroline say.

"I have, my lady," Kate's voice answered.

"And it will turn hair lighter with…umm…no ill effects to the skin?"

Mary frowned, confused. Caroline's hair was already a lovely golden blond.

"Yes, my lady, as long as you remove it after twenty minutes."

"Twenty minutes," Caroline repeated. "And… umm…if someone was to eat it?"

Mary stopped on the stairs, startled.

"Eat it?" Kate sounded incredulous, as well she might.

"Accidentally," said Caroline.

"Well, they'd better not, nor get it in their eyes either. You have to take some care with this mixture."

Kate would never learn tact, Mary thought. Her tone made it plain that she thought the inquiry idiotic. It certainly was odd.

"Of course," said Caroline.

Mary went on down the stairs. When she reached the kitchen she found Mrs. Tanner stirring a pot on the stove. Kate was standing nearby, next to Caroline, who held a small bottle of pale liquid. Arthur sat at the long wooden table, clutching a lidded basket on his lap.

All eyes swiveled to Mary. "Hello," she said.

"Oh!" said Caroline. "I thought you were…that is, I came by to get one of Kate's marvelous concoctions." She held up the bottle, then thrust it at Arthur, who put it in the basket.

Mary looked from her to the boy, and back.

"I've been helping…" he began.

Caroline cut him off. "Arthur has been kind enough to accompany me and carry my purchases today." She reached for the basket handle. "Thank you very much, Arthur. I can take them across the square."

Arthur held on. "But you said I could go along with you to...finish up."

"I mustn't keep you from your work any longer." Caroline lifted the basket.

Mrs. Tanner snorted and muttered something about Arthur not knowing the meaning of work.

"But...won't you stay a while, have some tea?" Mary wondered.

"Grandmamma will be expecting me," Caroline replied and headed for the steps.

Mary looked at Kate, who gazed blandly back. She looked at Mrs. Tanner, who was tasting the broth from her pot. "What was that about?"

"Her ladyship wanted a hair dye," Kate answered.

"For a friend of hers," Arthur said. "Have we got any of them scones left, Mrs. Tanner?"

"No, 'we' do not," grumbled the cook. "You ate the last one this morning, Sir Greedyguts. That stomach of yours is a bottomless pit."

"I'm growing," Arthur declared hopefully.

Mrs. Tanner snorted again. "Well, grow into the scullery and finish scrubbing out the pots. I set a pan of hot water by the basin."

"Yes'm." Arthur jumped up and went out.

At least he seemed more reconciled to his job here, Mary thought. "It was kind of Lady Caroline to give you a commission," she said to Kate.

The maid merely nodded.

"I think El...the dowager countess might be kind enough to offer her patronage as well."

This would give Kate a great advantage, should she become…associated with the Jenkins apothecary, Mary thought.

"Yes…ma'am. She has said she would."

Once again, Kate was ahead of her. But what precisely was going on? "Have you taken any more concoctions to Mr. Jenkins's shop?"

"Just this and that."

"'This and that,'" repeated her mother grumpily. "She's brewing and straining until she hardly has time for her proper work. And in *my* way with the doing of it."

Mary retreated from yet another quarrel between them. As she passed the scullery doorway, she paused to say, "Mr. Bexley was quite impressed by your drawing of the steam engine, Arthur." It wasn't untrue. John had found the diagram noteworthy, though he hadn't been much interested in the subject.

"That's good," said Arthur, up to his elbows in suds.

He didn't seem nearly as pleased as Mary had expected.

Feeling somehow superfluous in her own house, Mary walked up the stairs, fetched her reticule, and resumed her interrupted errands.

❧

Hearing Fordyce's voice in the corridor up ahead, John turned to find a different route out of the Foreign Office building. He required some sustenance this early afternoon, but he didn't care to encounter the idiot. "Well worth the investment," he heard Fordyce say. And then he was out of earshot.

When he returned to the office, Conolly was back.

He'd been out on some errand for the morning. "What have you done to yourself?" John wondered. Conolly's left hand was wrapped in gauze, and his right boasted a long red scratch.

"Oh," was the reply. "Got an aunt with a tabby built like a Russian bear. Vicious thing."

"Is that where you were? It attacked you?"

"Whenever you visit, she insists you pet the blasted creature. And then wrings a peal over your head when it shreds your hand." Conolly made a wry face and spoke in a high piping voice. "'What have you done to poor puss, you great brute? I'm sure she wouldn't scratch you if you were gentler with her.'" He shook his head. "Cat just sits there looking smug."

John laughed.

Conolly sat down, letting his bandaged hand drop behind his desk. "Did you see the report from Hansen? I thought he was onto something."

"No." John looked down at the piles of documents before him.

"I put it there on top. You should take a look."

"Right." They fell to work in their customary easy rhythm. John was lulled, comforted by the details of his work. There was no upheaval among his papers, whatever mayhem they might report. He could study and analyze them with measured care. This familiar world was a kind of retreat from worries and plans.

When he had made his way through the pile, he turned to the private notes he had accumulated over his visits to the London slums. They still amounted to little more than hints and implications. And his sources continued to dry up. People were more evasive. They threw looks over their shoulders and retreated from conversations.

His guide Henry Tsing was restless as well. On their last foray, he'd said, "You don't live anywhere near Limehouse. You go off to your safe life and leave me here among them." Which was perfectly true. And all of it suggested that some new factor had entered Limehouse and was causing a change in his reception. He wanted, needed, to discover what it was. But the more he pushed, the more people resisted.

He riffled through the notes again. He had to find a way to discover more or his grand plan was going to come to nothing. He was set to go out tonight. He'd persuaded Henry, with great difficulty. This trip must yield some progress. John shoved the pages into a drawer and returned to his regular work.

❧

When she went down to the kitchen to let Mrs. Tanner know that John would not be home for dinner, Mary found Jeremiah Jenkins there, looking very much at home at the wide wooden table, with a cup of tea before him. He stood at once when she appeared. "Ma'am."

"Mr. Jenkins."

"I've just brought some attar of rose for Kate."

With his use of the maid's first name, Mary was not much surprised when Kate turned from the large pot she was stirring to say, "We're getting married." She was smiling, eyes bright, but otherwise she seemed much like her customary self.

"Ah." Mary wondered how this had come about.

There'd been so little sign that a connection had been formed. "I'm very happy for you. Both."

"Thank you…ma'am."

Mary suppressed a smile at that last reluctant word. Kate would no longer have to exert herself to defer to a mistress. She wondered if the young woman would find it easier to cater to customers at the apothecary shop. Probably she would, as they would be holding out their hands with payment.

"I'll have to give in my notice," Kate added. Steam had curled stray strands of her blond hair about her face, and she pushed one back.

Mary tried to look suitably regretful, though it would be a positive pleasure to replace Kate with someone who was glad of the position and better at it.

"I figured I'd stay a month, so's you can find someone else. And I can train her up, like."

So her staff troubles weren't completely over, Mary thought, foreseeing many rough spots in that process. "Thank you," she said. "That's very thoughtful. But if you would like to go sooner, I would not wish to…"

Kate took the gratitude as her due. "The rooms above the shop need a deal of fixing up," she replied, revealing a more likely reason for the delay than goodness of heart. "We've all sorts of plans for the place."

"Indeed." Mary's heart sank a little at the prospect of a month's perturbations. Kate would be preoccupied with the details of her new life and probably more difficult than ever over her household tasks. Though it was, of course, nice to see her happily settled.

"I'm installing a double-sized closed range in the back premises of my shop," put in Mr. Jenkins.

"Plenty of space for Kate's work." He gazed at his fiancée with pride.

"No more taking up space on my stove," said Mrs. Tanner. She looked as pleased as her pinched features could manage.

"We'll have a distiller as well," replied Kate. "*Our* shop will stock only the best."

If Mr. Jenkins noticed the changed emphasis, he gave no sign. "I must get back. I don't wish to miss any customers. And the carpenter is working in the upstairs rooms."

"Make sure he sets that new window just where we marked," Kate commanded.

With a nod, Mr. Jenkins took himself off. He showed no signs of realizing that a new power ruled in his household and that the days of his sovereignty were ended. Or perhaps he knew and was glad of it. Mary hoped so.

Eighteen

MARY STOOD IN THE DARKNESS OF THE GARDEN IN THE middle of the square and pulled her cloak more tightly around her. The night was cold, but she had a thick shawl under her cloak as well as a wool scarf tied about her head and fur-lined boots and gloves. The chill was endurable. Her determination made it easier to ignore.

As the minutes dragged into an hour, and part of another, she rubbed her hands together to keep her fingers supple. She knew John wouldn't like what she was doing. But she'd thought and thought about it and considered the risks. She'd planned it all out very carefully.

She leaned down and checked the dark lantern sitting on the ground beside her. It had taken her some effort to procure it, and she had spent time learning exactly how to work it as well. All she needed was the opportunity. She knew she would only have one. If she botched it, there would be no other chance. She strained her ears in the silence.

At last, when she had begun to shiver with the cold, she caught the sound of footsteps coming along the lane that led into the square. Silently, Mary bent and picked up the lantern. After a moment, she spotted John walking briskly along with his own simpler light swinging at his side. Mary looked away to avoid being dazzled by the beam of his small lantern. Her eyes had fully adapted to the darkness.

John moved across the square and paused before their door, getting out his key. He unlocked it and went in.

Now was the moment. Mary scanned the darkness. She'd posted herself near the place where the shadow following John had crouched the last time she'd seen it. She stood perfectly still, staring and listening. There was no sound. Wait. There was a tiny scrape of boot on the cobbles. It she hadn't been motionless and straining her ears, she wouldn't have heard it. Mary took hold of the dark lantern's catch. Scarcely breathing, she waited.

A shadow left the shelter of the street leading into the square, slipped across, and stopped not too far from her hiding place. All its attention was on the house as John passed the lighted parlor window. Mary took a breath, made sure her lantern was centered on the spot, and pulled back the panel. Light erupted, sending a shaft of illumination through the bars of the fence and washing over the watcher. Startled, the figure turned. Mary blinked away dazzlement and got a good look. Not tall. Cloaked. But clearly the shoulders of a man. From within the cloak's hood, an Asian face snarled at her.

Mary willed her hand not to shake. She kept the light on the man and stared, determined to memorize every detail of his face.

With a spring like a great cat, the man rushed at her, crashing against the wrought iron spears of the fence. Mary stumbled back a step. The lantern beam wavered. She steadied it on him. He leaped, but the spiked tips were still three feet above his clawing fingers, well out of reach. Landing in a crouch, he gripped the bars and shook them violently, but they didn't yield. He glared at her again, then turned and hurried away.

Mary shifted the lantern's beam to follow him across the square and over to the street entry. She held it there, waiting to be sure he was really gone, listening with all her might. He was making no effort to be silent now. Rushing footsteps receded without pause. She waited a bit longer to be certain he was gone, before letting herself out of the garden and running to the house. All the way, she kept the lantern open, scanning the empty street.

She'd barely gotten the front door open when John pounced. "Where have you been? I looked everywhere. No one knew where you were!"

"John, I saw the man…"

He gripped her shoulders and shook her slightly. "How could you go out alone, at night? Haven't I told you…? Where have you *been*?"

"I have to draw him!"

"Draw who? Now? What are you talking about?"

"You don't understand. I saw…"

"No! I don't. Do *you* understand how worried I was? Searching the house, not finding you anywhere. The servants with no idea…"

"The man following you, I saw him." Mary

wriggled out of his grip. She wanted to get to her easel and record the face she'd seen. Impatient, she jerked off her gloves and the scarf around her head and pulled at the fastening of her cloak.

"Mary." At his tone, she turned. His face was stony. "You cannot worry me this way. Haven't I enough to bear with…?"

"But if we find out who this man is…the one following you…"

"No one is following me! It's over, Mary."

His voice chilled her more than the night's vigil. "What is over?"

John made a throwaway gesture. "Creeping about the slums…playing spy, imagining…adventures like a silly schoolboy. It's all come to nothing. Tonight, no one would talk to us. They've closed ranks." He gave a short, humorless laugh. "Even in Limehouse, I am snubbed."

"You can try…"

He shook his head. "You don't understand. My guide and I were threatened. With knives."

Mary put a frightened hand on his arm.

"Something roused suspicions against us. I don't know if it was my manner or a stray remark…" He shook his head. "It doesn't matter. Suspicions are enough in a place like that. The word has spread. I can't go back to Limehouse—not without a platoon of soldiers at my back, which would rather defeat the purpose. I must face it. My plan has failed. I won't be uncovering vital information in the depths of London." He walked into the parlor. Anxious, Mary followed.

"Not everyone is cut out to shine," he added, going

to stand by the fire. "How could they be? There must be a mass of…others for them to shine against."

"You *do* shine," Mary insisted. "You're…brilliant…"

His answering smile was distant. "And there, perhaps, is the key to contentment. Think of the wives in houses across the city who believe exactly that about hosts of quite ordinary men. Are they not happy with a quiet, undistinguished life?"

"You are not ordinary!" Hot now, Mary thrust off her cloak and the shawl beneath and let them fall to the floor. "You can't just give up. I tell you I've seen…"

"Come over to the fire. We'll have a glass of wine." He took her hands and seemed surprised to find that they were not cold.

"Why will you not *listen* to me?" In her frustration, Mary pulled her hands free and grasped his coat lapels. She gazed up into his blue eyes. "It must mean something important that you were followed…"

He captured her hands again, dropping a kiss on one of them. "It's kind of you to…"

"I'm not being kind!" Would a sharp blow to his midsection make him pay attention?

"We'll sit by the fire a while and talk of more pleasant things," John replied, as if they spoke entirely different languages. He slipped an arm around her. "And in a little while, *do* more pleasant things. That should be enough for any man."

"John." Mary let him pull her to the sofa and draw her down, marshaling her thoughts. She must find the right words to get through to him, to convey what she'd seen. Why was he being so infuriating? He almost seemed like another man. Or… Mary looked in his eyes as they sat side by side. He was rather like the earlier version of himself that she hadn't seen since their honeymoon, she realized. It was as if that mild, distant fellow had returned and was in charge once more. His detached manner was back, the sense that he didn't really hear, that the deepest part of him would always be veiled.

She felt a flash of panic. She didn't want that man! She didn't want the trivial, unexciting life he offered. She'd fallen deeply in love with the new John, and she intended—longed—to spend the rest of her life with him. She had to get him back. How could she get him back?

She needed to think, but that was hardly possible when John was drawing her close, murmuring her name, kissing her. In this, at least, he hadn't lost himself. Her train of thought was disintegrating with the distraction of his touch. She had to push him away.

He drew back, surprised.

"After the last time I saw someone following you, I bought a dark lantern," Mary said. She realized she hadn't extinguished it; it was sitting on the floor in the entryway. She must do that. "I made sure I knew precisely how it worked." She spoke slowly, clearly, repeating the experience in her mind, demanding his attention.

John frowned. As she'd hoped, the minute detail seemed to sink in.

"I stationed myself inside the garden fence, near where the shadow had been before, and I waited, with the lantern closed."

"In the dark…"

"And the cold. You came home and went in. After a few minutes, the other man crept into the square."

John's gaze was fixed on her face. At last, he was truly listening.

"He stopped by the fence. I opened the lantern and saw him. He looked Chinese." Mary shivered a little at the memory of his snarl, the way he'd lunged at her. "He was *very* angry at being caught in the lantern beam."

"Angry?"

"Furious. He was not someone out for a walk, John. Or lost in an unfamiliar district. He was watching you through the parlor window."

John's eyes narrowed. "But I took great care, each time I left Limehouse, to make certain I was alone."

"He was amazingly silent," Mary told him, "and stealthy. I never would have gotten a look at him if I hadn't lain in wait. With the lantern."

"That was very clever."

Mary basked in his approval and in relief at seeing the calculating intelligence back in his face.

"This could be—must be—the person I've been hearing about in Limehouse for some time," John said slowly. "And he is probably the reason the place is closed to me now."

Mary nodded. She didn't know exactly what he meant, but she was delighted to see him back to his "new" self.

"Why?" he went on, as if thinking aloud. "Why follow and why shut me out? Because I was about to discover something important?"

"Yes," said Mary. She didn't mind now that he

was lost in his own thoughts. The tone of them was completely different.

"But how to find him again?" John wondered. "I don't think he'll come back here, after being caught like this."

"I'll draw him," Mary said. "I can give you a good likeness."

Her husband turned to look at her. "But I thought you saw him for only a few moments."

"That doesn't matter."

He looked appreciative but a bit doubtful. "That would be helpful."

Mary was filled with a fierce desire to help and to show him what she could do.

"He's been extremely elusive," John went on. "A 'presence' talked of in Limehouse but not seen. Clearly, he's well able to hide."

"We'll find him," Mary vowed.

It had grown very late. Mary put out the dark lantern on the way upstairs to bed. Once there, she put her belief in him, her confidence and love, into the touch of her hands, the pliancy of her lips. She assured him, in every way she could imagine, that he was masterful and desirable and all would be well.

❦

Though she itched to get to her sketchbook, she wanted daylight, not the wavering shadows of candles, to draw the face she'd seen in the garden. This must be the most accurate portrait she'd ever produced.

And so she forced herself to lie still as the hours of the night passed. She breathed, willing her agitation to ease. And slowly, slowly, it did. The silence of the house, the warmth of her husband's body next to her, and a dragging tide of fatigue finally combined to lull her. And sometime in the respite of that oblivion she wrapped herself around John, holding him like a rare treasure, so that the first words she heard the following day were, "Mary, let go."

She blinked awake and found John gently tugging her arms from his chest and easing his legs from under the one she'd flung over him. He loosed her clutching fingers and pressed a kiss on them before setting her hands on the coverlet. "I'm sorry to wake you," he said.

But she was glad to be roused. She sat up and reached for him again, touching his stubbled cheek and murmuring his name. He smiled and took her hands briefly again before slipping free. He climbed out of bed, away from her. "I must go."

"I'm going to draw the person right away." He nodded. She threw back the covers and rose.

An hour later, Mary sat before her sketchbook, pencil in hand, concentrating, demanding inspiration. Drawing was her lifeblood. It came as naturally as her breath. But this morning, that didn't seem the case. The page remained stubbornly blank. No portrait had ever been so important. Why could she not begin? The fate, the happiness, of the man she loved hung on her skill.

The hand she'd raised to the page trembled a bit. Mary went still, breathed, and waited for the pencil to move, as it always did. And waited. Time ticked past. Her pulse accelerated; her throat grew tight. She'd never had to try so hard to draw. Her hand could not have lost its innate ability. That wasn't it. She was anxious. That was all. In a moment, it would come.

Mary leaned in, put the tip of the pencil to the paper. A small black dot appeared. But nothing followed. Very well, if inspiration wouldn't descend, she would coax it to life. Mechanically, she laid down the folds of a cloak, sketched the hood with a blank oval within, put in the suggestion of the fence, recreating the general outline of what she'd seen in the lantern beam.

A knock came on the door, and Kate entered before she could speak. Mary stifled a curse. "I really mustn't be disturbed…"

"The servant said this was important." She held out a folded note.

Even in her frustration, Mary felt a flash of amusement at the way Kate said, "the servant." Clearly, she no longer saw herself in that category, and just as clearly, the change pleased her no end. Mary unfolded the note and found a summons from Eleanor.

She wanted to set it aside and push on with her work, but her neighbor said she had important news. With a sigh, Mary stood.

Grudging the precious minutes required to don hat and cloak and gloves, she made ready, then hurried downstairs. She was surprised to find Arthur struggling to open the front door. He had a large, obviously heavy basket hooked over one arm. It seemed almost more than he could carry. "What have you got there?" she asked.

The boy jumped and cried out. The basket tilted and two apples and a turnip bounced from under the cloth laid over the top.

One apple rolled across the floor to her feet. Mary bent to retrieve it.

"Don't bother yourself with that, ma'am," said Arthur, his voice unusually high. "I'll pick them up."

Puzzled, and a bit suspicious, Mary stepped over to return the fruit to its place. The basket was piled with various fruits and vegetables, she discovered. And nothing else. She looked down at Arthur. He *was* always hungry, but these were hardly his favorite foods. "What are you doing?"

"An...I'm..."

"Have you taken these from the kitchen?" Mrs. Tanner would make a great fuss. How had he even gotten this haul past her?

"No!" declared Arthur.

Mary waited. "You know you can eat as much as you wish," she added finally. "If you are not getting enough..."

"Ain't for me," the boy interrupted. "They're... they're for a charity, like."

"Charity?" Mary was utterly mystified.

"Lady Caroline is sending them to...somebody who needs 'em." Arthur's voice strengthened as he went on. "She asked me to help, like. She's that busy."

"A gift for the poor?" Why should Caroline employ Arthur on such a mission?

"Poor. Right. No money at all." He nodded and spoke even faster. "Her ladyship was asking about my family, see. And I told her how Pa wanted me to learn my lesson, because of that chicken and all." He gave Mary a wide-eyed look.

The oddities in his story tugged at her. But

other concerns pulled harder at her attention. "You shouldn't go into poor areas of the city alone," she said. "It's not Limehouse, is it?" she added sharply.

Arthur shook his head. "Never heard of that. This place is all right. I been there before."

She stood looking down at him. "Do you promise me that you are not up to some mischief?"

The boy gazed limpidly back. "Just doing as Lady Caroline asked me, ma'am." He opened the door. "For a good cause, she says." He scooted out.

"Well, be careful," Mary called after him. By the time she reached the pavement, he was already halfway to the street out of the square. She told herself she would have to make further inquiries and discover exactly what he was up to.

❧

"I saw Lady Castlereagh last night," Eleanor said as soon as Mary joined her in her parlor. The old woman was alone; there was no sign of Caroline.

Had two weeks really passed? Mary made the calculation and realized they had.

"And all is…well."

Mary's pulse accelerated with hope. "You don't sound certain," she replied as she sat down.

Eleanor frowned. "Perhaps I should say, all appears to be well for you and John. The drawing is…forgotten? Not that, but I've been assured that it will not be held against your husband or affect his chances at the Foreign Office in any way."

Mary waited for the flood of relief, but she didn't quite feel it. "Something in your tone leaves me uneasy."

Eleanor shook her head, seemed to consider. "I know I can speak to you in confidence, Mary, and trust you not to gossip about Emily Castlereagh…"

"You can," said Mary.

Her neighbor still hesitated, yet it seemed as if she wished to confide.

"I don't know anybody to gossip *to*," Mary added. "I'm not acquainted with anyone in her circle." Well, except William Conolly, Mary supposed. But she wouldn't tell him or indeed anyone.

Eleanor smiled briefly, then gave a nod of decision. "Your drawing had much truth in it, I think. As they so often do. Emily is quite troubled, underneath. I think it has to do with Robert, her husband."

The stately foreign secretary, John's ultimate superior, must have many concerns weighing on him, Mary thought.

"She gave me the impression that he's been depressed in spirits. She didn't say anything outright, you know. It was all implication. I think he doesn't like being hated."

"Who could?" Mary said.

Her neighbor nodded. "Since those terrible killings at Peterloo in August…well, I'm sure it's been difficult. Robert is obliged to support Lord Sidmouth in suppressing dissent."

"Sending soldiers into the countryside to stop the weavers rioting," Mary said. Some had begun to protest the ferocity of Lord Sidmouth, the government's home secretary.

"Byron wrote that mean-spirited satire, and even though he's run off to Italy, it seems this fellow Shelley has done another, even worse. And the financial panic in America is threatening to spill over onto…" Eleanor stopped and sighed. "Well, as you can see, Emily ran on a bit. I suppose she may be regretting it now. But in all this, your drawing is…rather insignificant. It was just the moment of exposure, I believe, that overset her. She's recovered and does not hold a grudge."

Now came the relief. Mary reached out a hand. "Thank you so much for seeing her."

Eleanor squeezed her fingers, nodding. "I'm glad I did. I shall go back, I think. Since I live so 'out of the world' now, perhaps she will feel she can talk to me and…ease her worries a little."

Eleanor was a truly kind person, Mary thought. And she was glad to know that a bit of good might come out of her social misstep.

Though eager now to get back to her sketch pad, Mary stayed a little longer, chatting. When she inquired about Caroline, Eleanor said that her granddaughter was out shopping. "Is Caroline much involved in charitable endeavors?" she had to ask.

"Char…? Good works? Caroline?" The old woman cocked her head. "Not that I am aware of. Why do you ask?"

"Arthur said he was helping her with some food donations."

"Really? How…gratifying."

"She didn't mention anything to you?"

Eleanor shook her head. They gazed at each other in mutual puzzlement. But neither had any more information to offer.

❧

Arthur was still gone when Mary returned home. It was eleven by the time she settled to her drawing again, and she no sooner picked up her pencil than Mrs. Tanner appeared at her door. She insisted that they discuss the upcoming changes in the household. After a while, Mary gathered that she feared she would have no say in choosing a new maid. Once she was reassured on that front, she finally went away. Mary locked the door behind her.

Sitting, she stared at the rough oval within the hood that she'd set down earlier. She closed her eyes and recalled the face that belonged there. She could see it. The image was as vivid as any she'd drawn in the past. She put a few lines on the page, a hint of eyebrows, a nose, a curve of jaw. But there was no life to it. It was the suggestion of a face rather than a portrait.

She sat still and summoned her abilities. She wanted more than anything to help John. Nothing came.

Mary stayed before her easel for hours, but try as she might, she could not transfer the vision, so clear in her mind, to the page. At a certain point, fear started to make the process even more difficult. Her special kind of drawing had been at the center of her existence for years and years. She couldn't imagine what life would be like without it.

Nineteen

JOHN WAS WORKING HIS WAY THROUGH A CONVOLUTED description of the escalating political tensions between Siam and Burma when he heard voices in the corridor outside his office. It sounded like…but it couldn't be. He half rose in his chair. And Frederick and George strode in, accompanied by a junior clerk. "Your brothers to see you, sir?" said the latter. His tone suggested he wished to verify the visitors' bona fides.

What were they doing here? John stood and nodded to the clerk. He departed.

Frederick looked around at the stacks of paper and well-used furnishings. "This is where you work, then?" Neither his tone nor his expression suggested approval.

"Is there anything wrong at home?" John asked.

"Not at *home*," replied George.

John's spirits sank. "This is my colleague, William Conolly," he said. "My brothers Frederick and George."

His brothers nodded as if Conolly was a negligible person. "I've made a special trip down here to set things in order," said Frederick. "Shall we get to it?" He looked around as if deciding where to sit.

"Things?" echoed John.

"The muddle you've made." Frederick moved toward John's desk chair. Conolly looked puzzled.

John snatched up his coat and hat. "This is not the place to discuss family business." He walked out before they could reply, forcing his brothers to follow.

He took them to an inn nearby; it had a number of comfortable private parlors that were often used for Foreign Office meetings, and he was easily able to procure one. He ordered ale as well, suspecting that he was going to need fortification.

"All right," said Frederick, throwing himself into a chair. "I've come all this way, at a most inconvenient time, I might add, to offer you a position on the estate."

This made no sense to John. "What estate?"

"My estate," his eldest brother answered, as if speaking to a half-wit. "The family estate."

"Why would I want...?"

"Mama wants you back home," said George. "We can't have you embarrassing the family and alienating important people. What if we need to ask the government for a favor at some point? What about Roger's chances abroad?"

"You can be my steward," said Frederick. "Though I already have an extremely competent steward," he added under his breath.

"Work for you?" He'd rather slit his throat, John thought.

"It won't be too difficult." Frederick nodded as if assuring himself of some point and murmured, "I shall keep Dobbs on."

"This is what you really think of me then?" said John.

His brothers looked at him as if they didn't understand the question.

"Nothing I accomplish will ever change your minds, will it?"

"Mama doesn't think the present muddle is entirely your fault," replied Frederick kindly.

As usual, he didn't seem to have heard John's actual words.

"She knows it's mostly due to that wife of yours," George said. "Mama sent along her apologies for introducing you to such a pushing, managing female."

Frederick nodded. "George says you've become erratic and abusive under her influence."

John felt as if his head might explode. Yet even in the depths of his rage, he recognized echoes of phrases he'd flung at Mary when he first arrived home. It was hard to recall how angry he'd been then that she wasn't the Mary his mother had chosen for him: submissive, quiet, empty-headed, boring. Thank God she'd changed! He wouldn't have that Mary back under any circumstances, he realized.

"John? Are you listening?" Frederick assumed a look of benevolence. "Everything will be all right. Don't worry." He spoke as if to a child.

How could an idea of kindness be so wrongheaded? John wondered. "Do not speak of Mary in that way ever again," he said. "Tell Mama I said so."

Frederick reared back in surprise. George nodded as if to say, *See?*

"I am not leaving my position at the Foreign Office," John continued. "And if you try to make trouble for me there, I will protest in ways that you will *not* relish." John disliked speaking to his brothers so harshly, but they couldn't seem to hear more reasonable statements.

"Didn't I tell you?" said George to Frederick. "He's lost all sense of what's owed…"

"I've lost nothing," John interrupted, "except the willingness to be considered a failure."

"No one used the word…" Frederick began.

"They simply thought and implied it." Leaving his untouched mug of ale on the table, John rose. "Let this be the last such conversation between us. I don't want—or need—your interference in my life."

"What are we to say to Mama?" George looked scandalized.

"Give her my love, and tell her the same."

"You'll find you're sorry when you come to ask for our help," Frederick declared.

"I shan't. Ask." John turned and left the parlor.

Through the walk back to his office and the first hour or so after, he sustained himself on outrage. But gradually, the anger faded, and other emotions came to the fore. He'd made his point most forcibly and perhaps alienated his entire family. His position wasn't wrong. He stood by it. But it was…lonely. If only they would *listen*…

At this point, his treacherous mind insisted on evoking memories of the many good times he'd had with his brothers, the countless loving actions of his mother and his late father as well. They did care for him. He knew that. His mother would be wounded by his curt message. He could imagine her sad, bewildered eyes only too well, and the thought made him wince. But then she would see his reaction as just another mistake. His family's expectations were like a net that it seemed he couldn't escape no matter how he cut and flailed.

John set off home with a stew of emotions churning inside. Mary was the only one who believed in him. But if only your wife believed in you, what did that say about your place in the world?

❦

The moment John walked in that evening Mary shared her news. "Eleanor went to visit Lady Castlereagh," she replied. "She promised that my drawing will not be held against you." She repeated her afternoon conversation, minus the parts she'd promised to keep secret. When she was done, he nodded. "Good," he said and held his hands out to the heat of the fire. "I'm grateful to the dowager countess. I will tell her so at the first opportunity."

He seemed rather glum this evening. Mary put aside her own anxiety and tried to cheer him up. "So…the scandal is finished?"

He looked at her over his shoulder. "You've done very well."

"Then why aren't you celebrating?" she wondered.

"It is to be overlooked. It won't be forgotten."

"I don't understand."

"I'm very glad the Castlereaghs are mollified. Very thankful for it, Mary, truly. But such…tittle-tattle leaves a trace. Others in the office will remember."

"But if Lord Castlereagh isn't angry with you, he would tell them not to…"

"Subordinates don't always ask. They make their own judgments about what their superiors would like and act accordingly."

"But then you could go to him and…"

"No. That would make things much worse." John sat on the sofa and beckoned. "But it is good news, and I thank you for it."

Mary sat beside him. He looked tired, she noticed. Or, more than tired. "Did you have a difficult day?"

His short laugh was mirthless. "Yes."

"What happened?"

He shook his head, gazing into the fire. "There's no need to talk about it. Indeed, I'd rather not."

Silence fell over the parlor. Mary waited, and dreaded, an inquiry about her drawing of the man in the square. Minutes ticked past, and it did not come. Finally, she had to say, "I did not…manage to do the portrait today."

"Umm?" He sounded as if his mind had come back from a great distance.

"I will try…I will do it tomorrow." The image would come, Mary insisted silently.

"Portrait?"

"Of the man who was following you."

"Oh." John brightened. "Of course. I was thinking earlier today that we could send his likeness to a man in Limehouse who has been very helpful to me. He knows a great many people, and I think he would be willing to show it to some of them."

Mary nodded.

"Solid information is the thing." He sat straighter. "That is the whole point, after all. And it will make a far greater difference, in all ways, than rumors and insinuation." He seemed to notice her worried expression. "Not that I am belittling your friend's help with Lady Castlereagh."

To Mary's relief, Kate came in and announced dinner. John rose and moved toward the parlor door. "Shall we go right in? I'm famished." The thought of taking action had energized him, Mary saw. She would have been delighted, if only she had the drawing to give him. But she would have—tomorrow.

"Mary? Aren't you hungry?" John asked, waiting by the door.

Her stomach was too knotted up for her to tell. But she rose and followed him into the dining room.

"I am remembering what you told me about the way you draw," he said when they had begun to eat. "How you capture the character of the…subject. It should make identifying this man much easier."

His kindly tone only worsened her dilemma, Mary thought. It was like a dream come true that had twisted into a nightmare. How often had she longed for recognition of her work as her mother complained of it? How it had stung when people had gossiped about the portrait of Lady Castlereagh, whispering that she only wished to attract attention to herself—undeserved attention.

Now John was eager for a drawing, respectful of her skills, and she could not produce one. The images that had poured out of her—even when she didn't want them to—had run dry. No. No, they had not. She'd been tired today and continually interrupted. It was just one day. She'd have it for him when he came home tomorrow.

"Don't you think?" John said.

"What?"

"Is something wrong?"

"No."

He smiled at her. "I've bored you, going on and on about Siam. I'm sorry."

"No, you haven't. I'm very interested in your work." And hadn't heard a word as he spoke of it. It was a bitter pill that she must pretend with him just when circumstances offered an opportunity to grow closer.

❧

When she was sure John was asleep, Mary slipped from bed and quietly put on her warm dressing gown and slippers. Rest was far from her tonight. Silently, she moved through the dark house, so different from its daylight self. In her studio she built up the fire, which had died to a few coals, and lit candles. Placing tapers on either side of her easel, she settled at the table and placed her sketch pad there.

The outline of the cloak with its empty hood stared back at her like a stubborn phantom. Mary picked up a pencil and held it poised over the image. No impulse moved her. Biting her lip, she thought, Perhaps it could be like a push to a waterwheel to get things moving. She made herself add a few folds to the garment and some detail to the spear points of the fence.

But it was no good. The face remained a vacant oval within the cloak's hood.

Start again then. Perhaps there was something off about this attempt. She'd gone wrong in a way she couldn't see. She turned to a fresh page in the sketchbook.

To her immense relief, her hand moved at once, and she began to draw. The strokes were quick and certain, bold and stark. But the face that formed under her hand wasn't the man from the square. It was her own, as clearly as looking in the dressing table mirror.

"No, No, No," said Mary. She seldom drew herself, and less often as she'd grown up. It seemed... vain or indulgent. But she was given no choice. Her hand continued to move as it would, creating a self-portrait without pity. Dark circles and lines of tension appeared around her eyes. There was an unhappy downturn to her mouth.

After an unknown length of time, her fingers went still, and Mary sat there, tired and frustrated. She should be glad of this evidence that her talent wasn't dead. And she was, she supposed, although she hadn't truly believed that. But she was annoyed that she couldn't command it. She'd drawn William Conolly when she wished to. Why couldn't she create the image she wanted now?

Mary looked down. Her worry and uncertainty were plain in the portrait—and unsurprising. She was well aware of those emotions. But there was something else. Her drawings always showed more, and they'd never steered her wrong when she accepted the offered insights. With narrowed eyes, she examined her own image. It showed strength, determination, and...even a dash of wisdom. She couldn't deny it; those traits were on the page. But there was more— what was it? This woman carried a weight of some kind, more than mere worry.

Mary looked and puzzled and pondered and finally

realized what it was. She felt that if she could produce the right drawing for John, he would understand and love her, and if she couldn't, he would not.

Mary stared blankly at the drawing. That wasn't true. Of course it wasn't. It was ridiculous. Her marriage, her life, was a matter of far more than one drawing. Her happiness most emphatically did not teeter on such a knife-edge. But…the woman she saw pictured—it felt like herself and not herself —the woman she'd drawn believed it.

Mary sat there, appalled, and struggled with this idea. Slowly, she came to see that it was there, somewhere deep down, the conviction that everything depended on this portrait. The admission came with a vast sinking feeling.

Her drawings hadn't mattered before, she thought. Not really. They'd comforted her and helped her, but they hadn't been a matter of…

"Are you here drawing in the middle of the night?"

Mary started violently, whirled, and knocked the sketchbook to the floor.

John blinked at her from the doorway. She hadn't heard it open. "I woke, and you were gone. There's no need to lose sleep over this drawing, Mary."

Was there not? "I couldn't sleep," she said. He stepped closer. She bent and snatched up the sketchbook, flipping it closed.

"Do you want to show me what you have so far? Perhaps I'd recognize…"

"No!"

John frowned at the snap in her voice. "Very well."

"I'm sorry. I didn't mean…" Her recent thoughts

were too raw. She couldn't talk to him right now. "I need to work in my own way."

John gave a brisk nod. "I didn't mean to interrupt."

The coolness in his tone tore at her. "John."

But he had turned away and disappeared into the darkness of the entry. She ought to go after him, Mary thought. She should say…something else. But she was so unsettled and so tired. Whatever she said just now would not be the right thing.

Twenty

MARY LAY IN BED, EXHAUSTED, AND LISTENED TO THE small sounds from the bedchamber next door. John was preparing for a new day. He'd been asleep again when she finally returned to bed last night. She'd listened to him breathe and told herself she was over-wrought and being foolish. This didn't help her sleep.

She heard him leave his room and go down the stairs. On another day, waking so early, she would have rushed to dress and join him for breakfast before he left the house. Now, she climbed out of bed slowly and dawdled. When she sat at the dressing table to brush out her hair, she observed the dark circles under her eyes. "You would not have them if you were a more sensible person," she told her reflection. "And, no, talking to myself is not a sign of good sense."

Mary waited until she was certain John was gone before descending. In the dining room she found cold toast and tepid tea. She had to go to the kitchen herself to renew them. Kate had almost stopped work-ing at this point—though she still saw herself as quite magnanimous for staying on. Mary had decided that she wouldn't replace the maid until she was married and away. She didn't want any new servant to learn Kate's lax habits.

She ate her breakfast looking out the window over the square and thinking that she must go to her studio and try again to draw. It was a lowering reflection, like knowing that you had to have a tooth pulled. Which was alarming. She'd never felt that way about sitting at her easel before.

Leafless trees reached toward a ceiling of clouds that promised cold rain. Wind tossed the branches. It was not an appealing morning for walking, yet there were two people rounding the corner of the garden—a woman and a child. The woman's cloak billowed at a gust of air. She turned her head, and Mary recognized Caroline with…Arthur?

Mary rose and went to the window. It was indeed her neighbor's granddaughter and Mary's…guest from Somerset. It was hard to think of Arthur as a proper servant. Caroline gripped his arm above the elbow and seemed to be urging him along toward Eleanor's house. Puzzled, Mary went to her front door and flung it open. "Arthur?" she called over the rush of the wind.

The walkers started and turned. Arthur had a black eye.

"What has happened?" Mary shivered as the wind raced through the entryway. "Arthur, come here at once."

They both came. Mary ushered them inside and shut the door behind them. "Have you been in a fight?" she demanded.

Arthur gazed at her, mouth open.

"Yes, a fight," said Caroline.

Arthur turned startled eyes on her.

"I encountered Arthur on the street," she continued. "And I thought I would just help him…"

"Conceal his misbehavior from me? With that eye?" Mary put hands on hips and frowned at him. "Who were you fighting?"

"It was…it was…" Arthur gulped. "Near the market. This…fella just…just punched me without a lick of warning. I didn't do anything. I swear!"

The last two words were so heartfelt that Mary couldn't doubt him. "But who…?"

"I didn't even hit back," Arthur added. "I… came away." He put a hand to his injured eye and winced. "Ow."

"Did you see what happened?" Mary asked Caroline.

"No." She looked down at Arthur. "You'll be all right." When Arthur nodded, she turned to go. "Grandmamma will be wondering where I've gotten to." She was through the door before Mary could even thank her.

"Come to the kitchen. We'll ask Kate for something to soothe that eye."

"Aww, Cook will make a great fuss," Arthur replied. "Can't I just go up…?"

"No."

He was right about Mrs. Tanner. She fluttered about the kitchen and exclaimed as Kate unearthed a bottle of lotion from the ever-increasing store of concoctions she was accumulating. Arthur was not only slathered with it, he was dosed with a tonic that he pronounced utterly vile.

"Do be quiet," replied Kate. "I know what's good for you."

"Oh, I suppose you know just about everything?" he sneered.

"Everything I need to know about you, you little ruffian. Hold still!" Kate surveyed his face to make sure she had covered all of the bruise.

"No, you don't then. Think you're so clever…"

"Clever enough not to be fighting in the street!" Kate snapped.

"Girls don't fight!"

"Because we're clever!"

Bested and reeking with the lotion, Arthur turned tail and escaped to his room.

Mrs. Tanner wasn't far behind. After making her displeasure at the lack of help, and the necessity for her to walk to the greengrocer, perfectly clear, she went out with a basket on her arm.

Mary found herself lingering in the kitchen, watching Kate wash a small funnel and ready a tray of bottles. "You simply tell people how skillful you are," Mary found herself saying.

Kate turned to stare at her. "Well, I am," she replied with a mystified expression.

"Do you never have…doubts?"

Kate simply frowned at her.

"What if someone doesn't think you are?"

"Who?" Kate raised her chin, belligerent.

"I don't…what if you had a customer at the apothecary shop who said your concoctions weren't any good? And they told other people that they…"

"Which concoctions?" the other demanded.

"I don't know, Kate. Any of them. Hasn't anyone ever questioned your ability to create such things?"

The maid finally seemed to comprehend. "Oh. When I started out, a course. I wasn't but fifteen when the duchess let me begin to help in the stillroom."

"So people did criticize you?"

Kate nodded. "Until I gave them samples, see? That shut them up pretty quick." She went to test a cooling lotion with a wooden spoon.

"Was there no one who could not be convinced?" Mary asked.

Kate shrugged. "I can't be bothered by idiots," she replied, as if this was the only possible attitude. "If you're staying, could you hold on to this funnel while I pour? It's liable to wobble. I've told Jer he must order a new set."

Bemused, Mary stepped forward and steadied the funnel. Kate asked for what she wanted with none of the diffidence of a servant. She was crafting a life on her own terms. And Mary still couldn't figure out where her assurance came from.

The phrase "can't be bothered by idiots" stuck with Mary well after she'd left the kitchen. What would it be like, to see anyone who didn't appreciate one's skills as an idiot? She'd found her reluctant housemaid annoying—she still did sometimes. But now she wondered whether she couldn't learn from her. You didn't have to assume that harsh judgments were correct. Kate acted as if her abilities were worthy of praise, and people seemed to go along.

Mary thought of Lady Castlereagh's party—the memory of all those avid, sneering faces still made her shiver a bit. But what if she hadn't shrunk back before them? What if she'd reacted differently, full of confidence? Could she have changed what happened?

Mary frowned. Perhaps. There was no knowing; the past was past. And other people weren't exactly her problem now.

The fears of the night came back as she entered her studio. Why was it easy to see that they were ridiculous and still impossible to banish them? Mary opened her sketchbook and looked at the drawing of the cloak with the empty hood. She took up a pencil and forced herself to go on with a rough suggestion of the face she'd begun there. But each stroke she made on the page seemed more wrong. This wasn't the man.

She flipped quickly past last night's self-portrait to a fresh sheet. Her heart leaped when this seemed to help, and she started to draw. But the image that quickly emerged was John, asleep. His profile against the pillow, half-turned toward the viewer, looked younger than his waking face, softer and more vulnerable. Gazing at it, Mary had to smile. There was this John, and there was the one who had defended her to his brothers, and the one who had put out the kitchen fire so masterfully, and the one whose blue eyes went smoky with passion. He had turned out to be everything she wanted in a husband, more than she had dreamed.

As if in response to the thought, her pencil limned him in other poses—active and pensive and even impatient. Every one of the images brimmed with love.

But no matter how she urged and berated herself through the afternoon, she could not produce a decent image of the watcher in the square.

When John reached home that evening, he found Mary at her easel. Crumpled pages surrounded her on the floor, which was something he'd never seen before. When she turned at the sound of the door opening, she looked worn out and disturbingly dispirited. He thought she might even have been crying. "What's wrong?" he asked.

"Nothing. I…"

"Mary, something is obviously wrong." What could have happened to make her look so woeful? he wondered.

"I…" She hesitated, then words came out in a rush. "I don't know… I've tried and tried, but I can't draw that man who was following you. I'm so sorry."

John stepped farther into the room. He could see now that the page on the easel contained the rough outline of a man, with no discernible features. "You're pushing too hard," he suggested. "I know how that is. You should let it be for a while, then come back…"

"I did that and everything else I could think of. Nothing works." She slumped dejectedly in her chair.

John hid disappointment, even as he realized that he'd started to count on the portrait to redeem his efforts in Limehouse.

"I'm so sorry," Mary repeated. "I've let you down." She started to cry.

John couldn't bear that. He hurried over to put an arm around her. "It's all right."

"It *isn't!*" She buried her face in his shoulder and sobbed.

This seemed an overreaction, but John knew better than to say so. He didn't know what else to say, however. Nothing he'd offered so far had reached her. He wanted that portrait, but he hated to see her this upset. So, he simply held her, waiting for the storm to pass.

There were open sketch pads scattered all over the long table under the windows, he noticed. It looked as if she'd been pawing through older work. As he patted Mary's shoulder soothingly, his eyes ran over the gallery of images set out before him.

There was Arthur to the life, squatting over a pile of pebbles. The boy looked as if he would raise his head at any moment and show a face full of mischief. There was Mary's Great-Aunt Lavinia Fleming, more formidable than she'd appeared when he met her. Beyond two portraits he didn't recognize was one of their cook and maid, pictured together. And by God, there was Fordyce, in all his sneering glory. She'd captured his sly malice and disgusting superiority. And she'd only seen the man once, briefly. Mary really was amazingly gifted, he thought.

Further along the table, his eye caught a picture of himself—gazing into the distance, a suggestion of the sea behind. He remembered her drawing that one on their honeymoon trip. He hadn't wanted to pose, but he'd indulged his new bride.

Staring at it now, he wondered, Who was this man? He looked…listless, ineffectual. It wasn't him. Or…it was, of course, and…not. This man needed to rouse himself; he needed shaking up. And so he had been, John thought. So he had been.

He smiled at the memory of just what a shaking he'd gotten in the Far East. It seemed an age ago now.

The old John had scarcely known what hit him, at first. He examined the portrait again. Something in this outdated image made him truly appreciate how much, and how permanently, he'd changed. He'd shown it, even been praised for it, but somehow he hadn't fully felt it until now. He'd been offered the chance, and he'd accepted the challenge, and the change fit him like a perfectly tailored coat. Through her drawing, Mary had held that metaphorical garment out for him to slip into. Her artistry made it plain. "You are amazing," he said. The words just slipped out.

"What?" Mary hiccuped. She raised her head and blinked red eyes at him.

John gestured at the array of images on the table. "Look at these. Look at how you've captured the essence of these people. It's astonishing."

Mary turned her head toward the tabletop and blinked again.

John pointed. "When I look at this picture of me, I see so much about myself that I might never have noticed otherwise."

"But I haven't been able to do the one drawing you really need." It came out as a wail.

He gazed down at her. Her eyes were pools of darkness—anxious, uncertain. She'd worn herself out trying to do this for him. Had anyone ever cared so much, wanted so intensely to support his cause? John felt an odd sensation, as if his heart had turned over in his chest. No one had. Nor had he ever cared so much for another person. "Whether you draw the man you saw or not, all will be well. But never doubt that you have a true gift."

Mary sniffed. "But his portrait was going to lead you to information in Limehouse. You thought it could be important to find him."

He felt a pang of regret. He still thought so, and the loss of this possibility was a bitter pill to swallow. However, the chance wasn't worth making Mary so nervous and unhappy. With a resigned shrug, he let it go. "The truly important thing is that you stop worrying." He took her hands. "As long as we love each other…"

"Do we?" she interrupted.

"What?"

"Love each other?"

Despite, or perhaps because of, the desperate way she clung to his hands, John felt something very like a laugh bubbling up in him. "Well, I can't speak for you, of course. For my part, very much indeed. It will be quite a blow, in fact, if I discover that you do not…"

"Oh, John, of course I love you! I thought… I was afraid…"

Tears pooled in her eyes. "Are you going to cry again?" He very much hoped she was not. She threw her arms around him and buried her face in his shoulder, so it seemed she was. He braced himself. But then she drew back and gazed up at him, radiant. John was delighted to see the change in her expression—from tense and woebegone to happy. He was equally glad to respond to her kiss. It was several delightful minutes before Mary pulled away. "Where are you going?" he asked.

"I can do this," she said. She picked up a pencil and turned to her easel.

John felt a flash of hope. But her eyes looked almost

feverish. And she was trembling. He reached over and took the pencil from her hand. "Not now."

"What? But I think…I'm *sure* I can…"

"You're exhausted. Have you been in here all day?"

"Yes, but…"

"Have you eaten anything?"

Mary looked around as if there might be food lying about the room. "I had breakfast. Some."

"Well, you will have dinner now. And some rest."

"But I want to draw!"

"And so you shall, when you are restored." He put an arm around her and urged her toward the door.

❧

Though she found she was nearly starved, Mary begrudged the time it took to eat. Her whole body seemed to be vibrating with elation and eagerness to try the portrait again. John's words sang through her veins. He loved her! Whether she produced the image he needed or not. He loved her. The knowledge fired her with an intense desire to create.

The chops and mashed potatoes did make her feel better, however, along with the glass of wine John insisted she drink. She'd needed the sustenance. Still, she practically ran back up to her studio when the meal was finally done.

"Mary," he called after her.

"I must," she replied without stopping.

In front of her easel, the anxiety returned for a moment. What if she was wrong?

She closed her eyes, told the questions and worries to step aside, and let her spirit grow calm. She visualized the face she'd seen in the garden. Even before she opened her eyes again, her pencil began to move.

The strokes were tentative at first, as if her fears hampered her hand. Then, slowly, they grew bold and sure. With joy and relief beating in her chest, she drew the face inside the hood.

It was angular, almost gaunt. Sharp cheekbones jutting over a pointed jaw; inky eyes, with a pronounced slant and a small fold in the lid; a broad forehead and straight nose. She captured the snarl he'd given as he lunged at her. Her pencil racing across the pages now, she did another study in which he did not grimace, sketching in black hair rather than the cloak hood. Even faster, confidently now, she added a full-length study, showing the broad shoulders filling out the cloak. Time ticked past, and pages of the sketchbook filled, before she was satisfied that she had put down all she could remember.

Finally, Mary leaned back and stretched. Leafing through the drawings, she saw that she'd done well. Her pulse quickened with excitement and a touch of caution at the look of the man. Her talent hadn't failed her. Beyond accuracy, the various portraits exuded ruthlessness, the uncaring single-mindedness of a man you wouldn't wish to cross. Not an evil person, Mary theorized as she absorbed the images. Yet iron inflexibility could yield unfortunate consequences. He certainly looked like someone who wouldn't be swayed by softer emotions if he saw the necessity of action or by scruples as to what that action might be. She shivered as she picked up the sketch pad and hurried downstairs.

John's expression when he looked up as she entered the parlor tore at her heart. It was full of hope and of a determination to conceal how eager he was, if need be. This drawing really was important to him, whatever he had said earlier. She was so glad she'd managed to do it that she felt she could burst. "Success," she said and handed over the open pad.

John took it and stared down at the face depicted there. He took in every detail, tried to compare this man with those he remembered from Limehouse. The truth was he found Asian faces harder to distinguish than English ones. The Chinese had said the same about Lord Amherst's delegation, often mistaking one for another or simply expressing confusion. Perhaps there was some mechanism of discrimination learned in childhood and hard to expand. But that would not do; he had to figure out who this was.

"I did a number of different views," Mary said.

He flipped the pages and examined all the portraits, inch by inch. And he couldn't recognize the man she'd drawn. He had a nagging feeling, increasing with time, that he should, that he might have seen him somewhere. He turned the pages this way and that, trying to jog a memory. He'd observed, evaluated, talked to so many similar men during his visits to Limehouse. Was this one of them? Or…more likely, someone who'd lurked in the background, watching. He squinted at the pages, racked his brain. Wasn't there something? There must be. But he couldn't pin down a memory of this face, if memory it was.

John reviewed every single drawing. Theories and possibilities niggled at his mind. But stare as he might, he couldn't place the fellow. He didn't know where—or, he had to be honest, even if—he had ever seen him.

John slumped a bit over the sketchbook. He'd counted on recognizing the man Mary had seen, he realized now. He'd planned to have an urgent, coherent story to take to his superiors, to be able to point out where he'd encountered him and what that implied. That would be so much more powerful than a nameless drawing of a suspicious character who'd followed him a time or two.

Suddenly, as if Fordyce was actually in the room, he could hear the fellow drawling, "Did you hear that Bexley's begun exhibiting his wife's scrawls at the office? Lady Castlereagh wasn't enough for her, it seems." John bent protectively over the page. He flogged his brain. Nothing.

Nevertheless, he must take these in. Whether this was some Limehouse tough marking his movements or a watcher from some other place, it had to be reported. The Foreign Office always came down on the side of more information, rather than less. They wanted to know things. They deplored and resented ignorance; they excoriated those who withheld even trivial facts. Agents who did so were punished, even dismissed if they persisted. And this might not be trivial. It probably wasn't. If only he could attach the least bit of fact to the image, have some certainty about how it would be received.

But he couldn't, stare as he would. Part of him jeered that Fordyce would have a field day. Another of your wife's famous drawings, Bexley? Really? Who is it this time, the prime minister? No? Ah, a sinister figure following you through the dark streets? My goodness, how dreadful for you. Are you so important, indeed?

Others would pick it up from Fordyce. That was the man's genius—to inspire a group to greater heights of sniping and mockery. Wildly embroidered stories would spread, just for the amusement of it. There were those who delighted in gossip for its own sake, true or false. Oh, God. His brothers would hear and start in on him again.

"Is something wrong?" Mary said.

He tried to compose his expression. It wasn't only him. They would laugh at Mary, too. He hated the thought of exposing her to more ridicule.

"I'm sure I got it right," she added.

She was looking anxious again. How could she continue to doubt her abilities? The portraits practically jumped from the page, they looked so alive.

"Have you seen him before?" she said.

He shook his head. "I don't… I'm not sure."

"You think perhaps you have?"

He simply didn't know!

"You should do as you suggested to me, put them away for a while and then go back."

He stared at her.

"Memory can be fickle," she went on, faltering a little under his gaze. "I know…sometimes I wrack my brain and nothing comes until I stop thinking about… whatever it is."

And as she spoke to him in much the same tone he'd taken with her earlier, John realized that Mary wasn't the only one who had unreasonable doubts even though she was an immensely capable person. Apparently, this was a lesson one had to continually relearn. How much easier it was to advise another than to follow the same advice. "I'll take them to the office tomorrow," he said. He would think of a trustworthy, open-minded person to approach…

"You think they will be a help?"

John set the sketchbook down, and turned his full attention to his wife. She looked so shyly hopeful. "Absolutely."

Her smile lit the room. It lit John's heart, and he could do nothing but smile back.

Twenty-one

MARY WOKE TO BLADES OF SUNSHINE THROUGH CHINKS in the curtains and the rush of a brisk wind outside. She stretched luxuriously in her bed, stirring the scent of lavender from the linens. Every inch of her felt wonderful, and her mood was euphoric. Last night had been positively glorious. When she'd first married, she'd never imagined such a melding of tenderness and heat, depth of emotion and intensity of sensation. Indeed, she hadn't known bliss like that existed. She and John had talked until very late as well. There hadn't been hours enough for all they had to share. This was happiness, she thought. She lay there for a while savoring the knowledge.

Finally, Mary threw back the covers and got up. The room was chilly. John usually added coals to the fire when he rose, thoughtfully leaving her room warm for her. She had a vague memory of exclamations today. She'd half woken to hear him swearing about being late.

She dressed and went downstairs to roust out Kate and breakfast. Then she went to speak to Mrs. Tanner about cooking some of John's favorite dishes for dinner. In the kitchen, Arthur wanted to tell her all about a street magician he'd seen and the astonishing tricks he could do. Thus, it was midmorning before Mary went into the front parlor. She was sitting there, mending a rent in one of her petticoats, when she saw her sketchbook leaning against the end of the sofa. They'd set it aside when their attention turned to other matters last night and left it.

John had gone off to work without the drawings. Had he changed his mind about taking them? Mary's doubts threatened to rise. Had he simply been humoring her when he said he valued them? No, she knew that wasn't true.

But how could he have forgotten them after all the emotion these drawings had roused and all their talk about what was to be done with them? Not to mention his plans for gathering useful information. He'd said it was vital to put the images before his superiors.

Mary picked up that sketchbook. It had been left open at the snarling portrait, showing the man lunging at her. For some odd reason, this made her think of her drawing of Lady Castlereagh, who would have snarled at her, if it hadn't been ill-mannered. Thank heaven Eleanor had been able to smooth over that incident.

And then it occurred to Mary that it would be quite difficult for John to present another drawing of hers to people at the Foreign Office, perhaps the very ones who had whispered behind his back about the previous one. The scandal had been so hard on him. He'd had to face it every day, as she had not. And he cared so much about doing well at his job. Mary still fumed about the unfairness of it all—that he'd been blamed for something she had done.

She should have thought of this before. But, no, she'd been too caught up in her own concerns to think about her husband's. She supposed he would have to persuade his colleagues to look at the portraits. Some of them—that irritating man Fordyce, for example—would be skeptical. He would have to explain and justify the necessity. She should spare him that. She should take the drawings to the Foreign Office herself.

Mary swallowed and folded her hands tight in her lap. She couldn't intrude at his office. She wasn't part of that area of his life. And anyway, he might have made some other plan this morning. He wouldn't have wakened her about that. He would tell her this evening. But the sketchbook leaning against the sofa didn't look planned.

She gripped her hands tighter. The truth was she was afraid to face strangers with her work and insist that it was important. She could still see that mocking circle of faces at the party. She told herself this was different, but it felt similar enough to make her stomach twist. So, asked a sharp inner voice, because it's a risk, you will push the task off on John?

"No," Mary said out loud. But she still wavered for some minutes—determined and frightened, resolute and appalled. But slowly, she stoked her courage. She would do this for John.

She hurried to gather what she needed before she could lose her nerve. Donning her hat and cloak, she told Mrs. Tanner that she would be out for quite some time.

❧

It was damnably difficult to concentrate in a meeting about events occurring on the other side of the world when your mind was full of other concerns, John Bexley thought. How had he left home without Mary's drawings? Yes, he had woken very late and rushed out without a bite of breakfast, but the drawings were rather more important than a mouthful of toast. He had come to a decision about them, and he had meant to follow through. He did not appreciate his mind playing tricks and making him forget their existence.

He could see the sketchbook sitting beside the sofa where he had placed it last night. He had walked right by the parlor door and left it there.

Not only that, but the face on those pages nagged at him. There was something…some wisp of memory in the back of his brain. It drove him nearly mad that he couldn't pin it down. If only it would surface. Then he could justify leaving the drawings for another day, when he would have a more complete story to tell. He concentrated. Mary had caught the man's features so vividly, the anger, the furious snarl.

And it hit John like a pugilist's fist. This menacing man had been lurking around his house. Mary's house. After he'd gone to great lengths to remain invisible, Mary had caught him in a lantern beam. She'd exposed him, and he knew where she lived. John half rose from his chair. Why hadn't he considered this before? He'd been so enmeshed in his own concerns. He could be there at this very moment. Just because he hadn't shown up yet didn't mean he wouldn't.

The man had no way of knowing that Mary could

capture his likeness so perfectly, John told himself. Or at all. It was a rare talent. But he wasn't convinced. John couldn't believe he'd overlooked this aspect of the matter. He'd let his own struggles threaten a person he loved more than life itself. She'd believed in him, supported him, and he'd left her alone in the path of an unknown danger. He stood. And faced a circle of startled faces around the table.

"What is it?" said Conolly. "Something in the reports?"

"No. I...I beg your pardon, but I have just remembered...a family emergency..." Ignoring the raised eyebrows and puzzled glances exchanged by the other men, he rushed out.

The watcher had only appeared at night, he told himself as he strode down the stairs and out of the Foreign Office building. He'd only followed, never attacked. But what if that had changed...? John started to run. At the livery stable he pushed past the surprised ostler and threw the saddle on his horse. If he lost Mary... His gut twisted. He wouldn't think about that—except to let it spur him on. Nothing was more important than preserving her, certainly not his own stupid pride.

John rode as quickly as he could through the busy streets. He would take the drawings to...Lord Amherst's secretary would be a good choice. He was exceedingly intelligent, and he listened. He'd have the man hunted down. And they'd set a watch on the house until he was caught. Mary would be safe.

John bypassed his usual stable and rode all the way home, tying his mount at the garden fence. He went in calling Mary's name. She wasn't in the front parlor.

Arthur Windly popped up the kitchen steps. "She's out," he said.

"Out where?"

"I dunno, sir. She told Cook she'd likely be away all afternoon."

Perhaps she'd gone on an outing with Lady Caroline, John thought. That was all to the good. It gave him time to arrange things. John scanned the parlor. The sketch pad wasn't there. Perhaps she'd taken it up to her retreat. What had she thought when she found it here? He headed for the stairs.

Arthur trailed after him. "You're back right early today. How come?"

"I...came to fetch something." John hurried up the steps.

Arthur stayed right behind him. "Is it for an adventure? I could help. I've..."

"No." That was far too...lighthearted a word for the urgency he felt.

"...been practicing."

What did that mean? But John couldn't spare the time to inquire. "Go back to your work," he said. He saw Arthur's face fall as the boy turned away. He would talk to him this evening or tomorrow—sometime—whenever he'd taken care of this pressing task.

He went into Mary's studio and rifled through the sketch pads lying there. Amid the jumble of faces, he couldn't find the right drawings. Wild with impatience, he had to slow down and check the sketchbooks one by one. But the drawings he wanted weren't there. He rushed to Mary's bedchamber, thinking she might have put them somewhere safer.

He looked everywhere and found nothing. What could she have done with them?

Struck by a sudden thought, John hurried downstairs. Everyone in the kitchen looked considerably startled when he burst in. "Was Mrs. Bexley carrying anything when she went out?" he asked.

The maid and the cook looked at each other, then back at him, clearly mystified.

"She had one of her drawing books," Arthur said.

With a stifled oath, John raced back to his horse.

⤜⤛

Mary walked through the portals of the Foreign Office with her pulse pounding in her ears. She gave the attendant a note she'd already prepared for William Conolly, and as it was sent up, she prayed he would heed her request not to tell John she was here. A few minutes later, Conolly appeared. "You didn't say anything to John?" she had to ask.

"I couldn't. He's gone out somewhere. In a great hurry." He eyed her. "What's going on? What have you heard?"

"Heard?" Mary thought he seemed oddly intent.

"Did that boy...what's his...Arthur say something...?"

"What?" Had William Conolly met Arthur when he came to dinner? She was sure he hadn't. "What has Arthur to do with anything?"

"Precisely," was his odd reply.

Was her appearance at the office this unsettling? Mary couldn't imagine why. She spoke slowly and clearly. "I need to see someone in authority who was with John on the China mission." She'd thought it over and concluded this made the greatest sense. "Someone…in charge."

"Why?" was the blunt response.

"I have something important to show him."

"What is it? And why don't you get John to…"

"He's not involved with this. It's all my own idea. He can't be blamed."

Conolly looked even more skeptical. "Blamed for what?"

"Can't you just direct me…?"

"Mrs. Bexley, I cannot do anything unless you tell me what this is about."

"I could just go upstairs and march into the first office I see," Mary threatened.

"No, you couldn't, actually."

Seeing that he was adamant, and right, Mary gave in. "I have some drawings of a man…a Chinese man, who has been following John when he returns from the slums."

Conolly appeared to be digesting this. "Drawings," he said finally.

"Yes," Mary answered defiantly, "drawings." The scandal over Lady Castlereagh trembled between them. "It is very important that someone see them and institute a search for…this man. Because of what happened…before, I do not wish to…embroil John."

"You cannot think to exclude…" Conolly hesitated, then said, "You will have to tell me the whole." He drew her farther away from the attendants at the door.

Seeing no alternative, Mary told the story of how the drawing had been created.

When she finished, Conolly was thoughtful. "They

must be shown," he said at last. "But Bexley should be the one…"

"I won't have him blamed for my drawings again!"

Conolly gazed at her, then sighed. "I would not give in, but I think you're right. This could be important. And urgent." He considered. "Lord Amherst's secretary would be best, I think."

Relieved, Mary tightened her grip on the sketchbook she carried. "Which way?"

"I'll take you up."

"I can go alone. I don't want you to be blamed either."

"You can't go upstairs without an escort," Conolly replied. "Come along."

He took her to an anteroom and spoke to the clerk occupying the desk there. Mary couldn't hear their quiet exchange, but it was clear the man objected to this unheralded visit. Conolly finally convinced him, however, as he told Mary when he returned. "You will have to wait a little while. But then you will be allowed in."

"Thank you."

"I shall stay here with you."

"No, you needn't…"

Conolly held up a hand. "It's best I do, to make certain you're admitted. And…" He smiled wryly. "I don't want to go back to my office and have your husband asking me where I've been."

They sat in a pair of chairs in the corner and settled to wait.

❧

John rode back even faster than he'd gone. At the livery, he threw his horse's reins to the ostler and hurried to the Foreign Office headquarters. He had a foot on the stairs when he thought to ask the door wardens a few questions. The answers sent him to the opposite side of the building from his office.

And there was Mary, with the sketchbook in her lap. "What are you doing here?" he said.

The clerk at the desk glared at him. John was peripherally aware of Conolly edging toward the door.

"You mustn't be here," Mary said. "I'm going to tell them you had nothing to do with this. It was all my idea to bring the drawings."

John reached for the sketchbook. "No! I'll show them. I was just at home searching for them. You must leave at once. I won't have you worried…"

She jerked the book out of reach. He lunged, caught a corner, and yanked.

They pulled back and forth in a desperate tug-of-war, each protesting.

"What is the matter with you?" exclaimed the clerk. "Stop at once."

"What the deuce is going on out here?" asked a deep, cultured voice.

John stiffened and turned. Lord Amherst's secretary stood in the doorway to the inner office, gazing at them with frowning amazement. "Sir!"

"Bexley?" The secretary frowned and looked at Mary.

"And Mrs. Bexley," said the clerk, a picture of disapproval.

"I've brought some…" Mary began.

"I have something to show you," said John at the same moment.

"No, it was my idea," Mary insisted. "John is not…"

"My wife was just leaving…"

"I'm not… You will not be blamed this time…"

"Perhaps you had better come in," their host interrupted. His commanding tone silenced them. They followed him into a book-lined office and stood before his desk as he sat.

"I suppose you know my name," Mary blurted out. "Because of my drawing of Lady Castlereagh."

John hated to see her cheeks redden as Lord Amherst's secretary nodded. "Mary, let me…"

"Then you know it was thought to be a striking likeness." She opened the sketchbook. "I have some others, of a man who has been following John." She laid the page before him. "It was all my idea to bring them," she repeated.

John saw a new resolution in her face. When she'd spoken of her portraits in the past, there had been a shyness, almost an expectation that they would be belittled. Now she presented them…with determined confidence. He felt as if something turned over in his chest. But he had to say, "I intended to bring them to you, sir. Mary should not be dragged into this." Before the other man could answer, he launched into the story of his explorations in Limehouse and of being followed. "Mary noticed the person first," he acknowledged.

"So I waited behind the fence in the square and caught him with a dark lantern," she said. Her voice quavered slightly. She pointed to the drawing on the desk. "This is the man." She swallowed. "It is a true likeness. I…I am very good at capturing faces."

"Indeed," said their host.

John listened for sarcasm in his tone. He didn't

think it was there, but he said, "Astonishingly good. My wife is extremely gifted." He saw her blink and prayed it was not tears he glimpsed in her eyes.

They all examined the pages. Lord Amherst's secretary bent closer, eyes narrowed. "I believe this man was on the ship coming back from China," he said.

"But…we did not hire on any Asian crewmembers," John said. He looked closer.

"After the *Alceste* went down," said the secretary.

With this hint, John was suddenly flooded with memories. "Yes! Yes, I saw him on *Lyra*, when we were pulled from the sea. I thought I must have encountered him in Limehouse. I didn't think…"

"Interesting." The secretary turned the pages, examined Mary's other studies of the figure. "A curious coincidence."

"You think he might have had something to do with the wreck?" The idea was startling. There had been high seas and rocks.

"Impossible to say. There are certainly many in China who want no diplomatic contact with the Western 'barbarians.'" He straightened. "We must find this fellow, as soon as possible."

John leaned forward. "I could go…"

But the secretary was shaking his head. "Not you. From what you say, your face has become too well known in Limehouse. We will send others there and into the surrounding areas. We can use these portraits." He turned to examine Mary. "Could you produce a few more likenesses, rather quickly, Mrs. Bexley?"

"Of course."

"Today, that is."

"In an hour," she answered.

"Splendid." His examination grew more acute. He shifted his gaze to John and then back, seeming to consider something. "As you know, Bexley, this is a rather delicate time in our trade relations with China."

"Yes, sir."

Lord Amherst's secretary looked at Mary, evaluating. He started to speak, thought about it, then went ahead. "The East India Company has begun to cultivate tea in Assam," he told her.

Mary felt the weight of his regard. This felt like a test somehow. "So that someone besides China can sell it?"

Their host nodded with what looked like approval. "Indeed, they intend to break the Chinese monopoly."

"And we would prefer that China not discover this new venture," Mary replied.

He smiled like a man who has proved a budding theory. "Precisely."

After that, matters moved very briskly. Mary was given a seat at a desk and a handful of pencils. She used the blank pages of her sketchbook for more likenesses of their quarry. John was closeted with others to review the routes he had frequented in Limehouse. By the end of the afternoon, men were fanning out through the slums to find John's shadow, and Lord Amherst's secretary was bidding his visitors a cordial farewell. "Thank you, Mrs. Bexley. You have done us a service. Good work, both of you."

Gazing into Mary's eyes, John saw his pride and affection perfectly mirrored there.

❦

In the street outside the Foreign Office John found a hackney cab. His horse was to be retrieved by a trustworthy fellow named Simmons, who would take the animal to its customary stable and then keep watch on their house for any signs of the man they were looking for.

Mary was still vibrating with triumph as they climbed into the vehicle. Her drawings had been received more enthusiastically than she could have dreamed. John had been praised, too. His superiors clearly valued him. She felt they'd erased the last stigma of their earlier disgrace. She wanted to bounce in the seat and crow or hang out the window and declare her happiness to pedestrians on the pavement. She settled for smiling at her husband as he sat beside her.

John put an arm around her and pulled her against him. Mary nestled close, reveling in the feel of his strong body along the length of hers. The lines and hollows of his muscular frame were familiar now but all the more thrilling because of that, it seemed. Bursting with love and kindling desire, Mary turned a little in his embrace, threw her arms around his neck, and kissed him.

His response was all a woman could want. His lips took up her kiss and deepened it until she felt as if she was drowning in a sea of sensation. His hands moved under her cloak with possessive tenderness. One found its way inside the bodice of her gown and teased taut flesh. Afire, Mary let her fingertips drift down over the buttons of his waistcoat, and farther, until they encountered unmistakable evidence of his arousal.

John groaned and drew away, breathing hard.

"We must stop, Mary, or we will arrive home in a scandalous state."

She let her fingers roam a bit.

"My darling…"

She loved the way his breath caught on another groan. With John she had learned the intoxication of the power to give pleasure. She exercised it again.

"Ahh. Really, Mary…Ohh. No." His hand closed over hers and drew it gently but decisively away. "Simmons cannot catch us climbing out of a cab half-dressed and panting."

Though the image this conjured made her laugh, Mary had to concede. Simmons had planned to ride with all speed and reach the square before them if he could. She would not embarrass her husband before his colleague. "Later," she whispered, inches from his ear.

"You may count on that," came the murmured reply.

❧

Moments after they unlocked the front door at home, Arthur popped up from the kitchen stair. "It's both of them," he called down it. "All safe and sound."

A rumble of complaint traveled upward in response.

"Cook's mad as fire about the dinner," the boy added. "Nobody told her you'd be late, and the fish has dried to shoe leather, she says." He regarded them hopefully, keen for information about where they'd been.

"Let her serve us whatever chewable bits remain," declared John in a voice that was only too likely to carry between the floors.

Mary was not surprised to hear an indignant reply

from Mrs. Tanner. "My dinner is not spoiled! Drat that boy."

Mary took off her cloak. When Arthur reached out, she gave it to him. "Is Kate…?"

"Off someplace with her fee-an-say," Arthur said.

"Ah." That meant Arthur would be serving at dinner, which he should not be obliged to do. Unless Mary wanted to carry the dishes up herself. Not for the first time, she counted out the days until Kate's wedding in her mind.

The boy waited and took John's coat and hat as well. "I'm going to fetch that bottle of champagne," John said. He'd started a small wine cellar in a corner of the storeroom. "We're going to celebrate."

"Celebrate what?" asked Arthur, who showed no sign of moving even though he was nearly buried in cloth. "Have you been…?"

"Life," John said, heading for the stairs.

Mary took pity on Arthur, who so clearly wanted to go after him, and retrieved the coats. She took them upstairs and left them, along with her bonnet, before tidying her hair and freshening up. Dinner was on the table when she returned, and the door to the kitchen stairs was closed. John was twisting the cork in a fat bottle. It gave with a pop. He filled two glasses. "A toast," he said as he handed her one.

She raised it and waited, warmed by the admiration in his gaze.

"To a marvelously talented artist," he said. "And all her gifts have brought us."

Mary felt her face heat with gratification. She sipped, then raised her glass again. "To one of the leading lights of the Foreign Office," she proposed, "and his certain continued success." She watched John's cheek flush as he drank.

He held out the bottle and refilled the goblets. "To the 'managing' woman I found when I came home from China. Thank God." He looked at her with shining blue eyes.

"To the masterful man who returned to me. Thank God."

They drank.

"If I hadn't been called away, we never would have…"

"Fallen in love?" whispered Mary, her heart hammering in her throat.

"Fallen in love," her husband repeated, holding her gaze with the promise of forever.

Mary held up her glass one more time. "To perfect strangers," she said.

John grinned. They drained the goblets. And Mrs. Tanner's dinner was left to congeal on the plates.

Twenty-two

DESPITE ALL THE FOREIGN OFFICE'S RESOURCES AND efforts, the man in Mary's drawings was not found. Days passed with no word of him. John heard from the agents who were combing Limehouse that they believed some people recognized the portraits, but none would give information. Fear and uncertainty seemed to seal their lips. Watchers saw no sign of him near the Bexley house either.

"You won't go looking for him yourself, will you?" Mary asked him one evening when he had shared this news of failure.

"I might have…" At her anxious gesture, he shook his head. "If I thought I could do better. But I can't. I've contacted Shen and every other source I cultivated. None of them had substantive news. The fellow knows he was seen and has gone into hiding. Very effectively. Perhaps he's even left the country."

"I hope he has!" Mary refused to be sorry for alerting him. Who knew what he might have done if she hadn't? John could be dead in a slum alleyway or before their front door. She prayed he was gone. The storm of scandal had passed. John was more valued than ever at his office. All had ended well. She needed no more excitement of that kind.

Thus, when John brought home an invitation to an afternoon reception at the Castlereaghs' country house, Mary didn't feel the triumph that the first such gesture had roused. On the one hand, it seemed the crown and justification of all that had occurred, a mark of favor that John fully deserved. On the other, there was the risk of new disasters. Not that she would draw for anyone's entertainment! Lord Castlereagh himself could beg on bended knee, and she wouldn't touch pencil to paper before the ranks of society.

"It is a large party," John told her. "Not exclusive, and we are not invited to stay."

"They expect people to drive down and back on the same day?"

"It can be done. It's a matter of twelve miles from Charing Cross. I shall hire a chaise. If we leave very early…"

"And return in the dark?"

"There's a full moon that evening. They planned it so, I believe. And there will be a number of carriages on the road. Quite safe."

"It is a great effort and expense for a few hours," Mary grumbled.

"If you don't wish to go…"

"No, no. It is an honor for you. Of course we shall go." She shook off her lingering reticence. Old habits tended to return, she'd found, even when you no longer wanted or needed them. They were like oak roots twisted deep into internal crevices. "Is William

Conolly going? Perhaps we could ride together." That would make the journey, and the party, easier.

"I suggested it," John replied. "But I'm not certain he's invited. He was…oddly evasive."

"That doesn't sound like him."

"Indeed, it's not. He's been a bit strange lately. But he swears nothing is wrong. I've been rather preoccupied myself."

Mary was too taken up with thoughts of the coming, not ordeal—she mustn't think of it that way—say rather pleasant duty, to do more than nod.

❦

On the day, they left at dawn, warmly dressed, with hot bricks at their feet in the chaise and drove southeast into Kent. The driver kept the pace brisk but steady, so that there would be no need to change horses. The team would rest during the party and take them home again later on. More than once, Mary wished that William Conolly and Caroline were with them in the coach. Not that she didn't enjoy the sole company of her husband, but their assurance and familiar presence had been comforting at the last Castlereagh gathering. Until Caroline's unfortunate idea had set her drawing, Mary thought. And she decided the present arrangement would do very well.

They arrived at midmorning to find a line of carriages already pulled up before the facade of Waletts, the Castlereaghs' country retreat. Guests stepped down and were ushered inside to be plied with mulled wine or hot tea. Mary welcomed the latter, cupping her chilled hands around the cup. Strangely, no one offered to take their cloaks and gloves. Mary examined the chattering crowd, hoping to see someone she knew.

Almost immediately, Lady Castlereagh's stately butler revealed the reason that the guests remained bundled up. A tour of her ladyship's menagerie was the first item of entertainment. He divided the herd of guests into smaller groups and sent them out a pair of French doors at intervals.

John and Mary were in the fifth group to exit. Arm-in-arm, they walked down a gravel path with their designated companions. The day was sunny, at least, and not terribly cold. Mary wondered what their hosts would have done if it had featured one of the cold, soaking rains common to November?

As they walked, people struggled to find something to admire in the winter garden. One woman spoke nervously of the tiger. "It is in a cage, Susan," replied her husband. "It cannot get at you."

A roar from up ahead made the woman jump.

And then the menagerie came into sight, a cluster of cages, sheds, and fenced enclosures housing her ladyship's collection. The tiger was immediately visible—right up front and clearly a great feature of the place. He was huge and striped and snarling as he paced his cage. He looked like he was longing to eat one—or more—of the people gaping at him, Mary thought. She didn't entirely blame him.

Lady Castlereagh stood in the midst of it all like a very superior sort of tour guide. "This creature is called a 'kangaroo,'" she was telling the group ahead of them. "It is native to Australia and was sent to me by the colonial governor there."

The odd-looking animal leaped as if it had springs. Its head seemed very small in proportion to its massive legs.

"I wager the convicts wish they could hop it like that," murmured a man near Mary.

"And these are African antelopes," their hostess continued, pitching her voice to reach the newcomers.

"Lady Castlereagh! Ma'am!" came a call behind them.

"Fordyce," said John. "One can never escape the fellow."

They turned to see Edmund Fordyce hurrying along the path. Two footmen behind him carried a large wooden crate, and he urged them on impatiently. As he passed John and Mary, completely ignoring them, Mary thought of sticking out a foot and tripping him. But too many people were watching.

Fordyce stopped before Lady Castlereagh and signaled to the footmen. "Put it down, put it down. Just there." They set the crate at her feet. "You may go," added Fordyce with a lordly wave. The footmen retreated.

Mary caught movement in the corner of her eye and turned to find William Conolly and Lady Caroline Lanford drifting up the path from the house. Astonishingly, Arthur Windly was with them, lurking behind Caroline's skirts. The look of anticipation on all their faces roused Mary's suspicions. She'd been so busy and preoccupied that she hadn't really paid attention, but... Various odd occurrences suddenly popped into her mind and linked together. Combined, they suggested that Caroline and Conolly had not given up the idea of playing a prank on Fordyce. Quite the contrary.

"I've brought you an addition to your collection," said Fordyce, voice pitched so that everyone within fifty feet could hear. "One you've been quite keen to acquire, I understand."

Lady Castlereagh looked interested. People moved closer, anticipating a show, forming a loose circle around the pair.

"As you know, I was a key member of the China mission," Fordyce went on. He was really as pompous as it was possible to be, Mary thought.

John snorted.

"And in honor of that historic voyage..." He paused for dramatic effect.

"Historically unsuccessful," muttered John. Mary pressed his arm in solidarity and to suggest that he might want to stay quiet.

"I present you with an exotic golden monkey from the wilds of the Orient." With a flourish, Fordyce lifted the lid of the crate. The crowd leaned forward.

A small round head popped up. The monkey's fur was gold, Mary saw, not smooth and brown like pictures she'd seen.

A pair of golden arms rose over the top of the crate. But...that was strange. The animal's fur *was* brown—a rather mottled brown—under its arms. There was a darker patch beneath its chin, too. Mary wondered if they were some kind of markings.

And then in a flash, the monkey was up and out, balancing on the rim of its prison, gazing this way and that with preternatural alertness. Fordyce put a proprietary hand on its shoulder. The creature bared its teeth, unexpectedly formidable, and snapped at him, nearly taking off a bit of finger. Fordyce emitted a surprisingly high-pitched sound and jumped backward.

Startled, the monkey gathered itself and leaped—directly at Lady Castlereagh.

She did not scream. Her hands went up as if to catch it.

The monkey twisted in midair, eluded her grasp, caromed off her shoulder, and hopped onto her head. Its hands scrabbled at her fashionable bonnet. Bits of feather and straw sifted down like flakes of sunlight. The monkey sat up and looked around like a statue at the top of a plinth. Mary choked back a laugh.

"No!" cried Fordyce, eyes popping. "Don't! Stop that! The creature is trained. I was assured it was well trained."

Lady Castlereagh reached up, her head shifting with the movement. Unable to maintain its perch among the false flowers and ribbons, the monkey wobbled, recovered, bounced off Lady Castlereagh's shoulder once again, and jumped to the ground. It started toward Fordyce, chittering as if trying to communicate distress. He backed away, fearfully fluttering his hands. "No. Down, sit, you wretched little…" The monkey ran at him, arms out, eyes wild. Fordyce aimed a kick at it. "Keep away from me!" When it bared its teeth again, he turned tail and raced for the house. He was surprisingly fast.

A nearby gentleman lunged as if to capture the animal. It flinched and scampered off to the left. Brought to bay by the circle of onlookers, it dithered, then darted toward a stately woman in a voluminous black cloak. The lady shrank back—she had been pointed out to Mary as a duchess—and then jumped and screamed as the animal burrowed in beneath her wide skirts.

The crowd froze in horror. Mary heard a gurgle behind her and knew it was Caroline. She didn't dare look at her or at Conolly.

The duchess screamed again and twitched. "Get it away, get it away!" She jumped and cried, "Help!"

Someone must do something, Mary thought. Where had those footmen gone? But they were nowhere in sight. Everyone else just stood about looking horrified. She heard John take a breath, and then he had dropped her arm and stepped forward. He made a bow before the duchess. "If your grace would forgive a…an intrusion?"

The woman screamed and jumped again. She shook her skirts, to no avail. "Yes, yes, just get it away. However you can!"

Like a courtier from the last century, John bowed even lower. "Be silent, please," he said to the crowd. Then he crouched so as to be closer to the monkey's level. With one deft twitch, he raised an edge of the duchess's skirts, averting his eyes from her flounced underdrawers. As a collective gasp passed through the crowd, he held out a hand to the cowering monkey. The creature shrank back, trembling. John remained still, hand extended. The animal watched him.

Finally, when John simply waited without threatening, the monkey crept forward. Tentatively, with some false starts, it reached out and took John's hand. He let the duchess's skirts fall behind it. The crowd exhaled. The duchess took a step back, and then another, and another. The crowd parted to let her by as she turned and headed full speed for the house.

The monkey whimpered. John encouraged it to come closer. When the crowd started to erupt in a babble of comment, he silenced them with a quick gesture of his free hand.

"Where is Bowman?" said Lady Castlereagh. To Mary's awed admiration, she acted as if nothing out of the ordinary had occurred.

A man who looked like an upper servant was already pushing his way through the press of guests. "Your ladyship. I beg your pardon! No one told me we had a new animal arriv…"

"We did not know," interrupted their hostess. She spared one glance for the path Fordyce had taken in his flight. "Do you think it should go back in its crate for now? Until we can prepare better quarters?"

"Let's see, your ladyship." The man hurried over to John and knelt beside him. Carefully, he held out a hand. "Now then young…lass," he said. "I expect you're sick to death of that crate. Wouldn't you rather come along with me and see what we can find for you to eat? Something right tasty, eh?"

As if it understood, or perhaps recognized the kind authority in Bowman's voice, the monkey released John's hand. With something that looked very much like relief on its little face, it went to the other man and wrapped its arms around his neck. "There we are," Bowman said in the same soothing tone. His voice was so reassuring, Mary thought; it positively made one want to do whatever he suggested. Bowman touched the golden fur gently, looking puzzled. "And some nice warm bedding, too. I expect you're tired out."

The monkey hid its face on his shoulder. Holding the animal, Bowman slowly rose. "I'll take her off to get settled, your ladyship."

"Thank you, Bowman." As he turned away, she added, "That fur?"

"Don't believe it's a natural color, ma'am. Which is right odd. Never seen anything like it."

"Yes," replied Lady Castlereagh, as if he'd confirmed her own conclusions. "We'll have to ask *Mr.* Fordyce about that, should he ever dare to show his face again." With a nod that promised retribution, she turned away. "If you'll come this way, we will see the aviary," she said, the serene guide once again.

Now, finally, Mary dared turn and find Caroline and Conolly and Arthur. From the way their eyes danced, she knew that they'd been behind this and that they were beyond pleased with the result. She started toward them.

She'd taken only a step, when something flickered in the corner of her eye—a flash of movement behind the backs of the guests. Mary peered around a tall man and saw someone running across the lawn. She caught the merest glimpse, but it was enough. "John, it's him! The man who was following you."

The fellow pulled a pistol from under his cloak as he ran. He brandished it at a small group of men coming down the path from the house. One of them was Lord Castlereagh, Mary saw. She pushed through the circle of guests.

The intruder aimed the pistol at England's foreign secretary.

"Robert!" screamed Lady Castlereagh.

"Get down, sir," shouted John, already running.

One of his companions pushed Lord Castlereagh down. The muzzle of the pistol followed his movement. John pounded across the grass still feet away.

He wouldn't make it in time, Mary thought. The man was going to shoot. Acting on instinct, she drew back her arm and threw her reticule as hard as she could at the assailant. The woven cotton pouch arced up turning in the air, drawstrings fluttering. It hit harmlessly on the man's shoulder, but the threat of a missile distracted him just long enough for John to crash into his midsection.

The fellow's arms flailed with the impact. The pistol swung wildly upward and discharged, shockingly loud, into the air. John's momentum carried them both to the ground. In another moment, a host of other men had piled on top of him.

The party dissolved into chattering chaos. Guests who had been frozen with horror recovered, gestured, and exclaimed. Women grew faint and called for vinaigrettes; men stamped about and blustered. Lady Castlereagh rushed to her husband and clung to his arm. The intruder was yanked to his feet, searched, and hauled off by John and others.

Now that it was over, Mary found she was trembling, her legs quite unsteady. She was wishing for a garden bench to sink onto when William Conolly appeared at her side. "Bravo, Mrs. Bexley. Very quick thinking."

"I didn't even think," she replied shakily.

"And that is even more laudable. You were able

to act when the rest of us stood gaping." He took her arm, and she leaned on him a little.

"I don't know why…"

"Because your drawings had prepared you for trouble. And John, of course. I see now why he was such a boon during that shipwreck."

Arthur ran up with her reticule. "That was champion!" he declared, handing it to her.

"You were magnificent," said Caroline, coming up behind the boy. "Oh, why didn't I think to do that? I just stood there like a ninny with my mouth hanging open."

"And eyes bulging," said Conolly.

Caroline struck his shoulder with a playful familiarity that made Mary examine them thoughtfully. But she had a more pressing concern. "What is Arthur doing here?"

Arthur backed up until he was half-hidden by Caroline.

"Allow me to escort you inside and get you some tea," Conolly said to her then, smoothly distracting. "I'm sure you could use a warming beverage. And I daresay you won't see John for a while."

But Conolly was wrong. Ten minutes later a footman came for Mary and escorted her to a book-lined study. She found her husband awaiting her there, along with Lord Castlereagh and a number of other important-looking gentlemen. The only one she recognized was Lord Amherst. John had pointed out the leader of his China expedition earlier. "I told you he had great promise," the man was saying to Castlereagh. He clapped John on the shoulder. "A sharp mind and not afraid to act. It's a rare combination."

John looked surprised, then moved. Mary nearly burst with pride. She was startled when Lord Amherst shifted his gaze to her and added, "And I believe my secretary's recent recommendation has been fully vindicated."

Lord Castlereagh smiled. "I thank you for your quick thinking today." He nodded to include Mary. "Both of you. I must ask, however, that you do not speak about it to anyone. Assassination attempts by foreign spies are not good for a country's morale."

"But won't everyone be talking about it?" Mary ventured. Indeed, she knew they already were. The buzz of conversation could be heard even through the closed door.

"We have people circulating through the crowd, making sure that the story is as garbled as it can possibly be," he answered. "And that the…unfortunate bits are decried as gross exaggeration. Others will spread the tale in town as we wish it to be remembered."

Could one really manage gossip? Mary wondered. Well, if anyone could, it was the Castlereaghs.

"I wanted to be sure you knew that you have my gratitude," the foreign secretary continued, "since your actions will not be a great feature in the tale we spread. Bexley, you've done more than your duty. I shall indeed expect great things from you. And, Mrs. Bexley, I understand you're a very talented young woman."

A part of her still wanted to duck her head and demur. Mary resolutely pushed it aside and stood straighter. She nodded, accepting the compliment. Yes, she was.

"It's been suggested that we might wish to call on

those talents, now and then, at the Foreign Office to help with our endeavors. If you are amenable."

This was more than she'd ever imagined. In fact, she couldn't quite believe it. "Make drawings, you mean? Of people who…"

"Are of…interest to us. Yes." The foreign secretary glanced at John and then back to her. "We would make certain that you could do it safely, of course, and completely confidentially."

"I'd…I'd love to!" Mary burst out. This was vindication beyond anything she could have imagined.

Despite the presence of his ultimate superiors, John took her hand. The pride shining in his face made Mary's eyes burn. Ferociously, she blinked back the tears. She was *not* going to blubber in this august company.

"Splendid," said Lord Castlereagh. "Thank you." The men around him gave cordial nods.

And so they were dismissed. A footman took them back along a private corridor and eased them into a quiet corner of the reception. Mary doubted that anyone had noticed their absence. Or…almost anyone. Seconds after their return, Lady Caroline and William Conolly pounced, Arthur trailing behind them. "Where were you?" demanded Caroline. "What's going on?"

"I'm nearly starved," John answered. It was the truth. But even more he needed to divert his wife's ever-curious friend. "Shall we go find the buffet?"

"But we want to hear all about…"

John interrupted her. "Speaking of hearing all about. Would you care to explain that debacle with the monkey?"

"Explain?" said Conolly blandly. "How would we be able to…?"

But John was gazing sternly at Arthur, clearly the weak link in their conspiracy. Under his eye, the boy squirmed and shuffled and then blurted, "It was an adventure, just like you told me."

"*I* told you?"

"Come further away from the others," Conolly said, leading the group to a spot devoid of other guests.

"You said I should have adventures," Arthur said then. "Instead of going to see the steam engine. So when Lady Caroline asked if I could help at the place where they were keeping the monkey…"

"Which hit you in the eye," Mary put in.

"It did, the little bugger. And I was only trying to give it a bit of fruit."

"So you, ah, welcomed the opportunity to join their plot?" John asked, pointing to Conolly and Caroline.

Arthur stood straighter. "I offered my services, like. I was in charge of feeding the…creature."

"With food from my kitchen," said Mary.

"Lady Caroline said you wouldn't mind."

"Really?"

Under her irritated eye, Caroline abandoned the pretense of denial. "I couldn't always be going out with a basket of vegetables. What was I to tell Grandmamma? Anyway, how could you object? Was that not the best prank *ever*?"

"Will you talk more quietly," hissed Conolly. Caroline's voice had risen in delight.

"We should find the buffet and fill some plates and discover a secluded place to talk," said Mary.

"I don't think seclusion is likely to be…" Conolly began.

"Perfect," said Lady Caroline, linking an arm with Mary's and setting off.

They did manage to find a circle of chairs well away from the crowds. And in the face of Arthur's defection and Caroline's glee, Conolly had to concede that they had engineered Fordyce's humiliation.

"Even though I thought it unwise," said John.

"I couldn't let him get away with treating you and Mary the way he did," Caroline insisted. "Especially because I…gave him the opportunity. I had to make it right. And we came across this monkey."

"Came across?"

Caroline shrugged. "Well, searched out then."

"It isn't really a golden monkey, is it?" Mary said. "Are there golden monkeys?"

John turned to look at her. "Surely you were not in on this?"

"No, but I should have figured it out, what with one thing and another."

"You heard me talking to your maid about the hair dye." Caroline shrugged. "I knew you thought it odd. They do have golden monkeys in China. I found it in a book. But this was just a regular monkey."

"A regular devil," Conolly added. "The owner was so pleased to be rid of the beast that he practically paid me." He shook his head.

"You actually dyed a monkey?" John couldn't quite believe it.

"A deuce of a job it was, too," Conolly replied.

"Was that when it scratched you?"

"It did that every chance it got, the wretch. I had no idea monkeys had such a set of claws. Or teeth."

"You told me you were attacked by your aunt's cat," John accused.

"I told you she has a vicious cat, which she does," his friend replied.

"Lying by misdirection."

"I work at the Foreign Office," said Conolly with a grin.

"The poor creature," Mary said.

Lady Caroline had the grace to look contrite. "I spoke to Kate again. She assured me the dye did no harm. Its fur will grow in brown. Perhaps it wasn't a good idea to…"

"Perhaps?" John interjected.

"The dyeing it part," Caroline said, unrepentant. "Otherwise it worked wonderfully."

"Did you train it to do that?" Mary wondered. "With the skirts?"

Arthur giggled over his nearly empty plate of food. Conolly made a face. "We had no need to train the beast," he said. "It had every bad habit possible to a monkey. And some I would have thought impossible. Although the fellow who sold it to us might have said that it…"

"Ran under ladies' skirts," finished John dryly.

"I swear we never imagined anything like that." Conolly looked sheepish. "We just thought she would…misbehave."

"Well, I think you've gone mad. If anyone connects you to…"

"I was exceedingly careful, John." Conolly's tone

was serious now. "Everything was done through several intermediaries, or people we can trust absolutely."

Arthur held up a hand as if taking an oath. "I'd die before I told anyone else. I told 'em if *you* asked me, I'd have to let on."

"The connection will not come out," Conolly finished. "I like my job."

"And we've found the poor beast a good home," said Caroline with an air of great virtue. "Which she did not have before." When they all turned to look at her, with varying degrees of approbation, she giggled. "Edmund Fordyce's face…" Her eyes locked with Conolly's. He snorted. Mary chortled. Arthur started to cackle. John felt a bubble of mirth rise in his own chest.

In the next moment, they were all laughing like lunatics.

Twenty-three

SITTING IN FRONT OF THE PARLOR FIRE ON A COLD December Sunday, John Bexley dangled a piece of string, twirling it rapidly to make the end wiggle. The gray kitten in his wife's lap rose on still wobbly hind legs to bat at it, then tumbled over on its back. Undaunted, he attacked the string with all four paws from that position.

"What shall we call him?" Mary wondered.

"Mouser?"

She laughed. "Mrs. Tanner might like that, though she wanted an older cat who could 'get right to work.'"

The kitten captured the string in its mouth and worried it with needlelike teeth. John tugged a little and elicited a tiny growl. "Arthur got off with no problems?"

Mary nodded. "We all walked with him to the stagecoach. Even Kate, to my surprise. I spoke to the driver about looking after him. His father will meet the coach at Bath."

"Has he reconciled to the idea that Arthur wants to study engines and mechanical processes?"

"So he says in his latest letter. I think he's grateful

that Arthur wants to study anything at all. He thanked you for 'setting the boy straight.'" Mary grinned impishly at him.

John grimaced in response. "An undeserved accolade! Although I still *cannot* see how Arthur interpreted what I told him as encouragement to join Conolly and Lady Caroline's…"

"Adventure?" Mary put in.

John shook his head at her, then laughed.

The kitten flopped over in Mary's lap, wrapping the string around its chubby body. She freed it gently. "It all ended well, after you took him to see that steam locomotive to…redirect his thoughts."

"And the coin stamp at the mint. Don't forget that."

"How could I?" Mary replied, widening her dark eyes. "It sounded so fascinating. Did you know that it has the capacity to…?"

"Stop!" John groaned. "If I had to hear Arthur enumerate the virtues of that machine one more time, I think I would have strangled the lad. I'm sure steam engines are a great invention, but their inner workings are astonishingly tedious."

Mary nodded, conceding the point. "To us, and not at all to Arthur. It just shows how we all have our own unique talents."

Their eyes met in a moment of perfect understanding. Smiles full of tenderness lit their faces.

Nancy, the new maid, came in with the tea tray and set it on a small table near Mary's elbow. "Thank you," Mary said. She lifted the kitten. "Take… Mouser to the kitchen, please. He *will* try to climb into the milk jug."

"Yes, ma'am," Nancy replied, with a curtsy and a smile.

She seemed quite happy with her position, Mary thought gratefully. And she got on well with Mrs. Tanner, even at the times when Kate visited and stirred things up. Mary poured the tea. "So what are we going to do about Christmas?" she asked her husband. "My mother will make a great fuss if we don't go."

"As will mine." John took the cup she offered and sipped. He'd been able to make certain that George's nosy friend heard about his commendation from the Foreign Office for extraordinary service. George had been very frustrated when he asked what it was for and was told the matter was confidential. Mary's part in foiling the assassination attempt, and her new responsibilities, were more secret. Could he bear to see his family treat her carelessly without being able to say anything?

"I was thinking we might spend a few days with each one," Mary said. "A few days only."

"They expect much longer visits," he pointed out.

She shrugged. "Perhaps they must learn to expect something different."

"We can hope." He gave her a wry smile as he accepted a macaroon from the plate she held out.

"I thought we might take some special…gifts."

"Of course we must…" He noticed the spark dancing in her eyes. "What sort of gifts?"

"Wait a moment." Mary rose and went out. In a few minutes she was back, holding two long rolls of paper tied with string. She carried them to the table under the front windows, where she removed the string and spread them out, one on top of the other. She had to weight down the corners to keep them flat.

John rose to look. Mary had glued together sheets from her sketchbook to form a bigger page. And there she had drawn a group of people, placed as in a formal portrait. A middle-aged couple sat in chairs in the center. Five younger women were grouped around them in a loose crescent. Mary was among them. "Your family," John said.

She nodded. "I left out my sisters' husbands because the page was getting crowded. Besides, they are…"

"Negligible?"

She laughed. "Not at all! At least…not in their own homes, where I'm sure they are benevolent monarchs."

"Only in your mother's?" John examined the faces. Of course he did not know the Bexleys as Mary did, but like all of her drawings this one revealed much. Her mother was so obviously the center of the family. Something in the way she sat and the lines of her face told a viewer that she organized and ruled this household, with Mr. Bexley's amiable agreement. And covert refusal to take responsibility, John thought. Here was a man who enjoyed the luxury of blaming the difficult things on his wife. He glanced at Mary. Did she see that in her father? He wouldn't have liked seeing such a thing himself.

He turned back to the drawing. Mary's sisters—John had to think a moment to name them all: Eliza, Lucy, Sophia, and Petra—showed varying temperaments. Something deep inside him thanked God he hadn't been married off to Sophia, sure of the feeling without really knowing why. There was much more to see, but he couldn't take it all in at once.

"It's the oddest thing," Mary said as he gazed. "I realized I had never drawn my mother. Well, not since…"

"Since?"

"When I was eleven, I decided to create a special portrait for her," she said, her eyes on the page. "As a Christmas gift, actually, I'd forgotten that. I spent hours on it. I took such great care. I thought it would please her…and show her…"

Her voice trailed off. John had an urge to take her hand. "But it didn't," he said.

Mary shook her head. "She seemed quite…shocked."

"I'd give a guinea to know what she saw in it. Some aspect of herself that she didn't wish to acknowledge?"

His wife turned to stare at him. Slowly, her melancholy expression shifted, and she began to smile. "Perhaps. I wonder if she remembers that?"

"She may have some memory. More than likely it doesn't match yours. People—families—seem to recall incidents from one's childhood…quite selectively. In order to fit them into a settled story."

She looked much struck. "That's very wise."

"Wise!" He shook his head.

"It is!"

She thought he was wise. And somehow, with her, through her, he had become so. John felt a bubble of joy in his chest that was becoming familiar but never old. "Dare I ask what is on the page underneath?"

"I think you know."

He lifted the top page and set it aside. And there was his family, grouped in the same manner, except that it was only his mother in the center of the four brothers. It was sad that Mary had never been able to meet his father. "Do not attempt to argue with Frederick," he said and was slightly startled at his own words. But it was plain to see that his eldest brother was not open to new ideas. He would never convince him to change his mind. It was amazing that Mary could catch this when she had met him just a few times.

"Roger may not be right. I only spoke with him for a few moments at the wedding."

Yet she had captured his youngest brother's insouciance and humor, along with a fierce determination John hadn't recognized till now. Suddenly, he was convinced that Roger's ventures in India would be a great success. A little hesitant, he looked at the portrait of his mother. "Disappointed?" he said.

"What?"

"Nothing. I…" What about her life had put that discouragement in his mother's eyes? He'd thought she was pleased and proud of her household and her sons—most of them. Was it his father's early death, or…?

"Are you disappointed? Of course I don't know them as I do my own…"

"No! It was…something I noticed."

Mary nodded as if she knew exactly what he meant. "Should I not have drawn…?"

"If they are to be gifts, we must have them properly framed," he said.

"Are they?"

She watched him. He understood the question in her eyes and felt that her answer was the same as his. "Great gifts," he replied. This time he did take her hand. "We should go to your family first, as it's farthest away, then stop at mine on the way home."

"It's a great deal of traveling for such short stays," Mary remarked.

He nodded, still a bit preoccupied.

"It's a pity that we can't just stay home and invite Caroline and Mr. Conolly for Christmas dinner," she said.

"They will be with their own families," replied John absently. He was imagining his mother unwrapping the portrait, George and Frederick looking at it. He would see if he could find something to say to his mother that lightened that disappointment behind her eyes. And if he did, would she begin to see him differently as well?

"They might rather be with each other," Mary replied. When he turned to look at her, she added, "Caroline and Conolly. I think they are becoming attached."

"Doesn't she come from one of those families Conolly spoke of? Who wouldn't consider him a good match?"

"Caroline's grandmother would take her part."

John felt a twinge of concern for his friend. "Her father is the important one in the matter of marriage. And our neighbor may turn out to be more conventional than you imagine."

"Eleanor wants Caroline to be happy," Mary insisted. "As do I." She cocked her head at him. "Mr. Conolly too."

John's mind filled with a host of complications. "I don't think it's wise to interfere in something so..."

"But I am a 'managing woman,'" she interrupted.

He nodded to acknowledge that he remembered—
and regretted—the phrase. "You are an extraordinary
woman, a talented woman, and the love of my life,
but…"

"But…?" Her dark brows arched. Her smile was rueful.

He gazed at the lovely figure next to him, dearer
than words could express, and thought how amazingly fortunate he had been in the end. His life could
so easily have gone otherwise. If he hadn't been sent
to China, if he hadn't returned changed, to find an
entrancing stranger, where would he be now? How
drab and pointless his existence might feel. Overcome
with gratitude and love, he said, "*And* I trust your
judgment implicitly."

Fortunately, his cup was nearly empty when Mary
threw her arms around him, so only a few drops of tea
fell, unnoticed, onto the sofa.

Read on for an excerpt from

The Bride Insists

THE SCHOOLROOM OF THE BENSON HOUSEHOLD WAS agreeably cozy on this bitter winter afternoon. A good fire kept the London cold at bay, so that one hardly noticed the sleet scratching at the windows. In one corner, there were comfortable armchairs for reading any one of the many books on the shelves. A costly globe rested in another corner, nearly as tall as the room's youngest occupant. Scattered across a large oak table, perfect for lessons, were a well-worn abacus, pens and pencils, and all the other tools necessary for learning.

"I am utterly bored," declared seventeen-year-old Bella Benson, sprawled on the sofa under the dormer window. "I hate winter. Will the season never start?"

"You could finish that piece of embroidery for…"

"You are not my governess any longer," the girl interrupted with a toss of her head. "I don't have to do what you say. I've left the schoolroom."

And yet here you are, thought Clare Greenough. But she kept the sentiment to herself, as she did almost all of her personal opinions. Clare's employer set the tone of this household, and it was peevish.

All three children had picked up Mrs. Benson's whiny, complaining manner, and Clare was not encouraged to reprimand them when they used it. "It's true that you needn't be in the schoolroom," she replied mildly. She sorted through a pile of paper labels marked with the names of world capitals. The child who could correctly attach the largest number of these to their proper places on the huge globe would get a cream cake for tea. Clare had an arrangement with Cook to provide the treats. It was always easier to make a game of lessons than to play the stern disciplinarian, particularly in this house.

"I won't do what you say either," chimed in twelve-year-old Susan Benson, as usual following her older sister's lead.

"Me neither," agreed ten-year-old Charles.

Clare suppressed a sigh, not bothering to correct his grammar. Charles would leave for school in the spring. Only a lingering cough had kept him home this term. He was hardly her responsibility any longer. Bella would be presented to society in a few weeks, effectively disappearing from the world of this room. And Clare would be left with Susan, a singularly unappealing child. Clare felt guilty at the adjective, but the evidence of a year's teaching was overwhelming. Susan had no curiosity or imagination and, of the three children, was most like her never-satisfied, irritable mother. She treated Clare as a possession designed to entertain her, and then consistently refused to *be* entertained. The thought of being her main companion for another four years was exceedingly dreary. Surely Clare could find a better position?

But leaving a post without a clear good reason was always a risk. There would be questions that Clare couldn't answer with the simple truth: *My charge is dull and intractable. I couldn't bear another moment of her company.* Inconvenienced, Mrs. Benson might well refuse to give her a reference, which would make finding a new position nearly impossible. Clare wondered if she could...nudge Susan into asking for a new governess? Possibly—if she was very clever and devious, never giving the slightest hint that it was something *she* wanted. Or, perhaps with the others gone, Susan would improve. Wasn't it her duty to see that she did? Clare examined the girl's pinched expression and habitual pout. Mrs. Benson had undermined every effort Clare had made in that direction so far. It appeared to be a hopeless task.

Clare turned to survey Bella's changed appearance instead—her brown hair newly cut and styled in the latest fashion, her pretty sprigged muslin gown. At Bella's age, Clare had been about to make her entry into society. She had put her hair up and ordered new gowns, full of bright anticipation. And then had come Waterloo, and her beloved brother's death in battle, and the disintegration of her former life. Instead of stepping into the swirl and glitter of society, Clare was relegated to the background, doomed to watch a succession of younger women bloom and go off to take their places in a larger world.

Stop this, Clare ordered silently. She despised self-pity. It only made things worse, and she couldn't afford to indulge in it. Her job now was to regain control of the schoolroom. She shuffled her pile of paper labels. "I suppose I shall have to eat all the cream cakes myself then."

Susan and Charles voiced loud objections. Clare was about to maneuver them back into the geography game when the door opened and Edwina Benson swept in. This was so rare an occurrence that all four of them stared.

Bella jumped up at once and shook out the folds of her new gown. "Were you looking for me, Mama?"

"Not at present. Though why you are here in the schoolroom, Bella, I cannot imagine. I thought you were practicing on the pianoforte. Have you learned the new piece so quickly?"

"Uh…" Eyes gone evasive, Bella sidled out of the room. She left the door open, however, and Clare was sure she was listening from the corridor.

Mrs. Benson pursed narrow lips. "You have a visitor, Miss Greenough."

This was an even rarer event than her employer's appearance in the schoolroom. In fact, it was unprecedented.

"I do not recall anything in our arrangement that would suggest you might have callers arriving at my front door," the older woman added huffily.

Only humility worked with Mrs. Benson. She was impervious to reason. "No, ma'am. I cannot imagine who…"

"So I am at a loss as to why you have invited one."

"I didn't. I assure you I have no idea who it is."

Her employer eyed her suspiciously. Mrs. Benson's constant dissatisfaction and querulous complaints were beginning to etch themselves on her features, Clare thought. In a few years, the lines would be permanent, and her face would proclaim her character for all to see. "He was most insistent," Mrs. Benson added. "I would almost say impertinent."

You did say it, Clare responded silently. "He...?"

Mrs. Benson gave her a sour smile, designed to crush hope. "Some sort of business person, I gather." Her gaze sharpened again. "You haven't gotten into debt, have you?"

It was just like the woman to ask this in front of the children, who were listening with all their might. She was prying as well as peevish, and...pompous and proprietary. "Of course not." When would she have had the time to overspend? Even if she had the money.

Mrs. Benson's lips tightened further. "I suppose you must see him. But this is not to happen again. Is that quite clear? If you have...appointments, I expect you to fulfill them on your free day."

Her once-monthly free day? When she was invariably asked to do some errand for her employer or give the children an "outing"? But Clare had learned worlds about holding her tongue in six long years as a governess. "Thank you, Mrs. Benson." Empty expressions of gratitude no longer stuck in Clare's throat. Mrs. Benson liked and expected to be thanked. That there was no basis for gratitude was irrelevant. Thanks smoothed Clare's way in this household, as they had in others before this.

Clare followed her employer downstairs to the front parlor. The formal room was chilly. No fire had been lit there, as no one had been expected to call, and obviously no refreshment would be offered to the man who stood before the cold hearth. Below medium height and slender, he wore the sober dress of a man of business. From his graying hair and well-worn face, Clare judged he was past fifty. He took a step forward when they entered, waited a moment, then said, "I need to speak to Miss Greenough alone."

Edwina Benson bridled, her pale blue eyes bulging. "I beg your pardon? Do you presume to order me out of my own parlor?"

"It is a confidential legal matter," the man added, his tone the same quiet, informative baritone. He showed no reaction to Mrs. Benson's outrage. And something about the way he simply waited for her to go seemed to impel her. She sputtered and glared, but she moved toward the door. She did leave it ajar, no doubt to listen from the entry. But the man followed her and closed it with a definitive click. Clare was impressed; her visitor had a calm solidity that inspired confidence. Of course she would endure days of stinging reproaches and small humiliations because of this visit. But it was almost worth it to have watched him outmaneuver Edwina Benson. "My name is Everett Billingsley," he said then. "Do you think we dare sit down?"

Clare nearly smiled. He *had* noticed her employer's attitude. She took the armchair. He sat on the sofa. Clare waited to hear what this was about.

For his part, Billingsley took a moment to examine the young woman seated so silently across from him. Her hands were folded, her head slightly bowed so that he couldn't see the color of her eyes. She asked no questions about his unexpected visit. She didn't move. It was as if she were trying to disappear into the brocade of the chair.

Despite her youth, she actually wore a lace cap, which concealed all but a few strands of hair the color of a fine dry champagne. Her buff gown was loosely cut, designed, seemingly, to conceal rather than flatter a slender frame. A shade too slender, perhaps, just as her oval face and pleasantly regular features were a shade too pale. Here was a female doing everything she could to remain unnoticed, he concluded. She even seemed to breathe carefully. Everett Billingsley certainly understood the precarious position of genteel young women required to work for their bread. He could imagine why she might wish to appear unattractive and uninteresting, to remain unobtrusive. Her attempt to impersonate an ivory figurine made his mission even more gratifying. "I have some good news for you," he began. "I represent the estate of Sebastian Greenough, your great-uncle." This won him a tiny frown, but no other reaction.

Clare sorted through her memories. Sebastian Greenough was her grandfather's brother, the one who had gone out to India years before she was born. She had never met him.

"Mr. Greenough died in September. It has taken some time to receive all the documents, but they are now in place. He left everything he had to you."

Clare couldn't suppress a start of surprise. "To me?"

Billingsley nodded. "His last will was made in the year of your brother's death. In it, he expressed a wish to 'even things out.'"

Clare sat very still. Mention of her brother still hurt,

even after seven years. It evoked a cascade of loss—from the pain of his death, to the callous eviction from the home where she'd lived all her life, to the speedy decline in her mother's health in their new, straitened circumstances. How did one "even out" a catastrophe?

A bit puzzled by her continuing silence, Billingsley added, "Because the entail gave everything to your cousin. He wished to make up for that."

After he was dead and could not be inconvenienced in any way, Clare thought but did not say. Sebastian Greenough hadn't expressed the least interest in her while she was struggling to survive her losses.

"It is quite a substantial estate," Billingsley went on. "There is some property in India still to be liquidated. But the funds already transferred, and conservatively invested, will yield an income of more than five thousand pounds a year." At last the girl looked up. Her eyes were a striking pale green. She looked stunned. As well she might; it was a fortune.

"Five thousand a year," Clare murmured. It was more than fifty times her current salary. It was unbelievable. "Is this some kind of…confidence trick?"

Everett Billingsley smiled. "Indeed not. I have not brought all the documents here. I would ask that you call at my office to look them over. But I did bring this as a token of the change in your circumstances."

He took an envelope from the inner pocket of his coat and held it out. Clare accepted it and looked inside. The heavy cream paper bulged with banknotes.

"Five hundred pounds. For expenses until all is in place," Billingsley added. She could leave this oppressive household, purchase some pretty gowns, he thought. He was glad to see more animation in her face when she looked up again. "I should explain the arrangement. The legacy has flowed into a trust. It is to be overseen by me and your cousin Simon Greenough, as trustees, until…" He paused as all the dawning light in her face died.

"Simon." Her cousin would never let her touch any money he controlled.

Billingsley cleared his throat. "It seems that Mr. Simon Greenough wrote your great-uncle to say that he was watching over you. Making sure you had what you needed in the wake of his inheriting."

"He has never given me a penny," Clare responded through gritted teeth. He'd even refused to lend them money to purchase medicine and other necessities for her mother when she was ill. As far as Clare was concerned, he had killed her.

"So I have learned," responded Billingsley dryly. "I believe he also argued, quite forcefully, in their correspondence that your great-uncle's money should be left to him."

"I'm sure he did." Her cousin—the son of her father's younger brother, who had married early and unwisely—had been reared to resent Clare and her brother, to want revenge for their very existence. His greed was fathomless.

"But it was not," finished Everett Billingsley. "And you can be sure that he won't get his hands on it. I will see to that."

Clare believed him. Something about this man inspired trust. "But Simon will be in charge of what I can do with the money?"

"Partially. Along with me."

Clare's fingers closed around the envelope Billingsley had given her. Simon would move heaven and earth to ensure that she saw no more of the legacy than this.

"Until you are married, of course," her visitor added.

"What?"

"On the occasion of your marriage, the trust is naturally dissolved. Your cousin will have no further say in any matters pertaining to the estate."

"Because the control will pass to my husband." Clare knew that was the law. Married women couldn't own property; anything they had automatically went to their husbands as soon as the wedding vows were spoken.

"Correct," replied Billingsley. For the first time, the young woman met and held his gaze. A startling fire blazed in those pale green eyes. Her face seemed altered, too. The visage he had marked down as merely pleasant now shone with a spirited beauty, a patent intelligence. Miss Greenough had arranged to be thoroughly underestimated, he realized, like an actor inhabiting a role wholly unlike himself. There was far more to her than he had been allowed to see at first.

Clare felt as if parts of her were springing back to life after years of dormancy, like unused rooms when the draperies are pushed back and the sun streams in. Her mind raced. Cousin Simon would do anything to thwart her. Everett Billingsley didn't begin to understand the depth of that man's enmity. She would have no real control of this amazing windfall, or of her life, until her cousin was removed from the picture. Fleetingly, Clare wondered if one could hire murderers with a great deal of money. Not that she would, of course. The idea was morally repugnant. And unlikely to succeed, for any number of reasons. She would have to explore more conventional paths. But one thing was certain—Simon would not best her this time. He would not beggar her again.

Author's Note

During the years after the defeat of Napoleon and the restoration of peace, England's foreign secretary Lord Castlereagh became extremely unpopular. In order to remain in the cabinet and continue his diplomatic work, he had to support hated measures taken by the home secretary, Lord Sidmouth, to suppress domestic unrest. He was also severely overworked, with the constant diplomacy required to juggle conflicts among the other major powers. In 1822, Castlereagh began to exhibit paranoia in a kind of nervous breakdown. He said, "My mind, is, as it were, gone." He seemed mentally disturbed during an August audience with King George IV (formerly Prinny). A few days later, although Lady Castlereagh had had his razors taken away, he managed to find a penknife and cut his own throat.

Thus, Mary's drawing of her ladyship in 1819, showing her growing anxiety, was prescient.

Once Again a Bride
by Jane Ashford

— ❧ —

She couldn't be more alone

Widowhood has freed Charlotte Wylde from a demoralizing and miserable marriage. But when her husband's intriguing nephew and heir arrives to take over the estate, Charlotte discovers she's unsafe in her own home...

He could be her only hope...or her next victim

Alec Wylde was shocked by his uncle's untimely death, and even more shocked to encounter his uncle's beautiful young widow. Now clouds of suspicion are gathering, and charges of murder hover over Charlotte's head.

Alec and Charlotte's initial distrust of each other intensifies as they uncover family secrets, and hovering underneath is a mutual attraction that could lead them to disaster...

— ❧ —

"A near-perfect example of everything that makes this genre an escapist joy to read." —*Publishers Weekly*

"One of the premier Regency writers return to the published world. Ms. Ashford has written a superbly crafted story." —*Fresh Fiction*

For more Jane Ashford, visit:

www.sourcebooks.com

Earls Just Want to Have Fun

Covent Garden Cubs

by Shana Galen

❧

His heart may be the last
thing she ever steals…

Marlowe runs with the Covent Garden Cubs, a gang of thieves living in the slums of London's Seven Dials. It's a fierce life, but when she's alone, Marlowe allows herself to think of a time before—a dimly remembered life when she was called Elizabeth.

Maxwell, Lord Dane, is roped into teaching Marlowe how to navigate the social morass of the *ton*, but she will not escape her past so easily. Instead, Dane is drawn into her dangerous world, where the student becomes the teacher and love is the greatest risk of all.

❧

Praise for Shana Galen:

"Shana Galen has a gift for storytelling that puts her at the top of my list of authors." —*Historical Romance Lover*

"Shana Galen is brilliant at making us fall in love with her characters, their stories, their pains, heartaches, and triumphs." —*Unwrapping Romance*

For more Shana Galen, visit:

www.sourcebooks.com

Secrets of a Scandalous Heiress
by Theresa Romain

— ✦ —

One good proposition deserves another...

Heiress Augusta Meredith can't help herself—she stirs up
gossip wherever she goes. A stranger to Bath society, she
pretends to be a charming young widow, until sardonic,
darkly handsome Joss Everett arrives from London and
uncovers her charade.

Now they'll weave their way through the pitfalls of the polite
world only if they're willing to be true to themselves...and
to each other...

— ✦ —

Praise for Theresa Romain:

"Theresa Romain writes with a delightfully romantic
flair that will set your heart on fire." —Julianne
MacLean, *USA Today* bestselling author

"Theresa Romain writes witty, gorgeous, and deeply
emotional historical romance."
—Vanessa Kelly, award-winning author

For more Theresa Romain, visit:

www.sourcebooks.com

Sinfully Ever After

The Book Club Belles Society
by Jayne Fresina

—— ❧ ——

To Rebecca Sherringham, all men are open books—read quickly and forgotten. Perhaps she's just too practical for love. The last thing she needs is another bore around—especially one that's supposed to be dead.

Captain Lucius "Luke" Wainwright turns up a decade after disappearing without a trace. He's on a mission to claim his birthright and he's not going away again until he gets it. But Becky and the ladies of the village Book Club Belles Society won't let this rogue get away with his sins. He'll soon find that certain young ladies are accustomed to dealing with villains.

—— ❧ ——

Praise for *The Most Improper Miss Sophie Valentine*:

"A unique historical romance...pleasingly edgy." —*Booklist*

"A true charmer of a read." —*RT Book Reviews*, 4 Stars and KISS nominee (favorite historical heroes of the month)

For more Jayne Fresina, visit:

www.sourcebooks.com

About the Author

Jane Ashford discovered Georgette Heyer in junior high school and was captivated by the glittering world and witty language of Regency England. That delight was part of what led her to study English literature and travel widely in Britain and Europe. She has written historical and contemporary romances, and her books have been published in Sweden, Italy, England, Denmark, France, Russia, Latvia, the Czech Republic, Slovenia, and Spain, as well as the U.S. Jane has been nominated for a Career Achievement Award by *RT Book Reviews*. She lives in Los Angeles.